$\mathcal{M}$ANITUANA

MANITUANA

Wu Ming

Translated by Shaun Whiteside

VERSO

London • New York

Verso acknowledges the financial assistance of Arts Council England and Italian Ministry of Foreign Affairs

This edition first published by Verso in 2009
© Verso 2009
Translation © Shaun Whiteside 2009
First published as *Manituana*
© Einaudi 2007

1 3 5 7 9 10 8 6 4 2

Verso
UK: 6 Meard Street, London W1F 0EG
US: 20 Jay Street, Suite 1010, Brooklyn, NY 11201
www.versobooks.com

Verso is the imprint of New Left Books

ISBN-13: 978-1-84467-342-1

British Library Cataloguing in Publication Data
A catalogue record for this book is available from the British Library

Library of Congress Cataloging-in-Publication Data
A catalog record for this book is available from the Library of Congress

Typeset by Hewer Text UK Ltd, Edinburgh
Printed in the US by Maple Vail

To Piermario
To Maria

Chronology

31 August 1142 In the area that lies between modern-day New York and Pennsylvania, following the preaching of the prophets Hiawatha and Deganawida, five great Indian tribes come together and form the Iroquois Confederation or the Five Nations (Mohawk, Oneida, Cayuga, Onondaga and Seneca).

11 November 1620 The Mayflower lands at what became Plymouth in Massachusetts. The pilgrims found New England, and the Anglo-Saxon colonization of North America begins.

26 May 1637 New England settlers, at war with the Pequot Indians, attack and set fire to the Misistuck village, killing women and children.

20 April 1710 The court of the British Queen Anne receives a delegation of Iroquois led by the Mohawk sachem Hendrick Theyanoguin.

1713–15 The Tuscarora, a Native American tribe of North Carolina, flee their lands after being defeated in the war against white settlers. They move north to become the sixth Iroquois nation.

1738 The Irishman William Johnson disembarks at New York. His destination is the county of Tryon, in the valley of the Mohawk River, where his uncle's estate is waiting for him.

1755–56 William Johnson is made a baronet and Superintendent of Indian Affairs for North America.

1754–63 The Six Nations supports the British troops during the French and Indian War. Many other tribes side with the French. At the end of the conflict, the French cede their North American territory to the British.

1763–66 In the Great Lakes region, Chief Pontiac leads a revolt against the British. At the end of hostilities, Pontiac and Sir William Johnson meet at the Ontario Lake and sign a peace treaty.

5 November 1768 Sir William Johnson and a delegation of the Six Nations sign the treaty of Fort Stanwix, which sets a boundary on the expansion of white settlements.

16 December 1773 The Boston Tea Party. A group of colonists in Boston, calling themselves the Sons of Liberty, board three docked ships dressed as Mohawks. In protest against British taxes and the monopoly of the East India Company, they destroy the cargo of tea. The British parliament responds with punitive measures that help unite the colonies in the coming War of Independence.

A solitary may be sober, pious, he may wear a hair shirt, and he may very well be a saint, but I will call him virtuous only when he has performed some act of virtue from which other men will benefit. While he remains alone he will be acting neither well nor ill; for us he is nothing.

—Voltaire, *Philosophical Dictionary*

Prologue

Lake George, Colony of New York, 8 September 1755

The sun's rays followed the squad, blood-light filtered through the forest.

The man on the stretcher clenched his teeth; there was a sting in his side. He looked down. Drops of scarlet dripped from the wound.

Hendrick was dead and many Mohawk warriors with him.

Again he saw the old chief caught under the bulk of his horse, the Caughnawaga rushing at him.

The Indians never fought on horseback, but Hendrick couldn't run or jump anymore. They had to hoist him up on the saddle. How old was he? Holy Christ, he'd met Queen Anne. He was Noah, Methuselah.

He had died fighting the enemy. A noble, perhaps an enviable, end; if only his corpse had been found so that it could be given a Christian burial.

William Johnson let his thoughts drift, a flock of swallows, as the bearers walked along the path. He didn't want to close his eyes: the pain helped him stay awake. He thought of John, his firstborn, still too young for war. His son would inherit peace.

Voices and a general hubbub announced the presence of the camp. Women shrieked and railed, asking about sons and husbands.

They laid him down in the tent.

"How do you feel?"

He recognized the surly face and gray eyes of Captain Butler. He tried to smile, and managed only a grimace.

"My right side hurts like hell."

"A sign that you're alive. The doctor will be here any moment."

"Hendrick's warriors?"

"I met them as I was on my way back here. They were scalping corpses and wounded men, without distinction."

William let his head sink back on his straw bed and took a breath. He had given his word to Dieskau: No one would attack the French prisoners. Hendrick had extracted the promise from the warriors, but Hendrick was dead.

A short man came into the tent, purple in the face, his jacket stained with sweat.

William Johnson raised his head.

"Doctor. I've got some trouble here for you."

The doctor slipped off his coat, helped by Captain Butler. He cut away William's breeches with a pair of scissors and began to wash and dab at the wound.

"You're lucky. The bullet hit the bone and bounced off it."

"You hear that, Butler? I repel bullets."

The captain muttered a word of thanks to God and offered William a rag to bite on while the doctor cauterized the wound.

"Don't get up. You've lost a lot of blood."

"Doctor. . ." William's face was tense and washed out, his voice a croak. "Our men are leading the French prisoners to the camp. There's an officer among them, General Dieskau. He's wounded, he may be unconscious. I want you to treat him. Captain, go with the doctor."

Butler and the medic were about to say something, but William was ahead of them. "I'll be all right on my own. I'm not going to die, I assure you."

Butler nodded without a word. The two men left. To keep from fainting, William pricked his ears and concentrated his thoughts on the noises.

Wind shaking the trees.

Cries of crows.

Shouting in the distance.

Shouting nearby.

Cries of women.

A sudden confusion ran through the camp. William thought it was Butler coming back with the prisoners.

He looked out of the tent. A group of Mohawk warriors: they were wailing and weeping, tomahawks high above their heads. They were dragging Caughnawaga, warriors with ropes around their necks, hands tied behind their backs. The women of the camp were tormenting these prisoners with kicks, blows and a hail of stones.

The squad stopped no more than thirty yards away. None of the warriors looked toward the tent: they had forgotten everything; all their senses were focused on revenge. The most agitated among them paced back and forth.

"You aren't men. You are dogs, friends of the French! Hendrick told you all not to bear arms against your brothers! He warned you!"

He grabbed one prisoner by the hair, dragged him to his knees and cut off his scalp. The man fell in the dust, screaming and writhing. The women finished him off with sticks.

William felt sweat freezing on his skin.

A second prisoner was scalped and the women kicked him before beating him to death.

William prayed that no white men were among those about to die. While it remained a matter among Indians, he could keep from intervening.

Hendrick was dead. Sons and brothers were dead. The Mohawk had a right to vengeance, as long as they didn't touch the French: they needed them for the exchange of hostages.

The third Caughnawaga fell to the ground with his skull smashed in.

At headquarters in Albany the ringleaders sent by England didn't understand. They couldn't fight as they could in Europe. The French were unleashing the tribes against the English settlers. Incursions, fires and pillaging. *Petite guerre*, they called it. The French had a name for everything. At British high command they needed the stomach to react in kind. What was at stake was control of a whole continent.

The arrival of new prisoners interrupted his reflections. White civilians, quartermasters, farriers and soldiers in ragged uniforms. One of the warriors dragged a boy out of the group. He was dressed as the regimental drummer.

William was exhausted. He struggled to catch what was being said, but the little boy's fate was clear. A second warrior confronted the first, who was already showing his knife.

With the feathers on their heads and their painted bodies, they looked like two fighting-cocks in an arena.

"He's wearing the uniform of the French. You can't take his scalp!"

"I heard him speaking Caughnawaga."

"Hendrick said the white prisoners were the responsibility of the English fathers."

"Look at his face, does he look like a white man to you?"

"If Hendrick were here he'd chuck you out."

"I wish to avenge him."

"You dishonor him."

"Do you want to wait for him to grow up and become a warrior? Better to kill him straightaway, now that the Caughnawaga traitors are in flight and afraid of you."

"Idiot! Warraghiyagey will be furious with you."

William Johnson heard his own Indian name being uttered. Warraghiyagey, "He Who Does Much Business." He hoisted himself up on his elbows; he had to intervene.

He saw the knife coming down toward the drummer boy's scalp. He filled his lungs to shout.

Something struck the warrior in the face.

A stone bounced to the ground. The man relaxed his grip, brought his hand to his mouth, coughed, spat blood. A quick little figure was on top of him, pushing him away.

A flash of boar skin and raven hair. It roared at the warriors, who recoiled in terror.

"You are without honor," shouted the young woman. "You say you want to avenge Hendrick, but its the Englishmen's money that you want, ten shillings for every Indian scalp!"

She walked over to the warrior, who was still clutching his dagger, and spat at him. The man was about to strike her, but she strode right up to him.

"He's little more than a child. He's never fired a shot. He could be the same age as my brother." She pointed to an alert-looking boy on the edge of the circle of women that had formed around the scene. "When you've collected your pay you'll spend it on rum. Those who today give themselves airs of being great warriors, tomorrow will roll in the mud like pigs."

The warrior made a gesture of contempt before retreating.

The woman turned to the others. "You think only of scalps, but scalps don't go hunting, they don't put food on the table, they don't grow vegetables. Are you so drunk on blood that you trample on our customs? Today many women have lost sons and husbands. They are receiving new hands in compensation." She looked the little drummer boy up and down. "We must adopt the prisoners as new sons and brothers, according to tradition. My mother's mother was adopted; she came from the Great Lakes. Hendrick himself became a Mohawk in that way. You would have killed him!"

The other women went and stood behind the young one. Together they confronted the warriors. The men exchanged uncertain glances, then walked away with feigned indifference and a lot of muttering.

William Johnson fell back on the stretcher.
    He knew that Fury, he had seen her as a child.
    Molly, daughter of the sachem Brant Canagaraduncka.
    She alone had stood up to the warriors.
    She had decided a prisoner's fate.
    She spoke as Hendrick would have.

Part One

Iroquireland

1775

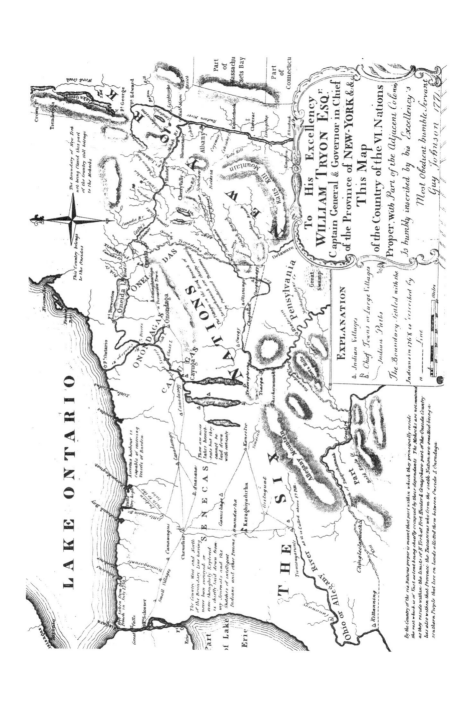

1.

They had brought the children along as well, so that they might one day tell their children and grandchildren. After many attempts, they had finally stood the pole upright. The Liberty Pole.

A birch trunk, properly cleaned and smoothed. A tangle of rope. A red fabric rectangle cut from a blanket. The banner of the Continental Congress.

The German Flatts committee of safety was approving its first document: its acceptance of the remonstrance that the Albany Committee had sent to the British Parliament. It was read out by Pastor Bauer. The text concluded with a solemn undertaking to "join and unite together under all the ties of religion, honor, justice and love for our country, never to become slaves, and to defend our freedom with out lives and fortunes."

The standard was just about to be raised, hailed by songs and prayers, when the sound of hooves interrupted the ceremony.

A squad of horsemen appeared outside the church. They brandished sabers, rifles and pistols. Someone fired into the air as the little crowd sought shelter among the houses. A few courageous people remained in the square. Frightened faces appeared from behind the walls, in half-open doors and at the tavern windows. A name flew from one mouth to the next, in a round dance of voices.

The name of the man who had fired his gun into the air.

Sir John Johnson.

Around him, the men of the Department of Indian Affairs. His brothers-in-law Guy Johnson and Daniel Claus. Directly behind him, Captain John Butler and Cormac McLeod, the Johnson family's bailiff and head of the Scottish tenant farmers who worked the baronet's land.

The only one missing was the clan's old patriarch, Sir William, hero of the war against the French, lord of the Mohawk Valley, who had died the previous year.

Sir John was mounted on a gleaming bay thoroughbred that trembled against the constraint of the bit. He slipped from the group and began to ride along the perimeter of the square, staring disdainfully at the members of the committee, one after the other.

Guy Johnson brought his horse into the shelter of a canopy and dismounted with some difficulty, because of his build.

"Come on, we're here to talk," he called to the houses. "That's what you want, isn't it?"

No one breathed. Sir John tugged on the bridle, and the horse stepped back and twisted its head before yielding to its master's will.

Then someone summoned the courage. The group confronting the mounted men grew denser.

Guy Johnson scowled at them.

"To address a petition to Parliament is legal, but hoisting a banner that is not the king's is sedition. One thing makes you look ridiculous, the other sends you to the gallows."

Silence again. The members of the committee avoided looking at one another for fear of spotting signs of indecision in the eyes of their companions.

"Do you want to follow the example of the Bostonians?" Guy Johnson continued. "Two gunshots fired at the king's army and it went to their heads. His Majesty has the most powerful fleet in the world. He is a good friend of the Indians. He controls all the forts from Canada to Florida. Do you imagine that the rebels of Massachusetts will get much more than a noose around their necks?"

He paused, as if he wanted to hear the blood boiling in the veins of the Germans.

"The Johnson family," he went on calmly, "possesses more land and commerce than all of you put together. We would be the first to take your side, if His Majesty really were threatening the right to trade."

A voice rang out loudly: "Your trade certainly isn't threatened. You are rich and well connected. We're the ones being throttled by the king's taxes."

A chorus of agreement welcomed these words. From the top of the roof Guy Johnson made out Paul Rynard, the cooper. A hothead.

Sir John's stallion shook its head and snorted nervously, and received another tug on the reins.

The baronet's riding whip struck the leather of his boot.

"The taxes are needed to keep the army," Guy Johnson replied. "The army maintains order in the colony."

"You need the army to keep us down," Rynard shot back.

Tempers flared, some of the horsemen instinctively raised their arms, but lowered them again at a nod from Sir John.

"Not yet," muttered the baronet.

Guy Johnson, red in the face, yelled from above: "When the French and their Indians threatened your lands, you cried out for the army! Peace has made you so arrogant and stupid that you want another war. Be very careful, freedom is no use to the dead."

"You're threatening us!" shouted Rynard.

"Get back to Ireland and your Papist friends!" called someone. A rock hurled at Guy Johnson just missed him.

A grimace of smug disdain crossed Sir John's face: "Now."

The horses moved forward, and the committee of safety dissolved on the spot. The men ran in all directions.

John Butler's horse knocked Rynard down and sent him rolling in the mud. The cooper stood up again and was about to escape toward the church, but Sir John blocked his way. The baronet whipped him with all his strength. Rynard curled up on the ground, hands over his face. Between his fingers, he saw McLeod unsheathing his sword and setting off at a gallop. He crept away, invoking God's mercy. When he received the blow with the flat of the sword in the small of his back, he shouted out loud, amidst the rough laughter of the horsemen.

As it dawned on Rynard that he was still alive, the men of the Department gathered in the center of the square. Guy Johnson got back in the saddle and joined them.

A light kick with the spurs and Sir John was at the bottom of the Liberty Pole.

He spoke so that everyone could hear him, wherever they might be lurking.

"Listen carefully! Anyone in this county who wants to challenge the authority of the king will have to deal with my family and the Indian Department." His malevolent eyes seemed to be unearthing all the inhabitants one by one, behind the dark windows.

"I swear on the name of my father, Sir William Johnson."

He slipped one foot from his stirrup. After a few kicks, the pole tumbled into the mud.

2.

Sitting in his armchair, Jonas Klug chuckled in the gloom. A blade of moonlight struck the eviction notice that he held in his hands. He gazed at it in ecstasy even though in the darkness he couldn't read it or even make out its words. He stroked it, running his fingertip over the grain of the paper, sniffing it like the perfumed letter of a lover. Perfume of wealth, perfume of earth, of the future.

The Indians, on the other hand, stank of the past.

Jonas Klug was tipsy: he had been celebrating. The sitting-room clock showed five to eleven. His wife was already in bed, the servants too.

Getting the Mohawks drunk was easy. Torrents of rum flowed in what they called the Longhouse, the name given to the land of the Six Iroquois Nations. Men and women wallowed in puddles of alcohol. Like the whites, or even more so, the drunken savages lost all restraint, they laughed until they dislocated their jaws, they bent double as they lost their balance, they fell and rolled in the dust or foamed with fury, starting scuffles that turned into brawls that turned into piles of raging bodies. One of their chiefs had died like that, drunk, falling into the fire.

If drink was ruining the Six Nations, why not take advantage? Klug was a businessman. He had seen a stretch of good land to the east of the village, five thousand acres of forest and hillside clearings, a few Indian shacks and the smallholdings of white tenant farmers—Papist Irish or Scots, who paid rent to the Mohawk in kind.

Klug was German. Twenty years before he had disembarked in New York dressed in rags. Years of indentured labor, shoveling other people's shit, and then redemption, freedom, a journey into the interior and finally the land. More land than he had ever imagined. He had broken his back, he had dug and built, in the hope of banishing poverty forever. Then war had come between England and France. A time of terror, barricaded at home for fear of Indian raids. In the end peace and prosperity had returned. Jonas Klug had even acquired a family of slaves who hoed the land in his stead.

Now those five thousand acres were his as well. With the money that he had saved he would be able to build a mill, a second farm, sell wood, sow barley and rye, produce beer and whiskey, raise animals. Or he could sell it again.

The law—the little law that there was—was on his side. The right side. God didn't protect the savages: Jesus was white, not Indian.

All the Indians wanted was rum. The most sober sachems had often spoken out against the devil's water, and the Old Man, too, before his death, had looked into the problem. Which amounted to saying that they had spoken out against breathing, and William Johnson, the baronet who protected the Indians, had been in charge of air. Rum was everywhere and it was there to stay.

As simple as knocking back a shot: three years back, Klug had got the right Indian drunk, the stupidest, most boastful one, Lemuel, Lemuel something, and friends of his, as stupid as he was. After they'd got drunk, before they threw their guts up, they had signed the transfer papers. With a lovely illiterate "X," which came to the same thing. Not that Klug was a man of letters, but from the little that he knew he had built a lot.

In the contract, Lemuel and company declared themselves legal representatives of the inhabitants of Canajoharie, owners of the land. A kind of tribal council, an Indian thing. Thereunder, they yielded four thousand acres in return for two cases of rum.

"X," "X" and "X," in front of witnesses.

Beneficiary: Jonas Klug.

Shortly afterward, on a night when the moon was full, he had sent a surveyor friend, who set out to map the territory. A thousand acres more than was stated in the contract. So he had sent everything to Albany and a year later had received the deed of ownership.

Rude awakening for the savages of Chief Tosspot.

The Mohawks had taken legal action, saying that Jonas Klug had acted in bad faith, that only the sachems could sign a contract of that kind and that the negotiation had been conducted without an official interpreter. They had moved heaven and earth, they had appealed to their baronet, to Governor Tryon, to the British Crown. Petitions in court, and other protests, and threats to go down the path of war. As if a court could find against an honest farmer faced with a horde of redskins.

Klug wasn't alone: he had people to protect him, and the Indians knew it. That was why they talked and talked, presented appeals like so many greasy lawyers, but didn't move into action.

Many of the settlers admired Klug for what he had done. Some couldn't wait to settle their scores with the savages, a stinking rabble that got into your granary when they were hungry, or pinched the apples from your trees, and if you weren't careful, threw up all over you as well. God could not have granted these primitive unbelievers a right to these lands.

Klug hated them. And even more, he hated the people who protected them: the Indian Department and the Johnson clan, with their court, all lace and porcelain. Especially that witch, Molly Brant, old Sir William's whore, with her half-breed children: one day face powder and plumed hats, the next seashells and war paint. Their estate covered hundreds of thousands of acres, in Onondaga, Sacondaga, Schenectady, Kingsborough, Albany, Schoharie. In league with the Six Nations and George, King of England.

Klug knew the arrogant landowners and wheeler-dealers very well. His father had wasted his whole life cultivating the fields of gentlemen such as these. Klug had emigrated to avoid being lumbered with them, and instead they were showing up here too. A blight on the land.

God knows where Lemuel and his friends had ended up—he'd never bumped into them again. Their brothers had probably beaten the living daylights out of them, perhaps they'd killed them, or chased them from the village. Who knows, they might have fled westward, they might have become tramps, every day cursing the time they'd got drunk, and drinking again to forget it.

The land would be his forever, or for as long as he wanted. The dispossession notice that he was clutching, validated by the proper authorities, was the last stage, the one most eagerly anticipated. A kick in the arse for Joseph Brant and the soul of William Johnson who burned in hell.

That was why Jonas Klug was chuckling in the gloom.

Then the clock struck eleven.

Silence again.

Klug heard a noise.

Joseph Brant had told the governor: the Mohawks' patience had reached its limit. His, to tell the truth, had been exhausted for some time. There was also his own land, on those five thousand acres.

There was a mood of exasperation at the village. Klug's was only the last in a long series of tricks set in motion by the settlers to steal land from the Mohawk.

Thayendanegea, "Two Sticks Bound Together," baptized with the name of Joseph Brant, wasn't one of the ones who got drunk. He was a survivor of the Franco-Indian War, a respected man, the interpreter for the Indian Department.

Governor Tryon had promised to do everything possible, but the situation hadn't changed. In fact, things were getting worse, and a black and orphaned future weighed on the nation's shoulders. The warriors were pawing the ground, still obeying the sachems but believing that they were too cautious. These things weren't a matter for the courts. Sir William wasn't around anymore, and many people wanted to resolve the matter in the old way: expose Klug's scalp among the trophies of war.

Joseph had suggested an alternative. He didn't want to end his days as a poor man, and the land and what was on it belonged to him and his people, who had always been allies of the king. But neither did he want the guilty man to be seen as a victim. With due pressure, he would obtain justice for himself and the others, within English law.

The village council had already given him carte blanche.

There were about a dozen men around Jonas Klug's house.

Joseph slipped to one side. Behind him his companions shuddered. They had approached downwind and poisoned the dogs. Two warriors had taken care of the African slaves who slept in the shack at the end of the farm. Half a dozen derelicts, whom Klug kept worse than animals. They wouldn't cause any problems now.

Joseph looked at his own image reflected in the windowpane. Two hours' marching didn't seem to have compromised the effect of his clothing: hunting jacket with horn buttons, leather trousers and horseman's boots. By the light of the moon he was merely an unstable outline traced in the glass: a shadow with its own retinue of shadows. He would appear before the German like a forest spirit.

Before marching off, Joseph had reviewed the unit. David Royathakariyo and two boys from the Bear clan had painted their faces. Joseph had only murmured something in a low voice, with a shake of his head: it was impossible to know what was going on in the young man's head. Anyway, as long as he didn't do anything stupid, everyone had the right to sort himself out as he saw fit. Certainly the painting testified to one thing: the will to war.

Jacob Bowman Kanatawakhon, August Sakihenakenta and a few others from the Wolf clan were the ones he most trusted.

They all seemed more or less sober, apart from the last to arrive, Johannes Tekarihoga. The most noble of the Canajoharie had turned up tipsy. He stank of rum and took long swigs from the bottle, offering some to the others as well. Joseph had spent a whole afternoon persuading him to take part. The presence of a figure of his rank gave legitimacy to the expedition. If the old sachem fell asleep along the road, they would pick him up on the way back.

Joseph rose up to his full height, motioned to the line of warriors to move away from the wall and with large strides covered the distance that separated him from the front door. The night air filled his lungs. His chest swelled under his jacket. He felt a cold, deep sensation: satisfaction. His appearance was elegant and martial.

Inside, a light was lit. Klug was awake. Better that way. Joseph knocked on the door with the ivory head of his walking stick, an old present from Sir William.

"Jonas Klug, open the door! Open up or we'll break it down!"

A low rumble came from the warriors. Joseph imagined the German throwing open the door and shooting blindly. Impossible: Klug valued his skin, he would try and wriggle out of things.

The door half opened. Joseph pushed the wooden boards with the sole of his boot. Klug, his face livid, presented himself to the Indians' view.

"What are you doing here? What do you want?"

By way of reply, Royathakariyo came up alongside Joseph and hurled himself at the German, teeth gritted.

"What are we doing here, eh? What do you think?"

The Indian's hands gripped Klug's throat. The German gasped for air. He emitted a labored grunt as Joseph tried to free him from the attacker's grasp. When he succeeded, Klug collapsed, coughing.

His wife came down the stairs holding a rifle. She tried to take aim, but Kanatawakhon gripped the barrel and pushed it up in the air. The woman began screaming like a thing possessed, imitated by the Indians. For a moment it was as if they were trying to see who could make the highest-pitched cries. Then the woman withdrew to the upper story, supported by her servants.

Meanwhile Klug tried to escape his fate by crawling away on all fours. The Indians were on top of him.

"Not his head!" Joseph commanded.

Blows rained down on the German's back and legs.

When he considered that the man had had enough, Joseph tugged the warriors off.

"That's enough! That's enough, I said!"

He bent over Klug and waved a piece of paper in front of his nose.

"This is a written declaration in which you, Mr. Klug, admit that you tricked my people out of their land. You will see what happens if you don't sign."

He had prepared the speech over the previous few days. It sounded good.

3.

In the morning she could hear the land breathing. At midday, she could hear the grass growing. In the evening, she could see where the winds were going to settle. Many invisible things were clear to Molly Brant, as clear as calligraphy, distinct as the outlines of the trees on a clear day. From her maternal grandmother she had learned to see where other eyes were blind, to hear where other ears were deaf. She had learned to capture the *oyarons*, spirits that guide people through dreams. And she had learned the right way to wake up. To open her eyelids, to thank the Master of Life, to count three breaths and get up straight away, before the body's laziness numbs the thoughts: that way the head remains limpid, dreams don't escape, the evils of the soul can be cured.

The light from the window cut through the darkness. The lower part of the bed remained in shadow, but above her waist the sheets were drenched in sunlight.

Nimbly, Molly got up. Her black hair fell back on her linen clothes. She poured water from a jug into the basin, washed her face. She dried herself with a piece of cotton and lifted her head.

In the mirror a network of faint scars, skin that smallpox had barely touched. Another battle won by Sir William's side.

The tickle of your hair inflames my passion, brings a blush to my cheeks.

The voice reached her on a breath of wind. Molly studied the reflection of her pupils. They could withstand anyone's gaze, even Molly Brant's.

Arendiwanen, "Woman of Power." Rich in things, in lands, in children. Capable of dreaming with great strength, as had happened in the days of her grandfathers, when Hendrick was young and the nation prospered.

In that night's dream the church was packed. Heads brushed the ceiling, like sacks of maize piled up for the winter. Bears and wolves crouched on the earth floor. Huge tortoises supported the altar on their backs.

The pastor, standing on the pulpit, flicked through the prayer book.

Peter got to his feet. He picked up the violin: the old Irish march that his father had played on the bagpipes before going into battle. Two sachems in black gloves and full mourning brought the coffin over to lower it beneath the altar, but the hole had not yet been dug.

The congregation came forward, one at a time. They picked up a spade and tried to plunge it into the ground. In vain. The earth was harder than iron. The handle of the shovel broke.

Joseph gripped his tomahawk to use it as a pick. A warrior came up beside him, his face in shade. He dug with his nails until his fingers bled.

Molly stood by the window. Clusters of men and women crowded the square outside the general shop.

An Indian hunter loaded down with furs and a seller of pots and pans wanted to engage her as an interpreter and conclude their exchanges. They offered a boatman provisions for the journey and pitch to mend a boat. Settlers from the neighboring farms had come for an extension of payment on their family debts. There were two German women from the nearby village of Palatine, one of whom the people called a witch but then crossed the river to her shop for a miraculous cure for toothache. There were dogs and children, old men and warriors, sachems and idlers waiting for their dose of rum. Women, young and old, came to swap dreams, to discuss the news and at the same time buy salt pork.

Even through the thick glass, dark and full of bubbles, Molly was aware of the excitement. The volume of the voices was higher than usual. The tone was animated. Not the ordinary chatter of people whiling away the time, but an avalanche of phrases.

Everyone was talking, no one seemed to be listening.

4.

Each time Canajoharie appeared, Joseph Brant thought of the fate of his people.

At the foot of the hill, the Mohawk River looped and enclosed the fields and wooden dwellings, built on the model of the longhouses.

When the nation was still large, the traditional houses had remained true to their name: one could hold as many as three hundred people. Now the whole village numbered that many.

The dimensions of the houses had become much smaller. There weren't enough men to fill them, and the Mohawk had become used to living like white men. Those of more elevated status had glass in their windows, and the poorest settlers looked at them with envy.

Only the territory of the Six Nations was still a Longhouse, however symbolic that might have been: the Seneca defended the western gate, the Mohawk the eastern one. In the middle the Onondaga guarded the fire. Cayuga, Oneida and Tuscarora helped the three elder-brother nations with their ancestral tasks.

On the path that climbed from the village, Joseph spotted a figure running toward him.

After visiting the Klug farm, half of the expedition had taken the wrong road, lost in clouds of rum. Their alcoholic shouts had woken all the dogs within a one-mile radius. Hunted down by the animals, the warriors had scattered all around. Some had fallen to the ground, vanquished by sleep. It had taken hours to gather them all together and get back on the road. Painted faces had become blurry, undignified masks.

"Fort Ticonderoga!" yelled Peter Johnson as soon as his uncle was within hearing.

When he had caught up with him, he went on: "The rebels. They've taken Fort Ticonderoga without firing a shot."

Joseph looked at his nephew. They had not seen each other often over the past few months. After his father's death, Peter had come back from Philadelphia only a few times.

"They're under the command of one Ethan Allen, do you know who he is, Uncle Joseph?"

"He's a bandit from the Green Mountains. He's been fighting the governor for years. Come on, let's go to your mother's."

Joseph sensed a shiver running through the men behind him. The warriors would have preferred to endure a hundred lashes rather than present themselves to Molly in this state. With various excuses, they dispersed in various directions.

Uncle and nephew walked on alone.

Along the path men and women quickened their pace, as at the first raindrops of a storm, then suddenly stopped, sucked into the crowd. The doors of the houses were left wide open so as not to obstruct the passage of the news.

There wasn't a young man who didn't want to act as messenger, running from the church to the boat jetty to the more remote farms.

The main room of the general store stretched a long way to the back. Amidst spirals of dust and smoke, the goods occupied every nook, every inch of shelving, when they weren't hanging from the roof-beams. Hempen ropes, wooden boxes of nails, wicks, tinderboxes. Boxes of paint for warriors, marked with Chinese ideograms. Mirrors for painting faces, candles, tools, flints, house paints; waxed blankets, skins, clothes of various styles and sizes; fresh and dry food, smoked and salted. Finally, in little barrels, the indisputable sovereign of every general store, shop or trading station for a hundred miles around: rum.

Joseph greeted his sister, who was busy trying to convince a customer that his shillings were fake, just enough for a miser's alms. Peter suddenly offered to subject the coins to an examination, guaranteed and infallible. His mother blessed him and nodded to Joseph to follow her.

Hidden behind a rough linen curtain there was a cosy room reserved for negotiations and respected customers. The low table and the rocking chairs rested on an oriental carpet. On the end wall, wooden steps led to the private apartments. Molly went to the stairs and ordered someone to bring her some tea. Then she arranged a cushion on the sofa, sat down and started keeping away the flies with a lace fan.

Joseph looked at her. She was eight years older than he was. Her long plait was shot with white hairs.

A young black serving girl came into the room with a silver tray of Chinese porcelain. Joseph recognized her. She came from the drawing room of Johnson Hall.

"Do you still miss the old house?" he asked.

Molly shrugged vaguely.

"I miss my things, the furniture I had chosen, the dishes I bought with William in the stores in New York. Sir John's governess told me they were melting down the silver in case the rebels confiscated it."

Joseph felt overwhelmed by the heavy atmosphere. A smell of leather, grain and cane sugar. Everything was within reach. Light filtered through the only skylight.

He blew out air through his teeth and swallowed the tea. "The settlers are becoming more and more arrogant. Since your husband died, the law of the white man has offered us hardly any protection."

"According to the law of the white man, Sir William wasn't even my husband."

From under his jacket Joseph pulled out a folded sheet of paper.

"They won't be able to ignore this." He handed the paper to Molly, who opened it and ran her eyes over it. "Klug's signature is authentic," her brother explained. "We must send a trusted person to Albany. It will be delivered to the colony court."

Molly smiled faintly and set the document on the tray.

"The morning mail brought news from the north. The Bostonians have taken Ticonderoga and are aiming for Canada."

Joseph nodded. "The rebellion's spreading," he said, "and the Longhouse will have to choose its war, before the war chooses the Longhouse."

A silence followed, interrupted only by the raised voices beyond the curtain. Molly rocked slightly in her chair.

"Many people say that it's a dispute between Englishmen, but the land is ours and we sealed our agreements with King George."

Joseph rose to his feet and drew the curtain aside.

Peter had persuaded the customer and was holding out the credit book for a signature. The boy wasn't slow off the mark. He lived in a big city, on his own and fearless, proud of his origins and his new knowledge. He spoke and wrote in three languages: English, French and Mohawk. He read music, played the violin and was learning his way in business. Soon he would demonstrate his courage to the warriors as well. Sir William and Molly had imagined a great future for their son. The boy wouldn't disappoint them. At his ease among the white men and in the Longhouse, even at the age of sixteen he embodied the future of the nation.

Joseph took a step back, turned and continued where he had left off.

"What would Sir William have done?"

Molly studied the dark surface inside her cup. She seemed to see again the waters of her dream, and the canoe sailing upstream toward the land where the sun sleeps.

"I'll ask him in my dreams. He would certainly have defended the valley. The world that he had built along with Hendrick."

5.

It was still the finest farm in the area. Solid walls, glass in the windows, land all the way to the river. Margaret, Joseph's mother, had inherited it from her third husband, the sachem Brant Canagaraduncka.

In the farmyard, a family of Irish tenants were lifting a cart to get one of the wheels onto the axle. The horses were drinking, tended by a little boy. A few Mohawk hunters repaired the keel of a canoe while their wives traded with the women from the neighboring farms, standing around a pile of blankets.

Usually Joseph stopped to exchange greetings and observations, but not today.

Susanna welcomed him in the doorway. Christina peered out at him from behind her skirt. When she recognized her father she gave him a shy smile. He brushed her cheek with his finger and the little girl hid again.

Before he entered, he looked into his wife's eyes and let her guess his worry.

In the darkness he noticed people around the table, who leaped to their feet. Herr Lorenz, Albany's armorer, waved to him and introduced the female Indian guide on his right. The other two guests bowed. The older one was about sixteen, and spoke on behalf of both of them. They were itinerant teachers, Shawnees. They had studied at boarding school in Lebanon, with a view to bringing Christ and the alphabet to the frontier villages. Every night they stayed with an old pupil from the school. They thanked him for his hospitality; they would pray for him.

Joseph sat down with them, but a figure in the corner drew his attention. A pair of eyes reflected the flickers of the fire.

"Isaac, come and say hello to your father."

The little boy approached. Joseph's firstborn was nine years old, not old enough to fight. Joseph wasn't sure that was good: in times of war the weak perish. He gripped his son's shoulders, as if to test his fortitude and also to pass strength on to him. He realized that the boy's cheeks were painted in red and black. As his grip grew tighter, Isaac tried to wriggle away, but had to yield to the adult's strength.

"These are war paints," said Joseph, as he vigorously cleaned the boy's face. "They're not for playing and you don't bring them home."

He let him go and Isaac slipped away toward the door. Children no longer had any respect for important things.

"Your son isn't to blame for the weight you bear in your mind," murmured Susanna.

Joseph ignored the rebuke and stretched his hand out to little Christina, but the child drew back and followed her brother outside.

Susanna served him his lunch. Joseph ate without raising his eyes from the plate, every sound amplified by the silence. When he had finished, he sat down in front of the fire to smoke his pipe, as the guests said good-bye, one after the other.

The last was Lorenz, who came over cautiously, with the clear intention of saying something.

He received an indifferent glance.

"They're asking me for rifles, Mr. Brant."

"Good for your business."

Lorenz shook his head.

"You don't understand. They're asking me for rifles. Lots of rifles. More than I can make."

"You'll get rich."

"Between Albany and here I ran into three militia roadblocks. They pointed their guns at me, searched the cart, turned everything upside down. What in hell's name is going on, Mr. Brant? Have they gone mad? Are they planning to do what they did in Boston?"

Joseph let the flames catch his eye as he took ample puffs on his pipe.

"In that case, we wouldn't be besieged."

The armorer hesitated, then realized that the Indian wasn't going to say anything else and took his leave.

Joseph went on staring at the fire.

Susanna called the children.

She was the sister of Peggy, his first wife. They were Oneida from the Susquehannah Valley. After being left a widower, Joseph had married her, as custom decreed. Isaac and Christina had become fond of her over the course of a summer. If things became heated, he would have to think of her and the children.

And of Margaret.

"Where's my mother?"

"In bed."

"Is she ill?"

"No. Sometimes she confuses day and night."

His old mother appeared on Susanna's arm. She sat down opposite Joseph, on a worn-out armchair that seemed to be cut for her like a piece of clothing. Bones, flesh, wood and fabric were molded into a perfect fit.

"How are you, Margaret?"

The old woman squinted as she tried to recognize him.

"Before I went to bed I asked God to take me in my sleep. Now that you've woken me up he won't be able to fulfill my wishes."

"Another time, then."

"Yes. Give me a smoke."

Joseph offered her his pipe.

"I saw Molly, down at the general store. She says hello."

"Tell her to come and see me before I die. I have things to tell her."

"Of course, Margaret."

The old woman savored the taste of the smoke. "Do you remember the first time William Johnson came here?"

"Yes."

"Your sister was very beautiful. The most beautiful girl in the whole valley."

Joseph still had clear images in his head. He had been eleven when his stepfather had put up that red-haired Irish gentleman. Molly was young and of marriageable age. Joseph remembered the adults talking about the war against France and her Huron allies, Abenaki and Caughnawaga.

He stroked his mother's white hair.

"Is the war still going on?" she asked.

"It ended twelve years ago."

The old woman shook her hair, keeping the pipe clamped between her wrinkled lips.

"Joseph?"

"Yes, Margaret."

"How many grandchildren have I got?"

"Ten. You have ten grandchildren."

"Yes."

Margaret nodded at her own thoughts.

Joseph watched her for a long time. He respected the past contained in that face, memories of old seasons that had come and gone one after the other, along with the current of the river. He wondered whether one day Isaac and Christina would look after him as he looked after Margaret. Perhaps they would look at him with the same compassion. Perhaps he wouldn't live long enough for that.

The old woman stretched a bony finger toward the fire.

"Look. The flames are turning green. They're on their way."

"Who?"

Margaret spat in the fire and didn't reply. Susanna called him to the window. He peered out. A canoe was coming along the path, carried by three men.

6.

They rested the boat against the wall of the barn and sat down under the awning to get their breath back. Joseph recognized their faces, dirty from their long journey. Bodies wrapped in layers of fur, hunting knives in their belts, long-barrelled Kentucky Jaegers: bear rifles.

"Don't forget that your mother doesn't want them in the house," said Susanna.

Joseph left without replying.

When they saw him they saluted him brusquely. They were chewing tobacco, or pemmican.

"The oldest of them spoke first. He used the Mohawk tongue.

"Greetings to you, Thayendanegea."

The bald, bony head, with the big flapping ears, protruded from the beaver fur like a tortoise's head from its shell. He hadn't shaved for many days. On his face, baked by the sun and harsh weather, his beard grew bristly and gray.

"Welcome to my home, Henry Hough."

"You remember my brother John?"

The young man grunted an incomprehensible greeting. He was cross-eyed.

Henry Hough pointed to the other man: "Daniel Secord is one of ours as well."

"May God protect you, Joseph Brant, and protect your house."

Secord appeared to be the same age as the younger of the two brothers, thirty at most. The Seneca amulets around his neck and wrists were a sign of vanity and superstition.

Hough raised an iron hook, showing the furs that hung from it.

"Your wife will be able to make you a jacket for the winter."

Joseph accepted the gift and sat down with them.

"What brings you to Canajoharie?"

"Daniel took a job. Reconnoitering the springs that rise around Lake Onondaga. On behalf of a fellow who wants to make some money. We're going with him."

Joseph ran a hand over the furs, soft and gleaming.

"You didn't choose the shortest way."

"We passed this way to hear the latest news. Strange rumors are circulating. That the colony is in a mess. That the Bostonians plan to attack Canada."

"They've taken Fort Ticonderoga."

Hough nodded without changing his expression. His two companions merely stared at the Indian, with the neutral expressions of people who pay little heed to misfortune.

"Things are getting serious," Hough observed. "What do they intend to do in Albany?"

Joseph wanted to leave. He struggled to speak.

"The militia was set up on the orders of the rebels."

Hough seemed to study those words, as if they had come from the Scriptures.

"You can sleep in the barn," said Joseph. "Don't show your face in the house or my mother will curse you again."

The younger man opened his eyes wide.

"So the old girl's still alive!"

The elder brother gave him a kick that sent up a cloud of dust. "A bit of respect, you son of a bitch." He turned back to Joseph. "You're a generous man, Joseph Brant."

He came back to them at sunset, with an oil lamp, rum, beer and a pan of stewed meat. He watched them eating in silence, sprawled on the straw, drinking in great gulps as their eyes turned red and the alcohol burned their guts.

Henry Hough had put on a worn three-cornered hat to protect his scalp from the cold of night. His long, scrawny neck stretched toward the food. He looked absurd yet unsettling.

"What do the warriors think?"

"They know the settlers want our land," Joseph replied. "If they attack us we'll have to fight."

"A thorny problem for your friends in the Department."

The younger brother belched and wiped away the drops that flowed from his mouth.

"If any peasants need bumping off, you can count on my rifle."

The elder brother glanced at him grimly.

"Johnny meant that we're loyal subjects of King George."

"You don't even know who King George is," the younger brother spluttered, trying to hoist himself up from his straw bed. "You're only saying that because that bastard brother-in-law of yours is with the rebels."

He got a bowl in the face and crouched down like a whipped dog.

"In a sense Johnny's right," Secord broke in. He had been silent until that moment. He looked less drunk, more stiff than the other two. The pendants to ward off the evil eye jangled when he lit the big cigar that nestled between his fingers.

"With the greatest respect, who has ever seen the king?" he went on. "He's on the other side of the ocean and he leaves us alone. On the other hand, down in Albany, there are thousands of them. If they take command of us they'll want to take all the land. First the Mohawk's land, then the Johnsons', and finally ours as well."

Henry Hough gestured toward his partner, then turned back to Joseph.

"There's a brain that's working properly. There aren't many people down our way who think like that. Bear it in mind, Joseph Brant."

The Indian stayed silent. Night had fallen over the farm and over the valley: a heavy, moonless night that choked the land of his forefathers. He looked beyond the river. New fires glowed in the distance, outposts of the imminent future.

7.

The face of Johannes Tekarihoga, the sachem of the Tortoise clan, was a thousand-year-old rock, the cracks of his eyes carved by a skilled chisel. The aged warrior proceeded impassively along the forest path.

Joseph walked beside him toward Johnson Hall. Without noticing, he ran his palm over one cheek. He wondered whether time would work on his face in the same way.

Joseph liked the old sachem. He had been a brave fighter and a fair and trustworthy authority in the controversies surrounding the Mohawk nation. He was also one of the most convinced supporters of the alliance with Johnson and the English Crown. A man of few words: serving as his interpreter was like solving an oracle. It required imagination and resourcefulness, talents that Joseph had in abundance.

He had not been back to the Johnsons' stronghold for months. Almost a year had passed since Sir William's funeral. It wasn't easy to get used to the absence of the superintendent, the great patriarch, Warraghiyagey. Now more than ever, when times were growing difficult and decisions more weighty.

The Indian Department had invited Tekarihoga to discuss the rebellion. Little Abraham, the sachem of the Fort Hunter Mohawk, would also be coming.

His mind returned to the road. It wasn't far now, just a few miles' walk through the forest. After hours of silence, Joseph felt the need for a human voice.

He turned to the sachem. "What can we expect from this meeting?"

Johannes Tekarihoga went on walking, with a broad, rhythmic stride. Minutes passed. The reply came in a murmur.

"Gifts."

Joseph noticed the merest hint of a smile in the man's immobile face.

The long avenue up to Johnson Hall was swarming with activity. Servants and workmen were transporting earth, logs, sacks. Indians and Highlanders mounted guard at the entrance to the avenue. Further on, the dwellings of the slaves, sundrenched. Children who were little more than infants rolled around among dogs and chickens. Black women were preparing food, chasing after children, pounding laundry. Toward the end of the avenue, other Indians and Scotsmen mounted a second, more solid guard, leading to the entrance of the main building.

Even after many years, Joseph was impressed by the great façade, by the number of windows, by the appearance of the wood that looked like white stone. For a long time it had been the home of his sister Molly, for almost twenty years governess and companion to William Johnson and mother of his last two children. Sir William had not forgotten them in his will: he had left them land and goods in abundance.

Joseph, too, owed much to the Irish baronet: Sir William had cared for him since boyhood, he had made him study, he had taken him on as interpreter to the Department.

On the steps leading up to the main entrance an elderly black man was waiting, dressed in old cloth livery. With a nod of the head he indicated the adjacent building, the one that Sir William, years before, had rechristened the Office.

Before entering, Joseph turned toward Tekarihoga, who stared back at him, as mute as he had been on their journey. Joseph thought that the Tortoise could not have had a better representative.

8.

The harvest of gifts was ample. Tekarihoga could consider himself satisfied, all the more because it was a difficult time for trade and commerce. Especially paints for face and body. Mirrors of all styles and sizes, carved or decorated with stones of various colors. A barrel of molasses and another of dried meat, because the stomach was equally honored. Woollen jackets, warm, hard wearing and well tailored, much better than the fur ones. Chewing tobacco of the best quality. Wampum necklaces. A big cow's horn full of gunpowder.

The main hall of the Office was very large. Sober decoration: a big central fireplace, benches and seats along the walls, an impressive table at the end, where Sir William used to sit. Hanging from the walls were portraits of the Johnsons, along with geographical maps, a long-standing passion of the Old Man.

The Department was fully represented.

Sir John Johnson, son of Sir William's first wife, was leaning on the long table, not sitting in his father's place.

On his left, a belly protruding from a seat with broad wooden arms, Guy Johnson, Sir William's son-in-law, chosen by him as his successor in the job of Superintendent of Indian Affairs.

A few feet further to the right, Daniel Claus, with frowning brow and arms folded. The German had made his fortune by marrying—he, too—a daughter of the patriarch and becoming superintendent of the Canadian Indians.

Opposite them sat Captain Butler, a rival of the Johnsons in the fur trade, but their loyal ally in politics. An old comrade-in-arms of Sir William, and a great expert on the Northwest Territories. An important nexus in the web of power that William Johnson had woven with a great deal of patience and strategic skill.

Little Abraham, a sphinx sitting beside his own pile of gifts, added a different brushstroke to the picture. Joseph and Tekarihoga sat down next to him, on comfortable chairs.

With a wave of his hand Sir John invited Guy Johnson to do the honors. The superintendent cleared his throat.

"Brothers," he said, turning to the sachems, "Thank you for coming at such a delicate moment for our community. When decisions urgently need to be made, the opinion of wise experts is like rain on scorched earth."

He waited for Joseph to translate, then continued in a more agitated voice.

"We have definite information that the colonial militia intends to kidnap me and demand concessions in return, inflicting an unbearably humiliating defeat on all of us. The roads of the county have become dangerous for those of us who have always declared loyalty to King George. Everything tells us that the rebellion is no longer only local to Boston. Since the taking of Ticonderoga, the Whig militias have controlled internal shipping between New York and Montreal. We risk remaining isolated."

Joseph finished the translation, and Little Abraham and Tekarihoga exchanged a meaning glance. The sachem of Fort Hunter was considered one of the best orators of the Longhouse, and his words were eagerly anticipated. Not least because no one knew what his thoughts were on the matter of the rebellion.

"The concerns of the English brothers are also ours," he began. "No one can enter the Longhouse, threaten a friend of my people and walk out the door like any old guest. Upon my arrival here, I was met by twenty warriors from our village showing their rifles. The dwelling of Warraghiyagey is a place very dear to the Mohawk, second only to the sacred fire of Onondaga, and as such we plan to defend it. Another twenty warriors are already on their way to Guy Park, because Guy Johnson Uraghquadirah is our superintendent and we have promised to honor him forever."

Once the translation was over, everyone expected Little Abraham to go on talking. Instead he sat back in his chair, a sign that he had finished, and it was Guy Johnson's turn to break the silence once more.

He thanked the sachem for his words, for his esteem and fidelity. Then, with all due care, he tried to make him understand that they weren't enough.

"The news that concerns me is like a leaf burning in a flaming forest. Pouring water on the leaf will not put out the fire. If it concerned only Guy Johnson, his family would be enough to defend him, without having to trouble men like Tekarihoga and Little Abraham."

Little Abraham understood English and intervened without waiting for the interpreter.

"Brothers, we are talking about a burning leaf, but no one has seen the flames. For that reason I have asked for a meeting with Philip Schuyler. He is the nephew of the man who brought Hendrick to London and his words carry great weight with my people. If he gives us a promise that no one will harm our superintendent, that promise may be wind that blows the smell of fire from our valley."

The sachem's words were intended to be reassuring and Joseph tried to translate their intention, but the wind that blew among the white men smelled like a thunderstorm. A meeting between Little Abraham and the rebel general certainly wasn't good news.

Captain Butler asked to speak. When a discussion threatened to lose its way, it was always he who put it back on the right track.

"Little Abraham is right," he said. "It is always good to check the rumors carried on the river, and none of us would have brought the sachems here without first doing so. Similarly, no one doubted that he would help us to defend Johnson Hall and Superintendent Johnson. And anyway, there are other fires. Farther away, but not far enough to leave us in peace. The smoke and flames from Lexington and Boston are clearly visible even from here. The words spoken by Ethan Allen at the taking of Ticonderoga are spreading by word of mouth. Talking to Philip Schuyler might be a good idea, but his promises cannot extinguish such big fires. The Mohawk will have to decide how to check the threat before the flames come and scorch them."

"In other words, brothers," interrupted Sir John, who until that moment had listened in silence, "what we want to tell you is that wars have the unpleasant habit of forcing you to choose sides."

Silence fell. Guy Johnson blushed with embarrassment. Joseph didn't translate Sir John's words, aware that the two sachems had understood very well.

Without moving a muscle, Tekarihoga began speaking the language of his forefathers, in a low, singsong voice. A few seconds, then he broke off. Little Abraham closed his eyes. It was the sign of his agreement.

Silence filled the room, while everybody, one after the other, turned to look at Joseph, waiting for his translation. He allowed the silence to become solid, a material that kept them at once united and divided from one another. What had Tekarihoga said? "If my house burns, my neighbor is in danger." Not enough for the white men. The meaning was: "If my problem risks involving other people, it isn't good to solve it alone. You have to consult everyone, starting with those closest to you, inform them of the danger, hear their point of view. Work out whether they're willing to help you." A remarkable weight for a few words to carry.

Joseph spoke in a serious, firm voice.

"Brothers, the wise and noble Tekarihoga greets and thanks you all. He shares your concern about the news we have received, and about the gathering clouds. The lands and goods that we share are tempting to many. We know from experience the greed of certain settlers. The fact that some of the children have decided to rebel against their English father is a misfortune. When brothers threaten one another with weapons and aim them at their fathers, it is always an evil, one that is to be avoided. That is why Johannes Tekarihoga says that it is very important to warn the Oneida, younger brothers of the Mohawk, our neighbors in guarding the eastern door of the Longhouse, before the fire takes everyone by surprise. If the threat against Guy Johnson is the leaf that burns in a flaming forest, that threat does not apply only to us. The Six Nations must know of the risk to their superintendent."

Joseph let the words float around the room, while Little Abraham and Tekarihoga smiled faintly to show their appreciation of the translation.

The white men exchanged glances. Joseph sensed mistrust. Since the beginning of the rebellion, the Oneida had been an enigma. Their preacher, Samuel Kirkland, was a supporter of the Whigs. Joseph knew him well: as boys they had studied together at the charity school in Lebanon. Sir William had always seen him as a troublemaker.

It was Guy Johnson's turn to put a brave face on things.

"The sachem's wise words have always been welcome to us. What Tekarihoga says is quite right, and we will contact the other nations, the Oneida first of all. If my brother Joseph will be so good as to write the message in Mohawk, the honorable sachems will be able to add their signatures."

Joseph congratulated himself. In the presence of the white men, even the noblest sachems counted for little without a good interpreter.

Written at Guy Johnson's, May 1775.

This is your letter, you great ones or sachems. Guy Johnson says he will be glad if you get this intelligence, you Oneidas, how it goes with him now; and he is now more certain concerning the intention of the Boston people. Guy Johnson is in great fear of being taken prisoner by the Bostonians. We Mohawks are obliged to watch him constantly. Therefore we send you this intelligence, that you shall know it; and Guy Johnson assures himself, and depends upon your coming to his assistance, and that you will, without fail, be of that opinion. He believes not that you will assent to let him suffer. We therefore expect you in a couple of days' time. So much at present. We send but so far as to you Oneidas, but afterward, perhaps, to all the other nations. We conclude, and expect that you will have concern about our ruler, Guy Johnson, because we are all united.

Johannes Tekarihoga
Little Abraham
Joseph Brant
(interpreter to Guy Johnson)

Joseph read this missive out loud, translating the text, trying to reproduce its formalities and civilities.

English was a rougher, more concise language; in the journey from eyes to mouth the words shrank, leaving part of their significance on the page. In the language of the Empire, every cause was followed by a consequence, to every action there was a single corresponding purpose, to every action the most appropriate reaction. On the contrary, the language of the Mohawk was full of details, run through with doubts, refined by constant adjustments. Each word stretched and expanded to capture every possible meaning and ring in the ear in the most consonant manner.

In the letter, the sachems and Joseph appealed to the Oneida as elder brothers; the words were chosen to reconcile the positions of the Mohawk of Canajoharie and Fort Hunter; the expectations and certainties of Guy Johnson were described in such a way as to confirm the friendship between him and the Mohawk without giving rise to any doubts about the latter's independence. Guy was called only by his name, without the addition of anything else, no flattering phrase to adorn his reputation. Although Sir William was never mentioned, the Oneidas would understand that a favor was being asked of them in his memory. Hence the final sentence: Joseph had written and rewritten it until he found the right tone, with which even Little Abraham would be satisfied. The younger brothers were being put to the test: what decision would they reach? Would they follow the inclinations of their Presbyterian reverend or come to the aid of the Mohawks, who were protecting Warraghiyagey's heir? The call for unity of the Six Nations was balanced on an orderly heap of nuances. The English language had scattered four fifths of them. What remained persuaded the white men. A messenger was summoned.

9.

The Delaware stopped and sniffed the air.

"The dog is near at hand."

The white man smiled. He nodded to the others and stepped forward, eyes plumbing the depths of the forest. Now that he thought of it, he was aware of the smell of bear fat. The savages used it to make a disgusting ointment to protect themselves against insects. Their guide, on the other hand, so as not to interfere with his sense of smell, had adopted the remedy in use among the settlers: smearing himself with mud.

The forest opened up into a clearing, the light struck the ground. The men were dazzled.

A shadow darted between the branches, about a hundred yards ahead of the group of hunters. The white men glimpsed it: the Delaware was already running in that direction.

Someone shouted. They launched themselves in pursuit.

Their prey clambered over shrubs and fallen branches, hurled itself across the clearing. Penetrating the forest was the only way for it to save its skin. It broke through the vegetation with the agility of a deer, but tall grass and uneven ground slowed it down.

The Delaware ran to the spot where the trees thinned, shouldered his rifle and took aim. A shot struck the air. The savage darted out of the cloud of smoke.

The troop of hunters saw him disappearing among the trees. They walked on to the place where the forest had swallowed him up and found him standing there, motionless by a big tree trunk.

The guide raised his rifle to the sky and uttered a shout of triumph. At the base of the tree lay their prey. The Mohawk, naked to the waist, clenched his teeth. He clutched his calf with hands that were soaked with blood. His sweat-drenched limbs trembled.

The white men rejoiced and tied up the wounded Indian. The first huntsman searched him and found what he was looking for: a folded piece of paper in the handle of the captive's knife.

After a quick glance he turned back toward the others.

"Damn, it's written in Mohawk!"

Nathaniel Gordon shook his head. That's what comes of educating savages, he thought. He wondered what the next thing would be. A monkey reciting the Psalms?

He squatted down and held the sheet in front of the wounded man's eyes. Fresh blood dripped between the Mohawk's fingers. The flies had started swarming.

"Read what's written on it, you dog!"

The Mohawk said nothing.

Gordon nodded to the Delaware, who took out his knife and made a cut on the prisoner's arm. He lifted a flap of skin, pulled it away, set it aside.

The Mohawk quivered, but didn't make a sound. The white man roared with fury.

He waved the paper in front of the Indian's nose again.

"It's an order from the Johnsons, we know that much. What does it say?"

Silence.

The Delaware made a fresh cut. Another piece of skin came away, this time from the chest. He set it down next to the first. He would turn it into a tobacco pouch.

The Mohawk hissed between his teeth.

"Speak!" the white man snarled.

One of the others stopped him with a hand on his shoulder.

"There's no rush, Nat. We should let the Indian get on with it."

The white men sat down a short distance away, to drink from a bottle, while the guide finished his work. In the end, Gordon got up impatiently.

"A waste of time, for heaven's sake."

He whistled to the Delaware.

"That's enough. We've done what we had to do."

The Delaware wiped his hands with a handful of leaves and pointed to the tortured Mohawk.

"Big man," he said.

The head huntsman looked first at the Delaware, then at the Mohawk hanging by his feet. He was still alive. He was panting, choking on the blood that ran into his nostrils from every part of his flayed body. Not a single scrap of skin remained. His inverted face, his eyes below his nose, was as alien as the face of an animal.

"Big man, eh?"

The white man walked over and spat on the lacerated face.

10.

It's the same dream, always. The church, the coffin. Peter plays the violin, Joseph grips his tomahawk. A warrior helps him dig.

Now I recognize him. Ronaterihonte.

The earth is hard. Blood pours from his broken nails, the earth grows wet. Every drop is a scarlet leaf.

The church disappears. In its place, a forest of maples in autumn splendor. Sitting on a rock, William blesses the efforts of Joseph and the warrior with a smile. His face is painted and he holds a tortoise rattle.

I walk over, sit down on his knees, stroke his lips.

"Who's in the coffin, William?"

He replies, but in an unknown language. A mountain wind carries his words away. A canoe appears on the river. Beside it, a girl. William comes up and holds out his hand to me.

"Come into the Garden with me, my love, come to the middle of the Water."

Joseph and the warrior load on the coffin, the canoe goes back upriver.

All of a sudden I find myself in the flat in Canajoharie, above the general store.

I shake the girl's hand. Her eyes are the color of the river.

The children are sleeping. I am about to wake up.

11.

A rare prey, in the Mohawk Valley.

The hunters thanked their good fortune.

The reddish skin shone in the sun, pearled with droplets.

The animal, up to its ribs in the water, lifted its head. Its muzzle streamed with water. Huge ears, downward-facing nostrils: it had the astonished expression of a massive mule. An impressive trophy spread from its forehead, as wide as a man's open arms.

The moose looked around, sniffed the air. One of the hunters wetted his finger with saliva and tested the wind. The breeze had barely changed direction.

The animal shook itself, turned its hindquarters and made off.

The old men said that the moose runs faster than any hunter, faster than a horse, but man runs for longer than any animal. The moose gallops as long as its heart holds out, but every now and again it has to stop and rest. Instinct warns it that the hunters are still on its trail, but it has to stop again, and then again, more and more often. With each stop the hunters get a little closer. Each time the moose starts running again, it gets slower. More and more uncertain. It isn't easy for such a big animal to shake people off its trail. Men can maintain the same pace for a whole day. The moose, exhausted, will await the knife as a liberation.

In the afternoon the clues became more frequent. The moose sought the depths of the undergrowth, leaving visible marks. The young wolves lengthened their strides.

Further on, still hidden from sight, the prey stopped running. It raised its muzzle to the sky and uttered a gloomy cry, ready for the last battle.

The hunters stopped on the edge of the clearing. The moose appeared, less than forty feet away from them. Protected by the shadows, Paul Oronhyateka pulled the trigger.

Behind the cloud of smoke, the animal collapsed.

The hunters ran toward it. They surrounded the body, a little crowd attending a funeral.

"We thank the Lord for favoring us with a good hunt. Let us give the blood of the moose, our brother, to the spirits of the earth, just as the Master of Life has always to be pleased with us. May the spirit of the moose be placated: its flesh will keep our people alive. Amen."

The oldest warrior bent down, knife in hand. From the animal's sliced throat a stream of blood drenched the earth and the men's legs.

"Find a place to butcher it, Kanenonte."

The others squatted down, supporting themselves on their long rifles.

Someone drank fresh blood. Someone filled the pipe. Time passed. Oronhyateka got to his feet. At that moment Kanenonte appeared beside him.

His eyes were open wide. He was foaming at the mouth with fury. He was trembling.

In the room the women formed a circle. In the middle were Molly Brant and an older woman, dressed in a skirt and a fire-red blanket. Between the two, a bundle of cedar branches was burning on a tray. What had been tree became smoke, thin spirals rising toward the ceiling without encountering drafts.

The woman in red collected the twigs, drew a circle with her right hand, murmured something. Molly voiced the most important question.

"Who is inside the coffin?"

"I repeat what I have already said, Molly Brant. I believe that Warraghiyagey is not satisfied with his funeral. He is going up the current to return to the island of his forefathers. Now he is in the real world, he sees things that we don't see."

Molly noticed that the smoke was reflected in the mirror. She brought her eyes to the reflection in the glass, then to the incandescent tips of the branches. The smoke quivered, as if filled with a breath of wind. The woman with the twigs closed her eyelids. Molly nodded.

"Send your *oyaron* to question him, Molly Brant. Your dreams are powerful; Warraghiyagey will speak again."

Molly nodded. Suddenly a buzzing noise arose outside. It was like the sound of a river when the current quickens before it cascades. Before Molly had a chance to reply, the murmur had exploded into cries of rage and horror.

In the middle of the crowd, young warriors were stamping their feet, their muscles trembling, their arms raised to the sky, they brandished knives and hatchets. The young men's legs were black with congealed blood. All around them, older men echoed their cries. They wept, shout, roared curses. Their voices were wounding to the ear.

The thing at the warriors' feet was offensive to the eye. The thing at the warriors' feet had once had human features. The body of Samuel Waterbridge was now a flayed prey, left to rot on the ground.

Molly knew death, obscene and cruel, but she had never seen it in the place where life is preserved. Not dragged into the middle of the village, not displayed so that young men could promise themselves revenge.

Molly entered the circle of furious bodies.

Around her, voices quietened. To her ears there came the panting of the warriors, the weeping of a woman.

"This killing calls for revenge, but your voices make the heart bleed. Youth and rage are no excuse."

She paused. In that frozen time nothing moved, but eyes flashed.

The woman continued her harangue. "A flayed body is a wound to the eye. Death has entered the village without a song being sung, without a ritual being performed. Madness passes through the young men's minds. Death must leave Canajoharie."

The men remained silent, even the young men who had collected the body. The women punctuated the speech with murmurs of approval.

Molly looked at Tekarihoga. The head of the Tortoise clan nodded.

"Those who brought the body into the village, let them take it away, then, and let that which is prescribed be done."

The young men picked up the corpse, which was merely a scab of blood and dust.

As they moved away, Kanenonte spoke to his companions through gritted teeth.

"While we waste time with the old law, they're slaughtering us."

12.

Guy Johnson became aware of a kind of creaking noise between his neck and shoulder, or rather a grinding sound, as when you break glass or walk on gravel. Sand between his vertebrae, something was wrong, he had slept badly. Anxiety sent him walking around the house, back and forth, halfway between an animal being led by the bridle and a recluse trying to stretch his legs.

Each morning he woke up and couldn't find peace. Each day he felt shorter and stockier, squashed as if in a press. From one hour to the next his back more bent, his legs more twisted. The weight of Sir William's legacy.

The weight of Indian affairs.

That afternoon he rolled his head all the way around, right, left, then chin up, chin down, and now his head tilted, left ear almost touching his shoulder, same operation to the right, but nothing to be done: something was out of place, it wouldn't fit.

He passed frantically from one room to the other, studied the windows, sat at his desk, rummaged among papers, picked up the letter from General Gage, got up, went back to the drawing board. Tried to calm his own state of mind, spilling his agitation out onto one of the big white pages. He drew and piled together squiggles, curved lines, until he sketched human figures that immediately struck him as sinister, ominous, presages of ruinous events. He crumpled up the pages, got to his feet and threw them into the fireplace.

Guy had always loved to draw. Sadly, his drawings had been burned in the fire that had happened two years ago. The house had been struck by lightning, the flames had devoured the wood, the map collection, the books in the library, important documents about land concessions. He had had the house rebuilt in stone, and he and his family had moved back in, less than a year before. Now Guy Park was an imposing building. Since the threats from the Bostonians, reinforcement work had been under way.

From Massachusetts the clashes were spreading and the number of rebels was rising. There was fear of an attack on Canada, the undefended stronghold of loyalty to the Crown. Hence the order that had just arrived from Gage: mobilize, leave. Cross the border with able-bodied men, including Indians.

Yeah. But how to tell the Mohawk that they had to go to fight in Canada while the valley was in an uproar?

*   *   *

Guy had been a boy when he left County Meath and Ireland. In America he had joined Sir William, a distant relative, and married his daughter Mary.

He had now spent more years in America than he had in his motherland.

And yet he remained an Irishman among Irishmen, just like the old man. If he tripped over a tree root or cut himself shaving, he still cursed in *gaedhilge*. When, ruminating about something, he counted on his fingers, he said, *a haon, a dó, a trí, a ceathair*. The old tongue.

And the old religion.

Like the old man and many Irishmen of the most recent generation, Guy was faithful to the Church of England. Adherence to the Anglican faith was a necessary condition for the *cursus honorum* in the ranks of Empire: no Papists among the trusted men of His Majesty. The Papists were Spain and France, enemy powers on both sides of the ocean. The Papists were sedition, stretching back over many centuries, in the closest and most riotous of the colonies: Ireland.

Sir William had been born and brought up a Catholic. In subjugated Ireland, few of his relatives had converted to the English God. Part of the Johnson family had supported the Jacobite rebellion to put a Catholic, James VII of Scotland, on the throne.

Beneath the bitumen that covered the hull of his soul, the old faith still pumped blood to his heart. Superstitions, good-luck formulas, recommendations to a saint, phrases from the Latin missal.

After their defeat, the Jacobite exile had touched America. In the Mohawk Valley, the eastern door of the Longhouse, a community of Highland Scots had settled. They had become part of the broader community, ready to take up arms to defend it.

For thirty years, intimate and unwritten laws governed the world that Sir William called Iroquireland. What Guy feared was the breakdown of the balance between Indians and white men, Crown and colonies, Whig rebels and Tory loyalists. That breakdown would leave America in flames. Not even the most solid stone walls would protect his world, his family, his property from those flames.

On top of that, Mary was pregnant again and the baby was due very soon. After all the girls, perhaps he would have a male heir, and now, of all times, he had to leave. Indecision gripped his innards. Given the worsening situation, only one person could help him.

"Father?" said a childish voice.

Guy, deep in thought as he was, had no idea which room he was in. He had been wandering like a sleepwalker. He looked around: he was in the library. Half-empty shelves, the backs of the few books saved from the fire. Esther, his firstborn, was standing in the doorway, twelve years of fair hair and green eyes.

"Does your mother need something?" he asked her.

"No, Father, Mother is well. But Mr. Joseph Brant is here, he asks to be received. He says it is very important."

Lupus in fabula.

Joseph Brant had never come to Guy Park except as an escort and interpreter. Not only an interpreter, but also a bridge between the two communities, united by their interests and their Anglican faith: working with Reverend Stewart, he had translated Mark's Gospel into Mohawk. And yet if you peeked beneath the veil of the Church of England, on one side you found Papists, on the other pagans. Two tribes of masked men.

Joseph was one of the sons of the agreement created by Sir William, a plant grown from a graft. Viewed with suspicion by Indians less in contact with the white men, with fear by white men less in contact with the Indians. Viewed with respect by those on both banks who were anxious to keep the bond firm.

The messenger had been discovered and flayed alive. Because of the situation, he wasn't even able to bring a message to the Oneidas, the closest of the brother tribes. They were isolated. What Joseph related made it even more imperative to obey the order that Guy had received.

Sir John had already said he wouldn't move from Johnson Hall. That he would do what seemed right to him. Guy decided that he would leave, taking his family with him.

"Joseph, my brother. If this rebellion were to turn into open war, what would the Six Nations do? Fight for King George?"

"The Mohawk are well aware that the rebel sons of King George are the same ones who are committing injustices against them. People like Jonas Klug."

"So?"

"The Six Nations are not subject to the Crown. In our language the word 'subjects' doesn't exist. Sir William knew that. He never treated us as subjects, only as allies."

"Sir William did everything possible to protect the Indian brothers from the settlers who are threatening your lands. He did it in the name of the king."

"My people will never forget that. But anyway, Sir William is no longer here."

Guy nodded bitterly.

Joseph went on: "To persuade my people to unbury the hatchet, Warraghiyagey would have requested a council. He would have spoken in Mohawk. After lengthy discussions the sachems would have accepted, in spite of the sufferings caused to the Six Nations by the war twenty years ago. We lost courageous men, we lost Hendrick, and we didn't get much in exchange. We would have fought not for the English king, but for William Johnson."

"I'm the superintendent now," replied Guy. "I'm a Johnson. My wife is Sir William's daughter, and she is expecting a baby who might be a boy, an heir in the direct line of Warraghiyagey. I don't know Mohawk, but I can speak in a council, with your help."

"I'm the Department's interpreter. If a council is held in Johnson Hall, I will do my job."

"Not here in the valley. It would alarm the rebels. It would supply a pretext for a sudden attack. We have to unite the Six Nations many miles away. In Oswego."

Joseph waited before replying. He looked out the window.

"That's many days' travel."

Guy followed the Indian's eyes. "Oswego is at the center of the Longhouse. The Nations will participate in large numbers. You are a war chief, persuade your people to come. This rebellion is the most serious threat that the Mohawk and the Six Nations have ever faced."

Joseph seemed to meditate on the last sentence.

Guy did not reveal the true reason for his choice. Oswego was on the way to Montreal. General Gage was asking for troops for Canada. If the council went as he predicted, Guy would be leading an Indian army.

He couldn't tell Joseph that.

His neck went on creaking.

13.

The echo of hammer blows, the ring of nails entering wood. The scrape of saws, banging beams. Gouges carving and planes smoothing. Work songs, shouts and curses.

Joseph went down to the river. Little fires spread the smell of pitch through the spring air. He reached the young men of his clan and asked Kanenonte for a report on the preparations.

"We've repaired seven boats. The others are falling to bits."

Someone lit a pipe and offered it to him. Joseph took a puff.

"It'll take at least twenty. What do you need?"

"Planks," replied Oronhyateka. "We have enough left for three boats. And barrels of paint, at least thirty. And boxes of nails, all the nails in the valley."

Joseph reassured him. A column of logs had been passing through Canajoharie's sawmill for several days: there would be no shortage of basic materials. As to everything else, Molly was expecting a cargo from New York. He asked if there was anything else, then rose to his feet and took the road leading to the general store. The sounds of work followed him down the slope.

For months he hadn't seen so much activity around the jetty. Since the closure of the port of Boston, the bad air blowing in from the coast had been stifling trade. Anyone who earned his living as a boatman was left high and dry, and the boats rotted on the banks of the Mohawk.

News had come in about Oswego. A council. The opportunity to listen to illustrious speakers, to meet friends and distant relations, reestablish alliances, celebrate births and marriages. Parties, rum, games of chance. Even more important: gifts. For the Department, bringing the Indians together meant showing their muscle, and without abundant gifts, even Sir William's son-in-law risked looking puny. The message had to come through loud and clear: the storerooms of Johnson Hall were always full, at the disposal of Guy Johnson's loyal friends.

The council meant business. Oswego was the most important port on the Great Lakes, a land of milk and honey, grain and salmon, where the English ships had never stopped docking.

In Canajoharie even the wealthiest families were now drawing on their stores, and the new harvest threatened to be poor. The smoke from the sacrifices didn't awaken the Three Sisters. Corn, Bean and Squash were tired and Saint John seemed deaf to their prayers as well.

They were short of tools and seeds. They were short of rifles and ammunition. Fur sellers didn't earn enough, and if they raised their prices they could keep their goods and die of hunger in the heat.

It hadn't required too much effort for Joseph to persuade his people. Many had taken the departure as the promise of a milder winter.

Reaching the general store, Joseph found the door locked. He knocked in vain several times, then sat down to wait, while the anxiety of leaving flooded his thoughts.

A long and tiring journey. A hundred and fifty miles huddled in the boats. At night, damp blankets and clouds of mosquitoes.

Sir John would stay with his family in Johnson Hall. Guy Johnson brought to Oswego his daughters and his pregnant wife. For his own family, Joseph was considering a different plan. He didn't want to have them with him, but he didn't want to leave them at the farm either. With so many warriors away, the valley was unsafe. They could go to their Oneida relations, eighty miles to the south. To Oquaga, a wealthy village far from the disturbances.

The touch of a hand interrupted his thoughts. Joseph understood and turned around without giving a start. Molly was quieter than a falcon. Some white men swore they had seen her changing into a woodpecker, taking flight and then settling again a little further away. Impossible, Joseph replied, my sister likes to walk.

She certainly hadn't left the shop to go for a walk.

"They've confiscated the cargo from New York," she said. "Yesterday morning, just outside Fort Hunter."

"Who told you?"

"One of the boatmen. He managed to find a horse and rode all the way here. If you want to talk to him, he's still at the inn."

"There's no need. I'll gather the warriors together and we'll go and get it all back."

"You know Guy Johnson," Molly replied. "He'll want to pay for another cargo instead. He doesn't want any problems before we leave."

"Another cargo could take weeks, and we need the hardware for the boats right now."

"I can get hold of something so we don't have to stop work. You've got a more important task."

Joseph remained silent.

"The dream is getting clearer and clearer," said Molly. "The warrior who's digging with you is Ronaterihonte."

Joseph stood open-mouthed. He hadn't heard that name for ages.

"You've got to go and call him. He'll come to Oswego with you."

Joseph spread his arms in disbelief. "With everything that needs to be done? It'll take us days to reach his cabin."

"It's the dream that wants him. The women agree."

"He doesn't obey dreams."

"But my brother does. You'll be able to convince him."

Molly untied a wampum bracelet from her right wrist.

"Bring him this," she said. "He won't be able to refuse."

14.

The outlines of things were visible, illuminated by the first suggestion of dawn. A table, two wooden benches, the andirons by the fire, the trunk. The rhythm of their breathing was a calm backwash. He became aware of the smell of the bodies under the bearskin, the warmth of his wife and daughter.

The echo of long-ago awakenings. In the wooden shelter the man was alone. His wife and daughter were no longer there, killed by the thirst for blood that had swept the frontier many years before.

Since then he slept little and always awoke before daylight. He got up without a sound. He glanced askance at the picture of the Virgin, cut from a French almanac, a gift from his old teacher, Father Guillaume. The artist had given the Madonna vaguely Indian features.

He picked up a book from the table, wrapped himself up in a blanket and went outside. The sky was pink and blue. The mist rose patchily from the ground, made denser by the morning half-light.

The sun was high in the sky when three figures emerged from the scrub at the end of the path. The man stopped sharpening his knife on his leather belt and picked up his rifle. Lately the forests had become dangerous again. Few of the isolated settlers still relied on their aim to defend themselves and their property. Many of them had built palisades, but the man wasn't a settler and had little to defend. His rifle was enough.

He recognized the visitors and lowered his weapon.

"Ronaterihonte, I am your brother," one of them said.

The man responded to his greeting.

"I, too, am your brother, Thayendanegea."

Joseph Brant introduced the others.

"You remember Jacob Kanatawakhon and August Sakihenakenta."

The two warriors greeted him with brief nods of the head as they rested their rifles on the ground.

"We've been traveling for two days," said Joseph.

The man opened the door.

"Come in. I've got some stewed venison."

Joseph contemplated the interior of the log cabin: the blackened wood seemed to have been born from the earth. A plank laden with books ran across the wall. He recognized *L'ingénu* by Voltaire, the *Spiritual Exercises* of Saint Ignatius, the Bible and Rousseau's *Émile*. Titles that came from New York, bound in expensive leather.

Philip Lacroix Ronaterihonte wasn't a seasonal hunter: he lived in the forests even in winter. For more than ten years he had forced himself into a retreat unusual for an Indian.

Joseph stared at his old comrade-in-arms. Since he had made that choice, shortly after the end of the war, their boyhood friendship had faded away till it survived only in memory. He wondered what was left: a thread as thin as a horsehair. He still didn't understand why Lacroix had appeared in his sister's dreams.

"It's Molly who sends me."

"How is she?"

"She's in good health. She left Johnson Hall and opened a general store in the village."

"And her children?"

"They're growing up. Peter is a man now. I already take him hunting."

"And yours?"

"Mine are growing up, too. Susanna is a good mother."

Joseph picked up one of the bowls that Lacroix had filled with meat. Jacob and August thanked him and started eating without ceremony.

Lacroix was still leaning on the mantelpiece. His hair fell on his shoulders like crow's wings. A carved wooden cross hung on his chest. His face betrayed no emotion. His resolute features could have belonged to an Indian or a half-breed, perhaps to the bastard son of a *coureur de bois*. His age was difficult to guess, although Joseph knew that they were contemporaries.

"Did you know about Massachusetts?"

Lacroix didn't reply.

Joseph gestured to indicate the northeast.

"The English Whigs have assembled an army to fight their king. They call themselves the New England Volunteers. They are besieging Boston and are about to wage war on Canada."

August and Jacob had served themselves again, without saying a word. That was why Joseph had chosen them: they were alert and discreet. He could trust them.

"The Albany settlers support the rebellion. There's a risk that they will attack the valley. Spies and assassins are on our trail. A messenger that we sent to the Oneidas was killed. Flayed alive."

Joseph waited for the hunter's reaction.

"Why did you come?" asked Lacroix.

"Guy Johnson wants to call a council. To ask the Longhouse to join forces with the king."

Lacroix threw another dry branch on the fire.

"You said Molly sent you."

"Yes. She had a dream."

The other man nodded, as if waiting to hear it.

Joseph held out the wampum bracelet.

"She told me to give you this."

Lacroix held it in his hands and stared at it for a long time. The white and black shells formed rhombuses and moons around a wolf's head. A gilded button stood out from the weave. It came from a French army uniform: the uniform of a drummer boy.

Joseph knew that this object was the pledge of adoption into the Wolf clan. It had been woven by Molly, for the boy that the French priests had christened Philippe Lacroix. The Mohawk had given him the name of a dead man, Ronaterihonte, "Keep Faith," and a widowed mother to look after. The bracelet represented new life, the life that Molly had given him when she rescued him from the warriors' vendetta. Joseph clearly remembered that day, even though he had been a little boy. The day of Hendrick's death and the wound to Warraghiyagey's side. The battle of Lake George had won William Johnson his baronetcy.

Philip had learned the language very quickly: at the mission where he had grown up there lived many Caughnawaga, who spoke a dialect similar to Mohawk. He and Joseph had received their warrior's initiation together and fought side by side until the end of the conflict, like young wolves. Once the war was over, Sir William had encouraged Joseph to study and settled down with his sister. Philip had taken a wife, and they had had a daughter. A brief period of serenity.

After the tragedy, he had done some terrible deeds. Since then Huron and Abenaki called him Le Grand Diable.

One day he had introduced himself to Molly and, without a word, had presented her with the wampum bracelet, giving up the life that had been given to him, and had moved to this cabin in the woods. He returned to Canajoharie a few times a year to sell furs, watched with fear by those who had known the war, and with reverence by the young men who were attracted by his legend.

"Molly says it's time for you to return to the nation. She says that's what the dream means."

The hunter sat down on a worn old chair, still staring at the shell belt.

When Lacroix looked up, Joseph felt a twinge of unease. "We will leave with the new moon. The council will be held in Oswego."

He had delivered the message. Now he was anxious to return: the journey to Oswego was not far off and there was still much to be done.

He gestured to Jacob and August to get up.

"We're going back. Thanks for the food."

When they were standing in the doorway again, Joseph turned around.

"Molly will want to know your answer."

Lacroix nodded again.

"Tell her I wish my dreams were as clear as hers."

15.

"We received the Game from the Master of Life, at the beginning of time. Our forefathers played it as God had ordained and we still play it that way ourselves."

Johannes Tekarihoga gestured broadly with his right hand. His arm and shoulder, naked, were still strong. His body, wrapped in a dark blue cloak edged with shells, was six feet tall. The players joined their hands at heart-height and lowered their heads. The old man went on, followed by all the others.

"Our father who art in heaven. . ."

The old sachem concluded the prayer, raised his head and exhorted the players with a few words.

"Play hard, but fairly. Don't lose your heads."

The field, the only uncultivated one, sloped gently toward the Mohawk River, not far from the groups of houses that formed the village. Two teams occupied it, about thirty men on each side.

Peter Johnson thought that one detail contradicted the old man's assertions. The Master of Life, at the beginning of time, had ordained that they should play *baggataway* naked and in war paint. But here everyone's legs were covered by leather leggings, and some players wore shirts.

And furthermore, at the beginning of time no one would have recited the Lord's Prayer.

Tekarihoga half-closed his eyes, whispered a few words and threw the ball in the air, right into the middle of the contenders.

One of the clubs struck it full on. The warrior uttered a long cry, then a cacophony of shouts invaded the playing field. The factions mingled, a single vibrating mass, a running horde.

The ball fell back down quickly, soon joined by the crowd of players. A wild affray broke out. Wood against wood. Wood against bone. At last the object of contention was dislodged from its lair of limbs and impelled at great speed toward the goal. In a mad dash, Peter reached the fugitive and knocked the head of his club against the deerskin globe with all his might. The shot was spectacular, if badly aimed. The ball traveled a long, tense trajectory to the forest rim. The players hurled themselves forward, waving their clubs, but noticed a presence at the edge of the playing-field. The group slowed down, the voices faded away to silence.

The man bent over the ball, which had rolled to his feet, and threw it back toward Tekarihoga. Even so, play didn't resume. The players looked as if they were under a spell.

Peter glanced at the old sachem: he nodded solemnly.

Molly was waiting with her arms folded, standing in the doorway of the emporium. A short distance away were some curious women with babies in their laps or slung in bundles around their necks.

The woman's eyes flashed. She was waiting for him.

"Greetings to you, Degonwadonti."

"Greetings to you, Ronaterihonte. Come in, the water is boiling on the fire."

Molly ordered the servant to make the tea, then invited Philip to sit in a black leather armchair, high-armed, comfortable and luxurious. For a long time the hunter's bottom and back hadn't rested against anything so soft. There was something sensual, almost obscene, about how comfortable it was. Lacroix abandoned himself to its embrace. He let his spine adjust, let his elbows fall inertly on the curved, gleaming wood, his buttocks and thighs sink in without tension. Some vague, dreamy minutes passed before the smell of the tea woke him. He found himself holding a saucer and a steaming cup.

"Sugar?" asked the servant.

"Yes, thanks." Sugar. No idea whether his tongue remembered the taste.

The servant finished her task and left.

The man and the woman took their first sips. The tip of Philip's tongue said *welcome back* to the flavor of liquefied sugar. The welcome was a hearty one; his whole mouth performed an elaborate ceremony. Philip couldn't help sighing. An untameable beast, pleasure.

After a few minutes of silence, Molly spoke.

"It was not I who summoned you, Ronaterihonte. It was the nation who called you: the dreams say so."

Philip took another sip. The cup warmed his hands.

"The nation adopted you and restored you to life," Molly went on. "Now it needs you. In the dreams you are beside my brother again.

"The dream has not yet disclosed itself; some of it is still in shadow. I can only tell you this: you must go to Oswego with Joseph and the warriors."

"I'm not a warrior anymore, Molly Brant. I'm not anything anymore."

"You're a Mohawk, and the Mohawk are suffering."

Molly stopped, summoned and assembled her words, inspected them and finally set them marching, one after the other. "Our name risks fading away, the jaws of time have already swallowed up whole lineages. Our land is being invaded and pillaged, a winter of hardship is about to fall upon this valley. I will stay in the village, because women, old people and children need me, but the future of the nation depends on what happens far from here. You and Joseph are part of it." She broke off and smiled. "You have to trust in dreams."

Philip stretched out in the armchair and brought the cup to his lips, as a whisper crept into his ears.

Welcome back, Ronaterihonte. The circle must be closed. The journey must begin.

16.

"Woman of the Sky had a daughter, who was fertilized by the west wind. When this daughter was still in her belly, the two grandchildren of Woman of the Sky argued about the manner of their birth. Left-Hand Twin didn't want to come out in the normal way. He traveled until he appeared from his mother's armpit, and by so doing he killed her."

Molly looked at Peter's face in the mirror and ran the razor over his skin. The boy was sitting cross-legged, motionless, his little sister Ann hugging one of his legs.

"The Twins buried their mother," Molly went on, "who became Mother Maize, from whom were born Squash, Bean and Corn, the Three Sisters who sustain life. From her heart tobacco was born, which is used to send messages to the World of Heaven."

She finished shaving the sides of his skull. A long tuft of dark hair was left, held together by a red ribbon. The mirror reflected the image of a warrior who was young, handsome and strong. His flesh a fine consistency, his bones well arranged. The eyes of the nation could be well pleased with him. The spirits of the forefathers would protect him.

"The Twins went on challenging one another. Right created the beautiful hills, the lakes, the flowers and the gentle creatures. Left, the steep gulches and the rapids, thorns and predators. Right was sincere, reasonable, good-hearted. Left lied, loved to fight, was rebellious by nature and walked complicated paths. Because Right created men, he is known as our Creator and the Master of Life. Never forget to honor him in prayer and recite the Psalms every night."

She fell silent and studied the boy. Sir William would have been pleased. His son was going to Oswego, to his first council. His hair braided in the traditional way, wampum belts to attest to his lineage. A true Mohawk, everyone would say. And educated, too, in the languages and science of the white men. Warraghiyagey's true son.

"Your father would have been as proud of you as I am."

The young man studied himself in the mirror. He turned his head, lifted his chin, lowered his forehead to gauge the effect.

"Something's missing," he said.

He got up, moving the little girl aside with a caress of his hand, and picked up the rifle. He turned to face the bigger mirror, hanging from the wall. With his gun resting on his foot, the image was perfect. The young man smiled to himself.

"It's a present from Uncle Joseph." He ran a hand over his smooth, dark hair. "Beautiful."

"Are you going to hunt deer with that, Peter?" his little sister asked.

"Yes, and I will also defend our valley." The young man seemed to reflect upon the words he had just uttered. "Who invented the rifle, mother?" he asked. "Right Twin or Left Twin?"

"Who was it, Mama, who was it?" Ann cut in in a shrill voice.

Molly appeared behind her son. She rested a hand on the little girl's head.

"The works of one may not exist without those of the other. You can't walk in the sun without casting a shadow. And you also need shadows when the sun is too strong."

"So it was Left?" Peter insisted.

"Stubborn son of mine," Molly smiled. "You know very well that it was the white man's skill that made rifles, violins, microscopes and the other things you like." She frowned. "But I don't know if it was God or the devil who put the rifle into the first armorer's head."

"The devil, mistress, it was definitely the devil."

Juba had come into the room, slender and quiet. She stopped and looked at the young man, who picked up his little sister. Ann fiddled with the tuft of hair that decorated his skull. She didn't seem interested in anything else.

The black serving-girl sought Molly's permission with her eyes, then placed her hands on the young man's head and murmured phrases of blessing in an unknown tongue. When she had finished she looked again at the matriarch of the Wolf clan.

"Bring the gift," Molly ordered.

"A gift?" said Peter, freeing himself from Ann's embrace.

"The rifle your uncle Joseph gave you isn't the only thing you might need."

When Juba returned with the box, Molly took from it a violin-case.

The young man gave a start. A new violin! He would have thrown his arms around his mother's neck, but he wasn't a little boy anymore. He delicately picked up the instrument and tested its weight, plucked the strings, sniffed the smell of gleaming wood.

"Music will keep you company on your journey," his mother said. "You will learn new songs and lots of other things."

"Play the one I like!" Ann begged him. "Go on, play it!"

Her brother needed no pleading. His bow darted and the little girl began swaying in time to the reel.

Molly looked at the scene, hiding her worry behind a smile. Many thoughts crowded her days, as dreams did her nights. William had given Peter education and knowledge, but had not had time to initiate him into the world of war. Now it was Joseph's turn to complete the work, to make a warrior of him. The time would come soon. Pride and fear challenged one another in the woman's mind, promising each other endless war.

Even in her dreams Peter played the violin, while William said something in the language of their forefathers. If only she could have understood those words, she would have bidden the boy a more serene farewell.

A little swarm of children invaded the room, shouting excitedly. Peter welcomed them with open arms and let them drag him to the ground.

Molly watched her children struggling together and rolling on the floor, laughing and joking. The time for games was about to end, and not only for Peter.

A shadow was falling over the valley, licking at its edges. Molly's task would not be easy: guarding the land of her grandfathers, protecting the children of the nation as though they were her own.

17.

Joseph didn't see who gave the signal, but the crowd began drifting slowly toward the river, Guy Johnson at the head of the group, Daniel Claus by his side. Joseph stayed aside and let the ranks pass him, checking that no one was missing.

One hundred and twenty white-skinned people. The dependents of the Indian Department and part of the Highlanders. Ninety Mohawk warriors. Johannes Tekarihoga. Families with women and children. Thirty fully laden boats. Weapons and tools, barrels of powder, bars of lead and bullet presses. Provisions, sacks of corn, salt pork, rum.

In the middle of the crowd, a group of women accompanied Mary Johnson, with her prominent belly, her hand gripping her sister Nancy's arm. The little daughters clung to their mother's skirt, as if they were carrying her train to the altar. The white and African serving girls held the straps of the rucksacks or waited apart from the others. Guy hadn't want to leave his pregnant wife and his children at home. He wanted to have them by him, where he could protect them.

Sir John had come to bid the expedition farewell. He shook his brother-in-law's hand first.

"Good luck. May God protect you and be with you on your journey."

"And help you defend our lands," Guy replied.

In front of many of the houses sticks were planted diagonally in the ground, a sign that the dwelling was empty and the spirits would punish anyone who dared approach.

Outside the general store, Mary Johnson saw a small cluster of women parting. Molly Brant appeared, with little Ann in her arms. The Indian woman raised a hand in greeting. Mary felt the creature in her womb stirring. She brought her hands to her belly.

Esther saw the scene. The eyes of that woman on her mother's belly, the vague gesture of her hand. She felt as if she were looking at a house of cards just before it collapsed. She came over to her mother and tugged hard on the rim of her cloak. She wanted to beg her father to stop, not to let everything fall to pieces, crash to the ground, but instead she said nothing.

The procession passed in front of Molly, who watched motionless from the veranda. When Joseph climbed the steps, Peter appeared beside him. The young man was kitted out for the journey in a leather jacket, powder horn at his side and rifle over his shoulder. Molly looked at her son with resignation, stroked his young face; the caress became a grip upon his tuft of hair. Peter gritted his teeth. Molly let go of him and turned again to Joseph.

"Lead him wisely."

They hugged.

The boy kissed his mother and came down to join the others. His eyes shone. Philadelphia and his years of study were nothing compared to the adventure that awaited him.

The last to receive Molly's farewell was Philip Lacroix, at the rear of the column. He replied with a nod of his head, with no need for words.

Joseph noticed three motionless figures on the edge of the slope. Susanna had brought the children to say good-bye to him.

He touched them once each on the forehead, a sort of blessing to protect them from the evil of the world.

Isaac's eyes gleamed. Tears barely contained, an expression of fury.

"He wants to come with you," said Susanna. "Some people are bringing their families," she added quickly.

Joseph understood the veiled request and his features hardened.

"You will be safe in Oquaga." He stroked Christina without managing to smile at her, then looked at Susanna.

"Take care of your mother."

He turned around and went down to the pebbly bank, where Butler and his son were directing the embarkation. As the men climbed aboard, the boats left the banks one by one. On the last boat were Joseph, Lacroix, the Butlers and the loyal members of the Wolf clan. They all clutched poles and oars and steered the boat into the middle of the river. The way to Oswego began against the current, going up the Mohawk. Seventy miles to Fort Stanwix, the first major staging post, halfway through the journey.

Joseph watched the lazy wake of the boat and thought about who was leaving and who was staying. The sun pierced the clouds. Every element of the landscape was drenched with rain. The men's limbs, the wood of the Longhouse and the cabins, the fields of rye and corn, the gardens of beans and pumpkins. He watched the line of chestnut trees that ran down the gentle slopes that led to the first loop of the river. Leafy cedars, lofty larch-trees. Everything faded from sight behind them.

Reverend Stewart said that reciting the Our Father closed off all breaches through which the temptations of the Devil might enter. Nothing bad could happen if the Lord's Prayer occupied the mind; travails would be confronted in a state of grace. Few took Stewart's advice literally, but there on the water the words of the Our Father came to the lips of the white men and the Indians. Joseph closed his eyes and raised his head toward the sky. It was filled with rays of light. He asked God to protect his family.

*   *   *

On the banks, the settlers witnessed the exodus of the Canajoharie Mohawk. The children waved, the adults watched with disdain. Joseph guessed that for many of them, seeing the Indians leave came as a relief.

The flotilla advanced, impelled onward by the poles and oars.

Joseph remembered this journey clearly. He had made it on other occasions, with Sir William. First to make war on the French, and then when the superintendent had gone to sign the peace between the Crown and the great chief Pontiac.

Where the sandy waters poured into the Mohawk, shallows and rocks choked the current, forming impetuous rapids. Several times they would have to take to the land, dragging the unloaded boats from the shore with thick ropes. To round the rocky precipices of Little Falls they had to load the boats onto their shoulders, climb through the woods for half a mile and then return to the water.

Joseph wasn't fearful for himself or for his companions: many of them had earned their living as boatmen. He thought of the women and children, who had never left home for so much as a day.

Guy Johnson turned to look for his wife and daughters. Two boats further back, Mary was standing motionlessly aboard, her eyes fixed on the little girls nestling at her feet. Nancy and the servant girls were on either side of her.

Guy glanced at Daniel Claus, sitting beside him, one of the few who knew the real reason for the journey. He brought a hand to his jacket pocket, where he kept the letter from General Gage. A hazardous risk: first deliver the obvious declaration of loyalty to the king from the sachems, and only at that point chain them to their duty as allies. He would display the order received by King George's highest representative in America and lead the warriors of the Six Nations into battle. He would show that he was a match for Sir William.

He listened to the silence, broken by the sound of the oars and the shouts of those in charge of the boats. One thing was certain: the river of life was leaving its old bed to flow in a new direction.

18.

Off they went. The Johnsons with servants, guards and savage friends. The devil alone knew where, and yet it wasn't important. At any rate it was a big moment. Judging by the preparations, they would be away for a while. Klug felt a space opening up in his chest, as if a stone had been lifted from his sternum. He took a sip of beer and rum and wiped his mouth with his sleeve.

He looked out the window, toward the river. His view was obstructed by a line of poplars. Behind it, the lands of troublesome neighbors. He imagined a valley without Indians, without wealthy Papists who had formed a compact with the nobility. Just honest working people. People like him.

His arms, back and legs still hurt. His bruises had passed from intense blue to red to yellow. And his feelings had changed color, too. He planned to denounce Brant and the other savages. The lawyer had reassured him: the signature was extorted, it wasn't worth a thing, the judges were bound to speak in his favor.

Klug thanked God. Reasonable people, the judges, at least in the colony of New York. Not like in London, where there was actually one who had taken it into his head to free the negroes. And the negroes knew it. The rumor ran from one farm to the next. You heard them chewing meaningless words, singing those refrains of theirs that might well have been hidden messages. They were passing on information, they were making arrangements to escape. If they set foot in England, they would become free men. And that was what they tried to do. They really escaped. It had already happened to Windecker, to Deypert, to Dr. Heyde. Cutting everyone's tongues out, that was the way to solve the problem of the negroes, when what they had to do was break their backs, not deliver sermons.

Klug shook his head. And the Tories? What did they have to say about it? Didn't they have slaves, too?

Klug felt hatred welling up in him. It was time to put a stop to it. Those people had given the signal. The king's army blocked the ships in the ports, stuff being confiscated, if anyone tried to say anything they threw them in jail. The Bostonians had the right idea. The loyalists were shot and thrown into the sea.

The Johnsons would buy the savages off with rum and drive them against other white men, against other Christians. No, you couldn't stand and watch, put out the red carpet, say make yourselves comfortable, just get on with it.

Klug made his decision. He would go to the next committee meeting. He would tell them what the savages had done. The next time they tried to touch him, a heck of a lot of people would pick up their rifles for Jonas Klug.

19.

The men from the Department spent dinner sitting in a semicircle, too tired to speak. They had been sailing for ten days and all of their faces showed the strain of travel. At sunset the convoy had camped on a steep riverbank, set up their tents and lit their fires. A little cluster of heat and faint light, rooted to trees and rocks.

Food and rum restored their strength. When Cormac McLeod reached the group, the smoke of pipes and cigars had already joined the smell of campfires.

The Scotsman wore a grim expression. He filled a dish and began to eat. "How's your wife, Mr. Johnson?"

"Not too good," Guy replied. "The journey is exhausting us."

As he lit the pipe, Joseph Brant studied the Irish gentleman. The fat that filled his clothes was less pronounced, and his face was reddened by the sun.

"I wonder what position the Oneida will take," Guy Johnson added, as if he wanted to dispel his anxiety about his wife.

"They'll come to the council, but they won't side with us," Claus observed irritably.

"You can bet on that," Butler added. "They're cowards. They may well have handed your messenger to the rebels," he said, making an abrupt gesture with his hand. "They will act the innocent, and so will the Onondaga and all the others. But if you offer them more rum than those damned Whigs and give them all the gunpowder they want, they'll soon be behind you, you'll see."

Johnson was about to reply, but McLeod interrupted.

"I'll just be happy to get to the council safe and sound."

"What do you mean?"

The Scotsman glanced at the darkness covering the trees.

"These forests aren't safe. A convoy of boats is an easy target."

"You're afraid of an ambush?"

"The rebels could have bought one of the local tribes."

Guy Johnson turned to Joseph.

"What does our interpreter think?"

The Indian shook his head.

"No one will do anything before the council."

"So that's what you've heard, old chap?" Butler cut in. "It's a bit early to start worrying about your scalp."

The Scotsman hunched up, wrapping himself in a blanket.

"I'll feel safer once we're past the Great Portage."

Joseph noticed that Peter was listening carefully. He got to his feet and gestured to the boy to follow him. They would take the first watch.

He led him to the old warriors' fire to receive Tekarihoga's blessing. They too were sitting in a circle and smoking. Some, already defeated by sleep or rum, were snoring under the stars. The old sachem was one of them.

They walked on to the outpost manned by Kanatawakhon and Sakihenakenta. Joseph told them to go and rest. Before they left, the two warriors pointed to a dark outline under an old willow tree. Peter went on the alert, but his uncle motioned him to look after the fire.

Lacroix was a shadow sniffing the air.

"What is it?" Joseph asked as he joined him.

"We aren't the only ones lighting fires."

He pointed to the tops of the trees. Joseph could just make out a thread of pale smoke, barely distinguishable, less than a mile away.

"Hunters?"

"Maybe."

Joseph went back to the campfire. Peter had made black tea. They drank in silence, holding the steaming cups to warm themselves.

"Uncle Joseph?"

"What?"

Peter nodded toward the shadow under the tree.

"You've fought together, haven't you?"

"Your father led us into war. We were your age."

"And then?"

"His wife and daughter were killed after the war. Since then he's withdrawn into the woods."

"Why do they call him Le Grand Diable?"

Joseph knew they would have to answer that question sooner or later. All the young warriors were still struck by Lacroix.

"It's a name given to him by his enemies. They tell stories about him. He took his revenge on his own."

For a while the crackling of the fire was the only sound.

Then Peter asked a question that Joseph hadn't expected. He stayed silent, looking at the bottom of his cup as if he would find the answer there.

At last he said, "Yes. He's my friend."

20.

Three weeks later the convoy was within sight of Fort Stanwix. Joseph had passed that way seven years before. He had gone with Sir William to sign the most important treaty. The sachems and the representatives of the Crown had established the border beyond which the white men were not permitted to settle: the River Unadilla, from Fort Stanwix to Pennsylvania.

Joseph remembered the size of the fort at the top of the embankment, the four ramparts and the palisade around it. Hard to imagine a log construction so solid and imposing, but the British garrison had left some time ago. A few winters of abandonment had weakened the pride of the place: the terraces were rotting, the casements were collapsing, the bulwarks were sliding into the ditch.

The convoy would stop off there for a few days. The boats were taking water. Stuffing straw into the joints was no longer enough; they needed pitch and paint. Some of the provisions were wet, and they would have to do some hunting and fishing. They would need to renew their strength and spirit before they set out for the Great Portage, along the muddy mule track that in four miles led to the other side, from the waters of the Mohawk to those of Wood Creek.

Beyond the plain lay Oneida territory. A delegation climbed to the fort to welcome Guy Johnson and guarantee a large presence at the Oswego Council.

Guy hurriedly organized a welcoming committee, made up of Daniel Claus, Joseph Brant and Peter Johnson.

In the approaching unit Joseph recognized the sachem who had celebrated Sir William's funeral. Shononses. His presence was an unexpected event. Ten warriors escorted him. He wore very expensive clothes and had birds' feathers tied to his single lock of hair

"I am your brother, Uraghquadirah," he said.

To welcome him in the proper manner, Guy Johnson had dusted off his red uniform with gold braid.

"I, too, am your brother, Shononses. We are honored by your visit."

Joseph showed off his elegant clothes and walking stick. He received the warriors' salute.

"The river brought news of your arrival," the Indian chief continued. "Before we left for the council ourselves, we came to wish you a safe journey. The river says that Le Grand Diable is with you."

"Yes," Guy confirmed.

A murmur rippled through the ranks of the Oneida.

"You remember Warraghiyagey's son," he added. "Peter Johnson. It's his first council."

The Oneida greeted the boy.

"Where is Le Grand Diable?" asked Shononses.

Joseph nodded to Guy Johnson and went down toward the river.

Lacroix was sitting with the young warriors. They were cleaning their rifles and filling their horns with black powder.

"The Oneida sachem has come to greet you. He wants to meet you."

Lacroix stood up.

"Don't sit with the Oneidas," hissed Jethro Kanenonte.

"Don't trust them," echoed Oronhyateka. "They're afraid of you and they will flatter you like girls. Don't go."

Joseph pointed the pommel of his stick.

"Hold your tongue."

The young man didn't lose his composure, but assumed a provocative tone.

"Joseph Brant knows the Oneidas are treacherous. It was they who sold their Samuel Waterbridge to the rebels, and they'll do the same with us. They have no honor."

"Shut up," Joseph snapped. "My wife and my children are Oneidas. The Oneidas are our brothers. I don't want any problems until the council."

The warriors fell silent and began cleaning their weapons again.

Joseph and Lacroix walked away.

Shononses launched into a long panegyric on the late Sir William, as if he had to be buried all over again. They were offered food and drink, as Claus improvised a welcome speech, which Joseph carefully translated. He couldn't bear the German's accent, it was like being whipped in the ear with a feather.

The Oneidas had brought wampum belts, beaver skins and multicolored blankets. Guy Johnson swapped them for gunpowder, knives and rope. Only after the gifts had been exchanged did he confront the matter at hand. He spoke of the unity of the Six Nations, the importance of the council, the need for reciprocal aid between the Mohawk and their junior Oneida brethren.

Joseph thought the speech was good, but it was missing something. He thought he spotted a movement, a familiar silhouette. The ghost of Sir William was sitting around the fire with them. He was listening to them and observing them curiously.

Shononses agreed about the need to remain united but stressed the neutrality of the Oneida. A conflict between Englishmen could not concern his people. The sachem's reply left everyone discontented.

Guy Johnson didn't seem impressed. "Even at the time of the Franco-Indian War the Oneida came here and declared themselves neutral," he murmured in Joseph's ear. "And yet Sir William did convince some of them. They even had themselves baptized."

It was time for tales of war. The stories mingled with the smoke that rose until it lost itself in the faint light of dusk.

Joseph looked again for the specter sitting at the edge of the circle, beyond the flames, but he didn't see anything. If Molly had been there he could have questioned her, asked her advice.

Later, at sunset, he found himself strolling among the ruins of the fort. In the last light from the west the crumbling bastions were the skeletons of giant beasts.

Among the groups of men camping there he saw some Oneidas staggering cheerfully. McLeod was pouring rum from a cask. When he saw Joseph he smiled and struck his chest.

"They're already on our side."

Joseph walked on, only to bump into Captain Butler.

The Irishman pointed at the impromptu tavern: "In the end, whoever has the most rum wins the war. The rest is just nonsense." He mimed a fluttering bird with his hand.

The hand accepted the cigar that was offered to him. Butler bent to pick up a twig from the nearest campfire and held it out to Joseph.

"Are you also sure that it's all going to turn out for the best?"

Joseph remained silent. White men tended to ask questions and answer themselves, for the pleasure of hearing their own words. Butler took a few puffs and continued:

"If the Oneida pull out, persuading the other Nations is going to be a major undertaking. Especially the Seneca, I know them well. They're a tough bunch and they hate the English, but they're the only ones who can marshal a thousand warriors."

Joseph thought that the old officer was right. Beyond the outer circle of the fort, the night was becoming impenetrable.

21.

The warriors stopped on the riverbank. Some of them trod on the muddy bottom. The water coming from the mountain had shrunk to a trickle.

Joseph exchanged a glance with Sakihenakenta. He turned toward Lacroix, who was staring at the forest on the opposite bank.

"What's happened to the river?" Peter's voice asked behind them.

Joseph said nothing. He needed to think.

They had gone in an advance party, to open the track for the expedition, which was about to cross the strip of land between the Mohawk and Wood Creek. That place was Deowainsta, the Great Portage of Canoes. Four miles of forests, their belongings on their backs, the boats dragged on wooden sleds. It would take them at least two days. And without the river they would be stuck.

"We could go down until we find water," suggested Sakihenakenta.

Joseph shook his head.

"It's too hard with this load."

If they came back with the news that there was no water to sail the boats, many of the men would give up the journey and go home. Joseph couldn't allow that.

"It isn't the dry season. A river doesn't vanish overnight."

Lacroix pointed to the mountain.

"But logs and mud can take it away for a long time."

Peter began climbing the stony bank.

"Then let's find it," he said.

The solution to the mystery came an hour later.

A mill. The indolent waters of the river slid into the half-full basin.

Someone was splitting wood on a log, to the rear of the building. The warriors approached cautiously, without a sound.

It was a short, squat man with a thick beard and a curious hat of piebald fur, white and brown. Suddenly he stopped, rested his ax and bent down to pick up his musket. He aimed it at the intruders.

"Who are you? You aren't Oneida."

Joseph raised his hand in a sign of greeting. "We are Mohawk from Canajoharie, and we're going to Oswego with a convoy of boats."

The man grunted and narrowed his eyes without lowering his weapon.

"Then you're here for the river."

Dutch accent, myopic eyes.

Joseph nodded. "The mill belongs to you?"

The miller gave a grunt of agreement and looked askance at the other warriors.

"My name is Jan Hoorn. It'll take another half day to fill the millpond, as God wills. Where are you camped?"

"Fort Stanwix."

"Then you needn't worry. By the time you've completed your portage, the river will have been full again for a while. Tell the men down there." He leaned on the log without lowering his rifle. "I'll give you a good price. Three shillings a boat. I can also do you gunpowder, salted meat, flour. No rum. A barrel of that swill isn't worth a mouthful of my beer."

Jethro Kanenonte said something in Mohawk, pointing at the cistern.

Joseph turned back toward the miller. "He says you're stealing the river. And I think he's right."

The Dutchman grunted again.

"The water in the river comes from the river. The water in my millpond is my water. My father's father acquired this land with a regular contract, in the year of our Lord 1701. My family has always lived in peace with the Englishmen from the fort and the Indians. My brother married an Oneida. We've never had any problems with anyone, as God wills."

Peter interrupted violently. "What's to stop us opening the sluice without your permission?"

The miller shook his head. "It would do you no good. When the river is dry you have to accumulate enough water to flood the bed all the way to the valley. We collect it in the millpond, set the wheels in motion and try to measure out just enough for the boats to sail. If you open the bulkheads now, all of a sudden, you'll manage to sail round the first loop in the river, but then you'll find yourselves high and dry again." He pointed to the mill basin. "Not enough, you see?" He lowered his rifle and sat down on the log. "How many boats have you got?"

Joseph took a piece of tobacco from his bag and offered it to the Dutchman. "Thirty."

The Dutchman snapped up the tobacco and talked with his mouth full. "Four pounds, special price. Nearly two crowns' discount."

"A deal, Mr. Hoorn."

The Dutchman twisted his mouth into something that was supposed to be a smile.

"As God wills."

"You'll have to sign a receipt for the Indian Department."

The miller looked at the piece of paper and the little pencil that Joseph was holding out to him as if they were bewitched. He picked up the pencil stub and traced a big X on the page.

"Fine."

Kanenonte smiled, pointing at the man's headgear.

"Funny hat," he said in heavily accented English.

The miller took it off and stroked it with his hands.

"Ya, ya, old Guus."

The Indian offered his knife in exchange for the piebald hat, but the Dutchman plonked it crossly on his head.

"No sir. They'll have to kill me to get this off me. He was the best hunting dog I've ever had, yes sir, I loved him."

Joseph studied him: perhaps he was older than he looked—knotty hands, few teeth, poor eyesight.

"Do you live alone here?" he asked.

The Dutchman nodded.

"My brother and his wife got the fever, three years this September. But a bear killed old Guus on me last winter." Again he touched the strange hat, from which two soft ears flapped. "It was a real shame, because he kept me company, and it was just as if he understood. Yes sir, he understood everything I said to him, as God wills. The bear opened him up from side to side, poor Guus spilled his guts all the way home. Giving him that death-blow was hard for me, but there was nothing more to be done. Before burying him I skinned him and with his fur I made this hat, to remind me what a great dog he was. Yes sir. And now here I am running this mill all on my own."

The man seemed to remember something.

"Is it true that there's a revolt?"

The Indians fell silent.

"A war could break out," Joseph replied.

"Another one? I hope it's against Massachusetts this time. Worse than the French, those guys. Always talking about God, but if they can cheat you they'll be more than happy." He spat on the ground. "Not that the people in Albany are any less disgusting. As God wills, I'll keep the mill and they can kill each other as much as they want."

Joseph smiled. Peter gestured to him that the Dutchman must be mad.

Joseph noticed that Lacroix was staring at the trees around the mill, his chin raised slightly. He went over.

"Let's get back," said Lacroix. "This forest isn't safe."

Peter shivered. His mother sometimes spoke like that. Phrases that hinted at some threat that was indistinct but all the more frightening for it. All of a sudden he wanted to get away from there.

He had been the first to go up, and he was also the first to come down.

22.

Two days later, Peter was carrying sacks of flour to the collection point.

The forest was a stretch of barrels and wineskins, boats and men, muskets and oars, bags of flints, powder horns, boxes of nails, ironware. The embarkation had not yet begun and the atmosphere was heavy with tension. Peter set the sack down on the ground and stopped to get his breath back. The porters silently overtook him, each concentrating on his own task. The last boats would be back in the water by midday. Uncle Joseph had already gone down to Wood Creek, to check that it was flowing again. With him he had brought only Lacroix. The warriors' arms were needed for transport.

Peter wiped away his sweat and studied the clearing that opened up among the oaks. It was dotted with white stones that peeped from the grass and the swamp. He saw the porters making the sign of the cross and remembered one of the stories that his father told him, the one about the five hundred fighters of Colonel Bradstreet, dead of exhaustion during the portage one summer day in 1758. After that slaughter the Crown had allocated sixty thousand pounds for John Stanwix to build the fort for the use of anyone who took that path.

For some obscure reason, since Peter had come down from the mill worry had not left him. Along with that there was the thought that somewhere, beneath his feet, the dead were sleeping.

He picked up the sack and wished it were much lighter.

By the river, which was still dry, they said nothing. They began the climb, silent as ghosts.

The air was sultry, heavy, and their shirts were drenched with sweat.

At the top of the path the mill appeared in the bright noon sunlight. They didn't approach it immediately; they waited for a long while, bending to study the surroundings. Joseph examined one detail at a time.

The water had stopped roaring.

Lacroix jumped to the opposite bank. They climbed cautiously toward the building, rifles aimed. The millpond was full of water, but freshly cut trees were piled up on the sluice.

Through the wood filtered streams of cloudy water, losing themselves in the valley. Joseph had seen bloodstained rivers before. He walked over. The Dutchman was facedown in the millpond. He had been scalped.

Lacroix emerged on the other side. He glanced down and crossed himself.

They began to move the logs, filled with silent anxiety. Joseph felt exposed, an easy target, as he struggled to liberate the sluice. A little waterfall appeared and plunged into the dry riverbed. It would take hours for the level of the river to rise sufficiently. They would have to spend the night down there, among snakes and mosquitoes, surrounded by a band of murderers.

When their work was done they didn't turn around. They should have pulled the body out and given it a Christian burial, but their instinct led them to pick up their rifles and run back down the hill.

The two warriors at the head of the group bent over the footprints in the mud. The others stayed where they were. Then, without breathing, they fanned out along the riverbank.

Joseph approached Lacroix and Royathakariyo, who were crouching on a mossy rock, their noses to the ground like bloodhounds.

"They disembarked here and advanced into the forest." Lacroix pointed in the direction in which they had marched. "At least four white men. An Indian guide. They're moving quickly."

The forest was dense and silent. Nothing but a fluttering of wings. All eyes were fixed on the canopy.

Joseph had spoken to Guy Johnson and the other men in the Department. If someone was following them, they had to find out who it was. They had given him the task of assembling the best warriors and beating the banks for trails.

He whirled a hand over his head. The group moved on, avoiding open stretches. There were fifteen of them, but if there were good shots on the other side, that might not be enough.

Every so often Joseph checked that his nephew was following him at a close distance. Peter clung to his footsteps, as he had been ordered to do. The boy was trembling, intoxicated by the company of the warriors. Beside him was Walter, the son of Captain Butler; by his father's account he was an excellent marksman.

They covered about half a mile. Royathakariyo and Lacroix squatted down behind a rock, the straps of their rifles running across their backs. The others sought shelter among the ferns. Joseph smelled Peter's scent behind him and glimpsed the tip of his rifle. He motioned to him to stay where he was and crept on until he reached the boulder. Royathakariyo pointed down to where the land ran steeply downward.

There were five of them, walking in single file. The guide was a Delaware. He was wearing Jan Hoorn's piebald hat, with the floppy ears on either side.

Joseph turned quickly toward the warriors and saw Kanenonte shouldering his rifle. He crept over to him and gripped the barrel of his gun just in time. Guy Johnson had been clear: don't rise to provocations, don't give them excuses to attack us. Not before the council. Discover who they are, how many they are, and return to camp.

Joseph said everything without speaking, but the men under him were aware of something, and they stood apart from one another and raised their weapons. The Delaware's eyes scanned the slope. Joseph and Kanenonte remained motionless, listening to their own breathing. The unit began marching again and disappeared among the foliage.

Kanenonte looked straight into Joseph's face.

"They must die."

"There might be others. The shots would summon them."

The young warrior put the gun back over his shoulder and prepared to follow the white men.

"Let them come. Before sunset we will wash ourselves in their blood."

Oronhyateka came up alongside his friend.

Joseph knew that if he let the two young men go the others would follow them.

"It isn't the time to fight. The day will come, but it isn't here yet."

Kanenonte could barely contain his fury.

"Do you want to wait for them to surprise us in our sleep?"

Joseph looked again at the grim faces. Royathakariyo seemed inclined to go into battle. Peter was in the middle, his eyes darting from one face to the other. Walter Butler looked on expressionlessly. He had grown up in his father's school and wouldn't retreat. He waited for the group's decision.

Joseph stood firm. He imagined himself as solid as a tree, fastened to the ground with deep roots. He spoke his words distinctly so that everyone could hear him.

"No killing before the council."

Oronhyateka began striding around, hissing into his ears. Joseph felt his breath on his face.

"Who is Thayendanegea to prevent us? He isn't a sachem, he isn't noble. He's a war chief refusing to make us fight. A useless chief."

Joseph remained impassive. "I've told you once before, be careful how you speak."

"Am I supposed to be afraid of you? Just because you fought in the war? I say too much time has passed and you've lost your courage."

The young man gripped his tomahawk. Joseph was about to strike him with the stock of his rifle, but Oronhyateka threw his weapon at Lacroix's feet.

"Let Ronaterihonte guide us against the enemy. Let him be our war chief."

The hissing stopped, the sounds of the forest resumed. Everyone looked at Lacroix, who was staring at the ax planted in the ground. He straddled it and took a few steps toward Oronhyateka. He threw the young man a careless glance.

"We're going to the council. Pick up your ax, we will follow Thayendanegea."

No one said another word. The line of men re-formed and set off on the return journey, Kanenonte and Oronhyateka bringing up the rear. Peter walked as if in a dream, sure that he had witnessed a crucial event, which he went on running through in his mind until they reached the camp. In front of him, Uncle Joseph and the Great Devil walked side by side. He observed their shadows darting subtly among the trees. He imagined they were those of the two boys who had followed his father along these same paths many years before, just as he, Peter, followed them now. He felt proud of that company. Proud to be a warrior of Joseph Brant, proud to be a Johnson.

23.

The boats proceeded in single file along the winding loops of Wood Creek. The current had become treacherous. Guy Johnson consulted the map, trying to protect it from splashes of water. Just twelve miles as the crow flies, but twenty-eight by river. The Crown should have financed the construction of a canal a long time ago.

It was midafternoon. Guy thought of the clouds of mosquitoes, waiting for darkness before attacking them. They had already resorted to bear grease. The smell impregnated their skins and clothes; it wouldn't go away. But now the odor was less pungent. He was getting used to it.

He thought of their mysterious pursuers. Cutthroats sent from Albany. They had to reach Oswego as soon as possible.

He looked at the pale, weary faces of Mary and the girls. This journey was the opportunity to renew the family's fortunes. He was traveling the same path Sir William had followed; that couldn't be a mistake.

He clearly remembered the last time he had confronted that journey, the welcome that the Indians had reserved for the Old Man, as if he were the king in person, the Great White Father. Now he had the best warriors with him, the last of a great race; the future of his line in his wife's belly; gifts in abundance—rum, rifles, gunpowder, mirrors.

His youngest daughter, Judith, asked where the river ended. Guy replied that it flowed into the placid waters of Lake Oneida. On the surface there were dark particles that the local people called lake flowers. No one knew what they were. Some people said they were chestnut pollen, others that they were rotten algae. Whatever they were, if eaten they caused vomiting, fever and diarrhea.

The little girl looked frightened. Guy stroked her cheek and said there was nothing to be afraid of. The lake was beautiful, it was filled with fish at all seasons. You had only to slip in a hook with a feather on it to catch pike and trout in abundance. The salmon weighed twenty pounds and the flying fish had wings that would make a falcon jealous.

Judith looked brightly at her father. Guy went on with his story.

They would cross the lake with sails unfurled, until they reached the mouth of the Onondaga River.

"Another river?"

The voice belonged to Sarah, his second daughter.

"It's another lake. The size of a sea. So big that you can't see land from the other side."

The children were open-mouthed. Esther, on the other hand, sat with her hands in her lap, straight-backed as she had been taught. Her skin was the color of a lily crushed between the rocks.

They stopped in a gorge, and some Oneida fishermen offered Mary Johnson a comfortable shack.

As the fire dried their clothes, the women helped Mary to lie down and wrapped her in blankets.

Her sister Nancy put her nieces to bed.

"When will we get there?" asked Judith, as she lay down on a woolen blanket.

"We'll soon be at Lake Ontario."

"And will there be lots of Indians?" asked Sarah.

"More than you've ever seen."

Esther wasn't listening; she kept her eyes fixed on her mother.

Nancy noticed the child's fear, caressed her and made her lie down beside her sisters.

"Go to sleep."

The little girl had green, watery eyes.

"Are they going to kill us?" she asked calmly.

"What's that you're saying? The Indians are our friends, and they respect your father. When we get there they'll give us a party."

Esther turned back toward her mother, lying at the end of the cabin.

"I have some thoughts." She rested her head on the fur pillow. "They were sent to me by that woman, Molly Brant."

"Sleep, I said."

"She may have put a curse on us," she insisted.

Her aunt gripped her arm. "Stop talking nonsense, you'll scare your sisters. Pray instead."

A whispered Our Father mingled with the crackling of the fire.

24.

Flaming backs, aching muscles, shattered vertebrae, the splitting heads of those who have been concentrating for too long. Even for the most expert boatmen the last twenty-four miles of the journey had been a nightmare of water and rocks. The rapids were numberless. Smooth Rock Rapid, the Devil's Horn, the Six-Mile Rift, the Little Smooth Rock Rapid, the Devil's Warping Bar, the Devil's Horse Race and Oswego Rift. Not to mention the waterfalls halfway along: twelve feet high and making a noise that was the echo of a hundred thunderclaps.

The convoy had avoided those, boats on their shoulders again, carrying the old, the injured and the sick, and a pregnant woman.

One afternoon in late June, the three forts of Oswego had appeared on the horizon. In the background, the blue of the water met the sky.

Fort George was a blackened skeleton, consumed by flames during the war.

Not far off, the ruins of another fort, a refuge for ducks and divers. The parade ground housed the cabins of the Indians who had come for the council. In front of each cabin were weapons, scalps, war trophies. A vague hubbub accompanied the comings and goings of men and women: cries, barking dogs, shouting children, merchants dressed in skins, shrieking the virtues of their wares. Fires were being prepared to light up the night.

Oswego meant "flowing quickly," but Joseph's memories were too dense to slip along so easily.

It was from this same plain that the expedition against the French had set off, sixteen years before. Sir William had led the siege of Fort Niagara: his greatest victory and a baptism of fire for Joseph and Lacroix. And the first time the Six Nations had fought together side by side with the English.

Fort Ontario was still in good condition, even though the garrison hadn't lived there for five years. Joseph had worked there as an interpreter. In a shed in the courtyard he had seen his wife Peggy give birth to Isaac, his firstborn.

"Brothers," the voice of Little Abraham rang out around the courtyard, after a brief pause. "The Six Nations have been allies of the English King for many seasons. They are friends of the Johnson family, of Warraghiyagey and his successor, Uraghquadirah, who has been taking care of our business for a year now and has never given us cause to lament the fact. But I don't think a man should always be dealing with his friends' disputes. If you come and tell me that someone has burned your house down, I will take my rifle and travel with you on the river, even for many miles, for whole days, until you have justice. But if you argue with your son because the water jug is empty and come to ask my help, I will tell you: 'Go, go back to your son and resolve the matter between you.' If I followed you home, I would only aggravate your argument. Brothers, I think the Great English Father has enough authority to sort out his rebel children all by himself. I can't forget that among them there are men like Nicholas Herkimer, Philip Schuyler and many others who have always respected our people, the sons, the daughters, the fathers, the mothers of the nation, the Longhouse and the Sacred Fire. Two months ago, when we were told that our superintendent risked being taken prisoner, we immediately sent the warriors to defend his house. We asked the most honorable men of the colonial assembly to guarantee that no one would harm Guy Johnson. Only then did we unload our rifles. Brothers, if the king's lands were threatened by a foreign army, the Six Nations would fight to defend them, as they have done in the past. For each blow dealt to the Longhouse, the Six Nations are prepared to deal a thousand back. But this won't happen today, and the friendship between the Six Nations and England remains a peaceful friendship, because no war has been declared. Brothers, I have spoken."

Little Abraham's speech concluded the first round of consultations. Upon his arrival Guy Johnson had immediately asked to hear the most influential chiefs of each nation, orators capable of persuading hundreds of men. None of them had questioned the idea of loyalty to the Crown. No one had adopted a position against the Whig settlers. Stripped to the bone, it was the same speech repeated six times. The differences running through the Longhouse were concealed behind nuances of tone and vocabulary, subtleties that the English were unable pick up.

The Oneida had been the least friendly. Kirkland's preaching was having a profound effect.

The Seneca stood and watched, intending to collect gifts from both sides.

The Tuscarora and Cayuga followed the Seneca like lapdogs.

The Onondaga, keepers of the Sacred Fire, had stayed midway between the two positions.

Joseph waited for a nod from Guy Johnson. The superintendent seemed calm; his expression was firm. He got to his feet and started talking.

First of all he thanked the orators for their sincerity, then recalled Sir William, who had died the previous year, during another council. Finally, he recited a few phrases that were received with great approval, nods of the head and shouts of "*oyeh*" that echoed from one corner of the square to the other. Joseph shivered. They were the words used by Sir William to persuade the Six Nations to besiege Fort Niagara. They were as much a part of Oswego as the elms in the ancient forest and the lake breeze. Guy Johnson had evoked the power of the place. What the Mohawk called its *orenda*.

Joseph began to translate. He could hear that the superintendent had touched the right cords, and tried to fill his words with all the energy he could muster.

At that moment, Guy Johnson slipped a hand under his jacket and took out a carefully folded sheet of paper.

"Brothers," he continued, "I have here a letter from General Thomas Gage." He waved the piece of paper and unfolded it in front of everyone. "The head of the king's army informs me that the rebels are threatening Canadian territory. You all know about the fall of Fort Ticonderoga. The goal of the traitors is to subjugate the possessions of the Crown. They will raze the cities and empty granaries and powder magazines, since they hardly have any food or ammunition, which you still have in abundance thanks to His Majesty's ships."

Joseph thought the argument was a good one, even though the Seneca didn't like to be reminded of it. A little over ten years before, in the days of the Pontiac rebellion, many of them had hoped to do without the whites, to go back to bows and arrows. Reduced to hunger, they had had to rethink. Joseph translated, trying to make the concept as inoffensive as possible. He was all too familiar with his brothers' susceptibility.

"The ones you call rebel sons," the superintendent continued, "are nothing but enemies of the king, just as the French were. That's why General Gage," again he showed the letter, his arm stretched above his head, "is ordering a military expedition into Canada. To attack from the north and go down to Albany, not to drag on this pointless conflict. No one who has just declared himself a friend of the king can deny him his support."

A nervous buzz ran through the crowd, beginning with those who understood English, and Joseph soon found a hundred eyes upon him. He hesitated, unable to repeat what he had heard. The *orenda* of words does not distinguish between languages.

Shouts of approval rose up from the crowd, voices too young to understand what was happening. The adult warriors and the elders had fallen silent, as if someone had got to his feet and pissed out the flames in the middle of the courtyard. Guy Johnson's confident smile dissolved.

At that moment Joseph understood. The superintendent's strategy was clear. To claim promises and cash them in all at once, thanks to an order that laid claim to warriors, not words. That was the real reason to call a council a hundred miles from home. To defend Canada, not the Six Nations.

Joseph studied the hardened faces of the sachems and the elders. He met Philip Lacroix's eyes. The Great Devil was impassive.

Someone touched his leg and pointed to the superintendent. Guy Johnson had started talking again.

"The English Crown," he was saying, "doesn't ask for your support without promising anything in exchange. At the end of the campaign, before the winter, every warrior will receive four pounds from New York. Furthermore,

General Gage solemnly promises that, once the war is over, all the lands contested between you and the settlers will be restored to the Longhouse. Any loss of land or goods will be indemnified in equal measure."

Joseph finished his translation to a silent assembly. In different circumstances, a similar promise would have raised roars of enthusiasm, but at that moment it was recognized as part of a game that had been fixed. It was just one more risk, to balance the one that had gone before. The sachems felt they had been cheated.

Joseph bit back his disappointment. As a war chief, he had spent thousands of words to convince his people. He had to show the muscle of the Six Nations, so the rebels would stop snarling. Meeting far from home, far from indiscreet ears, understandings and provocations, to come back in force and defend the valley. He had reminded them at every step, at every stroke of the oars, of the solid loyalty of the bond between the Mohawk and the Johnson family.

In exchange, Guy had made him an accomplice in a clumsy fraud, to force the council's hand.

Joseph returned to his post. Again it was time for the sachems to speak through their designated interpreter. He knew that the chiefs wouldn't be ruffled. Taking their time was an art that they knew to perfection.

As he was sitting down, a whisper slipped into his ear. The voice of Kanenonte.

"The day has come, Thayendanegea. Samuel Waterbridge will have his revenge. We all will."

Joseph felt he had no choice.

If he didn't want to lose face, he would have to be the first aboard the boats for Canada.

He would have to speak to the doubters, in spite of everything.

Play into Guy Johnson's hands.

25.

The fishermen's lanterns slipped across the lake and contested the primacy of the stars. Beyond the flames that lit up the camp, water and land swapped roles. The lake looked like a city and the shoreside villages were little fleets in transit.

The council was coming to its end. A night of celebrations and then, at dawn, every warrior would choose for himself. The Longhouse didn't make decisions that weren't unanimous, and the sachems had reached agreement on only one thing: accepting the presents of the Crown and giving thanks for the thought.

Chants, dances, games of chance, drunken stories, interpretation of dreams and the comical ceremony of the Seneca shamans.

Guy Johnson would gladly have spared himself the whole process. He had already done the math: two hundred warriors was the maximum he could expect.

Seneca, nobody. Mohawk, fewer than one hundred, Brant's men. From the other nations, scraps. Relations of the Mohawk, personal friends of the Johnsons, men chained by ancient treaties or recent dreams.

Sir William would have persuaded three times as many with half a sentence.

That was why he couldn't go to his wife. He couldn't abandon the ritual. He would have to show himself polite to the living and devoted to the forefathers if he didn't want to get to Montreal alone.

He had to keep the hearts of the Indians hot.

And even more, their guts.

Eighty gallons of rum, the powder keg of the evening. Madeira wine, Guy Park's special reserve. He hoped to uncork it, drink to the birth of a male. He would call him William, to reinforce the image of a dynasty strong in life and hope.

Nancy Claus received the woman in the antechamber.

"God be praised, are you the midwife?"

Lydia Devon held out a bony hand that reminded Nancy of a bird's foot.

"I'm Mrs. Johnson's sister. Come. The pains have begun."

"For how long?" Lydia took off her overcoat and followed Nancy into the bedroom.

"A few hours," Nancy replied, betraying her anxiety.

Mary was lying on the bed, her hands gripping the sheet and her face drawn. A small Indian woman was wiping the sweat from her forehead with a wet cloth.

Nancy introduced her: "This is Tabby. She has been present at every labor."

Lydia nodded, set down her bag and coat and looked around. A clay plaster whitened with lime covered the log walls. The furniture was reduced to the minimum. A narrow, Spartan room, more appropriate to the sleep of a passing merchant than to the pains of a woman in childbirth. She stroked Mary's face.

"Be calm, my love. We're here."

She turned to the other women.

"When was she last examined?"

"Before we left the midwife came," replied Nancy. "She said it would be at least three months. We shouldn't have trusted her, she hasn't even got a diploma."

Nancy spoke quickly, swallowing her words.

"My diploma is eight hundred and forty deliveries," said Lydia, "not counting the four I have given birth to myself. And you, Tabby, have children, don't you?"

The Indian woman nodded.

"How many births have you had so far, my love?" she asked Mary.

"Three. All girls," she replied, her breath beginning to break.

Lydia Devon laid a hand on her stomach.

"It's a little boy this time. Your belly's pointed."

The midwife knelt down on the floor, rubbed her palm with linseed oil and examined the patient. Mary held her breath. The walls of the room contracted with each spasm.

"I can feel him," Lydia announced a moment later. The news was received with sighs and blessings. Mary lifted her head from her chest and merely groaned. "He's lovely and big, you'll see, and because it was a bit tight he's gone skewed, he's trying to come out shoulder first, that's why it's so exhausting for you." She drew herself up, took the patient's hand and gazed into her eyes. "Now, Mrs. Johnson, we'll lay you down and try to turn him. Meanwhile Tabby will make you a compress of black wool, brandy and pepper—you'll find everything in my bag, my dear. And I've brought some tea to reinvigorate everyone. We'll need it."

The men of the council had been draining drink of a different kind. Most of them were already drunk when Guy Johnson got to his feet, apologized and climbed into the saddle with the man who had brought him the message. The child still wasn't born, and Mrs. Claus was asking for him.

As soon as he dismounted he went inside by the back door and dashed to Mary's room. A few steps and suddenly he slowed down, disoriented. His political obligations hadn't allowed him to be present at the birth of his daughters; he expected piercing cries, which would fill the room like air from an organ pipe. Now, confronted with silence, he didn't know what to think.

He knocked on the door, the serving-girl opened up, then stepped aside, and the mistress of the house came out.

"How are things going?" he asked.

Nancy's face darkened.

"Not well, Guy. It would have been better to call the doctor straightaway, as we did last time."

Guy's mouth twisted. "You know that Mary doesn't want to have men around her."

"That's why I called you. If she knew you agreed, she would, too."

"Fine," he sighed. "Just tell her that you've spoken to me. And keep me informed. I have to make another appearance."

He was about to leave, but his sister-in-law's voice held him back.

"And you're not going to tell me anything about your own delivery? Is there going to be war?"

"There already is. But the sachems prefer to pretend there's nothing wrong."

At that moment they both noticed three white figures at the bottom of the stairs: Guy and Mary's daughters. Their long nightshirts brushed the ground. They held each other's hands, and their eyes gleamed in the twilight.

"What are you doing here?" Nancy exploded at them. "Go back to bed immediately."

The little girls didn't move. Sarah was on the brink of tears.

"Mother isn't well," she said in a thin voice.

Guy met Esther's glazed eyes and shivered. He didn't know what to say. He turned around and left the house.

Nancy pushed the girls up the stairs as the youngest began to cry.

"If you love your mother, pray for her with all the faith you can muster."

It was a few hours before dawn when Guy resumed his place around the fire. The tales of hunting and dreams were endless. A lot of people were lying on the grass. He studied his own face reflected in the glass of a bottle and it seemed deformed, monstrous. He wished the Old Man were there, with his wisdom, to help him deliver the future. He wished time could run faster.

> Now many people are in this place
> hey in this our meeting place
> it starts when two men look at one another
> hey they greet hey one another
> we greet one another oyeh
> Heyyouheyyahheyahheyah
> Heyyouheyyahheyahheyah. . .

Spectral figures danced around the fire, reddened shadows, a Catherine wheel of sweaty muscles and feet hammering the ground. Enchanted by the flames, Guy inhaled fumes of alcohol that arose from everywhere. Beside him, John Butler was whispering incomprehensible words. The chants continued uninterrupted, accompanied by the violins of Peter Johnson and Daniel Claus.

> Then he thought: let us make the Earth
> So that some people can work on it
> I have created it and now it has happened
> we walk on it *oyeh*
> and in this hour of the day
> let us give thanks hey to the Earth.
> In our thoughts that's how it must be
> in our thoughts that's how it must be.

From the other side of the circle he thought he saw dark eyes staring at him. Joseph Brant, or perhaps his own image distorted by a play of reflections. It lasted just a moment, and then the whirl of dancers filled the night again.

> Heyyouheyyahheyahheyah
> heyyouheyyahheyahheyah

The woman in labor was lying on a chair with a pillow behind her back, and a Cayuga woman was supporting her by the armpits. Standing in front of her, Tabby was massaging her hips, as the midwife tried for the umpteenth time to turn the child.

"Be calm, my love," she repeated every now and then. "He's turned, he's ready to come out. The pains are regular, very promising. With the help of Saint Anne, nature will do its duty."

Mary Johnson no longer had the strength to smile. Her swollen face, pearled with sweat, was fixed in an expression of suffering and resignation. Her forehead was burning with fever.

Around the chair, the women took turns offering advice, reassuring memories, chicken-and-rum broth.

"Dr. Savage is here, madam," said a voice from behind the door.

The midwife picked up a towel and went to wash at the basin. Mary gestured to the Indian to stop massaging, lowered her nightshirt and asked the serving-girl to bring in the new arrival.

Once the ritual questions were over, Dr. Savage asked who the midwife was.

The woman came forward.

"Very well, Mrs. Devon. I would be grateful if you and the other women would carry Mrs. Johnson to the bed. May I ask you what she has been given so far?"

The woman said that she had applied a poultice to the patient's belly and chopped onions to her feet, had rubbed her temples with vinegar and given her tea and broth, half a cup of rum and one of syrup of Aaron's rod.

The doctor nodded. "Very well done, Mrs. Devon. But I fear we will need a more robust treatment than that."

He took a vial from his equipment bag, poured twenty drops into a spoon and approached the bed.

"Here you are, Mrs. Johnson. This will bring you relief. It's laudanum and in a few minutes it will eliminate all excessive muscular tension, which is due to false labor."

"Forgive me, doctor," the midwife broke in. "The labor is far from false, I have touched my patient several times, and . . ."

Mary Johnson blushed.

"Please, Mrs. Johnson, don't be embarrassed. Even if it is a true labor, as you say, Mrs. Devon, it is clear enough that my patient needs to regain her strength, or her muscles will be too weak to endure the strain. And you, too, if you want to rest for a few hours and send these women back to their families, please do so. I will need your help later on, when the labor resumes."

So saying, he slipped the tip of the spoon into the patient's mouth and gave her a handkerchief to dry her lips.

Soon, Mary Johnson was in a deep sleep.

As he did every night, Philip Lacroix met his wife and daughter. They walked together, in the tall grass, until they reached the front door. Wife and daughter went inside, and he remained on the doorstep cleaning his rifle. Once inside, he became aware that the woman was not his wife. She was Molly Brant. And the girl was not his daughter, but a little fair-haired girl. Molly walked toward him, untied a wampum bracelet from her wrist and placed it at his feet.

"To forget, you must know," she said. "To deny, you must also believe. When you received it, this bracelet had a value. When you gave it back, it had another. Settle the account or you will lose your balance. Do not come home empty-handed, Ronaterihonte."

The words were spoken, and the bracelet plunged into the ground, opening up an abyss in the middle of the cabin.

Philip woke up drenched in sweat and feeling strangely dizzy. The sun was up and the warriors were sharing out the gifts from the English. On the shore of the lake, a fleet of boats was waiting for its cargo.

Mary woke at four in the morning. The pains were back and a sudden attack of nausea seemed destined to get things moving; the baby would be born through her teeth.

The woman who woke her up hurried to lift her head, slipped another pillow behind her back and called for reinforcements. Tabby got up from the chair, followed by the midwife, who was resting on a few blankets. She immediately slipped on her cap, greased her hands and checked the situation. For the first time since the start of her labor Mary began screaming. Not real yells, more of a rosary of laments, modulated over a scale of notes from low to shrill. Penetrating enough to wake up Dr. Savage, who was lying on one of the benches in the antechamber.

"The pains are coming very quickly," the midwife explained, "but the baby can't get out yet. Perhaps the cord is around its neck. Tabby, will you give me a hand?"

The Indian woman came over and observed that Mrs. Johnson was wearing a necklace and that it would be better to take it off. With trembling arms, her back arched with tension, Mary slipped her hands behind her neck.

"And no superstitions," the doctor snapped. "If there's a risk of suffocation you have to intervene."

He resolutely took the forceps out of his bag, ordered the midwife to put its jaws in place, bent his knees slightly and began to pull.

Mary prayed, Tabby dried her forehead with a handkerchief soaked in vinegar, and Lydia Devon, astride her on the bed with her back to the patient, pressed on her belly to aid the expulsion.

The doctor got to his feet, leaving the instrument in position. He was sweating. He asked them to bring him a rag, had it tied tightly to the joint of the forceps and instructed the midwife to pull down on it, as he went on working the patient's arms.

Lydia reluctantly agreed. She took a sip from the bottle of rum, crouched down and did as the doctor said. A Seneca woman drew signs and symbols on Mary Johnson's belly.

Through the odors that mingled in the room—alcohol and sweat, fever and bodily miasmas, soup and herbal infusions—the midwife suddenly discerned the smell of blood.

She leaped to her feet, picked up the doctor's bag and rummaged in it with her still-dirty hands. She took out a big syringe and a glass ampoule. She handed it to Tabby. "Rub this on her loins," she ordered, "we have to stop the hemorrhage." Then she filled the syringe from a little bowl of water, the only one still clean, came and stood beside the doctor, knelt again, took out the forceps and inserted the syringe.

"In the name of the Father," she whispered, pumping in the first squirt of water, "the Son and the Holy Ghost."

She set the syringe down on the floor and stretched a hand toward the patient's face.

Mary Johnson was struggling to breathe. Her fever was rising and so was the sun, slow and clumsy, struggling to escape the embrace of the swamps.

Joseph wrapped his things in a blanket and tied it with a leather belt. He became aware of someone's presence. He turned around slightly.

Lacroix was standing behind him.

"Are you going home?" asked Joseph.

"What about you?"

"I didn't know about Gage's order. You aren't obliged to follow us to Canada."

Lacroix sat on a rock and started phlegmatically filling his pipe.

Joseph set his luggage down and joined his friend.

In the antechamber, Nancy Johnson wept silently, just tears and shaking, one hand over her lips to hold back her sobs, the other gripping her stomach.

As soon as she saw her brother-in-law, she walked toward him and tried to hold him back.

"Don't go in, Guy. Not now."

He brushed her aside with his arm and gripped the handle of the door.

The only person in the room was the midwife. She was holding the corpse of the child, wrapped in bandages. Six little amulets hung from its pale neck, covering its tiny chest. Lydia Devon was crying as well: since she started her profession only four unborn children had died under her care. Never a disaster like this.

Mary was lying in a pool of blood. Naked, motionless, the incision slashing her belly.

Guy quickly slammed the door, to banish the horror.

He clenched his fists and pushed away Nancy's hand. He felt as if the earth were shaking.

26.

When Joseph had lost Peggy, the comfort of those who loved him had softened his suffering. Molly and Sir William, Tekarihoga and the elders of the village, Margaret and the matrons of the clan, his friends Sakihenakenta and Kanatawakhon, Reverend Stewart. They had all had the right words for the widowed warrior.

Joseph had dreamed hard, and had entrusted the children to Molly and his old mother and set off for Oquaga. He had returned with Susanna and life had resumed.

In Oswego, on the other hand, Guy had the gruff comfort of Daniel Claus, John Butler and Cormac McLeod, along with a capital of polite conversation, a gift from other members of the expedition, to invest in an attempt not to fall to pieces.

Joseph thought about Lacroix, another tormented husband and father, the survivor of an even worse tragedy that he had confronted in total solitude. The man of the forests hadn't mentioned the death of Mary and the child; he had spent hours sitting on the lake shore and now he was there, among the crowd. His face betrayed no emotion, but between his throat and his breastbone there must have been a storm of memories.

The funeral of Uraghquadirah's wife brought the souls of the Longhouse together for one last day. The death of a child destined to be called William Johnson, the grandson of Warraghiyagey, was an anvil that had fallen from the sky to crush everything else. The tragedy had dissipated suspicions and grudges, had brushed them aside. Guy Johnson was just the head of a family, thunderstruck, stunned, left with three daughters and a journey to make.

Joseph and John Butler dug the hole and lowered the coffin. Tekarihoga and Little Abraham prayed to the Master of Life. The tears of Esther, Judith and Sarah drenched the cloak of their aunt, Nancy Claus, who was weeping on her husband's shoulder. The midwife, Lydia Devon, prayed with her hands clasped. The grave filled with earth and Guy Johnson couldn't look up from his own boots. Joseph looked at him and felt sorrow on his behalf.

The Christians recited the Our Father in English, in Latin, in Mohawk, in Oneida. *Onwari teconnoronkwanions. . . Pater noster. . . ise tsiati ioainerentakwa. . . qui est in caelis. . . Rawennio senikwekon. . . hallowed be Thy name. . .* The babel of Iroquireland bade farewell to Mary Johnson, buried with her baby in her arms.

Lacroix finished the prayer, *et non nos inducas in tentationem, sed libera nos a malo. Amen*, and he crossed himself. Joseph saw him walk over to Guy and rest a hand on his shoulder. The superintendent raised his head in surprise, eyes glistening. Lacroix said nothing; there was no need for words. The other man nodded. The man of the forests walked away.

Guy took a deep breath, shook his back as if a shadow had run down his spine, and moved at last toward Nancy and the girls.

"Today Le Grand Diable warmed a man's heart," thought Joseph.

The boats split the calm waters with their sails unfurled, but there wasn't enough wind. They had to apply themselves to the oars. The sky was clear, furrowed only by a few motionless white clouds, reflected in the mirror of the lake. Aboard, no one was talking.

Guy Johnson was sitting in the front boat, his eyes lost in the wake from the oars. After the funeral he hadn't said a word, not even to his daughters, whom he had left in Oswego with their Aunt Nancy. On the wharf, Esther had watched the boats moving away. Her sisters were asleep, but she had slipped out from the covers to see them leave. Guy had made a great effort to wave, but had received no response. The first ray of sunlight was reflected in the little girl's golden hair, stirred faintly by the wind. She had stayed there, motionless, as the mist from the lake gradually erased her from view. Guy had continued to feel her eyes upon him, out there on the water, as if the girl's clear eyes could reach him even here, or at the end of the world. He had prayed in a low voice for his wife, for his stillborn son and for himself. He had asked forgiveness from God, a strict father who seemed to have abandoned them. He had asked forgiveness of Esther, trying desperately to understand his own guilt.

He summoned all his courage. He had an expedition to lead and battles to fight. Canada was there waiting for him. He had to endure the grief, the weight on his shoulders and the creaks in his body. He had to go on.

27

"Two tribes were fighting over the earth. One of them lived to the north of the St. Lawrence River, the other to the south. The Master of Life, saddened by that war, decided to descend from heaven with a mysterious bundle."

The night was damp, but the smoke kept the mosquitoes away. Peter was telling the legend of Manituana, the place where they were camped. He had been told it by his mother, but he didn't remember it well.

With him were Walter Butler and three young Canajoharie warriors who had come during their watch with a bottle of whisky purloined from somewhere or other.

"The Master of Life unrolled the blanket and in it was a land of delights, created so that everyone might live in abundance and there would no longer be any reason to fight. He rested his gift on the waters of the St. Lawrence, an equal distance from the two banks, and invited the men to move there. For many years the people of the South and the people of the North lived in peace on Manituana. To talk, they mixed their languages, so that no misunderstanding might arise. The first children were born and many of them had a father from one people and a mother from the other. Each family wanted their descendants to learn only the language and customs of their forefathers. So, as the children grew and spoke their bastard language, the people of the North and the people of the South began to hate one another. The ones from the South returned to the South and those from the North to the North. Only the children who were of no people remained on Manituana, while their relatives prepared to fight, to decide which of them would keep the island. The shouts and war cries rose into the air and led the Master of Life to descend a second time. Reaching the earth, he understood that men were fighting once again over his gift. Then he picked up the blanket and took it away. But as he was moving aside the curtain of the sky, the blanket opened and the land plunged into the river."

Peter's voice grew deeper, the rhythm of his words slower.

"High waves rose up and the warriors assembled on the shores all died. Manituana shattered into pieces, fragments, pebbles. The Thousand Islands of the St. Lawrence."

"And what about the children left on the island?" asked one of the young warriors. "What became of them?"

Peter looked at the cup in his hands and supplied his surprise ending.

"We are those children. When the island fell from the sky, many were drowned, but others clung to a scrap of land and managed to reach safety. But they had had enough of the wars between North and South, so they sought another homeland and found it at last, in the Mohawk Valley."

Canajoharie's boys drained the bottle in a toast to Peter.

It was Walter Butler's turn: "I don't know any Indian legends, but I can tell you the story of Ethan Allen, the Goliath of the Green Mountains, the man who took Fort Ticonderoga."

"Do you really know it?" asked Peter.

"My father told it to me. He knew Allen before he became an outlaw."

Walter, pleased to have drawn attention, began the story.

"Ethan Allen was a bloodthirsty brigand, over six feet tall. For years he had lorded it over the Green Mountains, which were for a time part of New Hampshire. Then the land was bought by the colony of New York, which had sent its settlers there. Allen was a farmer who didn't want to pay any taxes to the people in Albany, because he hated them. He fired at the new arrivals, and he recruited a gang of criminals, the Green Mountain Boys, and pronounced himself their colonel. The king in person put a bounty of three hundred pounds on his head. He himself offered fifty to anyone who handed the governor over to him. Walter's father thought he was one of the most dangerous bandits in America. When the Whigs fired on the army in Lexington and Concord, and laid siege to Boston immediately afterward, Allen worked out that he could ally himself with them. They were angry with the governor of Massachusetts, as he was with the governor of New York. His intention was to proclaim the Green Mountains an independent territory, and with the help of the Bostonians he could do it. So he too became a Whig.

"They took Fort Ticonderoga while the garrison was drunk. Ethan Allen shouted: 'In the name of the great Jehovah and the Continental Congress!' The Green Mountain Boys had come in with rifles raised. Like when the Greeks entered Rome hidden in a big wooden horse, except that there was no wooden horse."

The Greeks in Rome? Peter was about to object, when he heard a sound of branches.

"Did you hear that?" Walter asked, turning suddenly toward the scrub.

He leapt to his feet clutching his rifle, his face pale. The sight of a familiar figure reassured him.

"Mr. McLeod," he said.

He saluted him discreetly as the Scotsman entered the circle of light.

"Three little bastards have pinched a bottle from my reserve. I saw them coming up hereabouts."

Peter looked around, embarrassed. The Indian boys had disappeared.

"They haven't passed this way," Walter said quickly.

"We could offer you some tea," Peter suggested.

McLeod grunted his thanks. He sat down and darted a glance behind him.

"You're not the only ones on guard this evening. There's that Indian, too." He pointed to the darkness. "Lacroix."

Peter turned around, as if he could see through the night.

"Where?" he asked.

"Down there, sitting in the dark."

"Impossible," Walter observed. "We haven't seen or even heard him."

"Sure," McLeod nodded, clutching the cup. "Just as you didn't see those three thieves, eh?"

Walter was about to retort, but again it was the Scotsman who spoke.

"I nearly bumped into him. Still as a tree trunk."

"He's a strange character," Walter said swiftly, "What do they call him?"

"His enemies call him Le Grand Diable," Peter replied. "Because of an act of revenge, I've heard."

"It's a story that happened long ago," said McLeod.

"You know it?"

The man poked the fire with a stick.

"Back from the war, he got married and went west to hunt, with his wife and daughter. One day he got home and found his family massacred." McLeod's voice thickened. "Huron Indians, disbanded and drunk. Rejects thrown out of the tribes." He spat on the ground. "They slaughtered them like animals."

He fell silent. The crackling of the flames was the only clear sound in the muffled chorus of rustling nocturnal beasts. Peter wanted to know how the story ended.

"He stayed away for a whole winter. He came back in the spring with twenty-seven scalps in a sack."

Peter gripped his jaw.

"I saw them with my own eyes," the other man said, his voice even hoarser. "They're buried beside the grave of his womenfolk."

McLeod stood up. "Gentlemen, thank you for the tea. Good luck with the rest of your guard."

The man walked away, and the two youths were left in silence. Walter said he would do the second round of guard duty, and wrapped himself up in his blanket.

Peter studied the darkness. He imagined the surface of the lake, a sea in the heart of the continent. The stories that night all spoke of conflict and reminded him that soon he would be fighting side by side with great warriors.

As he cleaned his rifle, he prayed that he was up to it.

28.

Smells of summer breathed from the banks of the St. Lawrence, and the open air dispersed the miasmas rising around the boats. The sun was already rising, and soon the Lachine Rapids would put the convoy to the test.

Joseph studied the profile of the banks, searching for footholds in his memory, in twenty-year-old visions, when he had first plowed these waters. He observed the shadow cast by the hull and noticed that Philip was doing the same thing. The solitary hunter's face rippled in the current.

The war against France had lasted seven years, but because of their youth they had only been able to take part in Sir William's final enterprises: the capture of Fort Niagara, where they had had their baptism of fire, and the taking of Montreal, the last French bulwark in America. The French had known by then that the war was lost, and the city had surrendered without resistance. And yet he and Philip had run their greatest risk then, as they traveled that river. They had escaped together and that had been the start of their friendship.

Joseph noticed that he was holding the oar tighter than necessary. A stiff, contracted grip that he was beginning to feel in his back. He tried to make his movements more fluid and went on rowing. He imagined that Philip, too, was traveling that path in his memories.

They were seventeen then, but that time they hadn't tried to hurl insults and fire from behind a tree as they waited for the warriors to resolve the issue. That time the smell of fear and death had poured in through their nostrils, descending to their bellies and rising to their throats.

They were scouting with two expert warriors, people who had fought under Hendrick's wing, killers of men, respected by all the chiefs in the Longhouse. General Amherst, who was leading the expedition, feared that the tribes allied to the French might launch an attack on the rapids. Sir William had offered to send a canoe on reconnaissance.

It was an important task, and Joseph remembered the pride he had felt. They had to disembark and patrol the shore, check whether anyone had left signs or traces on the path along the right bank of the river.

When the canoe approached the rocks, the warrior in the prow had gestured to them to stop. Silence, just the lapping of the boat and the roar of the rapids further down the valley. Joseph had only had time to touch his rifle before it happened.

All of a sudden, ferocious demons had emerged from the river, from the masses of weed that had concealed them. The warriors in the prow and the stern were dragged down in an inescapable embrace.

Joseph had seen his own fear reflected in his friend's face. Then Philip hurled himself out of the canoe with a war cry. Joseph saw him advancing up to his belly in the water, challenging the Abenaki. They had sneered, he was only a boy, they found the whole thing ridiculous, amusing. Nonetheless they prepared to kill him.

Joseph counted the rifles of the warriors in the canoe. Four including his own. Then he did the same with the enemies. He couldn't make a mistake.

He killed the first with a blow to the chest, without giving him time to approach Philip. The second he only managed to wound in the side, but Philip finished him off with his tomahawk. The third and fourth threw themselves against the young Mohawk, blinded by rage. Joseph struck only one of them, in the head. The struggle between Philip and his final adversary lasted only a few breaths, which to Joseph seemed an eternity. Then his friend emerged from the water brandishing his knife. He had a wound in his side. One step beyond him, his adversary was trying to get back to his feet, dabbing at his arm, which was cut to the bone. As he retreated toward the forest, he cursed them in his language and in French, unable to believe that he had been beaten by two boys.

With a mixture of rage and fear, Philip had thrown himself in pursuit.

Joseph had few shots left in his gun. Recharging would take too much time. As if in a dream, his mind's eye watched the body jumping into the water and running, knees lifted high, toward the riverbank.

He caught up to them among the trees. He had had to drag Philip off his enemy, who was still struggling under the knife blows. In spite of his wound, Philip was a bundle of nerves and muscles ready to spring—or to dissolve as soon as he lost his strength.

Without thinking, Joseph had looked at the dying warrior's face and raised the barrel of his rifle. The sound of the skull shattering entered his ears, never to leave them.

When they got back to the canoe, the little inlet was red with blood and the current rocked the inert bodies of the fallen. The two survivors had looked at one another without a word. Philip's wound was a deep one. They had to get back to the convoy as quickly as possible. Just one pair of arms to paddle, carry the bodies of their companions, hope that most of their enemies were far away. In that situation, firing had not been wise.

But you don't expect wisdom from young men.

Joseph had rowed with all the strength of desperation, anxious to glimpse the outline of friendly boats. The clash had taken place in the water, but blood drenched everything. Even their spirits.

The stream of memories made way for images of the present, another convoy, another war. Joseph went on watching Philip row. He thought there must be a meaning in the repetition of this journey. It was like going back to the start of it all.

29.

The Island of Montreal appeared in the blazing July sun. The Island of Jesus, the second post of the door into Canada, appeared behind it. The waters of the St. Lawrence parted into three courses, through easily defensible straits, to meet up again further to the north.

Peter Johnson had listened to the tales of that journey so many times that he recognized every detail, as if he had been there before. On the eastern bank, threads of smoke among the trees revealed the village of the Caughnawaga, who had once been renegade Mohawks, allies of the French. From the beach, women and children watched the boats.

Once they had turned the loop of the river, the larger island appeared, revealing its full length. The hill was scattered with fields and vegetable plots that sloped down to the city, firmly enclosed by its ramparts. The bell tower of the church of Notre-Dame stood out above the built-up area.

Peter wished he could say something, express his enthusiasm at having reached the end of the journey, perhaps even fire in the air to announce their arrival. But for many of them, approaching their destination was anything but joyous, because of the grief that had fallen upon the expedition and the few warriors who followed it. Silence dominated everyone's heart. Guy Johnson sat in the front boat, gloomy and taciturn, along with the men from the Department. Uncle Joseph hadn't said a word since leaving Oswego. The other warriors didn't consider Peter adult enough to let him chat with them. Furthermore, he had spent the last few years in Philadelphia, immersed in his studies, and had led too different a life. On the last stretch of the journey, if it hadn't been for Walter Butler, Peter wouldn't have had a soul to exchange two words with. But Walter was rowing on the Department boat, beside his father. Peter resigned himself to keeping his feelings hidden and rowed even harder.

Once, in New York, Peter had seen His Majesty's troops lined up on parade. Now, a step away from the war, the effect was very different. On the Place d'Armes, next to the church, the city garrison welcomed them with drum rolls. Peter was dazzled by the scarlet of the uniforms, which was echoed in the standards. Governor Carleton waited for the delegation in the middle of the parade ground, and together they saluted the flag. Guy Johnson and Daniel Claus, stiff before the Union Jack, betrayed no weariness. They followed the ceremony to the end, when the order was given to break ranks and return to guard duties. The soldiers quickly dispersed in little groups.

"Are we going to be fighting alongside them?" Peter asked.

Joseph touched his shoulder.

"Not just them, I hope. That's not a lot of people to hold the city."

The boy noticed the shadow that crossed his uncle's face. He didn't ask anything else.

Governor Carleton read the message carefully, his pupils darting from one word to the next. Then he folded up the sheet of paper and wearily handed it back to Guy Johnson.

"General Gage always has a thought for everyone."

His voice was slurred. Guy thought it sounded like the voice of a sick man. He exchanged a glance with Daniel Claus, who was sitting beside him, and waited.

The governor stretched his legs out under the table, letting his belly press against the wooden edge. Gray curls framed a hairless, sweaty face, reflective wrinkles rippled his receding hairline. He waved for a drink to be brought.

"It's very hot, don't you think?"

He drained a glass of yellowish liquid and wiped his fleshy lips with a lace handkerchief.

Johnson and Claus were still silent. It was true, in the commissariat the air was musty and stale. The light came in through only one window. They were sweating under their woolen jackets.

"He has sent you here to defend Canada. Of course." Carleton nodded to himself. "What the devil does Gage know about Canada? He's been barricaded away in Boston for three months and claims he's leading the military operations."

He struck his glass on the table and an attendant hurried to fill it again.

"You know, I sent him my best units. Now I'm forced to hold the position with a few thousand men, on a territory ten times the size of England, while he hides himself away." The last words were muttered between his teeth.

With a flick of his hand he unrolled a map on the big table and nodded to the two others to look at it, something that he had no need to do. Johnson and Claus craned their necks. The St. Lawrence Basin was reproduced there in all its length, from Lake Ontario to the ocean.

Carleton stretched his legs again.

"In London they don't understand." He was talking to himself now, staring into midair, hands folded on his belly. "The nature of the problem plainly escapes them." He ran his index finger along the edge of the map. "The size of this continent."

He sighed. He looked at the two gentlemen as if he had only just noticed they were there.

"We have a difficult task ahead of us. Civilizing a vast, wild and hostile territory. A heavy burden to bear, yes. And yet someone has to do it." He wiped away the sweat that pearled on his forehead. "It's very hot, isn't it?"

Again he had the glasses filled, and sipped his drink distractedly, listening to the vague sounds that reached them from outside, mingling with the ticking of the clock at the end of the room.

"I've asked for reinforcements, but no luck so far. I've also tried to recruit these French peasants. Pointless, they still see us as occupying forces, they will never fight for George III."

He stared at the two of them in silence, seriously, waiting for the answer to an implied question.

"And now Thomas Gage sends you, along with two hundred Indians." He smiled faintly. "What a masterpiece. Perhaps he thinks you should act like Leonidas at Thermopylae."

Johnson and Claus were two pillars of salt frozen to their chairs. Guy felt rage mounting, along with a sense of gloomy frustration.

"We can recruit a thousand," he broke in frostily. "Only if Your Excellency permits. With an Indian army we could go down to meet the rebels on Lake Champlain. Win back Fort Ticonderoga. Send them back where they came from."

Carleton listened impassively.

Daniel Claus leaned forward.

"With the greatest respect, Excellency, I have been acting as superintendent of the Canadian Indians for many years. Let us organize a council here, too. I have good reasons to believe that the tribes of these territories will fight on the side of the king."

The governor stifled a coughing fit.

"That doesn't mean that you, Mr. Claus, or you, Mr. Johnson, have any right to act as superintendent of the Indian Department."

The German said nothing, but Guy interrupted in a voice slightly more heated than etiquette might have called for.

"The late Sir William Johnson appointed us his successors."

"As I am sure you know," Carleton replied coldly, "Department posts are the prerogative of the Colonial Ministry."

Guy felt tired, put to the test by his recent struggle and annoyed by this man's stubbornness. He was tempted to forget the whole thing, get up and go home, abandon himself to events or even rage against them. He took a deep breath to banish the feeling.

"Excellency, by your own admission, you don't have many soldiers to defend Montreal. And if Montreal falls, the rebels will have a clear road all the way to Quebec."

Carleton interrupted him again. "If you're so convinced that the Indians will lend us their obedience, tell me, what would they claim in return?"

"Gifts. And the confirmation of what we promised in Oswego."

Carleton raised an eyebrow more expressive than a question mark.

"That those fighting for the Crown will be compensated for any territorial losses."

"Ah," said the governor. "Nothing less."

He shifted on his chair, but said nothing more. Guy spotted an opening and decided to exploit it.

"They won't ask you to put it in writing. It'll be enough for Your Excellency to say it in front of the war chiefs."

The grandfather clock, the clatter of the carriages in the square, the marching steps of the patrol, the shouts of children. The light faded, the sun gilded the outlines of things.

Carleton nodded, with slow, grave motions of his head.

"Now I'll tell you what I'll do. I will let you organize this council. Assemble all the warriors you can. The rebels are at least as frightened of the Indians as I am. They will be frightened and perhaps they won't attack us. And yet it will help us gain time. Anyway, I command you to stay within the Canadian borders. You won't go below the forty-fifth parallel, you will wait for the rebels cross it before engaging them in battle."

"Excellency. . ." Guy Johnson attempted to break in, but the governor's raised hand compelled him to silence.

"Gentlemen, here I represent His Majesty. Sir Guy Carleton will not enter the annals for unleashing the savages against English subjects, even if those subjects are traitors. They will hang from a gallows after a trial for high treason, not have their throats slit and their scalps cut off in the middle of a forest." He stared into both men's eyes for a long time. "These are my orders. Stick to them without exception."

30.

Honored Sir John,

The messengers I invited from Oswego will by now have given you news of the death of my wife and the baby she carried in her womb. An immeasurable loss for me and a bad omen for the expedition, which, I am convinced of it, has taken an indelible air of misfortune from this tragedy. Ill luck, in fact, has not abandoned us. Allow me to illustrate this with reference to the events of the last few months, and you may judge for yourselves.

We arrived in Canada in the middle of July with only two hundred warriors, receiving a rather cool reception from the governor, General Carleton. Of his antipathy toward our family we were already aware, but we didn't expect him to discourage an initiative that might bring him relief. He is, in fact, short of troops, having sent reinforcements to General Gage in Boston, and is under threat of an invasion by the Whig rebels. I have tried to explain to His Excellency that General Gage thought it a good idea to send us in return, along with the Indian irregulars, to support Canada, but the argument had no effect upon him.

Nonetheless, he agreed to confirm to the Indians the promises made in Oswego by the undersigned, in exchange for support for our cause, which is to say compensation by the Crown for all territory lost in the event of conflict with the Whigs. We pressured him to agree in front of a council of Canadian tribes, called for the occasion by our trustworthy Daniel Claus. Among the two thousand or so convened, Carleton's promises made a great impression, but we know that the enthusiasm of the Indians is short-lived, if it does not find an outlet in immediate action. Unfortunately the suspicious indecision of the governor toward the Indians has revealed itself to be an obstacle more difficult to overcome than any rapids or straits that we encountered on our way here. He does not trust the Indians and he does not want them to fight alone, for fear of losing control of them and being accused of savagery. It is His Excellency's firm will that our warriors should fight alongside the regular troops in mixed regiments, under the command of British officers. The order received has been to hold the position and wait for the offensive from the rebels or the arrival of fresh contingents from the motherland.

To this we must add that the Whig rebels have wasted no time in trying to corrupt the tribes, buying their neutrality with gold.

The Caughnawaga were persuaded by three hundred pounds.

Yet more serious is the fact that a week ago an Oneida delegation came to our camp, advising the warriors to sign the peace with the Albany rebels and pointing out that the Mohawks of Fort Hunter would already have done so. If this is so, then our valley and our possessions are exposed to a grave risk, without any Indian tribe willing to defend them, and you and your family are in danger.

Heavy-hearted with this news, we were resolving to turn back in great haste, when further news reached us: the rebels have resumed their northward advance. From Fort Ticonderoga they are going back up to Lake Champlain.

They are led by Montgomery, whom you will remember as an officer of General Amherst in the Franco-Indian War. He is Irish as we are: Sir William, your father, knew him well and would today be surprised to find himself fighting against an old comrade-in-arms. We do not yet know how many men Montgomery is taking with him, but the news has led Governor Carleton to mobilize the Indians, albeit under the orders of an officer. Butler put himself forward. As I write he is leading the warriors beyond the St. Lawrence, to the outpost of Fort St. Johns, the first obstacle that the rebels will find in their path. Our Mohawks are with him.

It would be futile to point out that the morale of the Department is rather low. The fighters at our disposal are few in number, there is as yet no news of reinforcements from England, and it is beyond dispute that Montreal would be unable to resist a major attack. Our contribution to the defense of Canada is far from significant. So it is my intention to prepare myself to organize our return as soon as possible.

Because uncertainty about what might happen by chance leaves us prey to a profound anxiety, I ask you to send me news from the colony as soon as possible.

In the hope of meeting up with you again soon and wishing you all the best, I remain

Your devoted brother-in-law,
Guy Johnson

31.

Around the dancer, whites and Indians were clapping their hands. The tune of the bagpipes and the tight rhythm of the drum seemed to be coming from underground, buried by the hubbub, the cries of encouragement. The man at the center of all the attention hopped back and forth on alternate legs, knees lifted high, right hand raised above his head, left hand on his hip. He was wearing the traditional headgear of his people, the one that the English contemptuously referred to as a cowpat. The kilt and clocked socks had been left at home, in a little farm owned by the Johnsons.

From the first note, Peter had recognized the music, a march. The steps, on the other hand, were indecipherable. It wasn't so much a dance as a play of the legs to disorient one's adversary and surprise him with a dagger blow.

Lying on the sun-yellowed grass, two swords formed a cross. Peter knew that the challenge lay in striking the feet beside the blades, now in one square, now in the other, without ever trampling on them. Not a simple game, with the usual corollary of bets: dancing on the swords was one of many ways of obtaining good luck. The Mohawks were very keen on it. His father had sworn that it was the Highland War Dance, rather than the exhausting councils, that had persuaded the Six Nations to fight the French.

"That's nothing to be surprised about," he'd said. "The Scots are the most Indian of all the peoples in Europe."

The drumming became urgent: the musicians were really showing warlike enthusiasm. Their shouts grew together into a chorus. Peter looked at the dancer: he was flying, hovering an inch above the ground, his feet so fast that they were floating on the dust. A warrior capable of moving like that would be an impossible target for anyone.

The circle of spectators tightened. The Highlanders came forward with long suspended strides, in a dance step. The others tried to imitate them. They looked like a marching army menacingly encircling the last enemy standing. In reality, they were approaching to check that their champion wasn't treading on the weapons. If he succeeded, the next day they would repel the rebel assault and Peter's baptism of fire would end in victory.

The dust obscured their view of the swords.

The summer twilight softened lines and contrasts on the Fort St. Johns parade ground. The sentries on the ramparts also cocked their ears to the music, which was speeding toward its final, furious gallop. There was a collective start, then the voices fell silent, hands stopped clapping and pointed to the cross at the dancer's feet. The whole of the first row was aquiver with squabbles and arguments, then the one behind it and the one behind that. The circle of men held their breath. In the sudden silence, Cormac McLeod walked toward the dancer, who was waiting at attention by the swords.

The great chief of the Scots knelt solemnly by the crossed blades, blew in the dust, then looked up at the warrior. McLeod gripped the weapons, lifted them high in the shape of a cross and struck the swords three times against each other.

"*Bualidh mi u an sa chean!*," he cried at the top of his lungs.

"*Bualidh mi u an sa chean!*," repeated the Highlanders in a roar of exultation, then threw themselves on their champion and carried him in triumph over their heads.

The Indians remained on the parade ground, still perplexed about the outcome of the dance, the battle and the bets. The evening star was already shining beside the moon.

Peter breathed in the night air. He had never seen such an old-looking building, not even in Albany, not even in New York. In actual fact the fort had been built recently, but the palisade, already moss-covered, seemed to have emerged out of the ground before the start of time. The British flag flapped lazily in the middle of the smoke from the fires, the faded colors of night making it look black and white.

The previous day, a salvo of hurrahs had greeted their arrival from the terraces of the fort. The garrison looked haggard. The 84th regiment, the Royal Highlander Emigrants, was in fact little more than a battalion. Recruited in Boston, New York, Canada, Nova Scotia. People who had only recently arrived on American soil: fishermen from Newfoundland, settlers from Carolina who had disembarked with very different hopes, had quickly made up their minds which side to be on. Soldiers in the green uniform of the Canadian regiments—they had been promised the red one, with kilt, saber and pistol, but it hadn't yet arrived.

Now the fort was swarming with activity, preparations for war. Powder-horns were being filled, rifles cleaned. McLeod honed the blade of his sword on the grindstone. They would get no sleep before the battle, just a few hours of unconsciousness to summon their strength and be on their feet at dawn. Peter certainly wouldn't shut an eye. At last the moment had come.

That afternoon Uncle Joseph and John Butler had studied the battle plan. The rebels expected to find a little contingent barricaded in the fort, and instead the garrison would be waiting for them along the river. The guides maintained that the best spot was a strait a few miles to the south, where the current would slow the enemy advance.

"The Scots have danced their dances," he heard his uncle's voice just behind his ear. "It's time for ours."

Peter sat next to him and took out a small mirror. Without speaking, he began to paint his face with broad red and blue squares, while Joseph finished cleaning his own weapon with the plunger and a soapy rag.

"They say the scalp is the essence of the man. But I say that the essence of a man is his rifle. The most intimate part of the rifle is hollow, empty. The soul of man is ungraspable, elusive. Without your rifle, you are just one more animal fighting to eat. The rifle, Peter, is the gift of God to the men of the woods, who made them lords over the animals." Joseph allowed himself a pause. He thought for a moment and concluded, "Of course, you have to be righteous lords, not tyrants." He set the rifle down and took mirror and paints from his leather bag.

Peter had never heard words like these. Joseph began painting his cheeks.

Philip Lacroix joined them. His hair fell loose over his shoulders; his war-paint was subdued. He had used only black, to paint a stripe on his eyes.

"Tomorrow, during the attack, you will stay close to me and Ronaterihonte," Joseph said.

Peter gulped. Not knowing what to say, he merely stared at the cauldron boiling on the big fire in the center of the field. The sweet flesh of bear was cooking in its grease.

As the hunter extracts the guts from the belly of his prey, the war chiefs would grip the boiling flesh with their bare hands. Peter and the warriors of his own age would serve it to the older ones, along with the gravy. The body and blood of the enemy would strengthen the men for war.

When dinner was over the Mohawks, too, would dance as hard as they could, stopping to get their breath back amid chants and tales of derring-do.

The light took over the sky as a cold breeze scattered the embers and dispersed the echo of dancing and singing. Peter, with his kit ready for hours and his face painted, studied the Highlanders standing outside the chapel for Holy Mass. In the dawn mist, with their rifles planted on the ground and their sabers at their sides, they looked like the illustrations in a book in Johnson Hall library. Knights, armed with lances and swords, ready to fight for their king. John Butler and his son were in their midst. They lined up in front of the priest and knelt down one after the other to receive the body of Christ, and each one lowered his rifle for it to be blessed.

Last of all Peter saw Lacroix rising to his feet and making the sign of the cross. Then he headed for the group of warriors. Peter quickened his pace, aware that his teeth were chattering behind his closed lips, to the rhythm of the Scottish war dance.

White men and Indians began leaving the fort in two long parallel lines, making for the forest. No more than five hundred men.

Two hours later, the scouts came back to tell them that the rebel army was advancing along the west bank of the Richelieu. At least two thousand men. Peter thought that was how courage was measured: confronting an enemy and making up for the disparity in strength with cunning and surprise. He felt he was on the threshold of a memorable ordeal.

32.

The rebels appeared along the path that ran beside the rapids. They patrolled the terrain and the surrounding forest, as the boats drew near the shore.

To Peter they looked like ants crawling over a tree trunk. They weren't wearing uniforms, and each one was holding a different weapon. In the distance, the Continental American army looked like a band of hunters.

Peter breathed deeply to check his agitation. The musky smell of undergrowth mixed with the sweetish air rising from the river. Lacroix, crouching next to him, didn't move a muscle. The whole line of fire was motionless. Butler had arranged the men along the edge of a little promontory overlooking the strait of the Richelieu. The 84th and the Highlanders in the middle, the Indians at the sides. They would strike them from above, from the shelter of the trees, while they were out in the open and halfway through.

Joseph crept along silently until he reached the edge of the rank, where he would take charge of the Mohawk fusillade.

Lacroix looked at Peter and guessed his state of mind.

"Control your fear. Don't let it out," he murmured. "When everything happens quickly, learn to be slow."

The rebels down at the river unloaded the boats to lessen their draft and let them pass through the rapids. Groups of them held the towlines and released them just enough to lower the boats without violent collisions. As they worked, they sank and slipped to their knees in the mud.

Peter realized the time had come. The Highland war cry rang out on the ridge, loud and picked up by dozens of voices. Panic spread along the riverbank, turning into terror when the first two hundred rifles opened fire from the forest.

Peter didn't know if he had hit his target. When the smoke cleared there were bodies floating in the water and others struggling to keep from drowning. Butler ordered the second salvo. The ants on the bank ran in all directions, in search of shelter, under the stones on the shore or in holes in the ground. Some tried to reach the opposite bank, but the current dragged them away.

One of the boats had run aground among the rocks; the others were stuck on the bank.

Someone returned fire, aiming blindly into the scrub. Peter's voice joined in with the Mohawk cry of exultation. The Indians were good at making themselves seem like twice as many.

The firing went on chaotically, each man shooting at his own hidden target.

Now they had them in their pockets.

Then earth and sky trembled.

Peter was assailed by a rain of rocks and soil, and a tangle of shattered branches came hurtling down from above.

Butler ran behind the line of riflemen, toward Joseph, but slipped and fell. A second explosion, and two ragged bodies were hurled into the air.

Butler got to his feet covered in mud, his face and jacket spattered with blood. He cursed as he reached Joseph.

"Those bastards are firing a mortar at us!"

He was yelling, deafened by the reports. Peter could hear something.

Joseph tried to locate the mortar in the rebel line.

"Where is it?"

Butler pointed to the loop in the river.

"Behind the rocks."

The third shot burst from behind a tree trunk, which collapsed on the rank of men. One of the soldiers cried out, his leg pierced by a splintered branch.

Peter spat out soil and tried to breathe; the air was thick with soot. The trees and the ferns trapped the gun-smoke, which turned into a dense fog.

"How can they see us from down there?" Joseph shouted with disbelief.

"They don't need to see us," Butler replied. "They're firing at random into the hill. With that thing they can bring the whole forest down on top of us if they want."

As if to underline the Irishman's words, a fourth cannonade crashed down a few yards above them, tearing up trees and plants.

The Indians were terrified, and on the point of scattering. Joseph ran along the rank, along with Butler, yelling with all the breath he could muster.

"Stop! Go on firing!"

Peter lost sight of him amid the smoke and foliage. Only then did he notice that he was pushing down with his palms to get to his feet: his legs wanted to run away, but Lacroix's hand was keeping him down.

The fifth burst of mortar fire opened up a corridor among the trees and bounced almost to the top of the slope. The falling leaves and branches buried half of the rank and kept them from firing.

McLeod yelled orders to his men, waving his sword. He swore on St. Andrew and St. Columbanus that he would disembowel anyone who turned his back on the enemy. The air was by now impossible to breathe and not a thing could be seen. Peter struggled to make out Joseph and Butler among the men lying around him. Mud and war-paint mixed on his uncle's face, giving him a monstrous expression.

Butler shouted over the noise of the disintegrating forest.

"We've got to split up into little groups and climb up to the ridge!"

Joseph shook his head.

"No. Up there we'd be easier targets."

"There's no alternative!" roared the Irishman.

Joseph looked at Lacroix. The two men stared at one another. He had lost count of the cannon shots, his ears hummed, he was coughing and spitting.

"Let's go," said Joseph.

He uttered a sharp cry and Kanatawakhon and Sakihenakenta emerged from the rank.

Oronhyateka and Kanenonte, their muscles gleaming with sweat, came up alongside Lacroix.

Joseph looked at the warriors and came up to Peter, so close that he breathed in his face.

"Going back up is as dangerous as staying here. So the only way of getting to safety is to go down. We have to get close to the mortar, you see? Where it can't hit us. Put it out of action."

Stunned, Peter nodded.

"Stay one step behind me," said Joseph. "Keep your head down and when I tell you, throw yourself on the ground."

He looked at Butler, waiting for his agreement.

"All right. Each of you take two rifles. I'll cover you as best I can. May God protect you, you damned lunatics."

They loaded their weapons and started down the hill at a jog trot, parting the ferns and thickening smoke. Without a sound they reached the edge of the forest and squatted down behind a big fallen tree trunk, about thirty yards from the rebel defenses.

After their initial dispersion they were reorganizing, trying to recover material and assemble their forces. The shots from the mortar flew high over their heads, whistling loudly. Then Peter spotted it, behind a group of rocks where the loop in the river created a little dip. It was some way from the bulk of the column, out of range, defended by a group of men posted behind a boat sunk into the mud to act as a trench. The mortar was a few dozen yards further back. When the wind opened up a gap in the fog, Peter could make out the artillerymen.

At that moment he saw Lacroix, knife and club in his belt, rifle around his neck, tomahawk in his fist.

Joseph started firing at the rebel positions, followed by the others. Above them, from the flank of the hill, the Highlanders were using up their ammunition, encouraged by the hoarse cries of Butler and McLeod.

It was then that Lacroix leapt out of his cover.

Peter Johnson watched what followed with disbelief.

Later that night, back at the fort, he had to break down and reassemble his memory of events, like a jigsaw puzzle, to make it plausible to his own imagination. Telling it would have been impossible.

Lacroix had reached the enemy defenses under cover of a cloak of smoke. Without running, walking quickly and silently.

Someone, perhaps an officer, on the other side had shouted: "Fire! Fire!" Too late. The Devil was already in their midst.

Captain Jacobs turned around, hands on his stomach. As he staggered he just had time to see the Indian smashing the skull of the second officer with a single tomahawk blow and plunging his knife between the ribs of the sergeant major. They were fluid motions, a dance. *My God.* He felt his knees giving way, he collapsed, spat the blood that rose to his throat and gasped for air with his mouth wide open. *My God.* Someone in the boat sounded the alarm. From behind the rocks they yelled at the men to keep quiet, because the loyalists were trapped on the hill, under the mortar fire. Captain Jacobs closed his eyes and opened them again. Everything was blurred. *The Lord is my shepherd.* Lieutenant Bones found a rifle barrel under his chin as he bent to pick up his own weapon. The shot cleanly detached his head and sent it flying. *He maketh me to lie down in green pastures, he leadeth me beside the still waters.* Donkers raised his rifle, but panic stopped him shooting straight and he found his guts between his feet, his hands groping to try and keep them in. *He restoreth my soul, he leadeth me in the paths of righteousness.* Abrahamson charged, bayonet in hand, teeth clenched. When the tomahawk broke his arm with a dry sound he froze, staring at the limb that dangled from his shoulder. Then he looked up to receive the coup de grace right in the temple. *For His name's sake.* Marteens slipped in the slimy mud as he tried to crawl away. A single knife-blow to the thigh sliced his artery and left him dying in the bottom of the boat, screaming like a slaughtered pig. *Yea though I walk through the valley of the shadow of death I will fear no evil, for Thou art with me.* The gunners were opening fire against the shadow that advanced slowly toward them. How do you fire at a shadow? *Thy rod and staff they comfort me.* Escape, Captain Jacobs would have yelled if he'd had any breath in his lungs. He saw Rodgers falling first with an ax in his chest. The men attached to the gun dashed furiously forward. The shadow bent down and crippled one as it struck the other with the butt of its rifle and finished both of them off with its dagger. *My God,* Jacobs thought, forehead resting on the ground, knees drawn up beneath his belly. He breathed in the damp scent of grass, mixed with the smell of his own blood. He saw the shadow coming back. *My God,* he thought again, before retching the last of his soul away.

The ramparts of the fort welcomed them in a protective embrace. The fighters tossed and turned, curling up under blankets and furs, beside the fire. Few had the strength to retell and relive the day of battle. There would be time for that tomorrow, when they had rejoined the world

Peter sat down, too exhausted even to blink. The words of Uncle Joseph and John Butler reached him in flurries. They had repelled the rebels, inflicted severe losses upon them, but soon others would come. They had to stand firm. Give Carleton time to organize the defenses of the city.

Peter was listening, but his mind was elsewhere.

He felt Joseph's hand on his shoulder.

"You did well today. Molly can be proud of you. Sleep now."

The boy lay down, but took a long time to get to sleep. Each time he closed his eyes he saw Lacroix's attack, and then the warrior waiting for them on the bank of the river, covered in blood from head to toe. Oronhyateka and Kanenonte stepped aside as he passed, fearful and admiring. And Lacroix's face: beneath the drying blood, every muscle had frozen. His lips were dry and cracked, the bed of a dead, sun-beaten river. The Devil walked on. They saw him stop fifty yards further on and take off his clothes, oblivious to everything, and walk heavily into the water, where he washed the blood from his skin with big, rough slaps. Peter had looked at his uncle. Joseph had stared for a long time at his old comrade-in-arms.

Peter twisted in the blanket.

Through his eyelids, he saw the flames flicker to the rhythm of the drum and the bagpipes.

A dance of war and death.

33.

Ramezay Castle wasn't a real castle. No towers and turrets, just the big chimney pots on the plunging roof. Transported to the Irish countryside, the governor's house would have looked like a big farm. In London it might have been mistaken for an army barracks.

For the first time since he had been in Canada, Guy Johnson left the building behind him and crossed the garden. Warm rays of sun drenched the haze. Three conversations with Carleton, so many stabs in the back.

That morning, a messenger from Sir John had brought news to the Mohawk camp. The rebels were throwing their weight about in the valley. They had arrested two Scotsmen as they were mounting guard on the road near Johnson Hall. The situation was rapidly deteriorating. According to rumors, the men from the Department were coveted prey. They wouldn't risk touching Sir John, not yet, but for all the others, going home was too risky. In Albany prison the gallows were ready.

The messenger had only just arrived and already McLeod was asking permission to pack. The Highlanders had come back from Fort St. Johns exploding with resentment. They had fought bravely, they had repelled the enemy. Two days later, Carleton had sent a company to replace them. Thanks a lot, back you go to the city, maybe we'll need you again one day. Used and set aside as soon as possible. Carleton preferred to defend Canada on his own, or deluded himself that the French peasants would give him a hand, rather than concede anything to the Johnsons and the Indian Department. No one wanted to fight for the governor anymore. Even the Indians were burning with disappointment. Fighting at the drop of a hat was normal for them, but they hated clashes without booty, without scalps, without honor and gifts to reward the warriors.

Your familiarity with the Indians would be very useful to us in Fort Niagara, Colonel Johnson.

Niagara, at the other end of Lake Ontario. The best place to go and rot, surrounded by Seneca, on the edges of the world.

Guy passed through the railing and dismissed the coach with a nod of his head. He wanted to walk, to stretch his bones. Perhaps the warmth of the day would dissolve the knot that he felt in his neck. Every day he felt lower, squashed like a snake under a rock, a rock warmed by the sun. He had to get out of this deadlock, make the right choice, go for broke. But what?

He wouldn't go to Fort Niagara, that much was certain. A place of soldiers and fur traders, where the only possible diplomacy involved licking the feet of a bunch of haughty and arrogant sachems.

Going back to Guy Park was too dangerous.

And then there was the more serious matter, the second dagger blow from governor Carleton.

Colonel Johnson, Lieutenant Claus: Let me introduce Major John Campbell, who has just arrived from England to take up the post of superintendent of the Canadian Indians.

John Campbell, the man from London, well connected in the capital's drawing rooms, stormed onto the scene overnight to oust Daniel Claus and remind Guy that his position was barely safer than the German's. Not safe enough to feel at ease, immune to further ignominies. Leaving the scene might mean disappearing forever, giving up being Sir William's successor.

What was to be done?

Not even the Old Man had ever found himself in such a maze. The more he thought of it the more convinced he was. There was little point wondering what William would have done in his place. The banal reply was that no Bighead Carleton would have dared treat Sir William like that. The Old Man had come to Montreal to conquer the city with six hundred Indians, not to kick his heels in a castle that looked like a farm.

St. Paul Street swarmed with carts heading for the market. The doorways of the shops selling tea, furs, spirits and cloth were framed with inscriptions that climbed up the façades all the way to the first-floor windows, declaiming the quality and the variety of the goods. From the backs of the open shops you could see the walls and a coming and going of porters that revealed the proximity of the river, with the waterfront and the masts of the vessels crowding around the wharfs.

In front of Our Lady's chapel, a group of Caughnawagas was chanting the rosary to earn alms from the passers by. The women going into the churches held little model ships. They must have been ex votos, symbols of prayers uttered for husbands at the mercy of the sea. Guy wanted to kneel down before the Virgin of the mariners, to ask for help against the gales of the past few months. He approached the door, but the red uniform he was wearing immediately attracted attention, and he changed his mind.

As he returned to the main road, with his hand around the back of his neck, a woman of the people started walking beside him.

"*Escusé*, sir, you *très mal*. Your shadow is heavy."

"What's that you say?" Guy asked.

The woman spoke quickly, a mixture of English and French, but neither seemed to be her language. She was of indefinable race: her features were European, her skin dark, her eyes slightly elongated, her lips the fleshy lips of the Africans.

"Your shadow is heavy," she pointed to the ground. "You will leave, you understand? Death follows you. Beyond *le lac*."

Guy gave a start and gripped her wrist. "Are you giving me the evil eye?"

"No, sir, Massoula not do that. The Virgin weeps for your grief."

Guy thought his brain was going to explode, that the street was the deck of a storm-tossed vessel. He clenched his fists, as he had when he had seen the incision. As he had when he saw the child, motionless under the bandages.

"*Bandoka* has made his nest *ici*," the woman touched herself at the nape of her neck. "Inside your neck, and now he hurts *très mal*."

As if woken by a necromancer, Guy remembered that he was in Montreal, in a side-alley off St. Paul Street, with a witch called Massoula, who knew lots of things about him, from his darkest misfortunes to the pains in his brain.

With a wave of her fingers, the woman invited him to follow her.

"*Venez*, just a piece of small change, come *avec moi*."

Guy hesitated. All he needed was a trick by a French pickpocket to bring the day to a fine end. The woman walked a hundred yards or so and disappeared into an inn below the city walls. A moment later she reappeared and waved her arm to summon him. Guy followed her, thinking that in an inn on the street there was no need to fear being ambushed.

Reaching the doorway, he thought again. On the wall, a print of King George was hung upside down. The eyes of the customers leaped at the stranger in the red uniform like hungry cats at a helpless lobster. No one seemed pleased to see him, and to judge by the curses and the spitting on the ground, no one wanted to demonstrate the opposite.

The woman was sitting in a corner and Guy hurried to join her. As soon as he was sitting down, the French mob went back to studying its cards and glasses. He thought he could hear the rustle of blades slipped back into scabbards.

"You have *bokú de bandoka*, sir, *vremàn bokú*. A wicked man is coming from *très* far away, across the sea, he too sent by *bandoka*. You must cut, Massoula tell you how. Then shadow light again, neck light, you free."

A wicked man, from very far away. In his mind's eye, Guy saw the elegant face of Campbell, his short wig and pale complexion.

"*Bandoka* take away the house, then the family, then the *travay*, then the *argent*, then the money. In the end he take away the shadow and you be lost."

Guy shivered and managed with some difficulty to keep from ordering a brandy. The list of misfortunes sounded like a ritual formula, but it was hard not to recognize in it the trickle of the last few wretched months.

"Tell me about the man who is crossing the sea."

"Yes, he bring *bandoka*, but also he bring solution. You must cut the root *du mal*."

The woman seemed about to finish the sentence, then lowered her eyes to the table, as though suddenly exhausted.

"What solution? Come on, talk, here's half a crown."

"You know this, not Massoula."

Guy gripped the woman's hand as she stretched out her fingers to grip the money. He felt he was being swindled, the usual cheap trick: they hit on a detail and then proceeded with nonsense and riddles. He was about to get up, but before his buttocks left the bench, he saw Campbell's face, heard his words in his ears.

The Colonial Ministry asks me to give you this letter and requests that you send as soon as possible a list of failures and complaints on the part of His Majesty's Indian allies.

Campbell had brought a letter from Lord Dartmouth, the Secretary of State for the Colonies. A list of complaints, that was what they were asking for in London.

Guy's grip relaxed and Massoula slipped the coin under her clothes.

"Always keep this with you, *monsieur*." The witch slipped something across the table. "To cut the root *du mal*, to face *le passage*."

The woman quickly got to her feet and reached the door before Guy could stop her. He looked at the little object on the table. It was only a pendant, carved from a pierced shell. He shook his head, picked it up and stuffed it into his pocket.

He left the inn, stunned and weary. He quickened his pace as the midday sun cast honeyed reflections on the rooftops.

34.

There's a bear in the forest.

Every night it comes out to cut the animals' throats.

Its blood-heavy paws scrape at the door.

The pallor of her skin, smooth as ivory, brought out the outlines of Molly's eyes and lips. She pointed out to Joseph the limit of the patch of trees, where the branches were violently shaken. Joseph was aware of the presence of the beast, and he was afraid.

Tell my son he must drive the leviathan back into the abyss.

Into the depth of the forest that gave birth to it.

Where the sun cannot penetrate.

Joseph wanted to ask why Peter had to be the one to risk the mortal undertaking.

Molly rose up hugely, her expression a black flame.

The road back takes you to what you were, not to what you will be.

Go, and what you must do, do quickly.

Or there will be no rainbows, nor good omens, nor harvest.

Why Peter?

Every link in the chain is in its exact place.

You cannot see the beginning of the chain or its end.

Not even I can do that.

Not even the dead.

A warning hoot came from the hills. When Joseph turned again to look at his sister, in her place a she-wolf was running toward the cry.

Wild animals took shelter.

The turtle slipped deeper into the mud of the pond.

The sun was eclipsed, the last ray of light touched the wings of an eagle.

From the center of the vegetation, the bear, vast and ferocious, came forward, breaking plants and branches.

When he woke up, Joseph found the warriors ready to leave. Many blankets were already rolled up and the first boats were on the water.

For the Mohawks the Canadian campaign was over. The larches were yellowing, it was time to hunt and prepare for winter. At home, wives and children were suffering the abuse of the settlers. Soon some would be returning to Canajoharie. The wisest of them, or the most compromised, would spend the winter in Oswego.

Cormac McLeod and his Highlanders were leaving as well. Sir John was in danger, and his guard of honor was returning to protect him.

Joseph was homesick for Susanna and the children. If he had been at home, that night he would have lain down in bed and forgotten all his worries, for a few hours at least, but he couldn't go back. He was Thayendanegea, Two Sticks Bound Together, destined to unite the Mohawks and the white men. The last request of Sir William on the point of death. In the end, what does an interpreter do if not bind together words, men and things? Joseph was a creature of the Department, he had grown up under the Johnsons' wing. If the family sun darkened, he would be the first to be left in the cold, and after him the whole of the nation.

He also had to decide about Peter. The boy was a Johnson and he was a Mohawk. He had fought, he was up to it, but now Molly wanted something else from him.

He could have spoken of the dream with the oldest warriors, but Tekarihoga, too, was saying farewell. The turtle was returning to the pond, with goodwill formulas and crisp words of good omen for those who remained. Joseph could not have said who was in greater need of help from heaven, those who remained or those who were preparing to return. He saw Oronhyateka and Kanenonte, side by side. They were staring at the middle of the river. At their feet, blankets, weapons, two water bottles. He walked over to greet them.

"You go home too, Thayendanegea," said Kanenonte. "War, here, is not as we dreamed it."

"We will fight in Canajoharie," added Oronhyateka. "If you stay here, the spiders will spin their web around the trigger of your rifle."

"What happens at home still depends on what happens here," Joseph replied. "And that, too, depends on me."

Beyond the river, Joseph smelled rain, and felt a terrible stitch in the middle of his chest.

Oronhyateka thoughtfully scratched his chin.

"You are my brother, Thayendanegea," said Kanenonte. "But you speak like one of those white politicians."

Joseph smiled. "My lips will bathe themselves again with the water of the Mohawk. But not now."

35.

The most important thing for Colonel Ethan Allen: being treated as a gentleman. Woe to him who dared to do the opposite. He had a ready reply for anyone who provoked him, rich or poor, friend or stranger. He hadn't been able to study very much, but he did know how to talk and persuade. His fingers were stubby but they plucked the right strings. He had made memorable the taking of Fort Ticonderoga, an enterprise that had been considered impossible, by pronouncing a perfect phrase. He had had the fort delivered to him "in the name of the great Jehovah and the Continental Congress." A great phrase, one of those that roll beyond misunderstanding, strong in one single meaning: Ethan Allen was impelled by the finger of God. His fame had barely left home, and already the light of legend was rising behind the hill. Colonel Ethan Allen was a conqueror and that was his strategy.

In the name of Jehovah? Not really. Ethan didn't believe in the God of the Anglicans or of the Papists. He didn't believe in the Lord of the Bible, a furious avenger, a sender of rape, slaughter and pillage. His God was the higher force that governs the universe, and he prayed to him with Reason, not with psalms or by eating insipid bread. Ethan's God was the intelligence that bridles and organizes nature. The Supreme Being who enlightens Man and enables him to affirm his Freedom.

The most important thing for Colonel Ethan Allen: being treated as a gentleman. Immediately after the taking of Ticonderoga he had betaken himself to Philadelphia, where the Congress was in permanent session. He had demanded to be received and to speak before the representatives. The new stage of his strategy: those gentlemen could not refuse to welcome the man who had fought in their name and in the name of Jehovah. How could one do wrong to the Goliath of the Green Mountains?

Ethan had spread the rumor of his coming, the crowds were filling the streets of Philadelphia to catch a glimpse of him. In his oration he had asked for recognition of the Green Mountain Boys as a fighting force, allies of the Continental Army. For those bandits turned heroes, he demanded the same payment as the other soldiers. He claimed their right to choose under which officer to serve. In exchange, they would continue to risk their lives for the cause of Freedom. The Congress had consulted General Schuyler and fulfilled his every request.

Ethan Allen's problem: his leg sometimes failed in its stride, and his foot was left hanging in midair; it fell back and dragged his whole body with it. Ethan feared those moments.

Twenty-third of September, 1775. An evening like no other, along the eastern bank of the St. Lawrence. Ideas flooded his mind. The most burning of all: to take Montreal. He had persuaded Major John Brown: a sudden attack, a daring, spirited action. They would take Montreal with their men alone. The last blow of the chisel, Allen had thought. To finish the masterpiece begun in Ticonderoga five months before. To take Montreal before General Montgomery, to get there ahead of the Continental Army.

He didn't yet have the phrase ready. The verse, the distich, but in warlike prose, well-rounded, polished, to be spoken at the right moment, a projectile of syllables to be fired all the way to London. Everyone would repeat those words. Nonetheless, first he had to line them up, and every syllable counted, every scrap of imagery that he could blow toward the enemy. When you elaborate a big theme, you also have to take care of the tiny details.

Ethan Allen would cross the St. Lawrence at Longueil, on a moonless night, and reach Montreal from the north. Brown would cross the prairie before heading south. At the first light of day, pressing on both sides, they would catch Montreal in a vise. No, that image wasn't quite right: *pulling* on both sides, they would open it by force. Like the doors of a wardrobe, pulled barehanded from their hinges to reveal history. The sole preoccupation: to make sure the reach matched the grasp.

The night was the bottom of a well, nothing could be seen, the blanket of cold air weighed down on his neck and back. Ethan felt the wind faintly stinging his hands.

A hundred and ten men, including eighty Canadians willing to fight with the patriots. There were few canoes and they had to make three journeys, with the danger of being surprised halfway across the river, one foot in Longueil and the other in midair.

The crossing of the St. Lawrence took all night. Ahead of them, their eyes saw nothing.

Dawn was still a snail trail when Allen placed sentries all around the camp. He had crossed his Rubicon. Who can say whether Caesar spoke his most famous phrase straight away? Was it born as it fell from his lips, or had it been considered for a long time, molded by the leader, his tongue uniting with his teeth? *The die is cast.* Perfect, lucid, immortal.

Allen resolved to wait for the signal: three loud shouts would come from the throats of Brown's men, tearing holes in the dawn mist.

The birds were already busy with their orchestra rehearsals. Allen cocked his ears.

Two hours later, half the sky was bathed in light. The dew was melting away, leaving the fields, and still no shout had been heard. Where had Brown got to? It had been his idea, the sudden attack, the daring action. Allen looked around: the men were losing the will to fight, to throw themselves into the imminent future like bears on a hive of honey. A night's crossing and hours of waiting slacken the nerves, dampen the powder that fires the heart. Nothing but kicked heels, shrugged shoulders, rubbed hands and yawning. They looked at each other furtively, spoke in an undertone, pointed to Allen with brief nods of the head.

Allen was sure of it: Brown wouldn't come. They couldn't have discovered him; the air and the St. Lawrence would have carried the echo of battle. He wasn't there and that was that, no point wondering how. The Rubicon was behind them, but the die was only half cast. His foot was heavy and, as it fell, it unbalanced his body. Meanwhile blue was conquering the sky.

Allen toyed with the idea of going back, crossing the ochre river, setting foot in Longueil. Impossible, it would take hours, the enemy would discover them. The only thing to do was maintain his position, but for how long?

Ethan sighed. The day of mysteries and impossible choices. The enemy would come.

And give battle, then.

36.

The news arrived quickly: the rebels were close, very close, and preparing to attack. It wasn't the Continental Army that was threatening Montreal—these were irregulars, and they were under the command of Ethan Allen.

They had to go out soon, with all their available forces. Engage in battle before the conqueror of Ticonderoga was in sight of the city.

The men of the Department—Joseph, Philip, Peter, Guy Johnson, the Butlers—joined the makeshift force that would block the way of the Green Mountain Goliath. Barely forty regular soldiers, merging with a multitude of militiamen, in jackets and hats of every shape and color. Civilian volunteers in hunting outfits, rangers, warriors of the nations of Canada, especially Caughnawaga.

Peter stared at the warrior next to him. Le Grand Diable. He thought, Whatever happens, I will follow him.

He thought of the man they were about to face. He was said to be practically a giant. Peter remembered the tales around the fire, Walter Butler's face beyond the flickering flames.

To follow Le Grand Diable. Peter discovered that behind his fear there was something else. Excitement and a new feeling, solid, unexpected. Determination. He already knew battle, the thunder of the cannon in your ears, the ground trembling beneath your feet. He had seen death. The only way to avoid it was to win.

The two formations made contact at around two in the afternoon. Volleys of rifle fire exchanged in the distance, from one end of a wide clearing to the other. And yet the enemy was changing shape, losing its compactness, thinning out in chaotic flights.

Suddenly, Lacroix waved his hand. The men moved.

Joseph, Lacroix and Peter advanced slowly, heads held low, with Walter Butler and a little group of Caughnawaga, over an arc about fifty yards across. They clung to the bushes and slipped along the side of the enemy forces. The bullets buzzed above them, heavy, clumsy insects.

The men took up position behind large pine trunks on the edge of the clearing. The rebels hadn't noticed anything.

Peter saw a tall, stout man shrieking orders amid the rattle of the rifles. He strode along the rank of rebels, kneeling behind the tree trunks and in holes in the terrain. His unsteady, nervous gait was that of an animal in a trap. He furiously roared commands, he clawed the air with his hands, pointed where to shoot. Peter understood: the man in front of him was Goliath.

The boy took a step forward. Fear gripped his innards. He forced his body to move again, until he found himself beside Lacroix. The two men exchanged a long look.

Peter's mind became clear and light. His decision ignited in the blink of an eye, a flash.

Peter emerged from hiding. He moved smoothly toward a rock that seemed to have been placed in the field by the hand of God.

Joseph and Lacroix followed him. Once they were hidden again, Joseph gave Peter a nod of approval. The boy threw himself forward. Joseph sent a signal to the Caughnawaga, who went on the attack, rushing to the side of the rebel armies.

The enemy retreated, scattered, took flight. Two stopped to fire on Peter. Joseph took aim while running and wounded one in the shoulder. Before the other man could work out where the shot had come from, Lacroix struck him down with the butt of his rifle. Peter went on with the chase.

Ethan Allen had already run a mile. Every now and again he stumbled. Another few steps and he fell, exhausted.

Peter was on top of him, panting. He aimed the rifle.

"You're defeated. Surrender."

His voice breaking with exhaustion, Allen replied, "My men will not surrender arms without the guarantee of honorable treatment. I demand your word."

Peter, confused, looked behind him. Uncle Joseph and the Great Devil calmly approached.

"Order the savages to stay away from me," said Allen.

"You are my prisoner. You have my word," replied Peter.

Allen surrendered his saber.

Peter raised it in the air, turned toward the warriors and uttered the war cry of the Wolf clan.

37.

Night enfolded the Island of Montreal, the city, the camp outside the walls. An owl hooted through the mist rising from the river. From inside the tent, Guy could see a quarter moon partially hidden by the clouds.

He was sitting at the field table, by the faint light of a lamp, rubbing his aching neck. He observed the first shadow on the oilcloth. It looked twisted and deformed.

Your shadow is heavy. You will leave.

In his head, the cry of the owl mingled with the witch's words. Guy stretched out a hand, as if to grasp his own silhouette. Without thinking he drew out the amulet that the witch had sold him. From the day of that encounter he had always carried it in his pocket, solely out of superstition. He set it down on the table, under the flickering light of the oil lamp, and suddenly he felt ridiculous. Half smiling, he thought that he'd had a little luck after all: now he had a famous prisoner, the great Ethan Allen, locked up in the corral and under the strict surveillance of trusted guards. The last ones remaining.

Guy sighed and turned serious again. They had all gone away, the Scots, the Mohawks. He was alone with a decision that had to be made. It meant the choice was his, but that didn't make things any easier.

Fort Niagara or Mohawk Valley. Or perhaps staying there, waiting for the rebel army to appear on the riverbank. But there was no point in waiting. Carleton's position was plain: the governor had no intention of defending Montreal, and never had. Each order had served only to gain him time and send Guy's men away. Now Carleton would retreat to Quebec, where he could count on the support of the fleet.

Guy felt it was no longer a rock that was squashing him, but an avalanche, a whole mountain collapsing on top of him. His neck was stiff and tense. He started rubbing it hard. What had the witch called it? The nest of *bandoka*. Of course, misfortune.

He dismissed the thought of that woman and began rereading his letter to the Secretary of State. He had listed in detail the remaining territorial issues and the infringements by the settlers against the Indians. He had written well, but looking at the page he had a sense that it would condemn him to oblivion. He had even signed it.

He got to his feet and walked into the darkness, back bent. It wasn't just his stiff neck; the lice were driving him crazy. The camp was infested with them. He returned to the opening of the tent and studied the night again.

Sending that letter had been an act of abdication. They had asked him to tell the government about the remaining issues in the Mohawk valley, because other people might be able to sort them out. What remained in store for him was the same treatment that had surprised Claus. Discarded after years of honorable service.

The German had shut himself away in stubborn silence, even though some people maintained that they had heard him cursing in his own language during the night. Curses meant for Carleton and Campbell, in all likelihood.

Guy sat on the bunk, head in hands. He wished his wife were by his side, he wished he could feel her warm hand massaging the tension away. He missed her. And he missed his daughters. He had to think of them too, left behind in Oswego. On his lips he formulated a prayer for Mary's soul and asked God to protect the girls.

He went back to the table: pen, inkpot, blotter. The little stick of sealing wax and Sir William's seal. If they unseated him, he would keep it as a memento. He turned it around in his hands. It represented the patriarch's coat of arms: two Indians holding a shield with three shells in the middle. At the bottom, the Old Man's motto. *Deo Regique Debeo.*

I am indebted to God and the king.

Guy froze. His eye ran to the witch Massoula's pendant: a shell. It wasn't the coincidence that gave him gooseflesh, but the echo of her words.

The man crossing the sea bring bandoka, *but he also bring solution.*

Campbell was coming from England. The solution he was bringing was not the request from the ministry. The solution was crossing the sea.

Guy gave a start. The idea stuck in his mind, so much so that it canceled the pain in his neck.

Cut the root du mal.

Win back the warrants of appointment.

With the help of God and by the will of the king.

"You want to take the letter to Lord Dartmouth *in person?*"

Daniel Claus uttered the question with eyes wide, his hands clutching the arms of the chair.

John Butler's reaction was calmer. The old captain didn't move a muscle, but it was plain that his ears were cocked.

Guy Johnson glanced first at one and then at the other. He had the look of someone who hasn't slept a wink, but for the first time in weeks he also looked determined.

They were in his tent. Guy had summoned the two others only mid-morning, so as not to alarm anyone, not even the directly interested parties. He didn't want one of Carleton's spies to learn of his intention. It was hot and activity in the camp was sluggish.

"You understood correctly, Mr. Claus," said Guy. "And on this occasion I will request an audience with His Majesty. To draw his attention to our family. The Johnsons have served him faithfully for more than thirty years, and he can't deny what is owed us by right. I am referring, obviously, to the warrant of appointment to the post of Superintendent of Indian Affairs."

After days governed by a black mood and muttered insults, the German roused himself.

"It's three thousand miles of ocean and winter is on its way."

Guy nodded without losing his composure.

"So there's no time to lose."

Butler looked into the bottom of the hat that he held in his lap.

"None of us knows London, let alone the labyrinth of the court. Our fortune is here in America."

"I am well aware of that, Captain Butler," Guy replied, "but at the moment it seems to have run out. Without warrants of appointment we can no longer administer the Indians, no one will defend us, our names will fall into oblivion. Sir William would never have accepted such an unworthy end. I say we must try."

"It will take us months, years, to obtain an audience with the king," Claus objected.

"That's true. But we will bring a gift to His Majesty. And it is hard to deny a welcome to those who bring gifts."

Puzzled, the two gentlemen stared at Guy.

"The leader of the rebels, gentlemen. He is the man who took Ticonderoga, and we have taken him. We will drag him in chains to the feet of George III."

An evil smile spread across Claus's face: "Like Vercingetorix before Caesar. This is a stroke of genius, Mr. Johnson."

"With all due respect," Butler broke in, "it sounds more like a stab in the dark."

"Perhaps it is, Captain," Guy replied, "but I don't think we have much to lose."

"Superintendent Johnson is right," said Claus. "All roads are blocked."

"It's clear that we have to bring Indians with us," Guy continued. "Someone who speaks on behalf of many and can impress the court."

The German thought out loud: "Our sachems have left."

"We have Joseph Brant," Guy suggested. "The only one who hasn't yet abandoned us. He's a war chief, and he speaks English. And don't forget the little David who slew Goliath. Peter Johnson will be our *passepartout*. For the name that he bears."

Claus's eyes flashed again.

"We have an Indian delegation. All that remains is to find a ship."

They both turned toward the old Irishman.

"Do you still keep your reserves, Captain?"

John Butler got up energetically and took a step toward Guy.

"Listen to me carefully, Johnson. I will be very open with you. I have learned one thing from Sir William: Without the Indians we are nothing.

They are our strength, our guarantee. The Indians don't look at warrants of appointment, they look at faces. You won't find the solution to our troubles in London."

"So you don't want to be of the party."

Guy's tone was embittered and sincere.

"I'm sorry," Butler replied. "My son and I have decided to go to Niagara. This war is taking an ugly turn. The Seneca have more warriors than any other tribe, and they're the ones we have to convince. Not some London fop, with the greatest respect."

A moment of silence followed. Then Butler pressed his hat down on his head and shook hands with the others.

"Good luck, gentlemen. May God go with you."

They watched him walk away in the day's bright sunlight.

"You didn't have to insist too hard to convince him," said Claus.

"He had already made his choice. Perhaps it's better that way."

Guy sat back down at the table and stretched his legs. The German pressed him: "What will we do now? What about our families? You can't plan to leave them in Oswego."

"Of course not. We must recruit an escort and go and get them. I entrust that task to you, Mr. Claus."

The German fell back on the bunk bed. That morning's news had weakened him.

"And what about you?"

"I will go to Quebec and spend the last of the Department's money," said Guy. "We need a trustworthy ship, captain and crew. I will make sure that upon your return you find a quick means of transport to join me."

"You need someone who will protect you, sir."

The Irishman nodded to himself as he poured spirits into a pair of glasses and passed one of them to Claus.

"I have an excellent bodyguard. Joseph Brant. And I recommend one for you: Philip Lacroix. His name inspires respect all along the St. Lawrence."

Guy clinked his glass against the German's.

"To King George and our voyage."

Claus gulped his drink down without a word, somewhere between enthusiasm and apprehension.

38.

Standing on the wharf, wrapped in a heavy red blanket, Joseph watched the fishing boats setting their prows northward, toward the estuary and the open sea. Only a few returned upstream. Migration time: flocks of migrating birds crossed the sky. How far from home were they?

At first, Joseph had been stunned by the decision. It sounded like the words of a madman: not Fort Niagara, but London. Being received by the colonial ministry, if possible by King George in person.

During the passage of the migratory birds there were some species heading northward, in the opposite direction to the flow of wings that plowed the sky. Winter's flying children, who sought refuge in its icy, open jaws. If the Lord had granted so much courage and resilience to these feathered creatures, he must have granted all the more to man, or at least to certain men, Joseph thought. Daring had become necessary: the vise that gripped the People of the Flint had broken at the handle.

Joseph could turn Guy Johnson's desperate move to his advantage, to the advantage of the Mohawks and the Six Nations. The superintendent needed him and he made no secret of it: if he wanted to show that he had the Iroquois on his side he had to bring representatives of the League with him. If he managed to have himself received at court, Joseph could extract direct pledges, concrete guarantees about the lands and borders that would have to be respected. Hendrick had already managed to do this many years before. As a gift they were bringing the head of the rebels, escorted by the warrior who had captured him, a young Mohawk who was the son of the great William Johnson. It wasn't crazy to imagine a warm welcome in London.

Going back upstream to the icy heart of Empire was an act of courage, not one of irresponsibility.

From the wharf, Joseph had observed the Abenaki boatmen tying up two canoes. They were escorting Daniel Claus and Philip Lacroix to Oswego, to bring back the Johnson women. Less than twenty years previously the men of that tribe had fought beside the French against the Mohawks. Now they took orders from Le Grand Diable, the most feared of all their former enemies. The team had left quickly and quietly, the better to avoid having many rumors head downriver faster than they themselves could travel. Members of the Johnson family were a precious cargo.

When the little convoy had taken to the water, Joseph and Lacroix had greeted one another with a nod of assent, as they had done years before. Over the past few weeks the bond between them had solidified. As ever, Molly's visions proved to be impressively clear.

The sound of footsteps attracted Joseph's attention. The figure of John Butler was approaching.

The old soldier came and stood beside him.

"You and Lacroix would be very useful to me in Fort Niagara," he said. "The Seneca admire courage."

"I'm a man of the Department," Joseph replied. "I have given my word to Guy Johnson."

The Irishman nodded.

"I hope you don't come to regret it. God be with you, Joseph Brant."

Joseph shook the hand that Butler offered him. The flocks pursued their course.

39.

The air didn't yet smell of sun when Esther felt the blanket slipping away and a voice telling her to get up, quickly, they had to go. She shook off the straw and tried to do the same with her sleep, but it remained stuck to her eyes. It had been a hard night. The attic where they had been put up was full of corncobs and Esther remembered what her mother had said, not to play in the granary, because snakes are greedy for corn. If her mother had been there, she would never have agreed to their being made to sleep in such a place. But she wasn't there any more, and Esther hadn't slept.

Before leaving Oswego, Aunt Nancy had brought her and her sisters to leave a bunch of flowers on the grave. They had a long way to go, to reach their father. He was waiting for them in the port at the end of the Great River, where the ocean began.

Why he hadn't come to collect them, Esther couldn't understand. He had sent Uncle Daniel, with Indian boatmen and the man they called the Great Devil. Crammed into bark canoes, they had crossed the lake and entered the river.

In the big kitchen, Judith and Sarah were making breakfast: milk and biscuits. Esther hated that. Listening to four mouths chewing on that stuff made her stomach churn. She asked for bread and honey, but there was none left. Aunt Nancy offered her a biscuit smeared with grease.

"Eat something, you have some walking to do today."

Esther asked no questions; she was no longer a child. On boat journeys you had to walk as well, she knew that now. It mattered little whether the danger to be avoided was a rapid, a shallow or something else besides.

She opened the door and breathed in cold air. The sound of a liquid ripple betrayed the presence of the river, hidden by a blanket of trees and fog. Esther threw the biscuit to the pigs and looked around.

In the farmyard, the Devil was speaking in French to the master of the house, a gentleman with a braid who stank of garlic and tobacco. The Indians were crouched over the remains of the fire, eating strips of roast meat.

Uncle Daniel and the serving girl came out of the farmhouse in total silence. On their backs they carried Judith and a cousin, in the Indian slings that are used to carry children. They lined up behind the boatman who was acting as their guide, while the others loaded the canoes onto their backs, to bring up the rear along with the Devil.

"*Adieu. Bon courage,*" the Frenchman called from the doorway.

The road wasn't a wide one built for coaches and horses. They walked between brambles, amidst grass and mosquitoes. Their feet sank into the mud and didn't come out again.

Sarah began complaining after half an hour's march. Her face looked as if a cat had jumped into it to sharpen its claws. She was crying, her feet hurt, she was thirsty.

As the serving girl passed her the water bottle, the Devil came over and offered to load her onto a canoe. Esther expected that her sister would start wailing. One evening, to frighten her, she had told her that the Indian really was Satan and he had come to take them to Hell. Instead she sniffed and offered her arms to the Devil, who lifted her up and set her down in the boat.

After a quick and inedible lunch, pemmican and honey, Aunt Nancy's older daughter also caved in, and ended up sitting in the other canoe. Esther resumed her march, proud that no one had to transport her like the other girls.

It didn't take long. Soon her weariness vanquished her pride. She hadn't eaten since the previous evening, her clothes were torn, her skin stung from the scratches, blisters swelled her feet. Her legs no longer responded, they were tree trunks that had to be dragged through the forest, and with each obstacle they came to a standstill.

Esther slumped to the ground, her head spinning. She saw the Devil coming over and instinctively hugged his knees, as if seeking shelter from an icy wind. Suddenly she felt extraneous to the scene. She observed herself from the vantage point of a bird perched on a branch. She watched herself stretching out a hand, taking the water bottle that was offered to her and bringing it to her lips.

Maple syrup and water. Even better than honey.

As she drank, she felt an arm slipping around her back, another under her thighs. In a moment she found herself on his back, with her throat tight and her thoughts upside down.

He hadn't lifted little Sarah like that. He'd picked Sarah up under the arms, as you do with a child who wants to play.

Esther was no longer a child, but often grown-ups didn't notice.

The Devil had understood.

The fire slumbered in the shelter. The Devil was sitting down, for the first time since they had left, puffing on a thin pipe. He and the boatmen had erected the shelter with sticks and oilcloth. He had roasted trout and squirrels, and Esther was surprised to find that they were good to eat. Aunt Nancy and the serving girl had put the girls to bed and flung themselves down to sleep, too exhausted to say goodnight. Uncle Daniel was snoring beside her and she couldn't get to sleep. She thought back on the day, on the scratches and the swollen feet, on the smiles of the little girls in the canoes, on the Devil's embrace.

A faint sobbing joined the calls of dormice and owls. Hiding in the blankets, Judith wept. Esther turned toward Aunt Nancy, to check whether she had heard, but the women were snoring, plunged in a far-off world. She was about to get up, but saw the Devil coming toward them and preferred to stay lying down, pretending to sleep.

Behind her half-opened lids she saw him kneel and run a hand over her sister's hair. She heard him whisper something, as the sobs faded away. It must have been a lullaby, one of the ones her mother knew, and which Esther would have liked to listen to as well.

The Devil's voice fell silent. He caressed the girl once more, then picked up his pipe and went back toward the fire.

Esther wasn't sure that she could see clearly, but she thought she was aware of a gesture, fingers brushing his eyes.

She felt confused.

She had always known that the Devil was strong.

He could also be handsome and nice, and flatter people.

But that he could weep, that was something she had never heard.

40.

Quebec was a big city carved from the rock. A fairy-tale castle dominated the river, the spires of Our Lady, the massive houses within the city walls.

Esther read the name written in gold letters on the prow of the ship.

A-DA-MANT.

Compared with this huge vessel, a giant with its belly in the water, the brigantine that had collected them in Montreal was a river sprite.

They had arrived the previous day, safe and sound, although Aunt Nancy was a different person: hollow-cheeked, puffy-eyed, her face caught in a net of scratches. The girls looked like animals that had escaped from a trap after days of struggling.

Their father had listened to them praising God, when they should really have been thanking the Devil.

Esther was unaware of her own appearance. She hadn't found a mirror to look at herself in: just enough time to have a hot bath, eat, sleep for a few hours, and already the need to leave was pressing.

They could put it off no longer, the storekeepers said at the port of Quebec. They would have to get a move on, before ice and storms blocked the river. They talked about London as they loaded the boat. They answered "London" to the questions of curious passers-by. The name of the capital filled their conversation, buzzed over their heads, was the constant refrain whatever they happened to be talking about .

London? Impossible, thought Esther. London was beyond the ocean. It would take them months to get there, one of those journeys you take once in your life, in search of your fortune.

ADAMANT.

She stamped the name in her memory, as she climbed on board behind her father, who was leading her two sisters by the hand. She turned. The Great Devil was at the foot of the ramp, with a sack on his back, and he glanced at her. Esther quickly turned round to hide her face. Her cheeks flushed.

41

The St. Lawrence estuary was a half-breed. A hybrid of different waters, saltier than a river, fresher than the ocean. A battlefield for opposing currents, high waters and tides that influenced navigation all the way to the lakes, in the heart of the continent. Peter thought of himself, an estuary between two peoples, both a way out and an entrance.

"It's like the barrel of a rifle," he said, pointing to the map.

"A rifle?" Daniel Claus asked, puzzled.

"One of those rifles that broaden at the end."

"And that makes us the bullets?"

"Sure. A bullet of wood, cloth and flesh."

"Which would mean that we're firing on England," Claus objected.

Young Johnson shrugged. The game really didn't seem all that important to him.

"More like a hunting horn," the other man broke in.

"What would that make us?" asked Peter, not to be outdone.

"We're the hunting call. The king can't help hearing us."

The St. Lawrence estuary was the darkness of the hold. Thirty men in a wooden box, six yards a side, a bucket of putrid water, a basin to relieve themselves in, scraps their only food. Ethan Allen had tried to rebel, to demand that they treat him as a gentleman, spare him the humiliation of fetters, let him speak to Mr. Watson, the owner of the ship.

"I'm a colonel in the Continental American Army," he had protested. "This is how you treat animals, not army officers."

Big black rats swam in the bilge that came up to his calves. Allen had struck one of them with an angry kick, sending up splashes all around him. From the window-slit a pair of yellowish eyes stared at him, standing out against dark skin. It happened when you least expected it. He lifted his head and those bovine eyes were there, as irritating as the flies drawn by the faeces in the slop-pail. Probably the negro didn't even speak his language.

"We're men, not animals!" Allen yelled exasperatedly at those dead eyes. "The world will know how King George treats his prisoners!"

He hurled the metal basin at the window-slit, missing it by a fraction.

When a cavernous voice issued from behind the wooden door, the prisoners raised their heads from their own bitterness. No one had addressed a word to them since they had been brought down below.

"Do you know who I am, Colonel?"

It was hard to tell whether the voice belonged to that face, because the window-slit didn't reveal the whole face.

Allen, panting with fury, said nothing.

"My father was the son of a prince," the voice continued. The words had a deep, sonorous quality. "White men loaded him onto a ship like this one, along with many others. So many that they could not even sit down in the hold. Half of them died on the crossing. You, Colonel, will reach the other side alive. You are fortunate."

"I am a free man and I am an officer!" thundered Allen feverishly.

The eyes did not reply. The slit closed again.

The St. Lawrence estuary was a slow farewell.

Hundreds of miles separated Quebec from the ocean. Joseph looked at the snowy peaks that the *Adamant* was leaving behind. They seemed to close up as the ship passed, like the waters of the Red Sea over Pharaoh's army.

If you can't get back to your starting point, your only choice is to continue. To go on, force yourself onward.

Joseph had woven tapestries of thoughts. In London, like Hendrick many years before. How many times had he heard that story? Hendrick at the court of Queen Anne. With him was the father of Canagaraduncka, Joseph's stepfather, known as "Brant." Hence the surname that Joseph bore.

Canagaraduncka had told him many times about the four Indian kings who had been received with full honors. In London, Hendrick had negotiated for the queen the support of the Six Nations in the first of the wars against the French. He had pleaded for an alliance among equals. He had been taken to the theater and to court receptions. Famous artists had painted his portrait. Everyone had bowed as he passed.

On that voyage, Hendrick must have been Joseph's age.

The St. Lawrence estuary was an unexpected reply.

Behind Guy, sitting on the straw, Nancy Claus was entertaining the children. She explained that the river, thousands of years before, had dug itself a path to the sea. It had eroded away the granite, dragged earth from the banks, felled forests.

Guy thought that the story told in this way made it sound as if the river had decided where to go.

In fact the St. Lawrence had eroded as much granite as the current allowed, not a grain more. It had felled forests as far as the floods could climb, and dragged away as much earth as allowed itself to be dragged.

If you considered it carefully, even with all the power of its waters, the St. Lawrence had had to make do with the only bed possible. Its volition was only an idea, a restricted point of view that didn't take too many details into account. Similarly, he thought, men convince themselves that they have choices, but the road they take is always the only one at their disposal.

Guy was the river. He thought he had made the best decision, but only because it was the only one possible.

The river had had to open up the way to the sea so that it wouldn't dry up and die.

The Crossing
1775

The rocking rhythm was deep and stomach-clenching. The wind was free up here, it filled the lungs. Philip Lacroix was engaged in a curious face-to-face with the gulls, which were intent on their wonderful acrobatics. For a long time his mind lay empty, freed from all burdens, and his body reacquired its vigor after the forced immobility of stormy days spent below deck. Simple, essential gestures: breathing, perceiving his heartbeat and controlling it, coordinating his limbs and brain in fluid movements that dissolved the accumulated tension.

As soon as he reached the top, Lacroix had looked down at the deck of the *Adamant*. He was aware of a certain level of activity, a coming and going of tiny figures, not without grace. The distorted echo of orders and imprecations muffled and devoured by the wind. Poor things, humans observed from above. He had turned his attention elsewhere. The ocean swelled around on all sides. He felt no terror at the sight of its vastness. He felt the stiff, biting cold. He felt the power of the mass of water.

All of a sudden he noticed a pinprick, a faint ache rising from his feet. He looked down. He spotted a very small, blurred figure. He tried to make out its contours in the majestic morning light. Guy Johnson's eldest daughter, Esther. The girl held a strange, primitive power. Her pain and hurt at the death of her mother had made her even more sensitive and close to ghosts. Like Molly.

He became aware of a new presence, someone else climbing the mainmast.

Joseph reached the top and sat down beside him. He filled his lungs with fresh air.

Lacroix went on looking at the ocean.

"Do you think the king will want to meet us?"

"The queen met Hendrick," Joseph replied.

"Hendrick was a chief. You're Guy Johnson's interpreter."

"Not anymore," Joseph replied. "I'm the ambassador of the Mohawk nation. This time the words I say will be mine. Ours."

Lacroix nodded, as the words made way for the calls of gulls and sailors.

"We need justice," Joseph added at the top of his voice.

"English justice?"

"The settlers stealing our land are enemies of King George. This rebellion is our opportunity to reestablish our rights." Joseph clenched his fist to give greater force to the idea. "The sachems don't understand, they think things will go on as always. And in fact everything's changing."

They fell silent again, for longer this time, listening to the wind and watching the sails billowing below them.

Philip Lacroix took another deep breath. Freed from the stench of men, the brackish air wasn't bad. He smiled faintly.

Joseph, too, relaxed his features. For a moment, fleeting as the tail-end of a dream, he felt as if he were in a canoe again, on the river, carrying two young warriors toward adulthood.

The sailors moved quickly. Some of them smiled at her, but most of them didn't even see her. A huge black man coiling a rope over his elbow bared his white teeth. One had a metallic glint. Esther was scared and moved toward the poop deck. She stopped beneath the steps, where the wind couldn't flush her out. She sat down on a barrel that someone must have put there for the purpose. Voices came from above, and she recognized the voices of her father and the man with the wooden leg, Mr. Watson.

". . .will have a tremendous effect," he was saying. "It'll drive them mad."

They were above her. She could hear the sound of the limping footstep, the *tump tump* on the planks of the deck.

She poked her nose over the parapet and looked down, into deep foam-striped blue. She imagined the dark recesses that cradled monsters.

She stood on top of the barrel. Her eyes gazed down into the waves. She raised one foot to the edge. The dark mass was calling her to it.

Esther.

A whisper in her ear. The blink of an eye. Enough to see a woman's black eyes mirroring her own. She hesitated.

Then she heard a shout, a loud cry, from the foremast.

"Land ahoy!"

The girl saw it: a dark shadow insinuating itself between sky and sea, breaking the waves and marking the end of the journey. The Other World. On the deck, the excitement was contagious. The captain started shouting orders.

Someone grabbed Esther by the arm and dragged her from her hiding place. For such a small woman, Nancy had a very strong grip.

"So this is where you've got to. Get down off there, your sisters need looking after."

Colonel Ethan Allen scraped the crust of dirt from his forearm. He could no longer smell the stench of bodies, or it had stopped bothering him. The noise on deck had woken him from his half-sleep. He checked the notches cut in the wooden plank. Yes, they could be within sight of the English coast. In the wolf's lair, he thought excitedly. He would have to come up with something, rack his brains. The hero of Ticonderoga certainly couldn't disembark like any old prisoner. He needed a memorable phrase, a speech, something that could travel from mouth to mouth, set the powder ablaze. He could appeal to the Whigs of the motherland. Motherland? The Green Mountains were his motherland. There, perhaps that was what he should say. But no, what did the inhabitants of England know of his country? . . . Down with tyrants. Maybe that was the idea. When he was tried for treason, he would defend himself with a speech on the freedom of the people. Those who rebel against a tyrant aren't betraying freedom, they're serving it. It would be transcribed and printed in thousands of copies. Ethan Allen, *On Freedom*. A title that would travel around the world.

Allen scratched his head, dislodging lice as he did so. He pushed aside the bulk of one of his men lying on the floor, and tried to stretch his legs. Two steps forward, two steps back, that was the space available to him. "A new world is advancing along the path of history." It sounded good. But abstract concepts couldn't be enough: he had to evoke something tangible that everyone could understand. He trod on a hand; someone protested. Allen delivered a couple of kicks to gain a few inches and leaned against the wall. Above his head the hubbub continued. England wasn't far away. The sound of bulkheads, furled sails, shouts.

Allen thought of the boy he had surrendered to. A half-breed, no less. He had handed over his sword to a bastard. He clenched his teeth with rage and studied the mass of lowered heads. There they were, the patriots. A thought began to assume a shape. What was that pathetic little island, England, compared to America? The New World, a great nation rising from the ashes of Empire. He smiled with excitement. The slit in the cell door opened up and the warder peered in.

"Hurry up, Colonel," said the yellow eyes. "We've reached the place where they're going to hang you."

The inns around the port had run out of gin before midday. It was Friday market in Falmouth, and news had arrived that the *Adamant* was about to come into harbor. A sloop had landed early that morning to announce the vessel's arrival. Some sailors and an officer had stepped out. The officer had entered the admiralty buildings and inspected the prisons.

The rumor spread. The ship was carrying prisoners, including Ethan Allen, the famous conqueror of Fort Ticonderoga.

In the street the crowd had become a roaring throng. The muddy streets had been invaded by vendors of alcoholic swill, tripe and Dublin Bay prawns, sellers of guaranteed louse-free wigs, children with bunches of flowers, beggars, jugglers, first-, second- and third-class shoe-shiners. The cries of the almanac sellers merged with the chants of the knife sharpeners. The pickpockets would earn a month's income in only a few hours.

As the rumor of the landing spread, the crowd shifted toward the dock: aristocrats from the nearby villas, the unshod poor, servants on their day off, merchants, sailors, farmers who had come to town for the market.

The people who lived in the houses overlooking the pier came down to the street offering exceptional seats for the enjoyment of the spectacle, far away from all the pushing and shoving. The owner of a sawmill tried madly to erect a stage. The work remained unfinished: with the first chime of the afternoon the *Adamant* furled its sails and entered the harbor. A double row of soldiers pushed their way forward, kicking and shoving.

As the vessel approached the dock, the crowd swayed. Many people felt that the position they had obtained was not the best one: the more discreet merely lifted themselves onto their tiptoes, but most of them started elbowing each other out of the way, trampling on feet and lapdogs that had slipped away from their mistresses.

After a great deal of confusion, the crowd reached a precarious equilibrium and held its breath.

There they were. A group of men was walking along the gangway. They looked English, but some had darker skin. In the middle, almost a foot taller than the others, a man in chains.

Ethan Allen.

The crowd began hurling insults, shouting abuse. Some vegetables were thrown, but no one wanted to risk a reaction from the guards.

The soldiers presented arms. The captain in command saluted. A fat, well-dressed man emerged from the group that had recently disembarked and proclaimed in an Irish accent:

"Captain, I deliver to you thirty-three prisoners, enemies of the King of England, and their leader Ethan Allen. He surrendered to this brave youth, Peter Johnson, son of the late Superintendent of Indian Affairs, Sir William Johnson. The other men who took part in the enterprise were the Iroquois chiefs here present, proud allies of the king, Joseph Brant Thayendanegea and Philip Lacroix Ronaterihonte."

There was a roar of amazement and approval. The captain stepped forward to receive the prisoner. Before the soldiers dragged him away, Ethan Allen raised his voice above the noise of the crowd.

"I am the fire that consumes Babylon! Death to all tyrants!"

Ethan Allen passed beneath a rain of insults and rotten vegetables.

Part Two

Mohock Club

1775–76

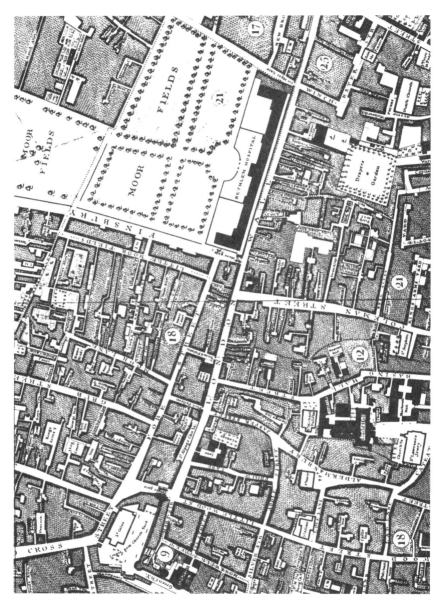

Detail of the map of London made by John Roque in 1747.
At the top, the St. Mary of Bethlehem Royal Hospital, known
to Londoners as Bedlam, the oldest mental hospital in the world.
Bottom right, beside the number 18, Lad Lane and the Swan with Two Necks inn.

1.

The carriage passed along the street as the two giants of St. Dunstan's on Fleet Street struck two. The coachman was fighting sleep: one sip too many from the bottle under the seat. The fog was dense, and he had to trust the instinct of the horse, a compass set for the stable.

The cry of a wild beast pierced the night. The man gave a start and pulled on the reins. When the wail was repeated, it came from closer by. The coachman felt a pain in his guts.

A milk-white wig poked out of the window.

"What the devil is happening, Giles?"

"I'm not sure I want to know, sir."

The coachman glimpsed a movement out of the corner of his eye, on the other side of the coach. He quickly turned around: a fleeting image, then nothing but fog.

"Come on, Giles, let's go!"

The servant clenched his eyelids, and his thoughts went to the bottle under the seat. He couldn't have seen what he thought he had seen. A naked man?

He shook his head violently and was about to whip the horse when a sharp thud shook the coach. The passenger shouted in fear.

There was no doubt about it: an arrow had landed in the door.

"Whip that damned animal, Giles, for the love of God!"

The servant cracked the whip, but the horse snorted and shied, then reared up on its hind legs, stretching its head high above the cobbles. In the faint lamplight two arrows could be seen protruding from the animal's neck.

The gin had nothing to do with this, Giles thought. Perhaps his time had come.

He was aware of presences, creeping shadows.

"What do you want?" he yelled, to give himself courage. Meanwhile he had picked up the big pistol that he kept beside the bottle and loaded it with a trembling hand. He pointed it into the fog, where he heard their footsteps. They were running alongside the carriage; here and there he saw the white flash of a body. "You come near, you die!" he roared from the box.

The passenger appeared at the door.

"Tell us how much you want and leave us in peace," he exclaimed loudly.

In reply, a second arrow struck the coach. The head retreated into the shell of the coach.

"Never fear, sir, we won't give up without a fight," Giles assured him, but he just had time to turn before he received a blow to the head. As he felt gravity getting the better of him and light making way for the darkness of unconsciousness, he managed to grasp one final waking image: a big Turkish crescent tattooed on the forehead of a brute with a painted face and a single tuft of hair in the middle of his head. A great ugly face, Giles thought as he slumped to the ground and blacked out.

The gentleman called the coachman, then worked out that he had been left alone to the mercy of the beasts. He saw outlines darting past the window, heard whispers, animal cries. When a shadow stopped threateningly by the opening, he brandished his walking stick and struck a downward blow. He took advantage of the confusion that followed to open the door on the other side and jump out. He tried to run, but stumbled, and when he was on his feet again he found himself encircled. He counted at least five of them, all with shaved heads and bare chests. A trickle of blood ran down one face. The man saw long guns, pointed sticks, a sword and a pitchfork.

"Emperor!" exclaimed one of the savages behind him. "This man is offending me by showing me his arse."

"Base insult!" echoed a man with a crescent on his forehead. "Punish him according to Mohock law."

The savage delivered a thrust to the gentleman's posterior. The man swung around, revealing his rear end to another member of the gang, who immediately gave him a second blow, forcing him to whirl around once more; but already a third blow had come, and then a fourth, while everyone shouted as if possessed, "Mo-hock! Mo-hock! Mo-hock!" while stretching out their arms, stamping their feet and crashing powerfully into one another.

All of a sudden the one they called Emperor raised an arm. His subjects stopped.

Their victim was bent double, clutching his knees, gasping for air. At a second nod from the ringleader, they lifted him up by his feet until every coin had fallen from his pockets.

The Emperor collected their ill-gotten gains, then bent over the unfortunate man.

"My name is Taw Waw Eben Zan Kaladar II, Emperor of the London Mohocks. After sunset, this is my hunting-ground." He took a deep breath and the crescent creased with wrinkles. Then he pulled the white wig off the gentleman's head and tied it to his belt.

"You may go," he added. "But go quickly. You need a bath."

The poor wretch struggled to his feet, clenching his teeth, and started running blindly toward the end of the street. With a swift movement the gang leader picked up his bow, took aim and fired an arrow into the fleeing man's backside. The man just managed to yell before he passed out.

The other attackers exchanged confused glances.

"What if he dies?" one of them complained. "Given that he's a toff and all that."

The madman barely deigned to glance at him, as he slipped the bow over his shoulder.

"Then we'll be famous."

No one said a word. With their chief at their head, one by one they re-entered the fog, creatures of a nightmare before waking. The last of them uttered the animal war cry again, defying the London night.

2.

Along the street the houses grew denser as the countryside made way for the suburbs. Philip Lacroix thought again of the exodus that had brought him from the forests of Canajoharie to the capital of the Empire, from the valley of the Mohawk to the valley of the Thames. He thought again of the voyage upriver; of the impetuous torrents that they had shot through at breakneck speed; the waterfalls and ridges rounded with their boats on their backs; the winds that blew over Lake Ontario; the Thousand Islands of the St. Lawrence; and the ice storms of the North Atlantic, capable of tilting the yards of the *Adamant* until they kissed the waves.

And yet the past five days, two hundred miles on the rambling lanes between Falmouth and London, had been the hardest. Perhaps it was just a matter of habit: Philip had little experience of wheeled vehicles. Perhaps his unease had something to do with speed: the stagecoach moved more quickly than the spirit of the passenger, which was obliged to follow it. He wrapped himself up in his beaver fur and looked at the friend sitting beside him.

Joseph Brant was lost in thought. Outside the window were more and more impressive buildings. The daylight was running out, and the city looked like a dark mass preparing to swallow them up, a giant animal, its breath hanging in the air, dense and visible. Joseph had been to New York once, but this was something completely different.

He shook himself, making an effort to smile at Philip.

"Welcome to Babylon," he murmured.

The shadows of great buildings loomed in the darkness. The air smelled of burning, dung and rubbish, but Peter was taking deep breaths as he tried to see through the smoke. He would rather have arrived in broad daylight; the dusk left you hostage to your sense of smell, and too tired to get your bearings and keep out of trouble. He yearned for fresh energy and enough light to explore every alley on either side of the street.

The convoy of coaches stopped. The horses stood panting, the exhausted passengers peered from the windows. Someone from the Department, at the head of the column, had entered an inn to book rooms for the night.

Peter saw a boy his own age holding a long pole with a little flame at the top. He stepped up to poles and lit them one by one, making them cast a yellowish light over the pavement. Shadows flitted under each halo, emerging out of nothing before immediately vanishing. He found himself thinking of a window looking out over an inverted world, from which it was possible to observe the strange creatures that peopled it. This wasn't how he had imagined arriving in the capital. They had been ordered not to get out of the carriages. He craned his neck, but couldn't see past the next vehicle.

Joseph cleaned the tobacco from his fingers by rubbing them together. The sweet smell mitigated the stench of London. Guy Johnson said the acrid smell of burning came from coal, and from the fog. Hard to imagine that a rock extracted from the ground could be used to make fire.

The coaches had been waiting for half an hour: the Golden Helmet had two rooms fewer than expected. The staff in the inn were doing all that they could to find an alternative.

"In Quebec we were all in one room," Peter observed between yawns. "Don't they do that here?"

"Here we are ambassadors of the Mohawk nation," his uncle replied. "The king of France's envoys wouldn't have consented to share a room."

Peter closed his eyes and slumped back in the chair. Joseph turned to offer a pinch of tobacco to Philip as well, and discovered that he had slipped out of the coach.

He needed to be upright, stand on his feet, free himself of the grip of the journey. He took a few steps toward the nearest lamp, to look at it close up. Between that one and the next there was still a stretch of pitch darkness: the world appeared in disconnected pieces, and the intermittence of light made it impossible for his eyes to adjust to the night. Beyond each feeble cascade of light, nothing could be seen. A luminous image rose up from the well of his memory: Father Guillaume's bony fingers pressing down on his desk. "Remember, Philippe. There is no Light without Darkness. A single principle and its opposite. To confront darkness you need faith, because you will never see beyond the step that you are about to take. That is our earthly trial."

A noise brought him back to the present, a sinister squeaking noise that approached it was hard to say where from, for the fog spread around in all directions. Suddenly he was aware of a presence below him. A monstrous creature touched his knee, emitting incomprehensible sounds. It was a man, or what was left of one. Its trunk rested on a plank of wood, moved on little wheels propelled by its hands. A compact coating of scabs and colorless rags covered its body, and you could hardly make out eyes, mouth, a few fingers. Philip felt an instinctive urge to chase away the horror, but remained motionless, enthralled by the immensity of such ugliness. "Our earthly trial." The creature stank and spoke, a singsong chant, obscure except for two words: "Sir" and "Excellency." At the end of its twisted fingers it held a little tin plate. The creature was asking for charity. Philip felt disgust, repulsion, fear. He pushed away the beggar's claw and returned to the coach.

Joseph saw him coming back, pale and frowning.

"What is it?"

"This place stinks," said Philip.

His friend shrugged.

"So does bear grease. But what would you do without it?"

A sound of hoofs echoed on the cobbles, the outline of two horses dragging a vehicle in the beam of light from the lamps. The man sitting in the box drew himself upright.

"A moment's attention, please." He separated his words, as if to be certain of being understood. "My name is Jerome, at your service. I come from the Swan with Two Necks, on Lad Lane. My master asks me to tell you that we are ready to receive you as best we can. Our inn is not equipped for long stays, but we have managed to free two quiet rooms for you. The staff will be at your disposal."

Philip picked up the bags and climbed down into the street. "One room is enough for me," he said. "And I believe that Peter will happily share it."

The boy woke from his torpor and joined the Great Devil. All Joseph had to do was follow them.

Jerome hurried to transfer the cases. Before returning to his box, he made sure that the passengers were comfortable.

"Gentlemen, if you will permit me, even though it is foggy, I will loosen these beasts' bridles. The streets of London are not well lit and driving is risky after dark."

The two Indians said nothing. Joseph merely nodded.

When the wheels started moving, Philip looked out. He thought he could still hear the squeaking sound, fainter and farther away.

3.

At least sixty men, a dozen horses, five dogs. Lots of chickens in a single cramped cage. Four children chasing a fat piglet. Gulls chattering in flight. The Creation.

Voices and noises floated up to the balconies like steam from boiling soup, filtered through every door, woke the guests one by one.

Philip's sleep was a net with a wide mesh: most sounds passed through it without breaking it. Yet even in his half-sleep, he was able to give a name to every sound, to assess its volume and its distance. He had learned that as a child, and by now it was a habit. Lots of Caughnawaga had worked at the mission, and it was one of them who had taught Philip that and the other rudiments of hunting. The priests hadn't opposed this as long as hunting didn't distract him from his studies and prayers. So, because he couldn't stay in the forests from dawn till dusk, he had come up with a series of exercises to keep his reflexes, senses, and muscles awake. The Creation was one of them. It had been given that nickname by Father Guillaume, who was always careful to introduce God into anything that concerned one of his pupils.

Philip slipped out of bed. Peter was still asleep. He took the clothes from his wardrobe and began to get dressed. Simple clothes, but made of the best materials. He put on his boots and went outside onto the balcony.

The Swan with Two Necks was a wide, plain building that enclosed three sides of a courtyard. The central body held the rooms, with access to the outside via wooden balconies lined up along the façade.

Below him the paths of men, vehicles and animals crossed in the mud. A drunk dragged his feet out of the tavern. Porters seemed to be collapsing under impossible burdens. A boy ran on thin legs to deliver letters and parcels. Two horse carts collided in a bid to pass first through a big archway. Postilions called for the way to be cleared while clusters of children besieged the passengers with offers of combs, sponges, razors, mirrors and orange fruits that Philip had never seen before. In front of the stables, stagecoaches waited for horses or repairs.

There was something familiar about the atmosphere of the place, Philip thought. In the Mohawk Valley, the big houses were always inns, stables, post offices, shops and storerooms for boats and armories. The people came and went, lives touched one another, and that had been enough to teach him about more things than Canajoharie had contained. He stepped onto the stairs and went down.

He barely had time to look around before he was surrounded by sellers of trinkets, all of them scandalized that a man like him could even think of facing the day without acquiring any of their merchandise. He paid for one of the unfamiliar fruits, slipped it into his pocket and broke free. He took a few steps toward the entrance, but a fellow with worn-out clothes and a haughty air managed to hand him a sheet of paper.

"An exhibition that you can't miss, sir. Only three shillings." He seemed to be reciting these words from memory.

"The porcupine man?" asked the Indian, reading the advertisement.

"A man with spines instead of hair on his body, sir. Sensational. Never before seen in any town in the kingdom."

The phrases bounced out like a playground-chant nursery rhyme.

"What does the exhibition consist of?" Philip asked.

"The porcupine man will show you his chest and his legs. You will be able to touch the spines and notice that there is nothing fake about them, just a joke of Mother Nature's. Then you will see him behaving like a porcupine, walking on all fours, stiffening his spines, hunting for worms."

"This man eats worms?"

The other man winked. "No, that's just to gull the jossers and rake in a few shekels."

"What's that you say?"

The man opened his eyes wide, as if caught in the midst of committing a crime. "Nothing, sir, nothing. Sensational. Never seen the like. The porcupine man." And with these words he walked away with the packet of papers pressed to his chest.

"Nothing to worry about, sir. It's the market."

Philip turned around and saw a smartly dressed man of about thirty. An open-mouthed smile spread toward his ears and cut his face in two, like a tree trunk waiting for the final blow. The man wore a big hat. Beside him, a tall, fat Negro, also elegantly dressed, held a leather bag.

"Let me introduce myself, sir. My name is Maugham—Frederick W. Maugham; the 'W' stands for Winslow. This is my secretary, Mr. Cornelius Pigou. You are a foreigner, that much is immediately apparent, sir. . ."

"Philip Lacroix."

"A Frenchman, then."

"I grew up in Canada."

"First time in London, am I right?"

"Yes, that's correct."

"You will have to get used to people like that rogue. Aside from the intrusiveness of those who try to sell them, goods do little harm. Good money drives out bad, if you are free to chose, and London is *the capital* of freedom of choice. In no other part of the world do so many goods circulate." Maugham spread his arms wide, as if to embrace as much of the world as possible. "In no other city is the market regulated with such admirable balance."

Philip tried in vain to give these words a meaning. Maugham must have understood this, because he changed his expression, lowered his voice and began his speech again in a calmer, more patient tone.

"Mr. Lacroix, the ragged man just offered you one of the most desirable goods there is: enjoyment, distraction, the shiver of the unfamiliar. Every day, people with simple tastes are excited by the sight of the porcupine man and who knows how many of his colleagues, true or supposed *lusus naturae,* dwarfs, giants, hermaphrodites, duckbilled women, men with four testicles. Most of them are swindles, staged for the gullible. Coarse goods, crudely advertised. If those who sell these spectacles remain in business, it is because the business operates in special conditions, artificially limiting one's freedom of choice. Do you follow me?"

"Follow you?"

"I mean, do you understand what I am saying? This kind of spectacle is suggested to people like you, met outside taverns and coaching inns. People in transit, in London for the first time, are in search of powerful sensations, but they do not know what the city has to offer or have time to discover and choose the best offer at the most advantageous price. So you find yourself seeing the porcupine man, and perhaps spend the evening being fleeced in some dive where the food is off and the wine is colored water, and conclude your *excursus* in an alleyway with a cheap whore. Often an accord will have been reached, where there is not a single interest involved: the employer of the porcupine man is also the landlord of the inn, as well as the whore's pimp. Your *excursus* has been guided from the start, so as to prevent you from knowing of other offers. This closes and blocks the market, and the quality of goods declines, which does poor service to the city, to England, to the Empire. And that's where I come in."

"You?"

"Yes, me. A loyal subject like Frederick W. Maugham cannot allow a gentleman like yourself to return to France or Canada convinced that the entertainments of London are second-rate, that the food is inedible and expensive, that the English whores have flabby flesh and sagging breasts. I have a mission: following market forces, I contribute to the wealth of the nation. The service that I offer to gentlemen is, no more or less, the possibility of exercising their own free will. As I told you before: bad money is driven out by good. I put good money in circulation."

Philip was intoxicated by the man's long speech. He was torn between the desire to go back to the inn and the curiosity to know what the point of it all was.

"Are you offering me something as well?"

Maugham smiled and nodded to his secretary.

"Pigou, open the bag."

The Negro obliged.

The bag was empty.

"What I am selling, Mr Lacroix, is *information*. You see what's in this bag?"

"I would say there's nothing in it."

"Precisely, precisely! Nothing. But imagine. . ." and he lowered his voice again, ". . .imagine that this bag is full of paper. Hundred and hundreds of sheets of paper. Black on white, everything that London is capable of offering a man of the world. Names, addresses, prices. The most beautiful women at the most reasonable prices. The most bizarre spectacles for selected customers. The best opium to be smoked with the most complete discretion. The *special* password-only receptions. The people to approach to satisfy less. . . usual tastes. Those who are able to offer these services turn to me, and I bring supply and demand together. They turn to me because I am the best, and I have become so without shortcuts, trouncing the competition thanks to the quality of my goods. Do you follow me, Mr. Lacroix?"

Philip said nothing. His confusion and curiosity had turned to contempt. The Negro closed the bag. Maugham continued.

"This is information that makes the economy go round, Mr. Lacroix. However, you understand, it is not information that can be shouted to the four winds. I am a patriot and a subject who loves King George, but I must say that the English authorities are still very backward. In the name of an outdated morality, they put inexplicable brakes on commerce and keep some goods and services illegal. Soon they will have to change their attitude and let the free market grow. Until that day comes, what should be in this bag is all in here!" He tapped his forehead with the tip of his right index finger. "You only have to ask, Mr. Lacroix. Would you like to enjoy someone's company? I can offer you young women, old women, fat women, skeletal women, or men, children, or others among God's creatures, if you catch my drift. What would you like to see? A fight to the death? Are you a betting man? There's a place where Negroes face one another with knives and sticks. All free Negroes, obviously. Pigou, too, is a free man. I am opposed to slavery: everyone has the right to sell himself, at the price he considers right. Ah, but where are you going? Mr Lacroix?"

Philip headed for the inn. Maugham and Pigou followed him for a few yards. "Mr. Lacroix? I have lots of other offers to make to you. Mark my words, you won't find anyone else who can give you. . ."

One of the ushers at the Swan with Two Necks saw Philip's tormentors, shook his fist and said: "Back again, you disgusting perverts? If you importune another of our customers I'll beat the living daylights out of you!"

The two men walked away. Philip entered the inn and left the world outside. He took a deep breath.

Behind him two rooms opened up, one connected to the other. Joseph nodded at him from a table by the window. He was sitting with a stranger, chewing on a piece of bacon. The stranger was spewing forth words in an incomprehensible dialect, with the air of someone who still has plenty to say. Philip took a chair and tried to trace the thread of the conversation. He looked at his friend: Joseph was listening carefully, nodding, and every now and again he raised his cup and took a sip of broth.

"Do you understand anything?" Philip whispered in the Mohawk language.

"Not a word," was the reply. "I'm getting used to the London accent."

The rotund figure of Jerome strode toward them.

"Gentlemen," he said remorsefully, "you shouldn't be eating here. I've reserved a room for you, special food. . ."

"Don't worry, Jerome," Joseph interrupted. "Here is fine."

"As you wish, gentlemen. Your inn has rooms free tomorrow morning, and although we will be sorry to see you leave. . ."

"We aren't leaving," Joseph broke in. "We're fine here. And you, Jerome, are a very kind man."

"As you wish, gentlemen. Your presence here is an honor to us." Their host was about to turn around, then stopped, rummaged in his waistcoat pockets and took out an envelope. "I forgot. A note for you." With a slight bow he handed it to Joseph. "Good day, gentlemen."

Philip watched his friend open the envelope and read the message. He glanced quizzically at him.

"We are invited to a reception at the home of a certain Warwick," Joseph said. "The *Earl* of Warwick."

4.

From the *Daily Courant*, 30 December 1775

A RECORD OF THE INTERVIEW WITH COLONEL JOHNSON, SUPERINTENDENT OF THE DEPARTMENT OF INDIAN AFFAIRS OF THE AMERICAN COLONIES

On the twenty-eighth of this month, I took my tea at the Golden Helmet Inn in Westminster, temporary residence of Colonel GUY JOHNSON, head of the Department of Indian Affairs of the American Colonies. The colonel is a sturdy man of medium height. He wears his hair short at his neck, combed back, as if to leave space for his refined and honest face. Although he has important duties, his speech is far from pompous, being concise and laconic, with a marked Irish accent. Following a brief correspondence, he very kindly agreed to receive me and answer some questions.

The American Indian delegation that crossed the ocean with him is also staying in our city.

Colonel Johnson asserted that those American tribes who are our allies are extremely confused by recent events in the colonies. Officers who fought together beside these tribes in the war against the French have begun to war with one another. . . In such a political hotchpotch the MOHAWK people wish to listen to His Majesty speaking in person and act only in obedience to his instructions.

A very similar visit occurred in 1710. On that occasion too there was an Indian alliance to be consolidated, and the splendor of London had to act as a counterweight to the lies of the French Jesuits, who told the tribes that Christ was born in Paris and crucified in England.

Queen Anne received at court Emperor Tiyanoga, whom the settlers called Hendrick, accompanied by the King of Maquas, known as Brant. The latter is said to have been the grandfather of Prince *Thayendanegea*, also known by the name of Brant.

I asked Colonel Johnson to give me news about our Indian allies. He showed me a map, drawn by his own hand for our new Secretary of State for the Colonies, LORD GERMAIN. From it I learned that the *Six Iroquois Nations* occupy the territory west of the colony of New York, up to the *Great Lakes*. The most important and authoritative people among them are the Mohawk, whose territories lie within the borders of the colony. Since the days of Queen Anne, the Mohawk nation has made a great deal of progress. They live in villages made of stout and worthy houses, they cultivate the land with the skill of an Essex peasant, they are all devout Christians and trade with the English merchants with a great deal of ease and comfort. As to military consistency, the entire federation can put FIFTEEN THOUSAND MEN on the warpath within a few days. According to Colonel Johnson, a clear and unequivocal choice of sides on the part of these allies would be enough all by itself to frighten off the Bostonians who are besieging Quebec. "Not by chance," he said, "a hundred warriors were enough to defend Montreal and capture the most dangerous of our enemies," referring to the captive ETHAN ALLEN, the rebel who a few months ago took *Fort Ticonderoga*.

I then asked why Prince *Thayendanegea*, having come to Canada to defend Montreal, had then left for London just as the continental army was lining up its troops on the bank of the St. Lawrence River.

Colonel Johnson rose to his feet, set the map down, and paused for some time as he considered his answer. When he spoke at last, the delicate nature of what he had to say explained his silence. He told me that the fifteen thousand warriors of the Six Nations were only waiting for a nod to intervene against the rebels and chase them all the way back to New York. He himself had led a small vanguard into Canada as reinforcements, on the orders of General Gage. Unfortunately, a disagreement had arisen between the general and the governor of Quebec about the use of the Mohawk militias, and his warriors had been forced to demobilize.

"Many officers fear that they are losing their control over the Indian troops," Colonel Johnson went on, "but this does not happen when someone the Indians trust is in command. Sir William Johnson, my uncle, dealt with Indian affairs for two decades. He died more than a year ago, but the Six Nations still have great confidence in our family. If their trust is confirmed by His Majesty, our alliance with these Indians can only bring benefits to the interests of the Crown."

With this important piece of information, the interview concluded, and Colonel Johnson gave me a further appointment, at which I shall receive a complete account of his audience with Lord Germain.

PANIFEX

5.

A smartly dressed pig with a sheep on its head.

The wig was too long; the sleeper's position made it drag on the floor. He was fat and far from tall. Rather advanced in years, too, one might have said. His cheeks hung slackly at the sides of his face, like a sow's. However, they were very well powdered, so that his flesh was the same color as his hair. His cheeks, like his lips, were brightened with rouge, and punctuated by a scattering of beauty spots. His breathing swelled his belly, which looked as if it were about to burst open, like the portal of a fortress under the blows of a battering ram. His shoes barely touched the floor; his backside was balanced on his hind legs. He stayed like that, tilted against the wall, rocking slightly back and forth.

Philip took his eyes off the strange creature and returned his attention to the master of the house.

"How I envy the Mohawk, Your Highness," the Earl of Warwick said, turning to Joseph, as he dabbed his own powdered countenance. "A people who paint their faces only when they go into battle."

Philip remembered that at the entrance to the drawing room a servant in a jacket covered with buttons had taken their hats and announced them as "His Highness Joseph Brant Thayendanegea, Prince of *Ganjahore*, and Mr. *Philippe de la Croix*."

Philip had been startled. By comparison, "Colonel Guy Johnson and Lieutenant Daniel Claus" sounded like simple members of their entourage; even Philip had received a warmer welcome, as a "victorious champion of the King."

He saw Joseph half-open his lips to reply, but the earl had already started talking again: "You have astounded my guests, who expected exotic warriors, barefoot, their faces painted, covered in plumes and feathers. At first they were disappointed to see you were such gentlemen. However, I assure you that you are the highlight of the evening," and he made a wide circular gesture with his arm that took in the vastness of the drawing room.

Philip studied the other guests: difficult to attribute human nature to most of these creatures crammed into gaudy clothes, balancing on ten-inch heels, fingers invisible under clusters of rings, heads sunk into their shoulders under the weight of wigs, making them look like stuffed birds. They were busy dancing, drinking, chewing on food, chatting.

Warwick, who seemed to understand what was running through the warrior's head, smiled and explained, "This. . . fauna is very different from that found in your forests, is that not so, Monsieur Lacroix? But I assure you that behind their ridiculous appearance, *ils ne sont ni plus ni moins que des bêtes féroces!*"

Joseph, who did not understand the language of Molière, frowned. Warwick came to his aid without looking at him. His eyes were empty now, as if he were talking to himself, forgetting his guests, in a state close to sleepwalking. "Wild beasts, your highness. Monsters that even Linnaeus, the great naturalist, could not have classified. After taking a good look, you might think them primates, family *Hominidae*, but some of them are nocturnal beasts of prey, others are insects, like termites, and still others cold-blooded reptiles. All are carnivores and hunters. They kill to eat, but their hunger is called boredom: they live with the perennial need to find something new, *someone* new, to distract themselves, to suck from others the authentic life, the *jouissance* that they themselves are condemned to simulate. When they find a prey they devour it, picking clean every bone, breaking the bones and sucking out the marrow."

Philip and Joseph were open-mouthed. The earl looked at them, shook himself from his trance and continued in a different register, "All right, tonight you will be the prey. You should have heard the nonsense talked about you just before you got here. Truly bizarre ideas about the Indians are circulating among the English aristocracy. Take for example the Duke of Sorethumberland, there at the end," and he stretched out his index finger. The two Mohawks followed its trajectory and in the middle of the motley crowd they discerned the likely object of his speech, a tall, very thin man of indefinable age, dressed in flame red. He was talking to a kind of barrel-woman, far shorter than himself, and his back was bent. The woman was carrying a little animal with long hair and a squashed face.

"What kind of animal is that?" asked Joseph.

"A lapdog. A pointless creature to amuse yourself with. Just think, my guests sometimes arrive with monkeys crouching on their shoulders, *et les singes, vous le savez, ils chient, juste comme les hommes.*"

"Monkeys?" thought Philip. "Monkeys shitting on people's shoulders?"

Warwick had already returned to his theme.

"The good duke was convinced that rhinoceroses run about on your lands, and that you Indians reduce their horns to powder to produce an aphrodisiac more powerful than cantharides."

Rhinoceroses? Cantharides? Now Philip and Joseph were both perplexed.

"As I was saying," Warwick went on, "they know nothing about our colonies. They have no idea where they are or who lives there. We are used to describing London as 'the heart of Empire,' but the heart pumps blood to the rest of the body, while here the opposite is true: it is the colonies that pump the blood that keeps London alive."

"So the city of your king is the head?" Joseph asked.

Warwick smiled. "If that were the case it would contain the brain. Look around: in theory, this drawing room holds the best of the king's high society. And yet, from the moment you begin to pass the evening in this place, I invite you to listen to the conversations. I assure you that you will find not a trace of ratiocination. I think these roads and houses are in fact the *buttocks* of Empire. They possess all the characteristics of the backside and its orifice: here is discharged every resource that the Empire sends to us. Except, by a whim of nature, these buttocks are *in front* of the body rather than behind it." The earl burst out laughing.

"You have a strange idea of your guests, My Lord," said Joseph. "Why do you surround yourself with people you don't hold in esteem?"

"Look at me carefully, Your Highness. I myself am of the same species. I, too, go in search of *jouissance*. I find my pleasure in disgust. I watch ridiculous and revolting spectacles with genuine pleasure. I arrange evenings like this one and observe the decadence of my time, one foot within and one outside the spectacle. It isn't a secret, everyone knows what I'm doing, and still they come running in droves, because no party is a match for mine."

Philip wasn't sure he had understood. Joseph was sure he hadn't understood. Warwick realized this and laughed again.

"You don't know the nature of the one who reigns over your white neighbors, just as we know nothing of them or of you. Certainly, we know that the settlers are in revolt on the other side of the ocean, but most of us have only the vaguest idea. The most frequent question when the subject arises is: 'Why do they hate us?' "

"They don't hate you," said Joseph. "Behind the veil of words lies my people. They want our lands and our dignity."

"Oh, of course they don't want ours," Warwick replied. "We haven't got any."

Philip saw a cat dart under the sleeping fat man's chair and knock it over. The man hit the ground with a thud and discharged a loud fart that aroused the noisy hilarity of the lady closest to him. The terrified creature sought refuge under the hem of her cloak, but the lady gave it a stout kick and sent it flying. Philip watched the ball of fur hurtling across the drawing-room and realized that it wasn't a cat; it was an opossum. It smacked into the back of one of the dancers, who acted as if nothing were wrong, merely keeping a fixed smile as he peered over his partner's shoulder. The animal dropped from his coat and landed in the middle of the room, where it risked being squashed by dozens of heels moving in time. At that moment Philip saw it more clearly and understood. It wasn't an opossum either. Or a rabbit. It was the biggest rat he had ever seen. After a moment of panic, the rodent headed at great speed in his direction. Philip stepped aside to let it pass, but a sharp blow nailed the rat to the floor. As if someone had burst a balloon, a ribbon of guts spurted from the creature's abdomen and landed on the back of the Duke of Sorethumberland, who turned, startled, thinking himself the victim of a prank. Someone pointed at his back and he performed various pirouettes before working out what had hit him. His lady just had time to spread her fan and vomit into a vase of flowers as her little dog began licking up the mess on the floor. Then the servants came to clean it up. Meanwhile someone was helping the pig-man to his feet. Philip was sure he heard him grunt, and had to clench his teeth to keep from laughing.

Joseph Brant lifted his stick and contemplated the corpse at his feet.

The Earl of Warwick quickly attracted the attention of his butler; a black man in livery and white gloves, he picked the rat up by the tail and carried it away amid the disgusted cries of the ladies.

The dancers started crossing the floor once more, in coordinated steps. The musicians' faces were masks of sweat and cosmetics. Peter had agreed after much simpering persuasion to display his skill as a violinist in concert with the band. Someone started praising the fact that a heroic soldier should also be interested in music and have such a light touch. Joseph couldn't relax his facial muscles, such was the stench that filled the room: a mixture of rancid sweat and rotten flowers. He had been told that the European aristocracy liked to wear perfume, but this certainly wasn't a pleasant smell.

He turned toward Philip, who was looking around in puzzlement.

"Perhaps they have to keep the mosquitoes at bay here, too."

The butler announced another arrival, and a deformed woman advanced into the room. Her hips were so broad that they brushed against the doorposts. A page had to help her pass through without getting stuck, then follow her closely to correct her path by prodding her gently at the sides. A staircase of ringlets crowned her head. Her dress glittered, as if woven through with fragments of mirror, so brightly that looking at her hurt the eye. Around her neck hung a rope of carved stones that fell to her massive bosom.

The butler loudly announced a considerable sum, and the four-poster woman looked smugly around.

"It's the price of the clothes and jewels that she's wearing," said the earl, turning to Joseph and Philip. "At the end of the evening we always announce a winner."

"Our women are also very good at transporting things," Joseph observed.

"To tell the truth, Your Highness, ours transport only their own vanity," Warwick sniggered. "An enormous weight, in fact. Allow me to demonstrate."

Joseph watched the earl nonchalantly approach the fat woman, kiss her hand, flatter her, and meanwhile slip the tip of his stick under the hem of her dress. Taking advantage of a burst of noisy applause for the musicians, he lifted the fabric slightly. An iron structure held up the weight of the dress, mounted on little wheels.

6.

Colonel Guy Johnson, in full-dress uniform, and Daniel Claus, in a white wig, were also watching the scene, from a vantage point some way outside the halo of interest and curiosity surrounding the Mohawks. In spite of his proud military posture, Guy was suffering from the weight of the journey and exhaustion of the past few months. His baffled contemplation of the London aristocracy had given way to a more serious train of thought concerning his mission in the capital.

London was a seething cauldron of humors and events, and there was a serious risk of being swallowed up in it. There were two doors he must open: Lord Germain's and King George's. He had to open them quickly, obtain those appointments.

At that moment all eyes in the room were focused upon "Prince Thayendanegea and his brave Mohawk warriors." The attentions of Lord Warwick and the morbid curiosity of the guests, he could tell, were destined to go on for some time. And it could turn out well: Guy trusted Joseph Brant, knew how much he valued Sir William Johnson and his blood-ties with the Johnson family. He knew he would do his part to honor the memory and precepts of the Old Man.

Guy was also grateful to have the "monk" Lacroix: he was hard to understand, but more trustworthy than most.

The Mohawks would act in the interest of their people and the Johnson family.

And yet, the risk of his being overshadowed by them was quite a real one. Perhaps he should call attention to his military successes against the rebels, above all his capture of that overblown buffoon Ethan Allen.

He should, but deep down inside him something had changed. The hump of weariness sat on his back, on his face the dark patina of grief. Shaking off *bandoka* was not an easy matter.

Mary and his male child. The responsibility had been his; he had wanted her with him. Since that night he had struggled to look his daughters in the face and had begun to fear the future. Perhaps that was the meaning of aging. Fear like a load of stones, getting heavier and heavier. Or perhaps he was only feeling the harshness of a journey begun many months before.

He was ending the year 1775 in the Thames-side residence of an aristocrat in favor with King George, among all these high-born whores and parasites of noble lineage. True, he was far from his own lands and possessions, and war was at their distant gates. Luckily, he had his daughters with him, in safety.

He was here to defend the honor and the wealth of the Johnsons. Make the right contacts, conduct good business. Sweep the dark shadow away.

Guy returned to his senses and noticed that he was holding a glass, but couldn't remember what it contained. He saw Peter following the music of the band on his violin. He was playing on a little dais, beneath a massive mirror with a gilded frame. The boy was at his ease. He had studied and received a good education, he spoke well and was already famous as a fighter. He could win the regard of the Crown. Guy looked back at Joseph Brant and the Earl of Warwick, a few feet away. The Indian was impassive: he didn't change his expression or open his mouth, but remained impeccably in character. Judging by the count's simpering, he might be able to ask a question.

Better not let himself be gnawed by impatience, keep moving at the right pace, know how to wait. He shook himself again and turned toward Daniel Claus.

"It seems that our *prince* has an irresistible attraction for the British aristocracy." He nodded toward the cluster of people listening with animated expressions to the loquacious earl. The German shifted his weight to his other leg and only grunted. Guy Johnson looked again at the glass he was holding.

The master of ceremonies interrupted the music and dance to announce that Lady Somersault, the strange self-propelling architecture of ringlets and jewels, was the winner of the evening, thanks to the considerable opulence of the load that she was bearing, valued at thousands of pounds. The information was followed by a round of applause, interrupted by the arrival of a new course of game at the long banqueting table.

The ensuing hubbub was immediate and unstoppable, as clusters of people broke up like a routed army. However, they were not in flight, but on the assault, so much so that some of the waiters only just escaped the crush. Tangles of hands dismembered pheasants and hares. Noises of mastication filled the room.

"Takes your appetite away, doesn't it?"

A disgusted voice. An uncertain step, the right leg stiff, the back as twisted as his smile. The man gave a faint bow.

"Sir Theodore Leed. Honored to meet you."

Guy Johnson and Daniel Claus returned his greeting.

Leed winked toward Joseph Brant, who was seraphically contemplating the banquet.

"With the greatest respect, gentlemen, unless the Six Nations have become a monarchy since I left America, your Indian is no more a prince than I am the king of Sweden."

He spoke with the abrupt tone of a soldier, and he looked like one, too. Guy and Daniel exchanged an eloquent glance.

"In fact, Joseph Brant Thayendanegea is a war chief, not a prince," admitted Guy.

"I thought so," the crippled man said. "I was stationed at Fort William Henry for the last war." He touched his leg, then his shoulder, with his fingertip. "French mortar, Scottish surgeon. Unhappy combination."

He allowed himself a bitter sneer.

Guy felt anxiety rising into his throat. He gulped a few times, trying not to think about his uniform, the valley and above all the watery abyss that separated him from home.

It was Claus who broke in, perhaps noticing his difficulty.

"Haven't you been back to America since then?"

"Sadly, no, I'm on terminal leave. Nonetheless, I keep myself informed about what's happening. I know that you've had problems with General Carleton about the Indians."

Claus stared at him with ill-concealed suspicion.

"I don't suppose that you, too, belong to the party opposed to their use in this war?"

Leed smiled. The question was an explicit way of taking his measure. He observed the ravenous horde leaving the table with the tired and satisfied look of those who have worked hard to earn their bread. The chattering resumed among the pairs and little groups, as the band put up a new score.

"I knew Superintendent Johnson in his day," Leed said at last. "I was sorry to learn of his death. It's rare to find a capable commander and a skilled diplomat in one and the same person."

"You haven't answered my question," replied Claus, his guttural accent becoming more noticeable.

"On the contrary, sir. A man like Sir William knew how to use the Indians against the enemies of the Crown and at the same time keep them under control. Give me another William Johnson and I will be the first to support the use of Indian irregulars."

"That's an elegant way of saying you're opposed to it," Guy put in.

"Far from it," the other man replied. "It's a way of telling you that I understand the delicacy of your mission. I think I'm the only one in this room."

"Nonetheless, you think the Indians are too undisciplined to fight on our side."

"Discipline, Colonel, allows us to delude ourselves that war is a game of chess among gentlemen." Leed spoke as if he were commenting on the taste of the wine, but his eyes were dark with an unease that seemed to be gnawing at the depths of his soul. "An idea with which we officers like to divert ourselves." His face twisted once more into a grimace. "But those who know America, as we do, know that this war will be a very unusual one. Without rules, and with unpredictable scenarios." He stared resolutely at the other two, a huge mental force battling within a flawed container. "Civil war, the bloodiest kind. The English know that, for it cost one of their kings his head. That's what frightens cowards like Carleton." A slight gesture was enough to express his lack of respect for the governor of Canada. "They know that the Indians are the ideal fighters for this kind of conflict, and they are afraid of them. Afraid of what might be unleashed."

Guy Johnson became aware of an irritating patch of sweat beneath his collar. He felt as if someone had stolen all of the noises in the room, as if sounds had ceased to spread. Mouths opened mutely. Peter's bow stroked the strings without drawing from them a single note. Heels and soles struck a cotton wool floor. Every body, every movement was absurd and inhuman. He felt as if he was surrounded by sheets of glass. The two square yards encompassing him, Claus and Leed was a fragment of an alien world, superimposed over the world of the party like a patch of oil on water, floating without being absorbed.

"Your words are truly unusual, Sir Theodore."

The veteran moved his stiff and asymmetrical torso like a marionette. "Do you find them inappropriate for a loyal soldier of His Majesty?" Leed embraced the room with a single gesture of his hand. "And if I were to tell you that in the face of the spectacle of these aristocrats I can't help feeling a scrap of sympathy for those who are weary of financing their luxuries with their own taxes, would you think I was a traitor?"

Guy exchanged a nervous glance with Claus. What was Leed getting at? Perhaps the mortar had struck his head as well, and beneath that wig his skull was deformed, his mind damaged.

"Well, you would be mistaken. And very much so," Leed concluded. "I would be willing to do anything to safeguard the unity of the Empire." He turned to stare at Guy Johnson. "What about you?"

"I don't understand what you mean."

The veteran nodded toward Brant, who was once more the object of attention of the master of the house and his guests.

"Stirring up the dogs of war against other Englishmen, even if they are enemies of the king," Leed declared. "It takes guts to do that. A great faith in God and in George III." He clicked his heels. "Gentlemen. It has been an honor." Again a half bow, a smile, and he walked away.

The two gentlemen stood and watched him dragging his leg, like an old wounded animal. The unease that they shared kept both of them silent.

"So this is what the Indians do. They stand apart and observe our strange customs."

Philip Lacroix swung around. The woman was dressed in blue, with a string of pearls around her neck. Her skin, pale as linen, was scattered with freckles that disappeared below her décolleté. She was solidly built, and carried herself with confidence. She seemed to have appeared out of nowhere, and had an adult face, with features barely softened by cosmetics. Her golden hair reflected the light of the room. Philip stared at her in silence. Then he seemed to recollect himself.

"I'm sorry, madam, I fear I don't understand."

The woman smiled. "I mean that you look like a student of natural history poring over illustrations of exotic animals."

Philip didn't know what to think. Were the woman's words a joke or something else?

The woman stretched out a hand. "Lady Florence Mowbray."

"Philip Lacroix."

The woman stood there, puzzled, waiting for her hand to be kissed, then opened the fan that dangled from her wrist and smiled. "I certainly wasn't expecting Hercules Kerkabon."

"And you aren't Mademoiselle de Saint-Yves."

"Thank heavens! You've really read *L'Ingénu*? What do you think of it?"

Philip replied in Voltaire's own words.

"A good fairy tale. I like the fairy tales of philosophers, I laugh at those of children and hate those of impostors."

Lady Mowbray's eyes betrayed sincere surprise.

"No one else in this room could quote it from memory like that. Allowing that anyone's read it. Are the *contes philosophiques* circulating in the American forests?"

"Many European things are circulating in the American forests," Philip replied.

Lady Mowbray screened her face with the circle of her fan and fluttered it in front of her nose to keep the sweat from melting her rouge.

"We don't really know anything about your country. We read Voltaire, who emphatically sides against America."

"He likes England," Philip commented.

"Perhaps. In fact I think he likes to vex his countrymen. He's a provocateur, the subtlest in Europe." She paused, as if deciding whether to risk going further or stopping. Finally she added, "Rousseau is a gray figure in comparison, don't you think? And besides, not French, but Swiss, a quite different race. Oh, forgive me, I haven't asked you if you know. . ."

". . .the Swiss?" Philip cut in. "No. But I have read *Émile*."

"Astonishing," said the lady, coming a foot closer. "And. . ." she weighed the question, ". . .which side are you on?"

Philip looked at her, puzzled.

"Of the two champions, which do you choose, which side are you on?" she specified. "You're no one today if you haven't an opinion on the matter."

"What matter?"

"Well, *you*, in a sense. I cannot miss the opportunity to be enlightened by someone directly involved."

"I'm afraid I don't understand."

She brushed his arm with her fingertips.

"The savage, the *ingénu*, the natural man. Do you think you're the model of the original man, virtuous and uncorrupted, or a latecomer to the world who has yet to attain a state of civilization?"

Philip considered the question and decided to say what he really thought.

"I belong to the People of the Flint, guardians of the eastern portal of the Longhouse. I am a son of the Wolf clan. I pray to God in the manner of the French papists and I have fought for the King of England. The philosophers have never set foot in America and have never met an Indian."

The woman smiled wide with wonder. "*Mon Dieu*, this is Alexander cutting the Gordian knot. You are right: declaring an opinion on everything, especially things one doesn't know about, is one of the sicknesses of the age. Typical of the French, I would add." She half-turned around him, glancing at the room and bowing her head slightly in greeting toward some of the guests. Then she continued.

"Your story must be rather more interesting than any little moral tale. I'm sure you're descended from some great king or other."

"I didn't know my parents," Philip replied. "The Canadian missionaries picked me up when I was two years old."

"So you're an orphan," observed Lady Mowbray, more seriously. "And a bachelor?"

"I had a wife and a daughter. They died many years ago."

The woman gave herself a slap on the hand.

"Excuse my indiscretion."

All around them, the room pulsed with movement and voices.

"Are you married?"

"Yes. I have bartered my virtue for a greater good." The words emerged through a forced smile. "A county, to be precise. But I had the good idea of demanding an education, so that I would not be as ignorant as an animal."

Philip didn't know what to say. She seemed amused by the effect of her own words.

"Lord Mowbray demands the utmost discretion from me, and asks that I do not contradict him in public. A cultured woman is more than these people can endure. As you see, Monsieur Lacroix, we English are truly civilized. We bargain over everything. That is why many philosophers take us as models."

Philip glimpsed the face of Joseph, who was being escorted by the Earl of Warwick toward a gaggle of overexcited women.

"But come now," Lady Mowbray suggested, without wasting any time. "Let us go to the aid of the prince, for the show is about to begin."

7.

The Italians were crazy about "machinery."

Not like the Germans. The Germans, at the most, erected an obelisk or a statue— a cherub, an angel with open wings, an equestrian in honor of the customer. Rough-and-ready works of plaster and cardboard, a few days of sweat, and the rest of the effort was spent on the fires: mixing the powders, testing the fuses. At the right moment, the obelisk or the statue opened up or burst into flames, and the rockets went off from inside.

Not so the Italians. The Italians built fairy-tale castles out of wood, canvas, and papier-mâché, with sliding or folding walls and an orgy of *trompe l'oeil* and fake perspectives. The Italians erected arches, domes, cathedral façades, with the fireworks hidden inside gargoyles and *hauts-reliefs*.

The machine: that was the important thing. Without the machine, the fireworks were "naked." That was what one of the master firework-makers had said, mixing languages as if they were different types of gunpowder: *Sans de machine, de fires sont nud, compris? Nud. Let de Germans being de Germans, we do different, con l'argent of de milord.*

Why Lord Warwick had insisted on using the Italians no one was allowed to know. Mr. Abbott, the Earl's master of ceremonies, preferred the Germans. Leaner, but precise and trustworthy. And yet, throughout the whole of Europe, it was the Italian firework-makers who enjoyed the best reputation. The Italians built their own glory on the embellishment of ideas born elsewhere, adding a flamboyant, clownish touch.

With them was an architect, one Guidalberto Rizzi. Abbott had seen his designs: a building with no recognizable style, a sumptuous façade supported by porticos soared upward in a forest of pillars and capitals, and at the top loomed towers and vertical cannon from which the fireworks would explode. At the very top was a revolving circular platform ringed with unicorns, Chinese dragons and lions like those of the Republic of Venice. Flames would emerge from their jaws, to be extinguished immediately by jets of water from the trunks of two wooden elephants hidden behind the trees, which would themselves be lifted up and then suspended in the air by a play of hoses before exploding in an orgy of red, white and blue flashes.

Lord Warwick was not one to quibble over costs, and had consented to every detail of Rizzi's design. Abbott had hired the craftsmen and laborers and got hold of the materials. A month of work, during which the avenues of the estate had been crammed with carts and overrun with bare-chested employees. Scaffolding went up, walkways spread, buckets traveled on pulleys and fell every now and again, narrowly missing people's heads. Warwick greeted these incidents with applause from the terrace; Abbott didn't know what to think. In the office cart, the pyrotechnicians mixed zinc, antimony and red arsenic.

Abbott was worried. Even the choice of orchestral accompaniment struck him as risky. *Music for the Royal Fireworks*. Everyone remembered the big bang of '49. That had been the Italians, too.

A disaster: premature explosions, fires, fatalities, injuries, brawls and arrests. The king and his retinue had fled, putting a seal of disapproval on the entire fiasco.

Abbott feared that he was about to witness something similar, though on a smaller scale. Horrible presentiments ran through his mind.

The sky was Prussian blue. The sole Germanic element of the display.

It took the servants a few minutes to extinguish all the lamps and candles in the panoramic drawing room. Gradually the great windows ceased to reflect the lights, smiles and dazzling colors of the assemblage, and became transparent. Everyone saw his double disappearing and found himself in the company of the dense, heavy blue vault of the sky.

Philip Lacroix Ronaterihonte had never seen fireworks.

Joseph Brant Thayendanegea had never seen fireworks.

Peter Warren Johnson had seen fireworks in Philadelphia, but he suspected that this spectacle would be a far richer experience.

With poles and winches, the workmen removed the canvases from the bizarre construction in the middle of the park, which was lit by long torches stuck into the ground and big lanterns hanging from the trees.

Peter looked around in search of his uncle and the Great Devil, but couldn't see them.

Boom!

The crowd gave a start and the windows trembled. The sky was still not illuminated.

A short distance away, a second explosion:

Boom!

And then:

Boom!

The third salvo was the signal. A flash silently lit up the sky. The orchestra launched into Handel's overture.

From a dome at the top of the temple a wall of fire appeared and became a cascade of red, white and blue flames. The Union Jack.

A sequence of frightening reports drowned out the music, as bright green trails emerged from every point of the building, climbed into the sky and brought ephemeral stars to life.

*   *   *

The Italians loved noise. Into their spectacles they always inserted the greatest possible number of "dark explosions," filled with black powder. "Abundance of grand noise, Mister Ebbott, is de Italian style, ssssssss, ka-boom! Boom, boo-boom! *Tutto scoppia, compris?*"

Abbott, standing on a little hill, enjoyed a good view of the machine and of the whole of the display. On the left he also saw the palace, the real one, with the fireworks reflected in the glass panes of the panoramic drawing room. One palace both opposite and inside the other, as if the stone one were being boarded by its flame-wrapped double and had given up defending itself, surrendered to a contemplation of its own destruction.

At that moment he understood the Italians' intent.

Philip understood, too. Leaning against the back wall of the drawing room, beside Lady Mowbray, he watched the spectacle over a horizon of wigs and tiaras.

Might not the artificial palace be a caricature of Lord Warwick's? The pointless pomp, the statues, the frills, the hanging colonnades. The firework-makers were confronting the English aristocracy with the spectacle of itself. The *jouissance* of the master of the house reached its peak in this bonfire of imperial vanities.

A lion puffed out a jet of fire, feebler than expected. It resolved into a rain of embers that fell onto the lawn, grazing the machine's façade.

So it was that a column in the portico caught fire.

Before anyone could intervene, the flames leaped to another column.

Meanwhile the elephants remained hidden.

From behind a hedge some bare-torsoed workmen appeared, each carrying a bucket of water.

By now the fire had spread to a third column.

Abbott hurled himself down the slope.

The fire was devouring the façade. Rockets were still going off, in a frenzy of artificial stars. They rose and fell with equal speed: definitive sunsets replaced by swift new dawns. Clusters of sparks surged and sank, reflected in the eyes of the audience.

Abbott reached the hedge behind which the *tireurs* were working. He saw the Italians and began to rage at them.

"Irresponsible idiots! I knew you would cause a disaster!"

The Italians looked at him as if he were a man possessed. One of them showed him the palms of his hands, either to calm him down or keep him at a distance.

"Calm, friend, *tranquille*! *Ça fait part du spectacle!* Is de Italian style, maybe forget?" Then, he turned toward the workmen, stripped to the waist, and ordered: "*Tirez la corde*, now"

Another pyrotechnist, covered with tattoos from his chin to his fingers, pointed behind Abbott and gestured to him to turn around.

At that moment the entire façade collapsed.
Abbott stood open-mouthed.

Peter, Philip, Joseph and all the others stood open-mouthed. The musicians stopped playing. A prolonged *ooooohhh* of astonishment filled the drawing room.

Behind the façade that had been destroyed by the fire there was a kind of pyramid. At the top of the pyramid, a disc of flame, a replica of the sun, cast a white light all around.

The pyramid rose, hoisted by tie-beams and winches. At its base dozens of rockets were lit, so that colored flames seemed to be thrusting the pyramid up from the earth, launching it toward the sky. A sky that lit up with stars and grew tinged, in one final big flash, with red, white and blue.

The applause was deafening. Everyone turned toward Lord Warwick to congratulate him. The master of the house smiled sardonically.

"And the elephants? Where are the elephants?" Abbott wondered.

"Weren't there supposed to be elephants?" he asked the Italians. "In homage to our Indian guests?"

The Italians looked at him as if he were a worm that had crawled from under a rock, before exploding with laughter.

"*Ils sont Indiens d'Amérique.* Elephants live in India, *imbezel!*"

Night. Peter, on his way back to the inn, felt ten feet tall. The wood and the fabrics of the carriage could hardly contain him. The excitement of the crowd, the music, the fireworks still rang out, echoed, exploded in his mind. They flowed in his veins along with his blood, dense and strong. His heart beat like a drum, a smile was painted on his face. The carriage jolted, but Peter felt no discomfort, as if his limbs, filled with excitement, were immune to unease or fatigue.

He was at the center of the planet, in the middle of a group of heroes whom London had welcomed, hat in hand. He was tipsy, with spirits and liqueurs and wines that had tasted like nectar, flavors very different from the rum of the colonies. The women and girls—some had looked at him, he had noticed—were nymphs, the drawing room where the ball had been held was Parnassus. The men had treated him with the respect due to a victorious young warrior.

Peter looked out of the window. The night was dark, and in many places there were no street lights. He felt the bulk of the buildings weighing down on the vehicle. London was a vast fortress, and its ramparts defended all its loyal subjects, reaching the four corners of the world, all the way to the Mohawk Valley, all the way to Canajoharie. Peter thought the future was all the colors of the rainbow.

8.

A damp cellar, without plaster or tiles. In the darkest corner, a gang of rats were gorging themselves on a dead cat. The heat of the stove was like a drop in the sea of icy air. Rays of pale sunlight and excited shouts filtered down through the air vents.

An ogre in an apron poured wine from demijohns into bottles, without filling them. A disfigured man polished a pewter tray. Another man, the thinnest of the three, scooped powder into a tea-spoon, poured it into the claret, and added water as he counted aloud:

"One hundred and seven, one hundred and eight, one hundred and nine. . ."

From the door at the back two individuals burst into the room, as elegant as lords compared with the others. Under their overcoats they wore rough linen jackets and woolen trousers. The taller of them even had a wig, threadbare and dirty, but well made. In his hand he held a crumpled broadsheet.

"Gentlemen," he announced with emphasis. "The *Daily Courant* has done us the honor of an article."

"Christ in a shitbucket! Read!"

"Hush. You're making me lose count. Where was I?"

"There's a letter from the blackbird we plucked clean the other night. He says if anyone doesn't believe him, he can go to Dr. Flint, and ask him what kind of a state he was in after his treatment from the Indians."

"Arrow in the arse. What horrors, Dr. Flint!"

"One hundred and eight. You'd got to one hundred and eight."

"Horsedung, one hundred and ten at the very least. I'll have to start over."

"Leave it," the newcomer stopped him. "We must talk."

"Some war paint for tonight?" asked the accountant.

"That too."

The disfigured man smiled. His one good eye was watery from gin. He had no plans for the last night of the year, apart from a little boy who owed him a favor.

"Bring the wine," the lordly man in the wig ordered the commoner in the apron. "I want to try it before you adulterate it."

He folded the paper he carried and went and sat on an abandoned wooden chest on the other side of the room. The other four dragged over boxes of their own and formed a circle. They passed him the bottle. He took a sip, then slipped off his wig and began combing it with his fingers. On his uncovered head was the tuft of an Indian warrior and on his brow a tattooed Turkish crescent. With a gesture he invited the other lord to speak.

The latter was a pale, fair-haired man, syphilitic-looking, with a beer belly. A beggar to look at, but not many people would have given him a penny.

"So," he cleared his throat. "The story is this: Here in Soho they're chucking everyone in solitary. Mobs, packs and screeves. The odd high-Toby on the Tottenham Court Road. Turnips like ours, there's only one who carries 'em off. Now, Dread Jack, he has a tightly run organization and plays a merry prank, he does: he thieves and he thief-takes, he steals and sells on, grasses up the buyers and pockets the takings."

"We'd no such bastards in Covent Garden," the thin man observed sadly.

"We had Judge Fielding's sleuths, on the other hand, and we had to make a run for it."

"Come on, you pieces of shit," the Emperor cut him short. "The move might do us good. The Garden was getting too thick. No sleuths hereabouts, just the dodderers of the Guard, you go *uh!* and off they run straight to the parish church. Put *Dead* Jack down below and the game is done. All the business is ours, and all the flimpers on our side."

"Smoothly done," spat the disfigured man. "But this isn't just any old goney. He won't give a fuck for a gang of gaffed redskins."

"Don't talk horseshit, Cole. We are the Mohocks of London, by my tuft we are that. And this thing here," he struck his tattooed forehead with his hand, "I didn't do it yesterday."

"We know that, Dave," the ogre recited the old chant. "Your grandfather was Hendrick, King of the Mohocks, who came to London and had himself a fine fuck."

"Exactly so. And now the whole city is slobbering over the Indians, just as they did back then. If we were Mr. Nobody's gang, he wouldn't even have written that letter to the *Courant*."

"And you reckon Dread Jack reads the paper?"

"He can barely write his name, but what has that got to do with anything? The herd need only hear our name to shit their little britches."

"And what do we get out of it?" The accountant wrinkled his nose in a catlike grimace.

"They shit themselves, they pay up," the Emperor declared. "Fear is the soul of trade. The city savages can't wait to join us. The old men of the Guard will pray to God; Fielding's sleuths will be curled up in their Bow Street kennel. *Dead* Jack will think twice before waging war on the London Mohocks."

Having said this, he drew from his pocket a little velvet-covered box, took from it a goose-quill toothpick and poked it between his gums and his rotten teeth.

"And our cargo of stolen wine?" asked the ogre, pointing at the demijohns. "They were cooking that one up."

"Exactly. Three days have passed. Have you heard them complaining?"

"No, but all in good time."

"Fuck time. This isn't a game of chess, we can't sit around waiting. We have made the first bet, and now let's up the ante."

"Up the ante? What with?"

The Emperor put the toothpick down, fished out a lump of something that looked like sugar and stuffed it into his mouth. With a look of disgust, he drained the bottle, gargled with it and spat the whole mixture on the ground.

"Alum," he said, his index finger pointing to his throat. "A kick like nothing else. A gentleman. . ."

"That's right, Dave," the ogre agreed. "*A gentleman is like a horse.* What in hell's name are we bidding, then?"

The other man pulled his lips over his teeth. "When you are conſtrained to ſpeak like thiſ and they're taking you up the arſe, how then will you earn your living? By ſucking cockſ?"

A rattle of chesty laughter echoed around the cellar. The ogre replied with a gesture, inviting his mates to take care of his own cock.

"What were we saying? Oh, yes, simple: we go, we introduce ourselves, and if they want a refund we'll gladly provide it."

Silence, broken only by the squeaking of rats. The disfigured man stood to open a new bottle. He took a long swig. It was one of the ones already treated; he didn't seem to notice the difference. The accountant was the first to speak.

"I'm in. When?"

The Emperor thrust on his wig and leaped to his feet.

"Tonight. Don't you want to celebrate? Tomorrow is the beginning of the Mohock year."

9.

One-Eyed Fred clocked the blowens from behind the bar of his inn. The inn stood in a courtyard off Tottenham Court Road, in the middle of Soho's Cutthroat Island. Twenty years before, Fred had abandoned masts and hulls forever to come on dry land, and with the few pennies he'd earned between stealing and smuggling, he had bought himself this hovel to turn into a dun jasper and drink in holy peace, and let saltwater go hang. It bore no sign, but from the day he'd opened it, it had had a name: One-Eye's Tavern. Business had been smart, earnings steady, no shortage of ackers in the bag, and just enough patter to inspire respect. The rest came from his blind eye, because one good one was enough to clock what needed to be clocked; a few scars to enhance his already expressive features; the twisted sneer and the four tooth-pegs left in his gobhole, sharp and rotten as a dead shark's. He had ended up a landlord.

Other times. Then dun, slack, flaying bastard old age had curdled his bones and guts, forcing him to take on a boss, a fly and shitty jasper he'd known since nipling days, name of James, now Dread Jack. Ran a gang of right nasties, cracksmen and flagsters every one. All day glugging gin and stuffing their gropuses with the fruits of their swailing and grifting.

One shitty year was ending, another beginning. Sod-all changed, and if it did it was for the worse, that was what One-Eye thought. The whores, in spite of the terrible cold, wore leather jerkins, as if they had nothing on underneath, with their backs and hams bare and their ninnies all on show, and wide skirts to protect the tools of their trade. The whores passed from one table to another, with gin and wobbling merchandise, at each grope a high, coarse shriek, and then they hooted, they hooted when one of Dread's thugs stuck his canister in their ninnies. In the end, One-Eye, from behind the bar, only had to pour gin and clock the meat on display, some of it fresh, some of it rancid.

Dread Jack slouched on a bench resting against a wall, tended to by Betty, known as Glut, along with Ellie, who was missing an arm but had in compensation received from nature two stupendous mams. Other thugs sat around with all the bloated swagger you might have expected of jaspers of such lowly rank. All swearing and belching and coughing up phlegm.

Things got interesting when all of a sudden the gob of Tom, known as Trombone, let out a roar like a wounded bear. Trombone Tom, the gang's chief night-prowler, had been sitting apart from the rest at another table for a bit, prating with Fat-Arse Mary. All of a sudden, gin and the horn and all, the sauce running in his veins had all gone to his head and Trombone, after giving that great yell of his, had thrown Fat-Arse's skirt over her head, slipped his cock in her notch and was hammering away at her from behind.

Now this, after a few initial shitty comments, had brought back a strange kind of calm: the women were no longer shrieking, and some were even chuckling, but quietly, and the slumped jaspers were absorbed as if watching a play or listening to a roadside storyteller. Mary groaned ecstatically from under her skirts. Trombone brayed and strained like the ogre he was. One-Eye, behind the bar, was well horned, and starting to give himself a good tug down below. God in a shitbucket, what a bugger it is to reach a dreary old age when no one strokes your knob. And here, right in the middle of the show, and thanks to the sad calm that had fallen upon the tavern, all of a sudden One-Eye heard a great loud bellow. It came from the gloom out in the street. Fred pricked up his earflaps, the only one interested in the thing going on outside.

> He flies like a hawk
> He darts like a sparrow

The bellowing roar was getting closer.

> Gets what he wants
> With his bow and his arrow

Fred heard the sound of rapid footsteps and then clocked the door opening with a bang and a jasper coming in with a frontage you wouldn't believe, wearing a mad tuft instead of hair and with a half-moon tattooed on his forehead, as he yelled with that same voice:

> The Emperor's ax
> Smashes bone to the marrow!

One-Eyed Fred barely had time to duck his canister under the bar before that mad jasper hurled his weapon straight ahead of him, landing it in the belly of a barrel just behind where the barkeep had stood.

A mighty great yell followed, like a battle cry, and behind the tufted jasper the ruffers started pouring in, with faces painted and carrying maces and cudgels and real bows and arrows ready for use. For Dread Jack's gang it was one shitty surprise, and the brawl that began was of epic proportions, albeit all one way. The ruffers dealt unbridled blows to canisters and gobholes, while the half-moon Emperor strode forward to grab the ax from the barrel and then climbed up onto the bar, right above One-Eye's hiding head. Up there, swaggering and triumphant, he began to clock the scene with the greatest joy.

Trombone Tom, cock still out, had just taken an arrow in that very region, and was wailing and howling like a dog; the blowens, Fat-Arse more than anyone else, were screeching like hawks and clustering in areas less riven with thrusts and slaps and blows; Jack's jaspers, stunned and plastered, had tried to get their mawleys on their swails, but the mad jokers were on them right away, reducing those smilers and gobholes to shapeless masks, sauce all over the shop and tooth-pegs, good ones even, flying out like spit. A consummate defeat.

It was then, from his pedestal, that the tuft with the ax called to the beaten and terrified jaspers with great waves of his arms and a honeyed voice:

"Ladies and gentlemen, pray lend me your ears. I, Taw Waw Eben Zan Kaladar II, Emperor of the London Mohock Nation, hereby officially declare the Mohock year open. From this moment, therefore, you all fall under my benign and balanced authority, from which you will draw nothing but good and a long and untroubled life. We have come to inform you, lest you be surprised by any of the, shall we say, changes that will from this very day beautify the existence of our neighborhood."

Dread Jack, who had pressed himself to the wall and used three strumpets as his shields, took a few steps into the open, raising a mighty great cudgel in one of his mawleys. Quite purple in the chops, he thundered in a hoarse, mean voice:

"And who the devil might you be, you stinking interloper, hurling all kinds of shit around in other people's houses without the slightest respect for anyone? Jump down here so that I can turn you inside out like a pair of shitten trousers."

"I knew it, it's the great Dreeead," said the Emperor.

And before he'd finished speaking he jumped down and landed the hatchet in Jack's skull, sending him sprawling. After a few squawks from the women, silence settled over the whole of the inn. Even the thugs of that shaven-headed jasper who called himself the Emperor looked scared and surprised. Taw Waw II delivered a kick to Jack's guts, as Jack drew his last few breaths in a pool of his own blood. Then the tuft straddled him and cleanly scalped him. Everyone looked on in terror. The man waved Jack's scalp in the air:

"Ladies and gentlemen. From today onward you work for me. That's all. Happy New Year." He struck the bar a few times with his open hand and added, "Old man, you can come out from under there, the customers need you. We're going now."

He turned to the thugs and quickly, one after another, just as they had entered, they left.

One-Eyed Fred, cautiously raising his face above the bar, found himself thinking that perhaps yes, the New Year would be different.

An Indian year.

10.

From the *Daily Courant*, 5 January 1776.

ON THE CRIMINALS DISGUISED AS INDIANS
WHO ARE RAGING THROUGH
THE STREETS OF LONDON

In the last edition of the year just past, we published a letter from a gentleman in Mayfair, telling of the ferocious aggression and robbery suffered by him at the hands of alleged *Mohock* Indians. Since then, many readers have written to us doubting the authenticity of the letter, or at least the facts therein described. Humble servants of the Truth, we had therefore gone back to the author and checked the circumstances, and were about to publish an accurate defense of his honesty, when a piece of information reached our Grub Street offices that, on its own, is worth more than one hundred such defenses.

On the first of this month, the first day of the year, shortly after midnight, a squadron of Indians burst into "One-Eye's Tavern" on Tottenham Court Road, assaulting the locals with hatchets and arrows, injuring divers of them and finally killing, with the barbarous ritual known as scalping, a certain James HOTBURN, thirty-one years of age, resident of Soho. The innkeeper and some women present have already given eyewitness accounts of these events to judges at the Old Bailey.

It is unnecessary to assert that the protagonists of these events cannot be the same Indians currently visiting our capital. Thoughts have flown straight to the sadly well-known MOHOCK CLUB, which Londoners still remember with horror and which we, for the benefit of younger readers and those with dim memories, will also recall in a few lines.

In the spring of 1712, two years after the visit of King Hendrick to Queen Anne, a group of ruffians who had christened themselves the Mohock Club began to overrun London at night, in search of passersby to molest, using methods of rare cruelty. Among these:

> closing the victim in a barrel and rolling him along Snow Hill;
> slipping fish-hooks into an unfortunate victim's cheeks and pulling him around on a line;
> overturning carriages into piles of filth;
> cutting off hands and noses;

crushing a victim's nose and pulling out his eyes with the fingers ("tipping the lion");

forcing victims to cut capers by waving a sword between their legs (the "dancing master");

turning ladies upside down and committing indecencies upon their legs thus exposed (the "tumbler").

It appears that behind the guise of those savages hid some scions of the city's aristocracy in search of distractions.

Today's Mohocks we are more inclined to believe are common, but dangerous, delinquents.

PANIFEX

11.

Orange peel and chewed tobacco bombarded the audience below like divine scourges, hurled by servants and lackeys hiding in the boxes, keeping the seats warm for their masters. In the dress circle, walking sticks and fans tapped the balustrade. Someone called for the actors, someone else for the Indian princes. These two factions exchanged spittle. The orchestra launched into a solemn melody, and shouts and general hubbub turned into song. The lyrics concerned the roast beef of Old England and its many advantages over the ragouts of the French. Joseph swapped a glance with Philip, but didn't say a word.

Warwick opened up a passage for them to the central bench in the front row, like an Indian guide on a trail filled with brambles. He moved the obstacles surely and methodically. A greeting to the right, a pinch to the left, the walking stick pointed straight ahead of him, the belly right behind him. As soon as his guests were seated, the earl sat down next to Joseph.

"The aristocrats of London think that the best seats in a theater are the ones in the boxes. They cost more than the others, *therefore* they have to be better. If all the seats were the same price, none of them would know where to sit. They would have to choose, ponder, expose themselves to the possibility of error. It is not the quality of the objects, but the sleep of reason that generates luxury."

Having said this, he brought his right hand to his heart and intoned the last verse of the song. The music speeded up to the final lines, drowned out by the whistles of people wanting the curtain to go up. An orange projectile brushed Warwick's cheek and landed on the parapet that protected actors and musicians from the excesses of the crowd.

"The first row in the middle is absolutely the best," Warwick whispered, as if dictating his last will and testament to Joseph. "The stage is in front of you, very close, and the thrown fruit seldom reaches all the way here. In the boxes, to follow the action properly you have to lean forward, and anyone overhead is waiting only for that to pour a glass of water, or worse."

At that moment the wings began to wobble and the applause of the public in Drury Lane accompanied the raising of the curtain. The Chorus entered: a tall man wearing a long velvet tunic and a soft beret. His stentorian voice rose above the roar of the crowd, which faded to a buzz.

"Two households, both alike in dignity,
In fair Verona, where we lay our scene,
From ancient grudge break to new mutiny,
Where civil blood makes civil hands unclean.
From forth the fatal loins of these two foes
A pair of star-cross'd lovers take their life;
Whole misadventured piteous overthrows
Do with their death bury their parents' strife."

A coarse cry rang out over the crowd.

"Hey! Those are the Indian princes!"

Rows of necks began to twist in all directions. The buzz grew loud again, eyes searched up and down for the cause of such amazement, until Joseph and Philip were identified. Neither of them dared to move a muscle: such people's attention seemed like a threat. Lord Warwick restrained a smug little smile.

"The Indians! By Jove, the Indians!"

"Let's have a look!"

"I can only see their heads."

"We want to see their faces!"

"Give us the Indians!"

The coryphaeus began to gesticulate and raised his voice again. "Gentlemen, ladies, please, we are here for *Romeo and Juliet*. . ."

"We can have them any day. We want the Indians!"

A few apples struck the head of the Chorus, who was forced to seek shelter behind one of the wings.

Lord Warwick got to his feet and struck his stick hard on the ground.

"Gentlemen, please."

A flying vegetable brushed his wig and persuaded him to sit down again. He looked at Joseph and shrugged.

"It's the price of fame," he said, amused, but his expression changed as soon as he saw that a gang of brutes had come down into the crowd and were trying to push their way through.

"If you don't let us see them we'll come and get them," cried the most excited one, meanwhile delivering scything blows with a walking stick. A few steps away, an officer in a red uniform unsheathed his sword. Someone shouted: "The guards! The guards!" A dwarf with a disproportionately large wig stood on a bench, drew a sheet of paper from his waistcoat pocket and started to read out heatedly, his voice rising to a falsetto at the end of each sentence.

"It's the Riot Act," Warwick explained, pretending to try and protect Philip while really using him as a shield. "Here in England the freedom of the individual is so dear that the guards cannot charge a crowd without first warning them by reading out these lines."

An elderly, elegantly dressed man strode onto the stage. He placed himself in the very middle and spread his arms, his palms open.

As the audience recognized him, the voices began to fade away.

Warwick leaned his head toward Joseph.

"The impresario, David Garrick. He's the most famous actor in London. He has retired from the stage, but he's still an authority."

Having gained a little more silence, the man smiled at the crowd.

"What attraction is so potent that it o'ercrows the Bard? Tell me, what retains you all here amongst the sinks of London rather than making for fair Verona?"

A few voices replied from the back rows.

"We want to see the Indians!"

"Right, Mr. Garrick, look, they're sitting in the first row."

David Garrick identified the two copper-skinned gentlemen within the crowd. With exaggerated elegance he pointed them out to everyone.

"Then I invite them to join me on this stage, because today Master Shakespeare must bow to those who have stolen his scene."

Lord Warwick touched Joseph's elbow.

"All you have to do is go up there, Your Highness, and bear in mind that the next steps you tread will be those of St. James's Palace."

Joseph looked at Philip again. He wouldn't go on his own. Philip nodded reluctantly and they rose to their feet. In the most total silence they approached Garrick, who received them with a graceful bow and with a slight gesture invited them to speak.

Joseph looked at that sea of curious faces and felt uneasy again. He had spoken many times at the assemblies of his people. He had taken part in councils and meetings. But he had always been seated in a circle, among equals. He had never found himself alone in front of—*against*, in fact—such an unfamiliar crowd. The more he thought about it, the more his unease mounted.

The Earl of Warwick, with his index and middle fingers, mimed a little man climbing a flight of stairs.

"Let them say something!"

"In English!"

"No, in their own language!"

"Their tattoos! We want to see them!"

"Do a war dance!"

A member of the audience leaned over the balustrade to bang his stick on the head of someone gesticulating below him. The man noticed, parried the blow and returned it. The other man riposted. Their neighbors were thrilled by the duel, and someone suggested betting on whether or not the man up above would fall.

Oranges and tobacco started flying again. Warwick's eyes pleaded with Joseph, who managed to find his voice.

"Brothers of London," he said, then waited for silence to embrace the Royal Theatre again. "Brothers of London, many of you will be wondering what led Thayendanegea, Two Sticks Bound Together, and his brother Ronaterihonte, Keep Faith, messengers of the People of the Flint and the Longhouse of the Six Nations, to plow the ocean to come here. Some say it is because of the quarrel between the American colonies and England. Others maintain that we are here to ask help from the king against those who are stealing our lands. All of this is true, but it does not diminish the curiosity and admiration that we feel for your great and magnificent city, rich in things that the Americans can only imagine. We feel stronger curiosity only for William Shakespeare, and for *Romeo and Juliet* in particular. If relations between men and women, here in England, are as Shakespeare describes, we wonder how it can be that London has a million inhabitants. If our people adopted the same kind of courtship, we would disappear within only a few seasons."

Applause. The public laughed, whistled, filled the air with a firework display of orange peel.

The two Indians walked toward the steps. The audience fell silent; it was the singular silence of those who do not know what to expect. The coryphaeus looked at Garrick with an air of bewilderment. Should he leave the stage and call for the curtain, or start again where he had left off? But after an elegant bow to the audience, the Great Garrick withdrew. The Chorus remained planted in the middle of the stage, not knowing what to do.

Joseph Brant was already descending the steps to return to his place in the audience. Walking behind him, Philip was aware of the embarrassment of the coryphaeus. He stepped over and murmured, "The fearful passage of their death-mark'd love. . ."

In the front row some mouths fell open once more. Without yielding to his surprise, the coryphaeus began once more:

"The fearful passage of their death-mark'd love,

And the continuance of their parents' rage, Which, but their children's end, nought could remove, Is now the two hours' traffic of our stage; The which if you with patient ears attend, What here shall miss, our toil shall strive to mend."

In the crowd, unable to contain his emotion, the Earl of Warwick was fidgeting in his seat. He shook hands to his right, his left and even behind him, then he hugged Joseph to check that it was really him, in flesh and bone.

"This city won't be the same when you've gone," he said sadly at last. "I'd even go so far as to say that not even Shakespeare will be the same again." He continued in a pleading tone, "You must promise me that you won't leave London before the summer. You have to promise me that or I will do everything in my power to postpone your audience with King George."

Joseph promised, then stared raptly at the stage, and the earl, his hands joined on the pommel of his stick, forced himself to remain silent until the end of the scene.

In one of the central loggias a group of gentlemen was pretending to pay attention to the play. Their voices were whispers; they kept their faces in shadow. Their elegant, sober clothes denoted their membership in the class of city businessmen. They sat side by side, but it was clear that one of them was the group's center of gravity. The faces of the others, tilted slightly toward him, were focused on his face, and the hissed comments that came from them were all aimed in his direction.

"That clown Warwick had to foist the Indians off on us . . . Next time it'll be the cannibals of Africa."

From a silver box, the leader took a pinch of snuff and snorted it, then wiped his nostrils with an embroidered handkerchief.

"The papers aren't writing about anything else," observed the shadow next to him.

"Do they really hope to bring the savages into fashion?" a third remarked contemptuously.

"They want to make us digest the idea that the Crown is entrusting the defense of its own interests in America to these primitives," added the one who had not yet spoken.

The man in the middle of the row took another sniff of his tobacco, then closed the little box and put it back in his pocket before glancing up distractedly. The duel between Mercutio and Tybalt was progressing on the stage—clean strokes with wooden swords. Some members of the audience were urging them on as if they didn't already know who would win.

"The problem, my dear Cavendish," said the man in the middle, still looking up, "is that the interests of the Crown are increasingly divergent from our own. With each day that passes this conflict with the settlers is costing us thousands of pounds. Half of our business contacts have gone up in smoke. The American ports are being closed, the goods are being confiscated or thrown into the sea. The army was supposed to reestablish order in a few weeks, and more than six months have passed already."

"They should have supported Burke. In the whole Chamber he's the only one with a bit of common sense: he predicted everything."

"In spite of your esteem for him, Mr. Pole, the government has a completely different opinion."

"Then perhaps we should have a change of government."

"Not before it has lost the war," declared the gentleman sitting in the middle.

"Do you really think our army could be defeated?"

"I know little of military affairs, gentlemen. Certainly, progress cannot be defeated. We are waging a war to guarantee the East India Company sales of its tea stocks in America. You realize that if things go on as they are, not an ounce will be sold? In fact, they tell me that the Americans have started drinking coffee in protest. This is what happens when you force the hand of the market. How many times have I repeated to the Ministry of Trade that the market must be free—free, for the love of God. Supply and demand, supply and demand. All the coats of arms in the world can't equal a good accountant."

"Are you aware that Mr. Adam Smith is sending his theories to the printers as we speak?"

"Thank the Lord, I will no longer feel like a preacher in the desert. He is a respected authority."

"We must set about financing the distribution of the work throughout London."

"Hundreds, thousands of copies."

The man pointed toward Warwick, in the front row.

"And in the meantime we have to put up with these old parasites? It's time someone upset the apple cart."

The whispers were drowned out by the roar of the audience at Mercutio's death. When the noise subsided, the man sitting in the middle began speaking again.

"They bring a few well-educated Indians here, Indians who know Shakespeare, and claim that we're all falling for them. Ridiculous."

"Shameless," added the shadow sitting to the right.

"Wretched," commented the one on the left.

"Sordid," concluded the last chorus member, after a moment's hesitation.

The man in the middle rose to his feet.

"The actors are slack today. Old Garrick could make a better fist of it playing all the parts himself."

"Even Juliet?" joked one of the others.

"Of course. Shakespeare may even have impersonated her himself."

"Unenlightened times," sneered the other man.

"No worse than these," the gentleman retorted. "Our American compatriots are asking for free trade and the government is so shortsighted as to fraternize with the scalpers. The world has been turned upside down."

The shadows slipped quietly away, leaving the box empty, like a gaping black hole facing the stage.

12.

Aunt Nancy kept telling her to hold her breath. As soon as Esther obeyed, a brawny servant pulled on the laces of her corset, compressing her ribs and trapping the air in her lungs. Esther thought she was dying, but her little body managed to maintain a certain amount of breathing space for itself, just enough to survive.

"Done," concluded the servant with a surly smile.

They turned her toward a mirror resting against the wall. Esther looked at the miniature lady in front of her. Her coiffure brushed the top edge of the frame. Decorated with gilded wires, velvet ribbons and strips of lace, her hair stood up straight on her head, like the branches of a plant on a trellis, before falling in perfect curls. She barely recognized her own face. A layer of white lead had made it flat and uniform, like the face of a porcelain doll. Her skirt brushed the floor, three layers of heavy fabric, and underneath were knickers that reached to her knees, and silk stockings. She wondered how she would manage to pee. Hampered by the corset, her breath was short and panting, and her heart thumped with panic at being imprisoned *in there*.

Aunt Nancy had explained that she had to make a good impression. She was a lady now, and society occasions required an effort. Would she do it for her father? She didn't want to displease him, did she? No, Esther didn't. Aunt Nancy said that up in heaven her mother would be proud of her, seeing her so beautiful. Beautiful? Esther looked at herself in the mirror again. No, she wouldn't have said so.

She tried to walk, and felt clumsy and slow. All dressed up like that, she wouldn't be able to run, or even quicken her step, let alone hide where no one could find her. She could only revolve on the spot, like the figure in the musical box that her father had given her the day before: a tiny lady moving in time to the music, on a wooden groove.

Esther turned toward her little sisters, sitting in a corner. They were looking at her in bafflement, as you might look at someone suddenly leaving. Esther understood that this was her parting from them, and yet she couldn't feel sorry. It had to be this way. She had to become a lady, learn to spin in place. She could do it. Use the carapace they had forced onto her and play the game. She looked again at the gleaming surface of the mirror and smiled at herself. From the backward world of reflections, her pale double curled a cold sneer.

*   *   *

In the carriage they sat her next to her father. Opposite them, Lord Warwick rested the small of his back against the edge of the seat and his hands upon the pommel of his stick. Beside him, Joseph Brant smiled vaguely at her.

Esther observed the wheels of the other carriages running quickly by. They sent up splashes of mud over the clothes of the passersby and the vendors' stalls.

Their coach reached a bridge crammed with a bustle of men and things. She had once seen a termites' nest broken open by the woodsmen. She immediately dismissed the image and took a deep breath to suppress her desire to retch. Perhaps it was the carriage bumping up and down, or perhaps the termites running through her head.

She heard her father speaking, his voice dampened by the noises outside and the sounds of the vehicle.

"Lord Germain is inclined to support our cause. He replied solicitously to my letter, asking me to put the unresolved questions in writing."

"That's good news," the earl observed. "Germain is the most treacherous Secretary of State for the Colonies we have ever had, but he's the only person who can resolve our problems."

Esther's attention was drawn by a group of little boys who had caught and bound a dog and were impaling it on a skewer. Its wails were heartrending. Meanwhile another group had tied three cats together by their tails and were whirling them around: a tangle of claws, hisses and miaows. She shivered as the carriage passed on. Then it slowed down and she found herself looking at a fat man on a sedan chair, lofted above the hubbub of the street by four servants. His big head was thrust out of the cabin and he shouted a series of insults toward another sedan chair coming from the opposite direction. Suddenly the man stopped yelling, noticed the girl, and stared at her with disapproval. She pulled her own head back inside the carriage.

Her father and the Earl were still talking.

"Do you think it will happen soon?" Joseph Brant broke in.

"Certainly. The presence of His Highness Joseph Brant is causing the right kind of sensation. After all, you are the prince of Canajoharie. They can't leave you waiting too long in the antechamber."

The Indian looked at the walking stick that he held between his knees, and shook his head.

"I am a warrior chief. It is a title earned on the field. My origins are not noble, Lord Warwick."

"They're like everyone else's," said the Earl. "It isn't God who assigns aristocratic titles, but force." He rearranged an untidy hair in his wig. "If you look carefully, the origins of the English nobility lie in rape and pillage."

Esther felt her father stirring on his seat. Her nausea was passing, but she had to let her head rest on the back of the seat and take a deep breath. She understood little of what the grown-ups were saying, but she could tell their state of mind. The earl spoke in a bored tone, as if everything were obvious.

"A long time ago a horde of hairy Frenchmen crossed the Channel, conquered these lands and exerted the right of the victors on the women of the island. Then they shared out the noble titles that we still bear today." Warwick gave an affected wave of the hand. "And here we are. Bastards, preoccupied with the idea of cultivating good manners so that our origins may be forgotten.

"The English lords lead the armies into battle," Joseph Brant cut in. "Courage and valor are the true source of nobility."

"Courage and valor? Qualities appreciated by a people like your own, who still take the ancient virtues into account," said the earl with another vague gesture of his hand. "But look out there. I wouldn't survive a day in those streets, let alone a night. These people spend their whole lives there. Talk about courage. Thieves, villains and merchants surviving everywhere, on everything. Like rats." Esther's head was spinning. Images and words, sounding vague and muffled, Warwick's face seemed distorted, Joseph Brant's had animal features. "It's a kind of insatiable hunger, which devours anything in its path. Do you think that courage and valor will change the course of events? Those are concepts for the allegories of our painters, whom we ask to depict us in armor and dress uniforms. A pathetic attempt to banish the thought that soon these people will be gnawing on our bones."

Her father spoke from a long way away: "And yet, milord, you can't deny that the aristocracy cultivates a certain form of excellence."

"I have, in fact, thought long and hard about what it means to be an aristocrat." Esther saw the earl draw a little metal flask from under his jacket, uncork it and offer it to the others. "A cordial?"

The two men refused, but Warwick took a copious swig before starting to talk again in the same tone.

"I have reached the conclusion that it means having someone willing to take the blows on our behalf. To prove this theory, the other day I farted loudly in the drawing room, in the presence of three of my servants. And not only did they pretend not to hear it, but when I vehemently accused one of them, he didn't bat an eyelid and endured the scolding with an air of the most utter contrition. So, being an aristocrat means acting with total impunity, despite all the evidence." The earl raised his flask again. "Long live King George." He took a second sip.

"Long live the king," the other two echoed unenthusiastically.

13.

The coaches slowed down, the horses drew abreast. The entrance to Vauxhall Gardens was full of life. Ionic columns rose up, supporting a kind of pergola. Philip noticed with surprise that the view spread far beyond the gate, although guided by the hedges and contained by rows of trees arranged by species. In some places the countryside opened up and the horizon was visible. Here, the ashen bulk of the city was a wrestler loosening his grip. Philip tried to fill his lungs, but the air still smelled of smoke and coal, of human and animal waste. Peter got out of the carriage and straightened his jacket with his hands.

Entrance was one shilling.

Esther walked ahead of her father. She answered his smiles with a smile, she introduced herself in the proper manner when Warwick decided it was time to stop, but she was concentrating upon the physical pain of the corset. And yet all the ladies seemed to adapt to it. Some had waists so tightly confined that two hands could have encircled them, thumbs and index fingers meeting in the middle, yet they seemed perfectly at ease under the white lead, the rouge, the patches, the complex coiffures.

Esther wanted to block her ears; she found the conversation boring and pointless. So were the people to whom she was introduced. She thought it was a real shame that the intimacy between herself and Peter had not increased in the course of the voyage. His status as a hero and the company of the adults had taken him away for good.

In the middle of the crowd, in Vauxhall Gardens, Esther Johnson thought once again about her mother.

The absence was deeper than the ocean they had crossed.

Her father stopped: more introductions, more chatter. She deciphered a handful of words. "Canada," "damned Whigs," "leading the Indians". . . The music of an orchestra came to them from the platform in the middle of the gardens.

Everyone seemed to have forgotten about her. Esther lingered behind. No one noticed.

The Great Devil was tired of the crowd. He glanced at Peter, absorbed in his contemplation of the musicians. He decided to move away from the group. Vauxhall seemed big enough to allow him some solitude.

One step after the other, Philip came in sight of the Rotunda, a massive circular building.

The interior was lit by chandeliers and mirrors. There were only a few people in it, all busy studying the frescoes that decorated the walls. The music sounded far away.

Ships. Most of the paintings were of ships. The English were well aware that they were great navigators. The scenes were the uninterrupted story of a vocation. He was struck by one in particular: the painter had captured the scene admirably, and the attention to detail rendered the individual characters highly lifelike. The subject was a surrender. A ship had been boarded, and the surviving crew were assembled on one side of the deck. On the other side were the victors, guns leveled. The faces of the defeated men revealed uncertainty and terror. Their lives were in the hands of an enemy drunk on victory.

The man of the forests observed each detail of the painting.

The scene was part of his own experience. He had found himself in both situations: prisoner and hunter of men.

He walked away from the painting.

Next to a statue, a familiar figure.

Esther emerged from the shadows.

Philip looked at her without a word. He was aware of the shortness of her breath, the unease that the girl was feeling in the finery they had imposed on her. He had a vision of a younger version of himself, dressed up for religious functions.

He didn't know how to break the silence, but something forced him to do so.

"Miss Johnson. Whyever aren't you with the others?"

His words sounded forced. Philip heard them echoing as if they came from a long way off.

"I got bored. They won't leave me alone for a moment."

Though Esther's voice was clear, it betrayed a certain embarrassment.

Philip couldn't remember solitude having value for him at that age.

The silence thickened again. He decided that it was his duty to disperse it again. "Have you seen the frescoes already?"

Behind her mask of white lead Esther tried to smile. "Ships. Just ships. As if we hadn't seen enough of those already."

Philip nodded. Esther suddenly changed her expression and took a few steps toward the Indian. In a low voice she went on, "Aren't you tired, Mr. Lacroix, of putting on these clothes? Don't you think these people are all as stiff as puppets?"

The girl had uttered the words in haste, without drawing breath.

Philip looked into her eyes. "Not just the clothes. It's the soul."

Esther looked startled, as if this were the first time an adult agreed with her. "When will we be going home, Mr. Lacroix?"

"I don't know," Philip replied. "Right now, let's get out of here."

Outside, the notes of the band barely touched them.

14.

Night. Fog. The countryside around Vauxhall: turnips on the left, onions on the right. Five ghosts were walking in a line along a ditch. The man in front was taking snuff to dry his brain of vapors. The second struggled to keep his torch alight and cursed into the wind: his curses acted as a lampshade. The third held an iron bar. The fourth and fifth were yoked together by a wooden ladder.

A patch of light drowned in the moist air. The ghosts seemed to be trying to reach it, but the icy mud slowed down their steps: hard as stone, a series of holes and crevasses. The rotten twigs scattered on the ground were steel knives and traps. Everything was stiff and pointed. Even the fog.

Once they had reached a tall fence, the march came to a halt. The light from the torches danced on their faces. A scar, a red nose, a missing incisor. Beyond the posts planted in the ground, they heard shrill laughter that didn't sound human.

"Shiiiit, Dave. You're the spit of that jasper up there!"

The ogre's admiration was sincere. With one eye he studied his mate's Indian mask; with the other, the image of a savage on an old almanac. The Emperor struggled to frame his face in a shard of mirror on top of a box.

"*Bastard* spit," the fair-haired man stressed. He approached the ogre and pointed to the portrait of the feathered native. "These are eagle, not chicken."

"Chicken your mother." The Emperor spun around: if they had called his mother a whore he wouldn't have taken it so much to heart. "It's called a turkey-cock. An American peacock."

"Turkey? What the fuck has Turkey got to do with it?"

"America, India, Turkey. All the same shit," the thinnest of them observed with disgust.

The Emperor struck his hand on his forehead, just below the turkey feathers. "This is a Turkish crescent, take a look, and you know who did it to me?"

"Yes, Dave," the ogre nodded politely.

"This shit is important," declared the Emperor. "I tell you, bullshit is the soul of trade. Bullshit makes a jasper important."

"Exactly." The fair-haired man was the only one who could afford to be so insistent. "If you had a good old rummage, you'd find eagle tufts in some hole or other. But no, you've gone off scrounging in the shitheaps of Vauxhall to scrape two hens together. All right, American hens, but so much the worse. Maybe having those tufts on you means something to a savage. It could mean 'I'm a twat,' and you, to act American, are going to the prince of the Mohawks with 'I'm a twat' printed on your canister."

"I could give one cold dead fuck about the Indian prince."

"A fuck? But you scribed him a brown-tongued papyrus!"

"God in a shit-bucket, Neil, what have you been studying? The letter isn't for the prince, it's for the *Courant*."

"Not for the prince?" the disfigured man said, astonished.

"No, fucking halfwits. Giving it to the prince is the purest humbug, it's a way to get the marks gandering. The marks gander, they tattle, they take an interest. The scribers tattle, they print, they fill their pockets. The ruffers shit themselves, the whores get fucked, everyone gets to work. The Emperor and his cronies shovel the shekels like there's no tomorrow."

Excited shouts greeted the chief's tirade. Even the fair-haired man seemed to set aside his doubts as he joined the chorus. The Emperor took out his toothpick and jabbed his gum.

"Go get ready," he commanded. "You're about to become the biggest savages in the whole of London."

15.

A yelling crowd lined the wide pavements of Pall Mall: rows on rows of wigs, hats and towering coiffures. Holding them back, like a long scarlet darning stitch, the red-sleeved arms and rifles of the Guards, reinforced here and there by the hoofs of the Household Cavalry. Two wings of people stretched for another half mile, from the northern gate of the Palace to Haymarket crossing.

Someone well-informed swore that the Indians would not appear, that the news, which had spread through all circles and been amplified by the gazettes, was without basis. Nonetheless, he used his own elbows to get the best possible view.

Others maintained that a brother, a cousin, a friend had already enjoyed the privilege of observing the savages from close at hand, and guaranteed that there was nothing to see, that the two men looked like any Islington squires in their Sunday best. Yet they, too, waited for hours to check this fact in person.

Someone laughed at them all, poor fools, waiting in the wrong place, when it was clear that the Canadian princes would be coming from St. James's Park. He tried to convince at least a pair of strangers to follow him: they had to trust him, it had to be that way. Nonetheless, he wouldn't hear of going on his own. If he was the poor fool, he wanted someone beside him to share his misfortune.

Suddenly a buzzing arose, first startled, then excited, then louder and louder, high-pitched and noisy, until the "aahs" and "ohs" shaped themselves into something comprehensible, an earthquake of shouts: "They're coming," "It's them," "There they are!"

A most luxurious vehicle was proceeding from the end of Pall Mall. The soldiers could hardly contain the vast crowd of shouting bodies.

Just then, behind a cluster of gentlewomen calling loudly for the prince of the Indians, other savages appeared.

"Let us through! We bring a letter for his highness," cried their feathered leader, attempting to force his way through the crowd and reach the carriage.

The ladies complied, because someone dressed in this way could really be a messenger of the prince, and slipping into his wake might be the quickest way to reach the front.

"They must be people from their entourage, servants or lackeys," someone said.

Someone else shot back that one of the savages lived in his own district, two yards away from his house.

"Give over! Can't you see that he's got red skin? Does this neighbor of yours have red skin?"

Still others observed that at least two of the Indians appeared to be drunk.

"Are you surprised? They drink all the time in India, everyone knows that. Worse than the Scots."

Meanwhile the savages took advantage of the confusion to get just behind the front row. They started pushing violently forward, so that the soldiers attributed the movement to the people in front of them. The guards rained blows on innocent heads. These unfortunates at first tried to justify themselves by pointing behind them, then they managed to step aside. Guards and savages found themselves face to face.

Prince Thayendanegea, crowned with feathers, leaned out of the carriage to check what was happening. The messenger of the savages understood that this would be his only opportunity. He gestured to his men to lift him up, and with a thrust he launched himself beyond the soldiers, arm outstretched and the letter clutched in his hand. The prince instinctively grabbed it.

"On behalf of the Indians of London!" shouted the messenger.

The London Indian felt himself being grabbed by the guards and pulled down. Twisting like a snake, he freed himself from the shawl that he was wearing like a cloak. He escaped their clutches, took a leap, gripped the carriage and scrambled up its side as swiftly as a rat. Climbing into the box, under the startled eyes of the coachman, with his clothes in rags and his tousled tuft like a crest, he spread his arms and opened his mouth into a crazed sneer.

"God save the king," he yelled. "Mohock power!"

With a ferocious cry he threw himself down in crucifix pose, landing in the outstretched arms of his companions. They, crushed among the crowd, didn't have room to lower him to the ground. They held him like the corpse of a martyr exposed to the crowd, and with blows of their hips, knees and feet they opened up a path toward salvation. Not wide enough to accommodate them all.

An hour later, as the ambassadors of the American Mohawks entered St. James's Palace to receive full red-carpet treatment, two London Indians entered Newgate with handcuffs around their wrists.

16.

The Earl of Warwick sat down at a desk of ebony and leather, next to the secretary of state, and studied the terrain.

George III, Queen Charlotte and nine princes. Good sign. The presence of the sons suggested curiosity. Curiosity produced questions. Questions produced points.

His Majesty appeared to be in a good mood. The ringlets on either side of his face were perfectly curled. George III didn't wear wigs. According to rumor, for fear that warming his head might damage his brain. In deference to fashion, he had his own mane combed and powdered as if it were artificial. An operation that made him nervous, often so much so that he had to cut it short, with tragic results for his hairstyle.

The queen, about to give birth, had chosen a pink dress, wide, with lots of lace. Her hair was curled on top of her head, without frills. Her gestures and posture said that an hour before, looking at herself in the mirror, Charlotte had not been disappointed.

The appearance of the little princes was unimportant; it was even hard to tell them apart with any precision. And except for the four adolescents, the men and women all looked very much alike.

At that moment the door of the study opened wide, the master of ceremonies entered, and the audience began.

"Colonel Guy Johnson," he announced, "Superintendent of the Department of Indian Affairs of the Northern Colonies."

The head of the delegation appeared in the doorway. He made his first bow right away, the second in the middle of the room, and the third at his destination, brushing with his lips His Majesty's ring and the queen's hand.

Movements that were not precisely those of a dancer, a slight uncertainty on the final steps, but all in all a good try: the colonel's sangfroid made up for his lack of experience.

Behind him, not much more graceful, came the other four. Daniel Claus, the worst by far. Clumsy, awkward, German. Luckily for him, the royal family was from the same part of the world, and set no great store by elegance themselves. Of the two Indians, the more striking was Prince Thayendanegea, in his red silk cloak, headdress of eagle's feathers, seashell belts, and necklace of bear claws. Philip Lacroix, much more sober in appearance, was in English garb. The boy, Peter Johnson, wore a suit cut by the best tailor in London.

On the king's face, no particular expression.

The queen half opened her eyelids.

The snotty-nosed youths remained composed.

"Royal Highnesses," said the colonel, "before introducing to Your Majesty's presence the men whose honor it is to accompany me, allow me to correct the announcement just delivered by the master of ceremonies."

Warwick grimaced with disappointment. This wasn't the speech they had rehearsed. The master of ceremonies was a touchy character. It was better to leave him be.

"It is not my custom to ascribe to myself titles I do not deserve," Johnson went on, "and I do not wish, for some trivial error, to pass for an impostor in Your Majesty's eyes. The tasks of the superintendent of Indian Affairs were entrusted to me by my predecessor, Sir William Johnson, and by the chiefs of the Six Iroquois Nations, but my office has not yet been confirmed by royal seal. The only title that I can boast, then, is that of colonel in the New York Militia."

A risky game, thought Warwick. This was the same Johnson who had introduced himself to the master of ceremonies as the superintendent. He had provoked the mistake in order to correct it and slip the notion of the appointment into the king's ear.

Now the master of ceremonies might decide to take his revenge. He was the ear of London within the royal rooms. He could spread rumors, disseminate doubts about the score, even if the secretary of state's transcripts were normally unequivocal. One point for every smile from the king, two for compliments, three for questions. Small talk was worth zero; irritable interruptions, minus two. A successful audience should come to at least eight points. Betting on the results was at least as attractive to high society as betting on horses.

The king raised an eyebrow and gestured to him to continue. The queen fanned herself.

One of the snotty boys was taken away to piss.

Guy Johnson finished the speech, stepped aside and with a gesture of his arm introduced the American delegation to King George.

It was the German's turn. He took a step forward, as the superintendent announced him in a loud voice. Claus had the weary air and pallor typical of the masturbator. His eyes, nose and mouth looked as if they were trapped in a box too small for them.

When he bowed to kiss the king's ring, he looked as if he were assessing the value of the stone. He made a short and agreeable speech—very short, so as not to offend the royal ears with his awkward pronunciation.

The queen snapped her fan shut and asked Claus which region of Germany his family came from.

Miracles of the Teutonic accent and Her Majesty's nostalgia for the stench of horses and sausages. Without even putting his brain into action, Daniel Claus had notched up a point and a half. Unfortunately, the queen's reactions were worth half those of the king, who remained impassive, his toad-like eyes directed toward the center of the room.

Warwick wove his fingers together under his chin. It was the turn of the champion, the showpiece, the man who could alter the character of the meeting and bring home the seven missing points.

Johnson introduced him flatly, a very bad beginning. No "His Highness," no "Prince." Just "Chief Joseph Brant Thayendanegea," and that was it.

The Indian came forward, the Apollo of the New World, a flesh-and-blood emblem of manliness and serene strength. He inclined his chest toward the king, kissed the queen's hand, and stepped back.

Warwick couldn't help covering his mouth with his hands. The prince, the American champion, had forgotten the king's ring! A whole afternoon rehearsing the ceremony with the dancing master, and then a trivial mistake sent all their work to hell.

Before giving in to his discomfiture, the earl studied the expression of George III, the expression on the face that represented the Empire.

There were no signs of anger. Lips pursed, complexion clear, no red patches, hands resting in his lap.

He looked at the secretary of state. He was recording the minutes with his habitual scruple.

His ears were pricked for the prince's speech. As if acting from a script, Brant had slipped one of his belts from his shoulder and held it up with both hands. The belt, he was explaining, represented the alliance between the Six Nations and the Crown of England. The Six Nations were ready to fight the enemies of their English Father, but before they did they wanted to be sure that the English Father was ready to fight the enemies of the Six Nations. Alliances, in fact, were either reciprocal or they were not.

It was the emphasis on the adjective "reciprocal" that explained to Warwick what had just happened. He clearly remembered the prince being carefully informed about the significance of each act of reverence.

The kissing of the ring was the tribute required of the king's subjects. Foreign ministers merely bowed. Speaking of alliances and performing a gesture of submission would have been contradictory actions. The prince had avoided the dilemma. There was no given score for such an act of brilliance, but it didn't matter. The whole of London would be talking about it.

Pursuing fantasies of glory, Warwick missed the queen's question.

The prince replied that his Indian name meant "Bind Two Sticks," or "Place Two Bets."

At the word "bets," Warwick's eyes glided to King George. His Majesty had a weakness for the horses. His regal lips trembled slightly. Warwick preferred not to look.

"What would be your double bet, Chief Brant?"

Warwick kept his eyelids half closed.

"I'm betting on the Six Nations, Your Majesty, and on the Crown of England."

From behind his eyelids, the count saw the king opening up into a smile that was the smile of millions of Englishmen. The British Empire was smiling at Prince Thayendanegea.

Five and a half more points, seven in all. It was almost done. Another smile from the king, a compliment from the queen. Nothing impossible, but it would be counted a good achievement for the boy, whose turn it was to speak. Warwick prayed that he was a match for his uncle.

"Peter Warren Johnson, the natural son of the late Sir William Johnson of Johnson Hall."

The boy took a step forward, quite confidently. He performed his bows and kisses, not forgetting His Majesty's ring. With a slow and deliberate gesture he unsheathed a sword and laid it at he feet of King George. The sword was Ethan Allen's. The boy explained that the head of the rebels had handed it to him in person, and now he was giving it to His Majesty, as a tangible and auspicious sign of glory for the alliance, etcetera, etcetera.

There was a buzz from the snotty boys, and then the oldest of them approached his mother and whispered something in her ear. The queen cleared her throat.

"Prince George Augustus would like to know how the capture of this famous bandit came about."

Warwick was excited: a question from the mouth of the queen. A point and a half. Paradise!

The boy delivered a winning account. Neither too long nor too succinct. King George nodded smugly. Once the story was over, he went on rocking his head back and forth, as if rocking a thought to sleep. Then he stopped, and parted his lips for the second time.

He congratulated the boy, praised his courage, and for a few minutes lost himself in a monologue about that precious virtue. Warwick had trouble following his reasoning. The king spoke in a strange sing-song voice that always made him seem emotional, as if he were about to burst into tears. He made ungrammatical pauses between one word and another, leaving his sentences hanging between conjunctions. The common people said it was a way of masking a stammer, but the better informed maintained that there was something behind it. The king had nervous problems, he was hypersensitive, he *really* had to hold back his sobs.

Tearful or no, the long digression ended in a question.

"Tell me, Mr. Johnson, what feature is it that leads you to consider the alliance between the Crown of England and the Six Iroquois Nations so solid and invincible?"

The boy was a revelation. As soon as possible he must find a way to reward him. Warwick had lost precise count of the points, at least ten. An audience like that would place him among His Majesty's favorites, surpassing the results of big shots like Carmarthen and Windelmere.

"I don't know what to reply, Your Majesty," the little star began. "No fish, in fact, could tell you why the sea is superior to dry land. It is his world and he can neither translate nor explain it. Thus for me is the alliance between England and the Six Nations. I am a subject of Your Majesty, as was my father, and I am a Mohawk of the Wolf clan, the clan of my mother and my uncle Joseph Brant."

King George smiled frankly, then got to his feet, a gesture never seen before. He picked up Ethan Allen's sword and handed it back to Peter Johnson.

"I don't wish to do you wrong, Mr. Johnson, by returning a gift to you, but we would like you to keep the sword that you have conquered. Promise only that you will bring it back to us when you wear a general's stripes on your chest."

Now it was Warwick who held back his tears. He must have a fever, for His Majesty's words reached him as if from another planet. He followed the rest of the ceremony as though under hypnosis: the bows, the greetings, the thanks. He said his own good-byes with the bowing and scraping of a mechanical doll and slipped out of the door behind the others.

The world of royal audiences would never be the same.

17.

The towers rose massively from the moat surrounding the walls. The central building, closed off by fortified gateways, stood out against the leaden sky. Strength and elegance combined. Quebec Castle wasn't much in comparison. He'd never seen anything like this except in illustrated books. Peter soaked up every detail with his eyes, he wanted to imprint it in his mind, to reconstruct that majestic building stone by stone when he was far away, to describe all its angles to himself, to see it again any time he wanted to.

The Tower of London, where the enemies of the king, the traitors and conspirators, were imprisoned. Perhaps Ethan Allen himself was locked up in the castle dungeons.

Father, if you could only see me, Peter thought. First in His Majesty's presence. Now in a place I knew from the tales you told me when I was a child, the dwelling place of knights and sovereigns.

He thought too of his mother, how proud of him she would be, knowing he was here in the carriage of an English aristocrat escorting him to see the Tower.

The carriage ran along the perimeter of the fortress and Lord Warwick pointed out the details of the building to Peter. They reached the square beside it and admired the ensemble of red uniforms and standards. Peter had been the one who had expressed the desire to see the guardsmen on parade, and Warwick had happily agreed. It was a reward for his extraordinary performance in the presence of the king.

The perfect geometry of the lineup, not a step taken out of place. The soldiers marched as if they were a single entity—a concrete reminder of the order that sustained the Empire. Peter smiled, thinking of the jumble of ragged men he had confronted in the Canadian forests. Compared to this wonderful solidity, the American Goliath seemed a dwarf. He observed the maneuvers from the carriage window and thought that those soldiers in their scarlet uniforms would not have let the rebels get away. All King George needed to do was send them across the ocean, and the rebellion would be over much sooner.

As the detachments made their way back to barracks, the earl pointed out Tower Hill, the place where executions were performed. "Ax-man's corner," he called it, sniggering to himself, but his face suddenly darkened and he added a bitter remark about the fact that anyone at all could find themselves putting their heads on the block, even the king and queen. He touched wood emphatically and began to speak in a smooth tone, listing the names of famous people who had received the executioner's services at that place. Peter couldn't remember any of them, but a vision of heads rolling between his feet made him shiver.

The carriage slowed to a stop and they both got out to walk along the river in front of the fortress. The wind flapped the earl's neckerchief. Warwick arranged it under the lapel of his jacket and Peter thought that the resulting swelling of his chest made him look like a strutting cockerel. Even his gait was a bird's: the count set his feet down carefully, studying the ground. He realized that the boy was looking at him and smiled, elegantly separating his syllables: "A horror of dung." He asked his young friend's forgiveness. He said that excrement was his obsession: stepping in something undesirable would make him first nervous, then sad.

From close by, the walls and towers were even more imposing. Banners flew on the pinnacles. A gentle touch from the earl brought Peter's glance back to earth.

Not far off, behind a crowd of onlookers and a row of bars, a large animal lay sleeping.

The royal menagerie included various beasts, but the lion of the Tower was the most famous. The earl said this as he opened a passage for himself and the boy with light taps of his stick.

It was only a huge cat, thought Peter. Moth-eaten tufts, stirred by the wind, stood out on its head. Its tongue hung from slightly opened jaws. Its stench was revolting. Had it not been for the slight movement of its tail, Peter would have thought it was dead.

Warwick rotated the stick, tracing a circle in the air to indicate the animal's dangling genitals. "Notice, please, the testicular diameter," he said. He shook his head. "What a waste, don't you think?"

Peter remarked that the creature didn't look terribly fierce.

The earl said that it had lived for so long in the Tower that it had forgotten its predatory instincts. He assumed a sad and embittered tone. "Here you have the emblem of England, the lion that roars from the coats of arms and the banners of the kingdom."

As if it had heard him, the animal raised its head and showed its jaws in a bestial yawn. People started backward with terrified shrieks. Peter too stepped back. Not so the earl, who instead leaned toward the bars, emitting an indolent answering cry not unlike a roar. The feline did not deign to notice. The earl, leaning on his walking stick, his head tilted on his shoulder, went on contemplating it.

Peter asked under his breath what he was looking at.

"A creature bored of living," Warwick replied gloomily. He blew his nose loudly, then invited the boy to follow him away from there, being careful where he set his feet.

They walked for some distance without exchanging a word. Then the earl checked his watch and with a sudden change of mood said that they had an appointment.

He couldn't stop looking at her. She was perfect. More perfect than the parade, more perfect than the castle. And yet she must have come from there, from the house of fairies and princesses. There must be a room, in the highest tower, where they guarded this enchanting creature. She was young. She smiled slightly, giving him a little stitch in his stomach. He stared at her, aware of his own rudeness. Eyes, mouth, curls, pale neck. Perfume. An essence that Peter couldn't recognize. That smell did not exist in America.

The earl was cheerful, speaking without haste and without pauses, a flow of words cradling Peter's astonishment at the creature sitting with them in the carriage.

"It's easy to talk of heroes, my boy. And what, in the end, is heroism? The rays of a fine star that light up our personal virtue." The earl took a pinch of snuff, accompanying it with a sip of spirits from his flask. "There are heroes in every war and there are also heroes on every street corner, lucky or despised by fate, rich and happy or married to a bottle of gin. But a man, ah, a man. Find me one in this Gomorrah of seduction and robbery, of pederasty and decadence, gnawed by rats like the carcass of some old beast. A man is a rare thing these days; you have to look for him with a lantern, like that man Diogenes."

Peter struggled to follow his argument, lost as he was in the girl's eyes. The earl didn't care; he was listening to his own words, absorbed in himself.

"You, my boy, come from a young, strong world. Red blood flows in your veins, not that bluish mixture that clogs our own. I have the honor—no, no, don't shy away. . . I have the honor of having been your mentor and guide on this festive day. Ah, the new man, who has not understood his own manly virtue. Warrior, soldier of the king, at once lusty and chaste. What your perfection still lacks allow me to add as a gift, or, if you prefer, a souvenir of myself. A personal touch, because where there is one for the Earl of Warwick, all the more reason there should be one for a truly noble man."

Peter didn't understand. He saw the earl knocking with his stick on the carriage roof. The coachman stopped the horses.

"This is my stop," announced Lord Warwick. He kissed the girl's hand, leaving her with his guest, bowed to Peter and with one sinuous movement stepped out onto the footboard. Before he got out, he scanned the ground beneath him.

Before Peter had time to realize what was going on, the carriage had already set off. He found himself alone and silent, in the cabin, with the girl. He felt he should say something, but his mind was empty and he couldn't take his eyes away from hers.

Then the fairy touched his hand and delicately brought it to her lap.

18.

The picked carcasses of a pheasant and ten partridges lay on a silver tray, in the middle of the round table. There was something sinister about the leftovers as a whole: the orderly arrangement of the bones on the plate suggested lucid brutality. The head of the biggest bird looked toward the southeast, as if regretting a truncated migration to a better fate. The other skeletons inertly awaited inhumation between the jaws of the cats to the rear of the club.

The waiter lifted the tray and removed the macabre remains of the dinner from the sight of the guests. Then he returned from the kitchens with a bottle of port, which the guests refused to have served to them, dismissing the man with an impatient gesture. They began filling the goblets on their own, giving themselves generous helpings.

"You were saying, Mr Whitebread," said the gentleman seated to the north, "that the prince of the savages refused to kiss His Majesty's ring."

A young-looking man in a black wig cleared his throat.

"It would be more precise to say, sir, that he did not do so. He merely kissed the queen's hand."

"And your pen will immortalize the moment in tomorrow's *Courant*, I imagine," the other man shot back.

"Not so much for posterity," broke in the man seated to the west, "as to feed London's gossips."

They all laughed, including Whitebread, who had to force himself to join in. He was never entirely at ease among the big shots of the City.

"Tell us about the speech," urged the man to the east.

"Is it true that he threatened the king?" asked the gentleman in the southwest.

Whitebread shook his head.

"Not really. He said that loyalty must be reciprocal among allies." He glanced at the other faces around the table, trying to catch their reactions. "And that the Indian tribes will fight alongside England only if the king guarantees respect for their borders."

The northern gentleman filled his glass again and passed the bottle.

"And what do you have to say about the brawls, Mr Whitebread?" His tone was insinuating. "We have the impression that since these Mohawks have been in the city, the climate has become easily heated, and the scum is rising from the depths."

The journalist nodded.

"A truly singular episode. It would seem that among the crowd there were agitators dressed as Indians." He paused, unsure whether to go on, but all eyes were upon him and he couldn't retreat. "A letter has reached the office of our newspaper. The sender maintains that he handed an identical one to the Indian emissaries on the day of the audience. He signed ours 'Emperor of the Mohocks of London.' "

Again everyone sniggered. Except the gentleman to the north, the one who seemed to enjoy the greatest esteem among the others.

"Mohocks of London? City Indians?" the eastern gentleman exploded in disbelief.

"Ridiculous," muttered North.

"Shameless," added West.

"Wretched," put in Southeast.

"Sordid," concluded Southwest. Then, replacing in his pocket a little silver stick, with which he had been cleaning his molars, he added: "Small wonder that the savages are showing solidarity toward one another. The stench of Soho and the forest scalpers, I mean. What distinguishes them, in the end?"

"Their dialect," the gentleman to the north observed distractedly, and took a pinch of snuff.

They laughed.

Whitebread raised his voice a notch to be sure of being heard.

"In the letter, the Indians of London ask to be recognized as the seventh Iroquois Nation."

A sudden noise stopped the laughter in their throats. The gentleman to the north had broken the stem of his glass with the pressure of his fingers.

Everyone turned around apprehensively, while North stared absently at the little cut on his thumb. He let a drop of blood trickle to the base of his finger, as if betting with himself on how long it would take. "You are right to sell, Mr. Cavendish. Dregs are dregs, whether they assemble in the stinking taverns of the East End, on the quays of Boston, or in the forests of Canada." He showed his open palm, where the drop had settled, making a little red stain. "And when the dregs come together, the Empire bleeds. You remember that man Spartacus," he added and stared at Whitebread, who was struck by a sensation of unease and harshness, as if his chair had turned to marble.

The eyes of Mr. North had turned to slits, barely letting out a blue gleam. The other gentlemen hung on his words, waited to catch his thoughts, perhaps even anticipate them.

"Given that they are unaware of this at court," he said, turning back toward the journalist, "perhaps someone could point it out to the public. Maybe our own Panifex."

"Certainly, Mr. Whitebread," East broke in. "You yourself should publish the letter from this Emperor of the city Indians. That way the people would understand the gravity of what is happening."

"Are you joking, Mr Pole?" exploded Whitebread, more and more uncomfortable in his seat. "Give space in our newspaper to the ravings of a lunatic?"

"Tell me, Mr. Whitebread, who is more of a lunatic?" Again it was North who spoke, his calm voice sounding sinister, even menacing to the journalist's ears. "The man who claims an Indian nation in the heart of London, or the man who is willing to gamble the Empire just to deny freedom of trade to the colonies?"

They were all silent again, turned toward North. That gentleman wiped his wounded hand on the tablecloth.

"The government invites these Indians," he went on, "and here they are, the darlings of the crowd and the street gangs, who are now demanding recognition for themselves. We even have a self-styled emperor raising his crest to challenge the legitimate authority of the Crown, as happens in America. Perhaps he, too, wants to be given the red-carpet treatment at St. James's. Or a seat in Parliament."

The men around the table laughed smugly.

"Bad choices have to be paid for," North insisted. "With political ruin by those in charge. In thousands of pounds by those like ourselves, gentlemen, who produce the wealth of nations."

"Well said."

"Wise words."

Whitebread could not meet the eyes of North, but in reality the stuffed buzzard's stare was fixed on the agitated men seated behind him. The journalist turned to follow the line of the pointed beak, saw the eager gaze of glassy eyes.

"Brawls, fights, a few local gang leaders who know how to read and write," North said with apparent nonchalance. "That's how it started in Massachusetts."

"Yes, Mr. Whitebread, write this in the *Courant*," broke in Southwest, unable to restrain his enthusiasm. "Write that these damned Indians are bringing nothing but trouble to the city of London. And if we aren't careful, we'll find the rebellion in the colonies happening on our doorstep."

As everyone nodded, "Panifex," real name Richard Whitebread, managed a polite smile, without finding anything to reply.

19.

From the *Daily Courant* of 2 March 1776:

ON THE DISORDERS THAT OCCURRED IN PALL MALL, THE WORK OF THE NOTORIOUS LONDON INDIANS

On the 29th of last month, at ten o'clock in the morning, Their Majesties King George III and Queen Charlotte received in St. James's Palace Colonel Guy Johnson, of the Indian Department of the American Colonies; the chief of the Mohawk Nation, Prince Joseph Brant Thayendanegea; and Brant's personal secretary, Mr. Philippe Lacroix.

The entrance at court of the American delegation was followed by a great crowd of Londoners, with the consequences that are usually apparent when too many people assemble in a single place: thefts, broken bones, injuries, and outrages. To this should be added the confusion generated by a gang of mountebanks dressed as Indians who were unwilling to abandon the insalubrious project of approaching the prince of the Mohawks even when confronted by the Household Guard. Two of these men, taken into custody, are now resident at Newgate, waiting for judges and witnesses to resolve two important questions. The first, whether these fake Indians are the same ones who the other night removed the scalp of a certain James HOTBURN, known as Dread Jack, at *One-Eye's Tavern* on Tottenham Court Road, and indeed the same who some days previously attacked the carriage of a gentleman in Mayfair, as described by the victim in person in a letter to our newspaper. The second, what was the motive for such obstinacy in attempting to reach the Mohawk princes; was it was an act of madness or a deliberate design? Upon the answers to these questions will depend the fate of the two malfaisants, *id est*, the asylum of St. Mary of Bethlehem or, as we would wish, the gallows at Tyburn.

Permit us to skip over the details of the reception at court, details which even the stones now know by memory, and to reveal that, apart from those directly involved, we alone, in the whole of London, have an answer to both questions. This answer is the letter that we reproduce below, the same that the Indians of London are thought to have handed to Prince Thayendanegea. A stranger delivered a copy of it to our newspaper office a few hours after the fateful encounter.

We have asked ourselves for a long time about the advisability of attributing these pages to the ramblings of a madman, and humoring his perversion by printing them. We replied to ourselves that beneath their guise of insanity, these lines conceal a lucid design, and although disseminating them may well play into the hands of whoever delivered them to us, keeping them hidden would be more serious still, because it would deprive our fellow citizens of the only resource they have in the face of such outrages: awareness and vigilance, knowing the day and the hour of the thief's next visit.

To the Prince of the Mohocks
His Highness Joseph Brandt Teyandegea

Brother

We write this letter in the awareness that the Colonial Office—and their beloved Guards—will not easily permit us to speak with you in a frank and calm encounter, preferring to bore you with pointless Receptions, Theatrical Spectacles, and Sword Fights.

Your Visit to the Cities of London and Westminster is for us grounds for inexpressible Pride and great Hopes. Pride, for the honors paid by the Capital of Empire to a Prince of Indian blood; Hope, for the opportunity that God has granted the Mohocks of the colonies and those of the Old World an opportunity to embrace one another and give birth to a single powerful nation.

For the sake of clarity let us say straightaway that we Mohocks of London—with the exception of him who writes to You—have not a drop of Indian blood in our veins, but we feel similar to you in every way. The so-called honest men, in fact, see us as savages and like to attribute to us the most cruel misdeeds, before remembering us when they need cannon-fodder for their armies. For a while we too were a proud and courageous people, dedicated to hunting and agriculture, desirous to live in peace, but the honest men stole our land, and with it forests, trees, animals and waters, forcing our grandfathers to live in unhealthy districts and become servants, soldiers, beggars or thieves. A fate that the English in America would also like to reserve for your people, as we should like to point out. The Mohocks of London, weighed down for centuries by deprivation and abuse, never had the opportunity to establish a pact with a sovereign. But they do have one advantage over their American brothers, which is that they live in the heart of Empire, a few streets away from the house of His Majesty, and that they can raise a loud voice of their own. Imagine the Indians of the Colonies and those of the Motherland joining forces to form a single great nation. The Mohocks of London would then be received as ambassadors by the king, an honor that would never be granted otherwise; conversely, the American Mohocks would have someone to introduce them in the Capital of Empire without having to cross the Ocean and return.

That is why we consider this union to be of great advantage to everyone, and we make a formal request, brother, to become part of your Confederation, as the Seventh Iroquois Nation. If a pact of this kind should prove impossible, we are even willing to perform an act of submission to your authority, asking the Six Nations to regard us as subjects, or to adopt us in the Indian manner, or *in extremis* to take us prisoner. All just to be Mohocks, as is our due.

So if you wish to do us the honor of accepting our invitation, we ask you, brother, to add these conditions to the pact of alliance that you make with His Majesty:

First, that the Indians of London and Westminster shall not serve in His Majesty's Army, but only obey the supreme chief of the Six Nations, Joseph Brandt Teyandegea, and the Emperor Taw Waw Eben Zan Kaladar II.

Second, that the Indian lands of the cities of London and Westminster, including the Borough of Southwark, shall be considered the Eastern Gate of the Longhouse, subject to the exclusive authority of the aforenamed Joseph Brandt Teyandegea and the Emperor of the London Mohocks. His Majesty's guards, soldiers, and militias shall have access to these lands only with formal authorization.

Third and last, that outside the aforenamed lands the Indians of London and Westminster shall be granted hunting rights, from sunset to sunrise, on the left bank of the Thames, in the reserves between Hyde Park and Tower Hill.

Trusting in your devotion to the common cause of the Indians of the Colonies and the Motherland, we are, BROTHER,

Your subjects and humble servants.

Taw Waw Eben Kaladar II
Emperor of the Mohocks of London and Westminster

We do not think there is much to add about the identity of the authors of this letter. They are clearly the notorious Mohocks of Soho, already rechristened as SOHOCKS by the people of London. The title of Emperor, in fact, besides being entirely incongruous to an Indian nation, is the same that appears in the statement of the Mayfair gentleman and of the keeper of *One-Eye's Tavern*. For that reason alone the two men arrested the other day should remain in the *Royal Inn* of Newgate, waiting for their just sentence. In addition, a letter written by these people in itself constitutes a serious crime, because, by the rhetorical device of analogy, drawn between the Indians of America and the Lower Classes of England, they are clearly inciting a vast number of subjects to join in their rebellion.

We are sure that Prince Thayendanegea is disinclined to view with sympathy the ravings of these *Sohocks*, but we cannot help noting that his presence has unleashed in the worst dregs of the city a dangerous desire for revenge.

The Six Nations are certainly a precious ally of His Majesty. Their military bravery is beyond dispute: one need only read the accounts of those Frenchmen who had the misfortune of fighting *les Iroquois*. Nonetheless, receiving them at court with great pomp, presenting them as the pointer of a most delicate set of scales, and dedicating to them Spectacles and Festivities means that many others will imagine they deserve similar attention. "What?" a butcher's boy suddenly thinks to himself. "Perhaps King George considers the savages more important than his own subjects? Perhaps my rifle cannot serve the cause of England better than the arrows of the primitives? And why am I not received at St. James's Palace, where I would never venture to humiliate His Majesty by denying him his proper reverence?" These are the words that we may hear in the streets of St. Giles and Whitechapel, in Soho and in the Garden. However distorted and unreasonable they might be, they place us on our guard. Might it not be the case that in order to thank an ally, important as he may be, the ministries of the Crown risk spoiling the alliance between the king and his people?

This is a risk that should be assessed with the greatest care.

PANIFEX

20.

Joseph swiftly held out the newspaper, as if he feared being spied by someone.

"Look at this."

Philip observed his companion. He looked alarmed. He took the paper and began to read. Joseph gazed over the parapet. The dome of St. Paul's rose over the roofs of the City. It was the biggest building he had ever seen. His eyes kept straying toward it, and its solemnity was confirmed for him each time he glanced in its direction.

The little boat went up the Thames amid traffic not unlike the traffic in the streets. Joseph and Philip had accepted the advice of a waiter in the Swan, who told them it was the only peaceful way to tour London. It hadn't been hard to work out that the owner and pilot of the boat was a relative of the waiter's, but in spite of the reek that rose from the river, the water tour had proved a good venture.

The water splashed over the sides of the craft. Distant echoes came from the banks.

Finally Philip broke the silence. "These people think you're a king."

"The same thing happened to Hendrick."

Philip waved his hand. "It isn't just that. There are people here who would like to submit to you, to the Six Nations."

"They're just madmen."

"You know what our people think: often the Master of Life speaks through the voice of the mad. What we have seen of this city is what they have shown us."

The words rang out in the air. Philip returned his attention to the *Daily Courant*. Gulls settled on the boat, uttering long squawks.

Philip watched the river flowing placidly and the boats moored to the jetties rocking in the current.

Joseph felt the weariness of the past few days. It had been a series of receptions, visits, interviews. His voice was rough when he spoke again.

"I accepted this role to open a door to the king. I have won his respect, his commitment to defending us. The rest is of no importance."

Philip began stuffing his pipe in silence.

"When we get back it will be time to choose," Joseph went on. "The Longhouse will have to decide which flag to fly. Someone will have to convince the warriors. Could Little Abraham do it? Shononses? Some other sachem?"

"No," replied Philip.

"I am Joseph Brant Thayendanegea of the Wolf clan, a relative of Sir William Johnson, interpreter to the Indian Department, friend of the king of England and darling of the people of London. Is there anyone in the Longhouse who can boast a more valid title to speak?" He shook his head.

He waited for Philip's reply, which didn't come.

The boat slipped slowly along in the afternoon light. The rays of the sun struck the water, blinding anyone who looked westward.

21.

The scrape of rimmed wheels on cobblestones and granite slabs, the din of axles jolting over holes and drains. Horseshoes on paving stones. Shouts of coachmen, cries of vendors, wails of children. Out-of-tune violins, drunken songs. Litanies of beggars, endless strings of lamentation, the shaking of boxes and tins, the rattle of dice and change. The air here was an insult to the nose, carrying sounds that were an assault on the ears, and the eyes were equally embattled. Bodies of wretched ugliness, dressed in rags, heads and bodies shaking from side to side, regularly as pendulums, a device more to keep themselves warm than to move others to pity. Chattering teeth, curses, a fight over a bottle. Emaciated huddles, alms given more out of fear than compassion. People wandered about like phantoms, seemingly at random. Distracted hands threw scraps of food from windows. Musical mendicants, grouped in pathetic little bands, strummed and wailed, attempted to dance. The luckiest among them defended meager dominions, as if some authority had granted them a street corner, a personal piece of pavement. Whatever the condition fate had assigned to them, the men and women here were all the same ashen color, as if the milky sky that hung over their heads had also taken possession of their flesh. All of them, beggars and coachmen, servants and masters, seemed to be absorbed in an occupation of vital importance. And they were: they were all engaged in prolonging their lives—eating enough not to die of hunger, drinking enough not to think, wearing enough rags not to die of cold.

Philip walked along Drury Lane, northward to where the city ended. Every now and again phrases from the letter written by the chief of the London "Indians" came into his mind.

So-called honest men, in fact, see us as savages and like to attribute to us the most cruel misdeeds, before remembering us when they need cannon-fodder. . .

The road swarmed with all kinds of people. The capital's belly opened up and out they came, filthy and yelling. The air was full of coal dust, thick with the smell of human and animal feces. He had walked the first hundred yards with a white handkerchief over his nose; after a short time, though, he had abandoned this protective veil, to avoid being too conspicuous. The last thing he wanted was to attract attention: eyes were already lingering on a stranger who hid half his face, whose skin was copper-colored from the sun. And besides, walking without stepping in horseshit was already quite a task. No point making it more difficult.

For a while we too were a proud and courageous people. . . but the honest men stole our land, and with it forests, trees, animals and waters, forcing our grandfathers to live in unhealthy districts and become servants. . . a fate that the English in America would also like to reserve for your people. . .

To reach the end of the metropolis, then the countryside, the same countryside he had glimpsed in Vauxhall. To fill his lungs with good air, giving new courage to a body put to the test not only by the smoke and stench, but also by food and drink of London.

Drinking water meant absorbing the disgusting fluid that ran in the city's underground elmwood tubes, exposed to all kinds of filth, maybe even the muck that rose from the Thames, sewage, water contaminated by all the foulness of London and Westminster. Apart from human waste, diluted in that water were the acids, minerals and poisons from shops and factories. Not to mention the corpses of animals and men, or the discharges from bathtubs, kitchens and urinals. Philip, who hated drunkenness, had had to resort to small beer, the least harmful of the liquids that quenched the thirst of Londoners. His body was beginning to swell and hurt.

He needed to breathe, spend a day on his own in the fields around London—set traps, perhaps, catch a bird, sleep under a tree.

Where the road crossed High Holborn, some little boys surrounded him. Taking their hats off and holding out their hands, in a dumb show of asking for alms. One of them drew out a little dagger, as it to persuade the stranger not to be stingy with his gifts to the poor. Philip showed them the big hunting knife that he kept hidden under his jacket. Cursing, the pack of little boys scattered. The one who seemed to be the chief, a snot-nosed boy with tousled red hair, gave him a look of loathing. The look of a mean animal.

Watching the little boys swarm along Red Lyon Street, Philip saw in the face of the ringleader who he really was. His features presaged his doom, his eyes were without hope, his sole certainty was a pointless death, his life one of self-absorption, an inability to find comfort outside himself. Winter would not spare him.

Further off, a desperately poor family carried a wooden chest nailed haphazardly together. The man, of indefinable age, was crying. The woman, skeletal and covered with a blackish shawl, wore a stunned expression. Supporting the burden, they advanced on uncertain footsteps. Behind them came a flock of half-naked children. A maimed dog tottered after them on three feet. As they passed, some pious souls raised their hats; others kicked the dog.

It was a funeral procession.

Philip hoped he would reach the countryside soon. The journey there was proving to be unbearable. A weight oppressed his chest: compassion and disgust. He had both heard and read over the years that this city had never ceased to accumulate, the urban deposit of Empire.

A fate that the English in America would also like to reserve for your people. . .

As he watched the progress of the sad procession, Philip had a vision: A London as big as the world. A single vast excrescence, made of low buildings and soaring towers, hovels, scenic boulevards, fountains and gardens, mazes of alleyways that the sun never reached. A man-made world, in perpetual motion, paved, cobbled, propped up; a world in continuous construction, stratified, violent, rotting; a world of artificial light and a great deal of darkness, salvation for the few and damnation for the majority: the noble cities of London and Westminster.

He pissed his last pint against a brick wall and resumed his walk until the landscape of the suburbs made way for countryside.

Philip reached the top of a hill and looked behind him. The first houses of London were now half a mile away. A leaden cloak weighed upon the city. The man looked around. There was a vague smell of spring in the air.

He decided the moment had come to set off for the fields.

"No, not here. There's someone down there, under that tree."

The man had just set down a little wooden box and was running a filthy handkerchief over his forehead.

"What do you think he cares, woman? Here is fine. Look at the children, they're tired. They haven't eaten since yesterday morning. And neither have I, for that matter."

The human puppies were sitting on the edge of the ditch, exhausted and shivering. Worn-out rags, tousled hair, huddling together to keep warm, a clump of thin flesh and bones. The woman was a portrait of miserable resignation. The man was a sad scarecrow. Patches of grayish skin appeared through erratically stitched patches of clothing, but he couldn't do without an absurd and antiquated wig.

"You and your obsession with formalities," he went on. "'We all have to say goodbye to Billy together.' Certainly, Madame. But I say it would have been better to leave the kids at home begging, so that at least tonight we could fill our bellies. Look at them, poor little bastards. They've had enough."

The woman burst into tears. "Let me see him for the last time."

The man assumed a penitent expression. He removed his tricorn from his head and opened the box. A dry, glassy little body, half-covered by a patched blouse and nothing else. Impossible to give it an age. It might have been four, five, six or seven, depending on how much food it had managed to consume before it collapsed.

As the woman wept and the children wailed, the last member of the family procession reached the burial-ground, tottering on three feet.

"I don't know what's keeping me from roasting you," said the man, delivering a kick to the dog. The creature whimpered without conviction. The man took a little spade from the belt around his waist. The woman's weeping grew even louder.

"God, God, why did you take my Billy from me?"

"All right, let's try and get a move on," the man cut in. "I want to take the bastards over the Thames at low tide, to see if they can find something worth selling. Or as God is my judge, I'll end up selling *them*."

The woman went on crying. The man had dug half a hole and already he had run out of strength. One of the children pulled on his sleeve. Someone was coming.

The stranger raised his right hand in a gesture of peace. By way of reply, the man brandished the spade, his eyes wild.

"What do you want from us? We don't have anything!" he roared.

"I'd like to finish the work that you have started, sir."

The newcomer pointed to the grave.

An imperceptible movement, a disturbance of the air: the spade changed hands. The woman brought her right palm to her mouth and emitted a little cry.

"I only want to help," said the newcomer.

The man, exhausted, collapsed onto his bottom. The woman started crying again. The stranger finished burying the box. Then he stood up again by the little grave.

"Look, husband. He's praying. . ." said the woman.

The man gulped. "Yes, wife. Papist prayers. I say, do you want our son to go to Hell?"

He was about to get up, but his wife held him back.

"Leave it." Her red, puffy eyes were filled with pain and resignation. "Do you think it makes any difference to Billy?"

The man bent his head as the sun grew still paler.

22

A gray light filtered through the curtains. The room was quiet and dark. Nancy delicately shut the door behind her: she liked seeing the girls sleeping. The little bodies were divided across two beds, the oldest one on her own. Under the blankets one could sense the rhythm of their breathing.

Nancy smiled. She crossed the room to the window and pulled the curtains aside.

The children moved. "Wake up! It's time to get washed and have your breakfast!"

The little ones began to sit up, yawning and rubbing their eyes. All but one.

"Esther! Wake up, you don't want to be the one to give a bad example!"

Then Nancy saw that the oldest girl's bed was empty.

"Where is Esther, girls?" Her voice betrayed her anxiety. The girls didn't reply. They merely looked sleepily at Nancy. "Esther! Where are you? Where have you got to?"

The woman came up beside the bed and lifted the blankets. The sheet was stained with a pool of blood.

He had slept in a sheep pen after asking the shepherd's permission. The man had been cordial, he had even invited him into his hut, but Philip had preferred to stay outside, under the stars, which were barely visible in that British night. The man had trusted him; even the sheep and the dogs had accepted the newcomer. He had traveled quite far and he would have to get up at first light if he was to keep his appointment.

His sleep had been agitated. Lines in Latin buzzed around his head: *pulvis es et in pulverem reverteris.* He had dreamed of getting up and leaving the sheep pen, following a familiar shadow. It was the ghost of his wife, smiling, she touched his hair like a soft breeze and led him into the middle of the field, where there were two boxes to bury, one of them very small. His heart was heavy in his chest, as if weighed down by a stone. *Your daughter*, the ghost had whispered. *Your daughter.* Philip had looked into the smaller box. In the bottom there was only an object: the button from a drummer's uniform tied to a lock of blond hair. He had tried to question the ghost, but its features had turned into the light of the moon. An oval face with its skin still smooth, and a long black plait, with a few white threads very visible. Philip had recognized her, half woman and half girl. Molly had looked at him severely, then pointed to the moon, red like the setting sun. *The moon is bleeding. An animal has been injured.*

He had suddenly opened his eyelids, as if until that moment he had been pretending to sleep. A glimmer in the east announced the dawn.

Now he was walking briskly back toward the city. The others were waiting for him at the Johnsons' inn, to attend the audience with Lord Germain.

Philip didn't want to go. Sleep occluded his thoughts.

This leaf is yellow and was painted by Grandpa Winter. This leaf is brown and was painted by Grandpa Winter. This leaf is red. . . No. No. No. What now? The moment had come. What moment? This leaf is yellow and was painted by Grandpa Winter. Blood, like Mama. No no no. Perhaps she should pray, certainly Nancy would have said, asked, ordered her to, but for some time Esther had been afraid of God. She was also afraid of admitting it, thinking it, feeling it. God. Fear. The blood between her legs. She wanted to touch herself. Fear. Was she going to die like Mama? No. She wasn't dying. Cold liquid flowed between her legs. She didn't want to pray. Mama's song of the colors. This leaf is yellow and was painted by Grandpa Winter, this leaf is red. . . The nursery rhyme said Mister Winter, but Esther liked Grandpa and after a while that was how Mama had sung it, too. Grandpa Winter was Sir William, even if she knew it wasn't true, but it was him. Grandpa. Mama. Where are you? Who will come and get me?

She wasn't dying. When she had woken up and noticed this disaster, she had thought she was, but not any more. Some things you can feel. Certain special things she could feel, like seeing ghosts, or horrible things to come. Grandpa William, for example, she saw him, every now and again. It was really him, but she hadn't mentioned it to anyone. He smiled at her, with a kind smile. Once he had gestured to her, and then told her to go on. Not her mother, though. Not yet, but she hoped she would come, too. The important thing was not to say anything, not to talk to anyone. Even about that awful thing. If not, she would understand that it was bad. Would someone come and get her? Aunt Nancy, her father? God? The Devil?

Her limbs were stiff with cold and exhaustion; it was day now. There was a yellow light, dirty with smoke, coming in through the windows of the shack where she had sought refuge. She was dirty. Her feet were numb and muddy. The blanket over her nightshirt wasn't warm enough. At any rate, she wasn't going to come out. They had to help her, but she wouldn't ask for help. Not from anyone. She wasn't dying. She was confused, dirty. She closed her eyes, drew in her shivering shoulders. She saw the house where she was born, beyond the sea. The big river, the valley, the woods. Then the outline of a woman, her face in shadow. She was waving to her before she left. There was Peter, too, he was in the doorway of Johnson Hall, dressed as a general, beckoning her in. He was saying, "Take your place."

The vision disappeared. Would she get back to the old house? When? What was her place?

Since the death of Grandpa William the world had begun trembling, more and more. The green of the Mohawk Valley meadows was turning blood red. Why?

Shivers ran down her spine again. Esther decided she would have to know more. About the blood. To test and defeat the terror. Not to be afraid of touching herself between her legs. Not to feel dirty. To find her place. To get home, to the green meadows.

As long as someone came to get her, because she certainly wouldn't be asking for help, and neither would she be going out alone.

He sensed the agitation in the house as soon as he crossed the threshold. In the middle of the big room stood the thin figure of Nancy Claus; she was shouting orders to the servants. Every so often she paused, brought a hand to her mouth and bit it, pressing her stomach with the other.

When she saw him she went toward him, but suddenly froze, and remained standing some distance away.

"Mr. Lacroix, they've been waiting for you for so long. They were wondering. . . my God, there isn't time, I can't explain."

The Indian came over, stinking of sheep and sweat.

"What's happened?"

"They all had to go to see Lord Germain, they waited for you for so long. . ." She bit the back of her hand again. She shouted at a servant to look again, to turn the inn upside down.

"What's happened?" Philip repeated.

Nancy gave a start, as if she had forgotten the Indian's presence for a moment. Philip noticed that she was still in her nightdress, covered only by a woolen shawl; curls fell untidily from under her bonnet.

"Esther," she said. "Vanished." She held back a sob. "Guy didn't want to go, it was Daniel who forced him to, that's why we came to London, for this audience, they couldn't. . ."

This time the bite left a mark on her hand.

Philip asked which room Guy Johnson's daughters slept in, dashed upstairs and reached the bloodstained bed. He sniffed. The stink of London had dulled his sense of smell, but he could still recognize moon-blood.

A cut that doesn't heal.

He came back downstairs and stopped on the last step. What does a wounded animal do? It finds a lair for itself. It hides.

He looked around. Nancy was saying something to him, but he paid her no attention. The nearest exit was not the main one, but a little back door.

Beyond the door was a courtyard, chickens and cackling geese. In the mud, little footprints led to a low shack at the far end, probably the woodshed.

Philip cautiously entered. The low ceiling forced him to bend down, the reek of sawdust made his breath come short. As soon as he was past the threshold, before his eyes grew accustomed to the darkness, he heard her voice.

"Keep away."

Philip crouched down in silence. The poisons of the bad air assaulted him again. He coughed, felt nausea and irritation. Dust you are and to dust you will return. He closed his eyes and restored his inner self to calm.

"Do you need help?" he asked into the gloom.

Silence again.

"I'm dirty."

The Great Devil spoke calmly. "So am I. This city is dirty."

"How did you work out I was here?" the voice asked suspiciously.

"I had a dream," the Indian replied. "In my daughter's grave there was a lock of hair, blond like yours. She would be your age today."

"She died as soon as she was born?" asked Esther, appearing from behind a tangle of dry branches.

Philip leaned against a pile of logs.

"She was very young."

"My mother's dead, too. And my brother. There was blood everywhere, all the blood in the world."

The Indian met her eyes in a gap between the pieces of wood.

"I've lost a lot of blood, too. Am I going to die?" asked Esther, rubbing her feet, red with cold and smeared with damp earth.

"One day, like everyone else," the Indian replied, getting slowly to his feet. "But not today. I'll go and tell your aunt to come and get you."

As soon as he turned around, the dry branches creaked.

"Why do they call you the Great Devil?"

Philip turned around.

"Because in war people like to frighten themselves. Then the war ends and the fear remains."

He was about to turn back, but she spoke again. It was as if she didn't want him to leave, as if she feared that once he left her, his sincerity would disappear with him.

"I dream about dead people too. Sometimes I dream about Grandpa William."

Philip smiled but said nothing. The girl had the gift, she was close to ghosts. He had noticed it the first time while he observed the ant-men from the mast of the *Adamant*. Now she was there in front of him, staring at him, as though waiting to solve a puzzle.

He did it without thinking. He slipped off his wampum bracelet and handed it to her.

"It'll protect you. From the living and the dead."

She took it and gripped it in her fist. Then she slipped her pale hand into the hunter's rough one. An old sensation returned to him, and he shivered.

Philip led the child out of the woodshed.

A flutter of impressions and fears filled the head of Guy Johnson as he made resolutely for the inn.

Guy Johnson, American, colonel, superintendent, subject of, successor of, son-in-law of, *father*.

A valet had handed him a message as he left the audience. Guy and Daniel still stood on the threshold, their faces still plastered with excruciating traces of the smiles that etiquette decreed. They lacked Joseph's *savoir-faire*, a confident, dreamy style, sleepwalking with power and pomp. In London, the Indian from Canajoharie had been reborn as a ceremonial beast, an exotic dog-show champion. No new life, on the other hand, for the German and the Irishman: just politics, a task to be performed with a weight crushing his chest, a result to be grabbed and brought home. A home filled with a whirlwind, a wind that swirled and splashed blood all around. *Bandoka*.

The note had been written by Nancy: they had found Esther. Philip Lacroix had found her. They had to thank the Great Devil for the second time.

She was well, but she was no longer a child. He had to remember that: the blood changes everything, there's a before and an after.

The icy blade that had been cutting his brain in two had melted, and the return journey was less painful. He actually managed to speak, to comment upon the audience, although some of his attention still flitted far away and back beyond the sea. Every now and again he gripped his lips between his teeth, the future was thick with smoke, decisions to take, requests and expectations. Who would go with him to confront it? What proof of himself would he give, and in front of which audience? He knew he had a part to play, and he didn't feel like an actor.

Frightened by her own blood, Esther had hidden in the woodshed.

She was no longer a child, and that was all the more reason for Guy to punish her. He had to punish her, show that he could be firm, in this circumstance *and in others*.

She had caused disorder and worry. She had violated a rule of obedience, she had run away. She had run away and had to be punished. He would have to do it, to set an example to the younger girls.

To set an example to everyone.

It was what was expected of him: punish those who run away for fear of their own blood. It went with his authority.

He knew he had a part to play, but he didn't feel like an actor. His prevailing feeling was relief that she was safe and sound.

He entered the room, where she was sitting on the bed, and she lifted her chin with what looked to him like sad indifference. He approached her with his back bent, as if about to wrap his arms around her. She didn't move. He called to her, and she shook her head as if to deny her own name. Her father raised his voice; she didn't reply. He bent down to look her in the eyes, lifted her chin with his hand. Again he called her by name. Shame, exhaustion, defiance, rancor, fear, filial love, distance. . . what was there in his daughter's eyes?

Guy held her tight. She moved her arms slightly and rested her hands on her father's hips, a reluctant hug suspended in midair.

They stayed that way without saying a word, in the room of an inn in the biggest city in the world.

23.

London, 19 March 1776

Honored Cousin John,

I am writing to you because I have learned of the provocation orchestrated against you and our family by the Albany rebels. News has reached the Colonial Office that the Indians of Fort Hunter have accompanied Gen. Schuyler to Johnson Hall to make sure that nothing happens to you, but you will be stripped of guns and powder. I think the contemptible behavior of the Indians may be explained only by offers of money, spirits or something else. I beg you to verify this hypothesis and above all to ascertain whether the rebels, contrary to what was thought, possess sufficient means to sustain a semblance of trade with the Indians. In that case, the Mohawks of Canajoharie must of course be rewarded for their loyalty with presents of at least double that value, so that the others see where the advantage/ their interest lies.

As regards the loyalty of the Indians, I would ask you to give me information about the activities of Butler in Niagara and the relations that the rebels maintain with the Seneca chiefs.

As for us, the goal that we established for this journey has now been reached. After two months of waiting, we have had the honor of being received by His Majesty and by the Secretary of State for the Colonies. The latter has proved so opposed to the conduct of Governor Carleton that he has sought to give Joseph Brant his official apologies for what has happened in Canada. The job of superintendent, in the end, was conferred upon me by the Secretary of State himself.

The future of Mr. Daniel Claus, however, remains uncertain. Therefore, it is necessary to remain in London for some time, the better to clarify the issue of his appointment. Meanwhile, Joseph Brant must meet for a second time with Lord Germain, to obtain orders regarding the territorial controversies that he has already presented to him. I shall not hide from you the fact that the presence of our Indians, more than that of the prisoners captured in Montreal, has been very useful to us. The people of London consider them on a par with princes and they have become such an attraction to the aristocracy that no one giving any sort of entertainment can avoid including them among the guests of honor.

I have nothing else to add, but remain, with esteem and respect,
Your affectionate cousin,

Col. Guy Johnson

After signing the letter, the superintendent blew on the ink, picked up the sheet and reread it from the beginning. It was a good letter. Yet he still felt a lump in the bottom of his throat. It had nothing to do with politics, diplomacy, the Indians. The fact was that he could not confess to anyone what it was that oppressed him the most.

Colonel Guy Johnson was frightened. The expedition to Johnson Hall was to all intents and purposes the first act of war in the Mohawk Valley. The new superintendent of Indian Affairs in the Northern Colonies would willingly remain in London until the following winter, and perhaps even beyond. Had it not been for all the wealth he had accumulated in the New World, he would have returned to Ireland, to his own people.

Where would he take his daughters? The exodus and the strains of the journey had already killed Mary and the baby, the heir he would have called William but who had died before he had a name. Esther and the little ones were the only family left to him. He couldn't allow the war to sweep them away too. He had to leave them in London, in safety. Find a good boarding school, go back to America on his own. See things in person, judge, judge what needed to be done. Quickly win back the lands of the Johnsons, rout the rebels, start living again.

Colonel Guy Johnson was frightened. He hated cannons. He didn't even like hunting. In London you could get away with it: no one claimed the Earl of Warwick was a good shot. In London you could be an aristocrat, a merchant, a judge, a minister. In America you were a warrior above all, like the Indians. In America you knew that sooner or later it would be your turn to fight, to risk your skin. In America, wealth, power, prestige all rested on the barrel of a gun.

Being frightened wasn't allowed.

"You have to agree, Doughty. Science cannot help but be objective."

"Objective in its ideals, but subject to circumstances, like all human affairs."

"In this case, it is a matter of opinion."

"And yet you remember the dispute between Wilson and Benjamin Franklin."

"Over the lightning rod?"

"Precisely. Which is more functional, a long and pointed lightning rod or one that is short and rounded?"

"I can't remember which of the two was right."

"Because the experiments didn't succeed in demonstrating it. Nonetheless the king decided to agree with Wilson, and now his theories are in the scientific manuals and his lightning rods are on our steeples."

"I don't see what you're getting at."

"Well, they will never be able to persuade me that that choice depended only on scientific arguments. Wilson was a Tory, Franklin a Whig. One from London, the other colonial. One was protected by Lord Whatshisface, the other was a commercial representative from Pennsylvania. Which do you think counted for more, scientific objectivity or the rebellion in New England? I bet you a guinea that in Pennsylvania they have pointed lightning rods the way we have rounded ones here."

Peter stopped listening in on the discussion between the two gentlemen, who went on debating undeterred. He observed the triangular room of the Royal Society with his nose pointing toward the ceiling, toward the wooden shelves, the rows of neatly lined books, packed tight as bricks, that seemed to support the walls.

Walking with his head tilted up he risked colliding with the other guests, who looked at him resentfully. He apologized and walked apart from them. The titles on the big shelves sounded bombastic and instilled a feeling of fear in him. The few people present at that hour of the day were holding discussions in groups of two or three, in lowered voices. They looked as if they must be resolving fundamental dilemmas, confronting them reverently, on tiptoe.

Lord Warwick, benefactor and member of the society by family tradition, had obtained membership for him as soon as he learned of his passion. For Peter science was an interest that dated back to Johnson Hall and his father's microscopes, which had always fascinated him.

"In London there's a place where scientists debate their theories and their experiments. The king protects them and ensures that everyone can enjoy the new discoveries and the inventions."

In his mind, the boy saw Sir William raising his face from the microscope and inviting his son to come over and look into it. A clear memory, from when he was a child. He felt the warm, heavy hand that had rested on his shoulder as he watched tiny creatures moving under the lens.

"Corpuscles, Peter," his father had said. "Microbes. Creatures so small that the human eye couldn't see them without the aid of this invention. Do you understand?"

Peter had nodded.

He had spent whole afternoons, as endless as they can only be at that age, in the Room of Science. The temple of the incredible, where every object could reveal a hidden side of nature. Mechanical models for perpetual motion, steam-driven spinning tops, the camera obscura that showed reality upside down. Again he thought of the microscope. How much room was there on a slide? How many things could there be on it? A whole world, a universe. It was no different from looking at the stars and imagining how many there were or how big the sky was.

"They move. They reproduce. They die," the voice behind him had said. "The aspiration of every scientist is to discover the secret of life."

Peter had raised his head and looked seriously at his father.

"Pastor Stuart says it's one of God's mysteries, and that wanting to know it is blasphemy."

Sir William had smiled.

"God has given us eyes, hands and an intellect. Do you think he would have done that if he had wanted to keep us in ignorance?"

Peter sat down on one of the stools in the conference room. He had always liked the strong smell of polished wood. The stench of Fleet Street did not reach the august halls of Crane Court. His chest swelled with emotion. Being there, in the place described by Sir William so long before, seemed a tribute to his memory and to the happy years spent in Johnson Hall, in the valley that had been his whole world, until they had sent him to study in Philadelphia.

That was why he had wanted to go there, leaping at the chance offered by Lord Warwick. Alone, accompanied only by the chairmen put at his disposal by the earl. Peter had walked, at the risk of muddying his shoes, and the two men had followed him with the empty sedan chair and puzzled expressions, stopping to wait for him outside the building.

"We aren't blaspheming when we try to know the laws that God has imposed upon the universe. Let us pay homage to his creative intelligence and celebrate his work. We don't claim to know the divine reason that has given rise to things, but we investigate their intrinsic mechanism. The long chain of causes and effects that make them the way they are. You understand?"

Peter remembered nodding again, desiring to please his father. The concept wasn't very clear to him, but the creatures doing battle under the lens piqued his curiosity and that was enough. But as he grew up he had come to understand that Sir William's faith transcended all denominations and at the same time ran through them all. In his valley there was room for everybody. The King of England and the Pope were far away, and the Master of Life worshipped by the Mohawks was not unworthy of being called God, even if he was addressed in savage and picturesque ways. Even as a child Peter had known that not all ceremonies in the forest were Indian. On the night of the Summer Solstice, in the depths of the forest, bonfires were lit and Gaelic was spoken, and masses were celebrated that the light of day would have forbidden. The Scottish refugees and his father's Irish settlers communicated in dialects as old as the rocks. The Language of the Night. Sir William used it when he wanted to tell Peter something intimate that others must not catch.

"It is the language of faith, of blood and war," he said. "They don't speak it by chance."

English, on the other hand, was used to command, to write and understand from one end of the valley to the other. In Philadelphia he had also been taught French, the language of the enemy.

But Mohawk was the language he preferred. Mohawk smelled of rum and furs. It was the language of trade and hunting, of councils and diplomacy. But above all, for him, it was the language of lullabies.

Molly's severe face appeared to him and he felt the grip of the strong little hands, so different from his father's. The Room of Science had never been her world, and yet she, too, was fascinated by it. She saw Sir William's instruments as interpreters, capable of giving an account of nature in the language of the white men. Molly was interested in the link between microbes and illnesses, in electricity as a form of treatment, in the practices of the English doctors. "It's a good medicine," she said, "but it cannot heal dreams." Dreams, amulets, ritual dances. Peter had learned to appreciate those too, as part of the life of the valley. His mother seemed to be the center of it, as important as the river or the meadows. It was as if everything down there gravitated around her. That wasn't just his childish perception: as he grew up, the idea had been reinforced, and even if he couldn't understand all of Molly's mysteries, he understood that her power thrust its roots through the night of time. The songs that had lulled him to sleep for years had been composed in the shade of the ancient pines and handed down since the beginning of the world.

Suddenly he realized that he was feeling nostalgic and sad. The news from home was not good. If the rebels had made it as far as Johnson Hall, they could reach Canajoharie in a day's march. Molly was in danger.

He said to himself, No, the people of the valley would protect her, and his mother was too cunning to be surprised. She might even have left, like Uncle Joseph's wife, taking her brothers and sisters to a safer place. The rebels couldn't take it out on women and children; it was John, his oldest half-brother, who was at risk. Peter shivered at the thought that the house where he had spent the first few years of his life might be sacked. The envious settlers had always aspired to empty it of all its furnishings, raid the cupboards and storerooms, the armory and the stables, and steal the slaves. They would also steal the microscope and the machines in the Room of Science, and there was nothing he could do to stop it. They were bound to think as Pastor Stuart did, or even worse. They would break his father's precious lenses, scatter the slides and test tubes, smash the camera obscura. Their god left no room for anything, he was small, mean and obtuse. The very image of his believers.

He got to his feet and contemplated the great Room of Science commanded by His Majesty George III.

It was time to go back. He had to fight those people, chase them back into the bog they had come from, prevent them at all costs from destroying what his father had built.

Now the capture of Ethan Allen seemed small beer.

He had to shoot straight. Defend his country.

25.

Being a doorkeeper wasn't as bad as all that, Lester thought. A lousy job like so many others, but the occasional tip made it better. Now, with the coal-heavers on strike for two weeks, the odd extra penny came in very useful. There was a difference between paying someone to bring the sweets home for you and having to go all the way to the dock with the wheelbarrow, all the way there, all the way back, and your spine cracked. A bit of a tip, that's right, even in the filthiest arsehole of the city, the Hospital of St. Mary of Bethlehem. Known to everyone as Bedlam, the Place of the Mad People.

Lester boasted of having invented it himself, the Bedlam tip, but it wasn't true, not a word. The patent was down to his old boss, a first-class fucker, who had shagged a laundress from St. Giles. Lester had taken the blame and Lord Garfield had had to fire him, as you to do servants who fuck each other. In return, the boss had found him this job, and so he'd gone from town-house doorman to madhouse doorman, which when you put it like that was a fuckover with bells on, but then the business with the tips had come out, because in London there were loads of madames and milords just dying to catch a gander of the loonies, hear them scream and especially see them naked. Among these weirdos, needless to say, was Lord Garfield himself, who in exchange for free entrance throughout his natural life would bring hordes of friends willing to shell out the pelf. A few months later, the lord had popped his clogs, so Lester had had to widen his circle, as you might say. Now he was picking up bookings, organizing visits on the quiet, and pocketing the tips as if he were a doorman at a theater.

An unexpected coach stopped outside the gate. Five of them got out and gestured him over. Lester threw his coat over his shoulders and set off down the avenue, which had been reduced to a path by the grass that besieged it. Four blackbirds and a little sparrow. They wore wigs and gilded buttons; she had a mountain of hair that stayed up by a miracle, and a tiny bonnet on top. If they were people of pelf, they certainly didn't splash out on sorting out their choppers. The half-smiles that greeted Lester would have scared off a flock of bats.

"We're here for the loonies," said the elegant man of the group, leaning knowingly on his stick.

"This is the place, sir."

"I am well aware of that, dear fellow. And I also know of a porter who organizes *scientific visits* to the hospital, is that not so?"

"I have heard as much. But I believe you have to arrange an entry time, you know? And be introduced by the old members of the Club."

"I understand," the man laughed scornfully, displaying his pegs as if they were pearls. "And tell me: do you think a guinea might be enough?"

A guinea? Christ.

"I really believe it might, sir. Please, this way."

A place of fear. What did the fine gentlemen get out of it, Neil wondered. Take a walk around the Abbey and you'll find as many as you want of these loony roughers. Take them one at a time you can have a good sneer at them, I wouldn't say no, one of them you just have to say a sparrow's name and zip, off come the breeches and he's tugging on it ready to slip it between your baps, but not altogether, no, in a great crowd they'd put the shits up you, no question, it's like a hell full of wandering souls, and if one of the grilles comes down, that'll wipe the sneer from your face.

Rob and Cole must have got a cramp keeping their buttocks tight, Neil thought. Or maybe not. Maybe there's respect between idiots, something like they can't hurt each other, something like that. Not that they're idiots, Rob and Cole, but the others, the idiots with the tufts, they don't even know, you just have to stay on the right side of the grille and they can't do anything more than spit on your shoulder or piss on your feet. Rather than staying on this side, let's say the whole thing comes down all of a sudden, you'd better get a move on, you bet, get Rob and Cole out of there and head for the hills.

What the fuck do they get out of it, these fine gentlemen from Nobshire. . .

Let's start the games, thought Dave, the Emperor. He'd been clocking the ruffers inside the cage at the end on the right-hand side.

"Gentlemen, milady, we find ourselves here today to repair an odious injustice."

A sudden motion and he had turned toward the thugs looking shitty and haughty. He was standing beside the host, who was clocking him with vexation. The Emperor, still for the moment in the garb of a jasper with no shortage of shekels, complete with wig and assorted furbelows, was launching into his number, with the thugs as ever clueless concerning the spicy details.

"Yes, my dears," he rested his right mawley on the doorman's shoulder, "a terrible, tragic injustice. Certainly my friends will be thinking about our two brothers, Rob and Cole, perhaps the best of us, lying imprisoned in this vale of terrible suffering. And who are we to say they are wrong?" He gripped the doorman's shoulders tightly. "Rob and Cole! Two honest patriots, judged as mad and locked up for daring to defend their own dignity and that of the people with whom they are on a par. Madmen, lunatics, loonies, crazies, maniacs, nutcases, bonkers, off their rockers, daft, demented, deranged, unhinged! That's what they are! What the stupid do not understand they call Folly. That is the truth. It is that truth that brings us here today." He bowed deeply to a baffled Take-a-Tip Lester. The thugs weren't getting much of it either. He paused like an actor. "Too easy, too convenient would it be for us to reclaim our dear friends and take them into our care. To reclaim those taken from us by force and trickery. Just and sacrosanct. But small beer. A greater task awaits us today."

At this point poor Lester grasped that it was time to intervene, that the hack was strange, and as he went on spouting and spouting, it would start making sense sooner or later. He was scared shitless—was the whole thing going to blow up in his face? The jasper wouldn't shut up. What the fuck was going on?

"Gentlemen, the laws and customs allow some men the right to assess the human mind. We are not here to question the value of your science or weep over your choices, decide whether they are correct or not. Instead, we are standing against the right of what they call honest men to choose for others incarceration for life in hospitals. Places that are nothing but terrifying prisons. This can no longer be tolerated. The Mad are the victims par excellence. They are men, these people here. Over these men, you must acknowledge, you have no advantage but force. It is to overturn this advantage that we are here. Dear boy, hand me the keys to the cages."

He pulled the knob on the end of the stick and drew out a blade, long and thin, which he put to Lester's neck, and opened up his gobhole, affecting surprise at the sight of his gold gnashers.

What a complete cuckoo, thought Betty, known as Glut, who was crammed into the finery of a woman of high estate. Even though she had seen and endured, God knows, so many whoremasters it would make you blush, even she couldn't help feeling a certain bafflement. There must have been some sense in all the bilge he was coming out with, because a madman like the Emperor had kept himself out of Bedlam, which must mean that the system wasn't working. But he was strong in his way. He had managed to get hold of the keys, all of them, and he had opened the gates to the cages, all of them. Then he had started shrieking like the savage he was. The thugs had come leaping out straightaway. Rob and Cole, filthy and twisted, hopped like quails down the corridor and toward the exit, because the great sacks of shit could already see themselves several leagues away. But Dave wasn't doing it on purpose; he was clutching the bars of the cage and yelling that they had to get out of there, the moment had come, justice had arrived. The guard wailed, asked for mercy, howled that this was dangerous. Surrounded by the thugs of the chief of the Indians of London, there wasn't much he could do but whine.

The loons looked scared. Some of them, half-naked, stepped outside the bars, but without conviction, and none of them dashed for the exit.

It was then that Betty worked out her role. She could hardly believe her peepers. That shaven-headed jasper was telling her to whip out her merchandise and get the show going. Yes, really, out with the ninnies and do those games she'd been so good at on the Tottenham Court Road. He was really crazy. Meanwhile, all the malchicks in the gang had turned to clock her, and with the frontages they had it wasn't easy to distinguish them from the rest. What dregs. Betty turned a grimace of disgust upon them all and then—what else was she to do?—started her number, because after all the stinking tosspots in the taverns of Soho were certainly no better. All she had to do was pretend she was at One-Eye's and just get on with it. Because what she did was hardly the Dance of the Seven Veils; it was just that when she got all filthy with her dugs all the sleazy jaspers got the horn. Fingering them, squeezing them, shaking them, bringing them to her mouth and running her tongue over them, all the usual.

The Emperor took center stage. The loons emerged from their cages, almost in orderly lines, as the London Mohock nodded to Betty to walk backward toward the exit. The Emperor had grabbed a torch, and as the long corridor filled up, he guided the herd like a shepherd. He sang his singsong louder, forced them to take their freedom, but Betty's huge mams were the secret of this exodus from Bethlehem,

But what a horrible business it was. It was scary being the bait for that gang of brainwrecks following her like puppies. Jesus, cocks of all shapes and sizes, standing proud from their owners, gripped in great mawleys, Jesus, the sight of it, unbelievable!

The gates of Bethlehem opened up on London.

26.

"If we guarantee freedom to the Negroes and America to the Indians, what are we left with, gentlemen?"

"Indeed. To whom will you sell your African slaves, if the Somerset ruling becomes law?"

"For my part, Mr. Pole, I could ask you where you will get the wood for your building sites in New York, if the inland forests remain in the hands of the redskins."

"*Touché*. But the root of both problems is the same; it is called America."

"Oh, no, Mr. Gilbert. America would be the solution. Myopia is the true villain: in trying to get a commercial monopoly, we will end up losing the whole market.

"Come on, don't be pessimistic, the spring counteroffensive is under way. His Majesty is sending troops to close the account with these rebels."

"I have heard that. German mercenaries, it would appear. That's what started the decline of the Roman Empire."

"Good God, how gloomy you are."

"Not gloomy enough, Cavendish. I expect the worst. But, as they say, a businessman has to be farsighted. We must allow the storm to pass. Then our moment will come."

"Difficult words for this hour of the afternoon. I suggest, gentlemen, that we move on to other topics. Is it true that our Corsica Boswell has sequestered himself in private with the prince of the Indians?"

"Yes. I believe they are having an interview."

"Nothing less, Mr. Whitebread. So the competition has beaten you to it."

"Little harm done."

"Perhaps Boswell will stop boring us with his Corsican friends and start advocating the Indian cause."

"If that should be the case, Mr Pole, you may be certain that we shall shortly see him with feathers on his head."

"While we are on the subject, rumors are circulating that the warrior savage has been affiliated to the Lodge of the Falcon."

"Chief Joseph Brant, a freemason? There must be some mistake. I'm sure he belongs to the clan of the Crocodile."

"That's jolly good. Who would ever have thought that we would live to see such stupidity?"

"Negroes, Corsicans or Indians, this obsession with the exotic must come to an end. As we predicted, it is beginning to do serious damage right under our noses. You must have read about what happened at Bedlam three nights ago."

"Certainly, it's unbelievable."

"Crazy."

"It has to be said. Women violated in the middle of the street. Men engaging in the most sordid indecencies against tree trunks and lamp posts."

"Unnatural acts. . . with dogs and chickens. It took two days to catch them all again."

"We had said that these city Indians were a danger."

"But the *flatus vocis* is not enough, gentlemen. And neither is the sharp quill of our friend Panifex here. We must put things in order."

"What do you mean by that?"

"Events have proved us right. This confusion must come to an end. We may not be able to keep them from abolishing slavery. But no more Indians going around London. Or in Soho. Or in our club. The two thousand Negroes crowding into the slums of the East End are quite enough, thank you."

"The Indian delegation will be setting off again soon. There is nothing to worry about."

"Fine. Very good, Mr Whitebread. So let us hope that their imitators disappear at the same time."

27.

From the *Daily Courant* of 8 May 1776.

FAREWELL FROM PRINCE THAYENDANEGEA
TO THE SECRETARY OF STATE OF THE COLONIES,
LORD GEORGE GERMAIN

On the 6th of this month, for the second time since their arrival in the city, the superintendent of the Department of Indian Affairs, Col. Johnson, and the prince of the Mohawks, Joseph Brant Thayendanegea, were received by the secretary of state for the Colonies.

At the end of the discussion I approached Col. Johnson for details of the meeting, who couldn't resist my request and asked his secretary to give me a copy of the speech that the prince had delivered to Lord Germain.

I reproduce it here, as I received it, for the delectation of our readers.

Brother (thus Prince Thayendanegea addressed the secretary of state for the Colonies!),

In our last discussion you replied with few words, saying that you would address the claims of the Six Nations concerning their lands, in particular those of the Mohawks, and that you would resolve them; that all this would be sorted out to our great satisfaction as soon as the troubles in America were over, and that you hoped that the Six Nations would continue to show the same attachment to the King that they have always demonstrated; in that case, they could depend upon His Majesty's favor and protection.

Brother, we thank you for you promise, and we hope to see it maintained and not to be disappointed, as has happened so often, in spite of the warm friendship of the Mohawks toward His Majesty and His Majesty's government; you have been reminded of this so often by the Six Nations that their inability to obtain justice has become a source of surprise to all the Indian Nations.

Brother, the chaos prevailing in America and the distance that separates us from our country allows us only to say that upon our return we will inform the Chiefs and Warriors of what we have seen and heard, and unite with them in taking the wisest measures to stop this uproar.

Brother, as we will soon depart for our own country, after being here for many months, we ask you not to listen to all the falsehoods that can be heard about the Indians, but only to the decisions coming in from our chiefs and the wise men of the Council, which will be communicated to you by our Superintendent.

It seems obvious, in spite of the references to the old treaties and the warm friendship, that the Indians of the Six Nations by now have adopted our own way of forging alliances, not so much in the name of some abstract loyalty, but more with a view to gaining something. We take cognizance of this, considering it a sign of their progressive civilization, which, as certain philosophers know, cannot help but overcome a certain purity of spirit. What we don't understand, in fact, is how they have reached the peculiar conclusion that His Majesty and the government should wait for the decision of the tribal chiefs concerning Indian intervention in the troubles in the colonies, when we learn that such an intervention has never been requested and that the tribal chiefs thus find themselves in the in the position of having to wait for a proclamation from His Majesty permitting them to marshal their warriors among the ranks of the army. The difference may seem subtle, but in fact it is major and is born, we believe, from a misunderstanding of the words of the secretary of state, who asked Prince Thayendanegea to preserve the attachment of the Indians to their king, without meaning to formalize thus a request for military support. We do not hide the fact, that events in America do not seem to us to require intervention by the allies, on one side or the other. As Sallust said, "there are allies it is better not to marshal." The only Indians we wish to see fighting with our redcoats are the *Sohocks* of whom London has gossiped so much over the past few months. For two weeks now no crimes have been attributed to these savages—who are, of course, less civilized than their alleged brothers—and according to various rumors they have been captured by a press gang and put on a naval vessel bound for the colonies.

Soon London will also be saying farewell to the authentic Indians. In a month the delegation led by Prince Thayendanegea will set off for New York. We hope that their deployment in battle will not, even on the other side of the Atlantic, inspire the scum and the rogues of either shore to commit crimes and demand tributes.

If we remember rightly, the criminals who attacked the ships in the port of Boston and threw the tea of the East India Company into the sea were also disguised as Mohawk Indians. A similar spirit of imitation has already caused enough disturbance. There is certainly no need to blow on this fire.

PANIFEX

28.

The troop marshalled behind the boy presented arms. Peter advanced toward the general. Drums and fifes sharpened their steps. The sun shone high, clouds ran eastward. Banners fluttered.

It was magnificent. All the beauty of martial life encompassed in a single scene, the vault of the sky like a stage set. At the end of his speech, General Burgoyne pinned on the medal: the ceremony allowed the decorated man to say a word of thanks.

Guy Johnson smiled. Without a doubt, this half-breed did the name of the Johnsons proud. Satisfaction shone from the superintendent's face: another success to add to the bag. But only another Mohawk, impassive as themselves, would have been aware of the gratification in the eyes of the two Indians.

Peter opened his mouth. The superintendent, the prince and the hermit pricked up their ears. A flurry of excitement ran the length of the parade ground. But the wind carried his voice away.

Only his last words were clear.

". . . there are still many of them, and more dangerous than Ethan Allen. I know my duty, and for that reason I ask of Your Excellency the honor of being able to serve the king and my country by joining your regiment."

The boy's eyes gleamed.

The Americans stayed stock still. It took only a glance at them to understand that Peter had kept everyone in the dark.

The moment seemed to go on forever. Dressed in his red uniform, Burgoyne looked at the young man for a long time, as though weighing up the request. Then he gave the lad a sardonic smile. And refused.

Peter took the blow without moving a muscle, but the general went on speaking. His voice, used to issuing orders, cut through the parade ground from one end to the other. Each of His Majesty's soldiers was fighting for the kingdom and for his own home, he said. That was why flag-bearer Peter Johnson would not enroll in a regiment that was bound for Canada, but in the reinforcements of the 26th Cameronian, which had just been detailed to the colony of New York. They would be leaving in two months. The young hero would be able to fight for his native land.

Peter seemed to stand even more to attention, as if trying to detach himself from the earth. But events would find him firmly in his place. He had made the best choice. His mother would be proud of him, the memory of his father would be honored by his son's victory over his old enemies.

That was how it should be. It was time to beat a path of his own.

Philip studied the boy's face and guessed his thoughts. He was ready. It was no longer a desire for adventure, and there was nothing that he wanted to prove. He had crossed the threshold. He had found a reason to fight, and he would fight to the end.

It had happened to him and to Joseph, many years before.

"It was up to us to take the boy to war."

Philip was waiting for a similar reaction from Joseph. He wasn't happy, either. At the end of the day melancholy came upon him, weighed unmistakably upon his back.

Joseph's face was grim. He had refused to take a carriage, preferring to go back on foot. Philip had decided to accompany him. After dusk, the streets were not safe.

"That's what we've done. That's why Ethan Allen is in chains and the boy can walk alone," he went on as he tried to avoid the puddles. He stopped in front of Joseph and looked him in the eyes. "You said we had to fight for the king."

Joseph's jaw tightened.

"I'm proud that my nephew is fighting in the king's army," he said. "But I wanted him by my side. I wanted him to fight alongside our warriors."

Joseph tried to move away. Philip held him by the arm and went on staring him in the face.

"He has chosen to fight with the whites, his father's people. Every man has a path marked out for him in heaven."

For a moment Joseph felt he had lost his bearings. Monstrous shadows crept along the walls, insidious as snakes. It was dark, and the lamplighters had not yet been on their rounds.

Night was falling. Without saying another word the two men quickened their steps.

29.

A flock of ducks flew across the clouds, one behind the other, an arrow point in search of the horizon. The Earl of Warwick reflected that those birds would see many more lands than he. A pair of wings could do more than wealth and quarterings of nobility. Nature imposes migration on certain creatures. And perhaps on certain men. Others are sedentary, the chains that bind them to places are heavy, rusty, though in certain cases gilded. Warwick tried in vain to count the birds: too mobile. The pleasures of gregariousness would never abandon them. They would remain a flock of ducks until death, until the next generation of ducks, and their kind would never succumb to boredom.

The Earl of Warwick studied the man posing for Mr. Romney: diadem of feathers, white shirt, silver bracelets at the ends of his sleeves. The portrait of Prince Thayendanegea in campaign dress would remain as eloquent testimony to their friendship.

"You are in good hands, Mr. Brant. Mr. Romney manages to put light into the eyes of his models. The soul shines through the tip of his brush."

Warwick's voice was even, without a hint of excitement. The painter modestly lowered his eyes; Romney was well aware of his own mastery. Each action was rarefied and shrouded in sacrality. Mixing the paints. Holding up the brush to measure the sitter. Spreading trails of different pigments over the canvas: quick dabs like a puppy's tongue licking a bowl of milk, strokes as broad as the current of a river when it reaches the plain.

"We're nearly finished," said the painter. "Please lift your chin a little, Mr. Brant."

Warwick looked outside again. The afternoon light was clear; it heralded the season of fine weather.

"Have you ever suffered from melancholy, Mr. Brant? I have. It always catches me at this hour of the day. In ancient times they would have said that my life was ruled by Saturn. Is there an Indian remedy for this state of mind?"

Joseph gave a confident reply.

"Hunting. Lying with a woman. Playing with the children. Smoking your pipe. Dancing. Or sitting and looking at the horizon. It's strange, but the most varied remedies seem to cure the same ill."

Warwick nodded.

"Tell me. Are you never homesick? What do you think when your mind turns toward home?"

The faces of Susanna and the children appeared in Joseph's mind. The farm. Canajoharie. Molly.

"Of my wife's breath, beside me at night. Of the skin of my children. Of smells. The scent of bilberries in the woods along the river, roasted maize and maple syrup. Of the good things in my sister's general store."

Warwick looked as if he were about to cry. "If I belonged to a place other than this one, I, too, would be homesick. I may confess to you that I sometimes feel something very similar. A longing for the unknown, of things unseen, unimagined. A longing for the lives of other people whose paths have crossed mine."

"You have been generous to us," said Joseph. "You have asked nothing in return but my painted image. This is. . ." he tried to find the right word in some cleft of his mind, ". . .flattering. I hope one day to be able to pay back my debt to you by acting as your host in America. You would be most welcome. We would cure your melancholy."

Warwick chuckled. He saw himself surrounded by a gang of Indian women and children, but suddenly he realized he didn't know how to imagine them: the only Indian he had known was standing in front of him.

Emotion gripped his throat and moistened his eyes.

He spoke in a hoarse voice.

"You know, in my life I have never traveled. Far from this island I would feel lost. London and I are two bad-tempered lovers. We tease each other, we allow each other fleeting betrayals. But we will never leave one another."

He shook himself and asked the painter to turn the painting so that he could admire it in the last light of day.

Romney did as he asked.

"You have surpassed yourself," Warwick observed after a moment's silence. "This is the soul of the American hero."

The painter bowed reverently and took his leave. He would come back the next day for the last retouches.

When he had gone, Warwick noticed Joseph's puzzlement as he looked at the painting.

"Do you think he was lying?"

The Indian looked at him.

"I don't think I'm myself," he said, pointing at the picture. "This man is white, like you."

The man in the portrait was an unreal American, his skin and his features those of a European. His eyes alone, vivid as flames, belonged to Joseph Brant.

"On the contrary, sir. The artist has captured the essence, the concept, the very idea that you embody." Rapt, Warwick brought a finger toward the canvas. "You see? Beneath the clothes of the Indian chief the gentleman appears. Nobility is not the prerogative of our old world: there is something older, something primitive, something that doesn't depend on coats of arms. It is the nobility of the soul, the old power that belonged to the Athenians and the Spartans, and which may be seen in this face." He turned to look at Joseph. "In you."

He made a bow, which Joseph returned.

"In a few days you will leave," the Earl went on. "At least I will have a tangible sign that you have been between these walls."

"Perhaps when the war is over and the alliance between our nations is consolidated, perhaps then we will see each other again," said Joseph.

"Perhaps," the Earl remarked bitterly. "Or perhaps we will have changed too much to remember what we are now." He shook off the cloak of gloom that had enveloped him and pulled himself together. "I believe it is customary for a warrior to give the tools of his trade as presents." He walked over to a cabinet and took from it a long, narrow wooden box. He lifted the lid so that Joseph could see the contents.

Two pistols with inlaid handles lay on a green velvet cloth.

"They were used only once, by my uncle, in a duel. The family honor was defended by an accurate shot that is still spoken of at family reunions." He smiled. "I'm sure you will make a better use of them than I could."

Joseph accepted the gift. He caressed the pistols, took them in his hand, weighed them.

"When I shoot at the king's enemies, it will be as if you are the one spitting fire."

"Fortunately not," said the Earl. "My aim is not a match for that of my late lamented uncle. I couldn't hit a cow if it came in through that door. But thanks for the compliment."

Joseph didn't know what to add. He glanced once more at his double, who studied the scene from his position on the easel, then he vigorously shook the Earl's hand.

30.

When her father released her from his hug, Esther felt herself growing suddenly cold. Once more he was leaving her behind, as he had in Oswego.

She watched him hugging Aunt Nancy and shaking hands with Uncle Daniel, who was staying in London to wait for his own appointment. He would remain with them until it was time for them to go back to America, once the war was over. Her father was preparing to leave, and she felt nothing. Once that fat, nervous man had inspired her with reverence and affection.

She watched her father saying good-bye to Peter. Her cousin was wearing a red uniform; he had become a soldier of the king. He, too, would leave for America, but later, with the army, to fight the rebels. Then Peter received a hug from Joseph Brant, who spoke to him in their language, with a serious expression but in an intimate, fatherly voice.

The servants finished loading the luggage into the diligence. Someone said it was time to go. The ships awaited them in Falmouth.

Although it was June, it was cold at that time of the morning. The sun had not yet appeared over the rooftops and a breeze swept gently over the lower half of the world. Esther wrapped herself tightly in her fur and felt a tickle at the base of her neck, which made her turn around.

Philip Lacroix was there. The girl instinctively touched the bracelet that he had given her in the woodshed. She wore it under the sleeve of her dress.

In her mind she asked him to take her back. Not to leave her in this dark, foggy city. She asked him as her guardian angel, not as the Great Devil.

She walked over to him. "So we won't be seeing each other again, will we?"

Philip looked into the distance, beyond the diligence, beyond the street and the port. Esther waited for him to examine the future. She hoped he could contradict her.

"If we do, I'll be happy," he replied, before climbing onto the box beside the driver.

Esther's feet were chained; her legs were made of stone. She burst into tears. The diligence set off. Her father was still waving from the window, but she didn't see him.

31.

The regiment was the biggest human formation that could be commanded by the human voice. The war would be music.

Peter marched and marched, thrusting out his chest, listening to the drums and bagpipes accompanying the movements on the parade ground. The first few days had been exhausting: bearing the regimental standard called for strength and self-negation. But with the passing days his body had grown used to it and his resilience as a young man of the woods was further strengthened.

Each company had one or two drums, and one or two bagpipes. Slow March, Quick March, Strathspey, Reel: when several companies came together, their musicians united to beat time to the steps and ease the men's weariness. The music strengthened their legs, relaxed their stiff arms, banished thoughts from their minds.

It was magnificent. Peter thought he could march forever.

Once the day's orders had been carried out, the troop wandered the streets of the city in search of beer. Before dinnertime, drummers and pipers marched through to tell the shopkeepers it was time to close up. Peter returned to camp awash with beer but still hungry for food. Sometimes he found himself in the arms of a camp follower, but never again did he feel what he had felt with the fairy of the Tower of London.

Music began his days and accompanied them—and brought them to an end, at least until someone complained. After dinner, there was time to exercise his fingers and let his mind fly.

"What's that march called, boy?"

Sergeant Bunyan had poked his head into the tent without asking permission. He was a stout man, advanced in years, crammed into his lobster-colored uniform. Peter set his violin down and turned coldly toward the intruder.

"*An Faire*, sergeant. It's a double jig. And please don't call me boy."

"Of course, forgive me. It's because you look so young, Mr. Johnson. The age of a drummer boy, more or less. I didn't mean to show a lack of respect."

Peter saw that the man was speaking in good faith. He decided he liked the lined face. "I accept your apologies, sir."

The sergeant's face opened up into a smile, a wider wrinkle among the others that furrowed his face. "Thank you, and I have a request, if it isn't too impudent: couldn't you play some good Scottish music?"

Peter smiled. "Sir, good Scottish music is Irish music."

The sergeant smiled in turn and took his leave. There were no flies on this boy.

It had been one of Sir William's favorite sayings. "Good Scottish music is Irish music." And also: "The most notable Scottish families all have Irish blood."

Sir William had been proud of his origins.

He had also been proud of being Warraghiyaghey. And of serving the Crown. He knew only too well what some people thought of the Irish, of their dubious loyalty. He also knew that the Scots weren't seen in a much different light. In London he had heard that the most visible Scots had formed a lobby that controlled the king. Londoners called these rumors "politics." But Sir William always said that Britain's strength lay in the fact that it was the United Kingdom: time would reveal who its best and most loyal subjects were.

The bow set the violin strings vibrating. *An Faire*. His father's favorite music, played on the new violin given to him by his mother. There had been a time when he hadn't liked playing this music, thought it was for old people. But now the simple five-note scales and the dance rhythms that he had heard a thousand times in childhood often emerged from the strings of his violin as if rising from the strings of his soul.

Longing for his mother: difficult for a soldier to admit, but not for a young Mohawk. Longing for Sir William, too. For Johnson Hall and the forests.

32.

The story had been told by Gwenda, a Soho Square blowen who always called in at One-Eye's for a bit of Dutch courage before going on the attack.

It had happened the evening before, right underneath her lodgings.

She'd been standing at the window, clocking the movements of all the ruffers and strutters, because since the Mohock invasion the pelfed-up jaspers kept their distance, earnings were tight and she had to resort to the filthiest scum in Soho.

With a bang from the other side of the square this sedan appears, with these jaspers inside you can hear singing and them dressed to the nines, all cloaks and white gloves, butter wouldn't melt, as if they're in Vauxhall for tea.

She'd got her mumbles out, sat them on the ledge and started rumbling out some dirty song, one of those ones you hear them it puts you in the mood. She's just launched off when her voice and everyone else's is joined by a third, a screech of stuck beasts, and suddenly a quadrille as bare as Adam bursts out of the square, with bows and arrows and all the gear of the Indian year. Them in the sedan leap out; them carrying it drops it and seeks hiding places in a dark alley, with the Indians right on their heels.

At this point, from Gwenda's window you can't see a thing anymore, just two molls appearing out of upstairs windows in the hovels along the way, one of them pouring swill from a tub, the other chucking who knows what, but right away you hear the amens of them as seems to be gulping it up down below.

After ten good minutes of everyone yelling and dancing about, the alley spews them back out, in a row like soldiers, the two chairmen at the front, then four naked men who must be the Indians, but now they've got their rugs in a bag and a net over them holding them together, and behind them come another five or six, strutters who'd passed by under Gwenda's window, and one fired at her and she recognized him, it's like he's the boss who cashes in the sawdust with a gang drawn from the sewers.

So the Indian year lasted only six months, thought One-Eyed Fred. The Emperor and his hooligans ended up in the navy—maybe they were sent to the colonies, to scrap with the real Indians. The savages of London were too base to form a nation, but fake enough to put on a uniform. The opposite of the ones on the other side of the ocean. Base enough to serve in the army but not too fake to. . . oh, you know, the opposite.

One-Eye realized the tavern was his again, and this time, if he didn't want to give it to the first cunt who came along, he would have to have a good think. Certainly, the first cunt who came in with four armed and stinking thugs would turn the place upside down. The main thing was to keep them out. If there was something those shitbrains had taught him, it was the phrase that the Emperor repeated most often.

Fear is the soul of trade.

By way of a start, a sign. One-Eye's Tavern, perhaps, to make things clear from the outset. No, of course not, One-Eyed Fred might have scared a child, but no one else. So what about the Emperor's Tavern, as if to remind you that the Emperor might come back sooner or later. The priests had been keeping the faithful down for centuries with that kind of rubbish, so why shouldn't it work for him, in those head-splitting years still left to him? If fear was the soul of trade, trade had a lot to learn from the Church of Christ.

The Mohock Tavern, that was good, or the Scalp Inn, that was it, because that lunatic the Emperor had let him keep it, Dread Jack's scalp, and you never know, now things were looking up, he could hang it on the wall behind the bar, beneath a pair of crossed hatchets, where he kept the charcoal portrait they'd done of him when he was quodded. Maybe with the Indian tavern he could go on serving up that disgusting swill of gin, mint and molasses that the Emperor was always glugging down him, and his thugs had to glug it too because he said it was his grandad's favorite tipple, him and all the other Indians who had come to see Queen Anne, before the krauts took her throne off her. And the swill was a good idea as well, to remind people that there, in One-Eye's Tavern, or the Scalp, the Seventh Nation still met up, pretending that the Emperor was coming back from America with beaver skins and strumpets for all.

Twenty gallons of mint syrup. If he managed to shift it all before the worms got into it, he'd have the words tattooed on his arse:

Fear is the soul of trade.

The Return

1776

No trace of the *Lord Hyde*. Joseph and Lacroix's brigantine had been separated from the convoy during the storm. Guy Johnson studied the horizon, hoping to see its masts appear.

Before the tempest, tedium and weariness had gone with them like a two-headed shadow. The tedium was a legacy of London; the weariness, perhaps, was an anticipation of ordeals to come. Days and days of sea voyage, strolls on deck to stretch the legs, distracted reading, visits to the other ships, revolting food.

The smell that rose from the hold and the cabins was an offence to the nostrils. Guy felt homesick for bear grease.

He leaned against the wall. The waves were long and dizzying. He had been advised to look into the distance, at a point on the horizon, or else he would give up his soul to the abyss, one vomit at a time.

The way to America. A wake of rubbish jettisoned from the deck, a trail of shit and vomit.

He felt like the machine-man in those French books he had flicked through in London. Needing oil in all his joints. The statue-man, linked to the outside world by a tunnel of senses, hidden inside a mass of inert matter.

Guy Johnson knew that his frame was too slender to sustain the weight of excessive flesh and fat. And if to flesh and fat were added the weight of worry and responsibility, then the body collapsed like a house of cards or a rotten tree struck by lightning.

Beyond the horizon, to keep from throwing up. Beyond the horizon, where Mars stalked the earth.

He could feel that his tedium and weariness covered something deeper.

Fear. Daughter of uncertainty, but also of self-consciousness. He thought of Esther and the children. He thought of his male firstborn, whom he would never call by name. He thought of his wife's shade.

He thought of all that he had already lost, and all that he still risked losing.

The thin, dark line was not the American coast, but the island of Bermuda. Captain Silas's announcement was received with a string of clench-toothed curses followed by hocking and spitting, a reaction of disgust for the adverse wind that had dragged them southward. The storm in the middle of the Atlantic had parted them from the rest of the convoy, then driven them six hundred miles off their route. But they were afloat. They were alive. They just had to roll up their sleeves.

The sea is treacherous, Philip thought as he listened to the captain speaking. You can't rest your feet on it, you're suspended over the abyss, a hostage to the elements. You slide over the sea. And when the wind wrinkles the surface, the plain becomes a mountain, then an avalanche that rolls you like a marble.

Monsters rise up from the deep. The satanic Leviathan of the Scriptures came from the ocean, and so did the serpents that devoured Laocoön and his sons.

The sea is treacherous and infernal. Dying at sea means not having a grave, a resting place.

And yet the ocean had restored the color to his face. The pallor of London belonged to the past: after the tempest, the sky had opened up above the ship, dense blue criss-crossed with very high clouds.

Being able to see a long way, getting one's eyes used to the open spaces after the confinement of the capital, meant trying to remove the veil that covered the days to come. Thoughts of what would be helped him to master his sense of the past, the distant past and the most recent.

Since they had been at sea he had spurned Joseph's attempts at conversation, speaking only a few words: *yes, no, perhaps.*

But now they were side by side again, leaning against the wall.

"What are you thinking about?" asked Joseph.

A shadow crossed Philip's face.

"Two London palaces could contain the whole of our people. If something went wrong, the name of the Mohawks would be lost forever."

Joseph's face grew hard and resolute.

"I'll manage to persuade the Longhouse. The king's army is vast; the men who will take up arms for him cannot be counted. We will win."

Philip didn't reply, distracted by something outlined in the distance.

A sail.

The two Indians watched a mystery unfold before their eyes.

"It doesn't look like a ship from the convoy," said Joseph.

Philip shook his head. Perhaps it was coming from the islands. In the distance, it was just possible to make out the name carved into the prow. *Argos*, he thought he could read. Joseph knew nothing about big ships, but he had been a boatman long enough to notice that its draught was very shallow. No cargo. It was lighter and faster than the *Lord Hyde* and coming toward them at great speed.

A shout came from the mainmast.

"They're taking the wind out of our sails!"

With an abrupt maneuver, the brigantine had slipped into their wake. Joseph heard their sails deflating, a sound like an emptied sack. Then a far-off bang and a column of water shot up in front of their prow, showering the deck as it fell.

Captain Silas cried out. The men were running everywhere, weapons raised.

Joseph turned toward Philip. He was already loading his rifle.

A second cannon ball tore into their sails. Silas ordered the men to prepare to fire. The sailors swung the ship's broadside to the enemy and aimed their cannons. The pirate ship responded with a risky ploy: drawing level and close to the *Lord Hyde*, to prevent them from using their guns. The two sides now lay a few yards apart, and the sailors shot at the pirates from behind the walls, using anything they had, firing iron marbles, nails from slingshots.

A voice called out, "Surrender to the United States of America! Hand over your ship and its cargo!"

At the same time, the *Argos* tried to cross the *Lord Hyde*'s bows. The helmsman of the *Hyde*, hampered b the damage to their sails, did what he could to prevent a collision. The two ships were aligned now, so close that they were touching. The rifle salvo went off first, then the pirate flung its grappling-irons, which the crew of the *Lord Hyde* hurried to unhook or cut, covered by fire from their gunners.

Joseph and Philip aimed at the figures visible on the poop deck and fired in unison.

Then the smoke grew too thick, obscuring their target. The men waited, resting their rifle-barrels on the parapet.

Joseph thought how sad it would be to die there in the middle of the sea. Not to see his home again. The children. Susanna. That wasn't how he meant to fulfill his destiny.

If he couldn't resist the will of God, at least he would put up a fierce struggle.

He murmured a prayer.

The echoes of the explosions, the cries began to fade away.

Silence fell upon the space beyond the walls. Water lapping, a breath of wind. The dark outline of the privateer could be glimpsed receding into the distance. The *Lord Hyde* had successfully repelled them.

Triumphant insults flew after them, but they were out of range. The bosun reestablished order with pushes and kicks, moving through the stench of shit and gunpowder.

"United States of America," thought Philip.

Leviathan had reached them in the middle of the ocean.

He saw Joseph approaching, still clutching his rifle. He understood that the nearness of death had banished fear. His face bore the resoluteness of a king of Israel.

No dream could have told him what awaited them on dry land.

Part Three

Cold, Cold Heart

1776–79

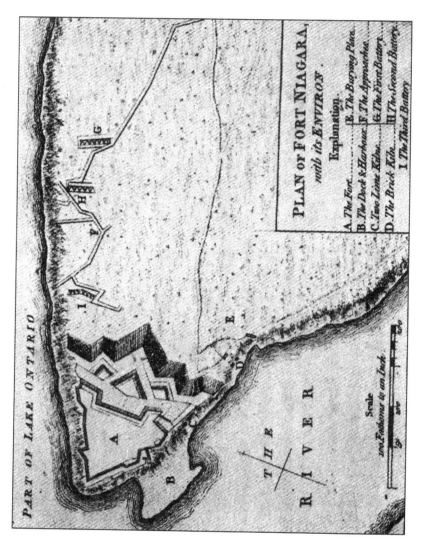

Plan of Fort Niagara (John Carter Brown Library)

1.

The Liberty Pole stood tall, pointing straight at the sky. The birch trunk had been raised once more, with the greatest care, with chants, dances, and renewed dedications. The oath had run from mouth to mouth: their pole would not be toppled by any loyalist property owner. The banner of Congress fluttered, red as the blood of the first martyrs. It was said that another banner fluttered elsewhere, but no one in the valley had seen it as yet.

Cotton-wool clouds drifted across the sky; the heat was oppressive.

Militia colonel Nicholas Herkimer sat down and fanned himself with a white handkerchief. A crowd of patriots, a new people in the making, filled the square in front of the church. Many of them seemed impatient. Since John Johnson and his mercenaries had left, the militia and the committee for public safety had been in control of this area of the valley. The days of fear seemed to be over, or rather, they were still there, but for the other faction, in a perfect reversal.

Herkimer had been a captain during the Franco-Indian War; he had always done his duty by the colony. For that very reason he had found himself on the right side. His motives were ideal rather than concrete. The subjects of the English monarch had been the envy of Europe for their freedom. For years, however, George III had been behaving like a tyrant, imposing scandalous taxes and humiliating duties on the American colonies and contemptuously disregarding their requests for representation in the government. Consequently, his "subjects" were nothing of the sort. They were no longer under any obligations. The document that he held in his hands proved as much.

This was a copy of the declaration formulated by Congress a short time before. From the moment of its publication they had ceased to be subjects. They were citizens, and the colonies were a new Athens, or a new Republican Rome. The proud English Tarquin could no longer govern their lives. The new Darius, arriving with a doomed army, would meet his Marathon.

Now it was a matter of explaining it, or rather, *translating* it to the throng. Since most of them were German and Dutch immigrants, English was a language they only half knew. Herkimer hoped he would be up to expressing these lofty concepts in the local Mohawk Dutch, a mixture of Dutch, English and German pronounced in a manner incomprehensible to outsiders. He looked around and wondered whether the majority would understand, even with the best possible translation.

Once more, Herkimer couldn't help thinking that all the problems in the valley had to do with an absence. Sir William: he had known him well, they had fought together, and no one could persuade him that a man like that would have turned his back on the call for freedom that was rising up from the whole colony. In the time of the Stamp Act, just two years after the end of the Franco-Indian War, Sir William had not spoken out against the Whig requests. He had merely declared that those arguments risked being put forward improperly. Over the years that followed he had always made formal acts of submission to the Crown; in his position he could hardly have done otherwise. But he died before the situation came to a head, before the motherland began to violate and frustrate the legitimate requests of the colonies. What other patriots said—that Sir William would have been on their side—was perhaps excessive. Certainly, however, he would have been intelligent and long-sighted enough not to side with a tyrant.

His children, his heirs, his Indians had been much less lucid. They had been frightened.

Herkimer surveyed the faces crowding the square.

"My dear friends, I see with pleasure that we are all present. When the Liberty Bell rang out its first chimes, we were certainly far fewer in number. We all clearly remember what happened the first time we raised this pole. Arrogance and abuse drove still more people to embrace our cause. And today we. . ."

Remember? Raise? Jonas Klug's lips pursed in a puzzled grimace. He had heard it told a thousand times, the story of the pole. People like Rynard never missed an opportunity to puff up their feathers: "I was there." As if saying, "You weren't, you arrived afterward, you woke up late, when less courage was needed." A thousand times, and on none of those times had Nicholas Herkimer been mentioned. He too had woken up late, but none of the braver men dared to correct *him*, no, with him they were silent as stones.

Meanwhile Herkimer went on explaining, saying something about independence, that the king no longer had any authority over the colony, that the citizens of the United States of America were free and had a right to happiness.

Fine words, certainly, but not much substance. Far from free. You wanted to give a lesson to a puffed-up loyalist? Sorry, no individual initiatives, orders of Colonel Herkimer. You wanted to make the savages believe the tune had changed? Nothing to be done. If you went to Canajoharie, you had to go there unarmed. Herkimer had made that promise to the Indian witch, perhaps receiving a screwing in return, or then again perhaps not. When you're filthy rich and you've got good land coming out of your ears, it isn't all that difficult to act like a gentleman, to respect the enemy, give ground and do all that other official stuff.

The sermon ended with applause and hats being thrown in the air. When the hubbub had subsided, Klug cleared his throat and spoke.

"There's one thing that isn't clear to me, Colonel. The savages who live in the free state of New York. Are they citizens too, or what?"

"If by savages you mean the Indians, sir, then no, they aren't, but they must decide whether they are friends or enemies of freedom."

"Excuse me, Colonel," Klug replied, "but if they aren't citizens, why are they allowed to live in our nation? If I buy a house and go to live in it, but find people inside when I get there, I make them move out, I make them clear off."

Klug's words prompted a hum of approval.

Herkimer gave a wave of his hand and retook the floor.

"You forget that this a country of just men, sir, which takes as its model the greatness of Rome and Athens."

Athens? Klug wondered. Never heard of it. Rome? Wasn't that where the pope lived? What did the pope have to do with the new nation? There were no papists among them, luckily enough.

"The property and safety of the Indians will be protected unless they explicitly act against Congress and against the United States of America. Before our ancestors came here from Europe, they already inhabited this land. Our task is to civilize them, not to expropriate them."

Klug gave a sign to indicate that he had nothing more to ask, but the reply had not satisfied him.

The savages had been in America since the dawn of time, what a discovery. So had the squirrels, but no one had asked their permission before cutting down a forest and growing rye. Klug was more and more convinced: he had to get rid of the redskins once and for all. Sooner or later, some gentlemanly general with a passion for squaws would convince himself that the Indians had a right to happiness, too. And the Negroes. And the squirrels and the forests.

If things went on like that, the United States of America would have a bear as ambassador, a Negro as a minister and Sister Squash with a seat in Congress.

2.

The wind commanded the army of flames. The wooden city was subjected to furious assaults, the very houses seemed to be fighting, struggling not to be taken by the fire, but the enemy was stronger and soon conquered them, set them alight, offered them in tribute to the night until they collapsed. All that remained were hills of ash.

Peter had disembarked only the day before. From the Bronx he had come to Manhattan, just in time to see it burn.

His Majesty's army had occupied New York after the Battle of Long Island. Washington's rebels had retreated in the fog, marching northward along the East River. Or maybe not: maybe they had transmuted themselves into flames.

In the big meadow at the edge of the city, refugees with blackened faces contemplated the destruction. They had chosen not to flee, not to let New York become a city of ghosts, soldiers and desolation. This was their reward.

The fire had been blazing for many hours. Now it was heading north and encountering no obstacles: the sky blazed, the color of bronze or pyrite, false gold. Impossible to tell that the sun was about to rise.

Rumors circulated among the evacuees. Everyone blamed the rebels. The fire had started in an inn near Whitehall, at the southernmost tip of the island, and had spread north and west on the arid breath of Aeolus, destroying everything in its path between Broadway and the Hudson. The old Trinity Church no longer existed; the fire had consumed everything, including its magnificent organ, worth eight hundred and fifty pounds.

Some people said that the fire had broken out in several different places and that at least one arsonist had been caught. He had brandished a knife and wounded a woman in the arm before being overpowered. His corpse, left hanging by its heels, must be ashes by now.

Had he been the one who had cut the handles off the buckets? And emptied the water cisterns? God knew how many people had conspired to start the fire. They had taken the city by surprise: there had been no bells to warn of the danger. The rebels had melted them to make bullets.

As more refugees arrived, the stories grew richer and more intricate. The crowd had pushed other arsonists, all Whigs, into the flames that they had lit. Rumors of summary executions circulated. In the inferno that had been New York, the wind threw up embers that had once been men, judged guilty in a moment and shot, stoned, stabbed, trampled to death.

The year before, from Lord Warwick's panoramic drawing room, Peter had watched multicolored fireworks and not seen in them the staging of this great fire. He had had to cross the ocean again before he understood what those master pyrotechnicians from Italy had been alluding to: the beginning of a war that would spare no one. And now he was a soldier in that war.

Shortly after setting foot on dry land he had tried to track Joseph down, but to no avail. He had boarded the ship they had directed him toward, but Joseph had left it a number of days earlier. Everyone remembered the Indian chief who had come from London, but no one knew where he was. According to some, he had fought on Long Island with General Howe's men. According to others, he had arrived only in time to return with them to Manhattan, where he made sure that the rebel army had been routed. Gossip. His uncle left a trail of legends behind him, as if they slipped from his back, garments too big for him, too cumbersome.

Before sunset, a navy official pointed out to him the ship where Guy Johnson was lodging. Peter took advantage of the little time left to him before the Cameronian gathering to climb on board.

A familiar voice responded to the knocking on the door.

"Who is it?"

"Peter Johnson, sir."

The cabin door opened up, revealing the stout form of Guy Johnson.

"My boy, when did you get here?"

"Yesterday morning."

They shook hands firmly. Peter noticed that Guy's hand was sweaty.

The superintendent ushered him in. There wasn't much space, and most of it was occupied by trunks and cases.

"What hell this is. You have no idea what's been happening here. I asked to be taken back on board. At least one thing is certain: fire doesn't cross water."

Guy moved a couple of bags and liberated a seat, which he offered to Peter. He sat down on the camp bed.

"Do you think it was the rebels who started the fire?" the boy asked.

Guy Johnson shrugged.

"That's what they say."

He moved a nervous hand toward the open bottle on the table and filled two glasses. One of them he handed to Peter, who took it without moistening his lips.

"I've been looking for my Uncle Joseph, but there's no sign of him. Can you tell me anything?"

"He isn't in the city anymore," Guy replied after gulping down the rum. "He left two weeks ago, heading for Oquaga, I think, to see his family."

"Lacroix?"

"He left, too. Heading for Canajoharie. That's all I know." He poured himself another glass. "The colonies have declared independence. Everywhere inland is in chaos: bandits and raiders have taken over."

Peter set down his glass and looked out of the porthole. He could see a scrap of sky and the dark line of the buildings of the port in the haze. It was hot, and sweat gathered under his woolen jacket. He thought of the men traveling across hostile territory. He thought of his mother, who hadn't heard news of him in months. Lacroix would reach her, he was sure of it.

He stirred. Guy had asked him a question.

"I'm sorry?"

"I asked you about your regiment."

"We've gathered under the command of General Howe."

"Good. Very good."

Guy seemed to notice the boy's uniform and stripes for the first time. He forced a smile.

"And what are you going to do?" Peter asked.

The other man's face suddenly darkened.

"To be honest, I have no idea."

Guy got to his feet and looked outside, at the columns of smoke still rising to the north.

"America is burning, my boy," the superintendent said gravely. "Taming this fire is not going to be an easy business."

3.

Outside the general store there was not a living soul, just dust and sun-scorched tufts of grass. Five days before, the Graafs' boat had unloaded its cargo, as it did every week. The goods had run out at midday. It had been like that for at least three months. Since the Albany rebels had taken control of the river, there wasn't a single boat on the lower course of the Mohawk that escaped their attention. Mr. Graaf received special treatment, in the name of old relationships and remembered favors. His merchandise was the only cargo allowed to sail undisturbed beyond Fort Hunter, and hence the only cargo supplying the store. A few hours of haggling, negotiations, exchanges, rationing, and the bookings for the next cargo were already being taken. Rum, rye flour and pork were the first to go. But also ropes, ammunition, woolen blankets and knives: with the army besieging New York, Graaf's boat, too, might soon be left high and dry. Until then, its weekly arrival would go on recalling distant families, faces that had been seen in the village, once, perhaps, people who now lived many miles away, along the tributary valleys, beyond the ranges that closed off the horizon.

Molly saw the strange woman crossing the square, and knew she wasn't there to buy anything. She closed her accounts book, told Juba to get dinner ready, and came down the stairs.

The woman introduced herself, said she had come from Schoharie, and in a few words explained the reason for her visit. The marks on her daughter's face had appeared that morning. After a night of fever and wailing, beneath the veil of tears and sweat, little pustules had covered her cheeks. Not too dense, but dense enough to leave no doubt.

The last great battle against smallpox had been at least ten years ago, before the child had been born.

Molly rummaged through the drawers of a massive piece of furniture, wrapped a handful of herbs in a scrap of fabric, and tied it twice with a piece of wire.

"I can't do much for your daughter," she said to the woman, holding out the package. "Dr. Brennon left the valley this winter. He was the one who put the mark on our people, at the request of Sir William, ten years ago. I don't know anyone else who knows how to perform the operation, and even if I did, the mark serves to keep the spotted disease far away, not to get rid of it once it's there."

The woman received the news with resignation. The long journey had been a pointless exertion.

"Forgive me, madam." Juba's voice broke the silence. "I know what you're talking about. The lady is right, the mark doesn't heal those who are already sick, but it can prevent many deaths. Juba can do it."

"You know how?"

The black woman nodded.

"In my land it is done when the sickness comes. My father did it. You need the tip of a knife and a little of the liquid that is in the spots."

The first to receive the mark were Molly's daughters. Over the next few days they had fever and vomited, but none of them developed the spots.

The sick child was staying in a house outside the village. She was slightly ill, and the disease that Juba took from her pustules was strong enough to prepare the body for battle without killing it in the process. Molly sent messengers up and down the river, to the slopes of the Adirondacks and the Oneida villages on the shores of the Susquehanna. She herself went to talk to Nicholas Herkimer, who had been a good friend of Sir William and commanded the county's rebel militia. She told him that in the course of a few weeks, during the period when the Graafs' boat put in at the village, men and women from all over the valley would be coming to Canajoharie, in much greater numbers than usual. She said that nothing strange was going on, except that smallpox threatened the sons and daughters of the Mohawks and they had decided to defend themselves. Anyone who came down to the general store to sell or buy would be given the mark that keeps the spots away.

Herkimer had often heard of the treatment that doctors called inoculation. The first time had been a few months before, when the redcoats had successfully defended Quebec, thanks to a smallpox epidemic that had broken out among the besieging rebels. It was said that His Majesty's soldiers were all inoculated and that Washington wanted to spread the practice among his volunteers as well.

The wind threw the first leaves to the ground, roaring in the branches, drowning out people's voices. Outside the store was a crowd whose like had never been seen.

Betsy, Molly's older daughter, stood in the doorway checking whoever came in, studying faces and arms to stop anyone already a victim of the spots, saying no, the treatment was useful only to the healthy and not to the sick, in spite of rumors that had given many victims hope.

Inside, the store's usual gloom was relieved by two large lamps. Molly welcomed the people who came in, hurried through sales and barterings with them, then pointed to a chair and nodded to Juba to continue. The operation was a simple one. The tip of the knife scratched the skin, and a sip of rum revived the spirit.

As a frightened old woman made herself comfortable on the chair and Molly sought to persuade her to accept the mark, the voices from outside suddenly exploded with excitement. It sounded like an argument, and Molly told herself that this was normal, that it had to happen sooner or later—a sick man who refused to be turned away, someone tired of waiting, or the usual drunk.

She calmed the old woman and made for the door.

Voices emerged from the uproar, but she didn't have time to make them out, to assemble a scrap of meaning.

Then she saw the familiar shadow framed in the door.

Ronaterihonte was back in Canajoharie.

4.

The general store was a graveyard of empty shelves and deflated sacks. Behind the clouded windows were the shadows of small boys attempting to peer through. Philip glanced at them and the little heads disappeared, but only for the blink of an eye.

Molly sat with her hands in her lap, ready to hear any news, whatever it might be.

"Many of you left and only one returns," she said. "My heart is trembling."

Philip let his weary limbs melt into the chair's embrace.

"There is no reason for that. Your family is well, Molly Brant."

The woman heaved a sigh of relief.

Philip pointed to the queue outside the store.

"I can't say the same about your people."

Molly nodded.

"The smallpox has attacked the valley, but we have stopped it in time. You too will have to be marked. But first, tell me. Why are my son and my brother not with you?"

Philip told her of Peter's decision to join the English army, and of Joseph traveling toward Oquaga to meet his family. He also told her about Daniel Claus, left behind in England, and of Guy Johnson, staying in New York.

"So the company has split up," Molly observed.

Philip didn't say anything.

"Things aren't going well," Molly went on, shaking her head. "I know of no treatment for the epidemic of rebellion. The settlers have declared their independence from the Empire, and their militias are growing by the day. Many people are joining, even people we would not have expected to have as enemies." Her face darkened. "Then there are those, like Jonas Klug, who have been waiting for an opportunity like this for some time. The forest is no longer safe, the river isn't safe, nowhere is. Even Johnson Hall has fallen into the hands of the militia. It happened in May. Sir John had to seek refuge in Canada. He left his wife here with their little son and another in the womb, along with an escort. A few days later the militia surrounded the house. They took Sir John's wife and son, and they're now prisoners in Albany. They also took away John Butler's wife and children."

She stopped speaking, her sad eyes fixed on the floor. She forced herself to look up. Then she seemed to recall something she had been storing up for some time.

"What is the king of the English like?" she asked.

She seemed genuinely curious to know.

"A man who lives far from his people," Philip replied. "In a palace as big as a *baggataway* field."

Molly put her hands together and sat back in her chair.

"You want me to listen. Speak sincerely."

"We cannot win, Molly," said Philip. "You can stop their sicknesses, but not the contagion that they bear in their souls. The white men will destroy us as they destroy themselves. It makes no difference what flag they fly. They are a whirlpool that spreads and swallows everything up."

This time Molly's sigh was serious and long.

"Men think of defeat as of the sun going out, the world ending. Women know that's not how it is."

Philip turned around: the figures of the children darted away, and he caught a glimmer of smiles as they vanished.

"We will do what needs to be done," Molly went on. "If war is what awaits us, we will confront it, as we already have done. Blood will be spilled, but I tell you that the People of the Flint will not die, if their sons do not deny them." She got to her feet and rested a hand on his shoulder. "You are back. It is good to have you here again, Ronaterihonte. You will help us to survive the winter."

"Is that why you called me back? So that I can be with you at the hour of your sunset?"

Molly's face remained impassive.

"I called you because every circle is closing. What this means for each of us we cannot know from the start."

Philip rose. He felt a great affection for this woman, and knew that their hearts would be bound forever, until the day they died. He sought words to say so, but she stopped him.

"On your journey something happened that you haven't told me." She gave him a sidelong glance as she bent to poke the fire. "Your wampum of adoption is not around your wrist."

"I gave it to someone who needed good fortune."

The woman nodded again.

"You are a generous man, Philip. The last time that bracelet passed from one hand to another it wove two destinies together."

Philip saw himself as a child again, a little drummer boy under the butcher's knife.

He nodded good-bye and went back to the inoculation room, lifting the sleeve of his shirt.

5.

The breathing of the forest was like the crying of ghosts. Joseph had been walking for weeks, alone, dressed as a huntsman, wearing nothing Indian that could betray his origins. Step by step, his sense of danger mounted, grew in his belly, weighed down his limbs more than their load of arms and provisions. His muscles contracted in painful knots, and his breathing was quick and heavy. The paths to Oquaga formed a single, interminable climb.

A bear had been crossing his path for days: he had heard it in his half sleep, he had seen its marks on the trunks of the pine trees, claw marks left as a kind of signature. It was the enemy's *orenda*, hatred transformed into fangs and claws.

The creature's presence was apparent all around; at times he felt he could even pick up its scent. The bear was following a trail, for sometimes bears anticipate a man's journey. Joseph expected to see it moving through the undergrowth.

In fact the bear, a solitary creature, was the least serious threat that walked those woods. The most dangerous of beasts moved in groups, without precaution, leaving obvious traces, as if afraid of nothing, as if defying fate: white men, Whig militias, rebels, raiders in search of booty. They felt they were the masters of the Indian lands, and they felt they were safe in them: the breathing of the forest was a chorus they could not hear. Voices of ancestors, past generations, flesh that was now worms and food for animals, hordes of men decimated by smallpox and the wars fought on behalf of distant allies. Those woods, Joseph thought, still belonged to the Indians. They would repel the strangers just as the body, with a good medicine, chases illness away. That land guarded the bones of the forefathers, and Joseph's forefathers had been loyal to the Crown: the medicine that would restore the land to health was the king's army.

Joseph Brant had been brought up to love the English. Now that the rebels insisted on being called *Americans*, he felt relieved.

The damp impregnated his clothes. He consumed his food in haste, he marched without stopping, exhaustion dragged at his legs and weighed on his chest. Joseph stopped to drink and catch his breath, leaning on his rifle. A flight of birds rustled the branches of the pines.

He had to move quickly, beyond the edge of human capacity. The world was a dangerous place.

He had to reach his destination. Oquaga and Unadilla were friendly villages, home to dozens of his relatives, close and not so close. Salvation would come from there.

He had to get back to his mother, his wife, his children. Look his flesh and blood in the face, see the living, concrete aspect of the ideal for which he had chosen to fight. If he distinguished himself in that war, people like Klug would not be able to get their predatory hands on the Mohawks' belongings. His mother would die in peace, and Mohawk land would guard her bones.

Joseph thought of his people. Since the days of his childhood many more Mohawks had died than were alive today. Philip was right: two London palaces could have contained the whole of the People of the Flint.

It was evening now: the orange light of the sun filtered through the branches. The days to come promised to be as dark as his march through the depths of the forest. Joseph wished he had le Grand Diable by his side.

The bear appeared suddenly, standing upright, cutting short the flow of his thoughts. The hairs stood up on the back of his neck, and Joseph aimed his rifle. The bear growled, turned its back on him and disappeared into the depths of the forest.

Joseph ran the back of his hand over his brow. A little black bear, it had looked far from threatening. The eyes of the man and the eyes of the bear had met. Perhaps it wasn't a bad omen; perhaps the bear was trying to tell him something, put him on the alert. He had to advance cautiously, take care to leave no traces, keep from resting until his nostrils caught the smells of home.

They were many: they occupied the whole of the clearing. Joseph held his breath, hiding in the brambles that covered the hillside. Giving up bear grease had been a good idea. From that distance, if the wind had changed, the smell would have given his presence away. There were plenty of Indians in the group. Joseph couldn't tell what nation they belonged to. In the semi-darkness he couldn't make out their features: they could have been Mingo, or Delaware, or even Oneida. They were about forty yards from him, and were speaking quietly. Not like the white men, who swapped noisy comments as they prepared their camp for the night.

The encounter had dispelled the exhaustion in his limbs and brought fresh lucidity to his mind. Retreat without a sound, get away from the clearing, circle at a distance, return to the path many miles to the west. Joseph entrusted himself to divine mercy and started moving.

He traveled the last stretch with the circumspection of a lynx. Closeness to home gave him strength. Soon the solitude of the journey would be behind him. Solitude, the saddest fate for a man, would be left behind in the belly of the forest.

The dogs barked, but Joseph was calm. Soon they would recognize him, welcome him with their paws on his chest, try to wash his face with their tongues as they always did. The faint light of an oil lamp filtered through the loose planks that closed the window.

The door opened, releasing a domestic atmosphere, liberating the smells of a peaceful life. A robust little boy came outside with a stick in his hand and turned toward the stranger as the dogs leaped, barking, around his legs.

"Who's there?"

Joseph smiled, but his voice sounded dark and severe.

"Don't you recognize your father, Isaac?"

The boy stood silent.

The tension of the journey melted away in Susanna's embrace. Joseph smelled the perfume of her hair and felt her hot breath on his shoulder. His wife stroked his face, as if to make sure that it was really him. Her fingers brushed wrinkles and scars, ran along his profile, in a slow sequence of touches and caresses.

"Joseph."

He was too tired even to speak. He abandoned the sack on the floor and collapsed into an old chair. Christina tottered over to her father, who picked her up and set her on his lap. The little girl hid her face in his chest. Isaac was still staring at him, his features screwed up enigmatically.

Susanna hurried to bring hot food. Joseph's eyes met his mother's. The old woman was sitting in the furthest corner of the room, wrapped in a blue blanket.

"How many French scalps did you bring, Joseph?"

6.

He came outside, taking his bearings in the still faint light that had filtered through the windows. He felt a need for clean, open air. Air wet with dew and imminent rain. Low clouds, bloated as oilskins, thundered close by. The dog welcomed him back to the courtyard with a yelp of joy. Joseph stroked its head. He lifted the bucket from the well to drink and wash away the sleep from his face. The icy water reinvigorated him, running down his neck and under his shirt. The buildings of the village were dark masses just starting to take shape. The river ran calmly not far away. The fires of war did not lick at Oquaga. At least not yet.

Turning around to go back in, he noticed a figure at the edge of the vegetable garden. He froze, then recognized his mother, her white hair ruffled by the breeze.

"Margaret," he called to her quietly, so as not to frighten her. "Margaret, what are you doing here?"

The old woman sniffed the air. She must have got out of bed without Susanna noticing.

"Do you smell it?"

Joseph sniffed, but recognized nothing that didn't belong to the woods or the cultivated fields.

"What, Margaret?"

She took another deep breath.

"The smell of carrion," she said. "It's carried on the east wind, along with the rain."

Joseph couldn't smell a thing.

"You should go back inside before you catch your death."

The old woman turned to look at him.

"You've come back, Joseph."

"I'm back."

"So why don't you bring me back home?"

"Soon, Margaret. For now it's dangerous. We must wait."

"Are you sure?"

"Yes, Margaret."

"It smells of carrion here."

"That'll go as soon as the wind changes."

The old woman shook her head.

"It's the white men," she wrinkled her nose. "They won't go."

She let him escort her into the house. Susanna had gone out to look for her and as soon as she saw them in the doorway she hurried to bring the old woman back upstairs.

Joseph sat down by the blackened fireplace. The embers glowed faintly under the ashes. He took the bellows and started bringing them back to life.

Soon afterward Susanna went back downstairs and put some water on to boil for tea. Joseph became aware of the density of her thoughts, the questions she had been brooding over since the previous evening, when she had seen him arriving, filthy from his journey through the forest.

"I must leave again soon," he said.

"Isaac and Christina are growing up without a father. Isaac in particular needs you to guide him. He needs to learn and grow."

"He also needs a place where that is possible," Joseph replied. "He must know that his father will fight for him and for the Mohawks."

Susanna couldn't lift her eyes from the teapot.

"I'm living like a widow."

Joseph got up and walked over to her.

"The time will come to stop and set down our weapons," he said.

She gripped the pot without pouring the tea.

"When?"

Joseph took the teapot from her and filled the cups. The dense perfume pricked their nostrils and aroused physical sensations that he hadn't felt for weeks.

"When we have won."

7.

They arrived three days later. It still hadn't stopped raining and the world was cloaked in grey. In the village streets you plunged up to your calves in mud, so that walking was a huge effort. People stayed at home, or in the stables looking after the animals.

A little boy came to warn Joseph. For more than an hour the three men had been perched on the fence like crows. No one had worked out what they were waiting for.

Bent under their tarpaulins, their tricorns wilting in the rain, they watched him approach without moving a muscle. Only Henry Hough stretched his tortoise neck every now and again, to spit lumps of tobacco into a puddle.

Johnny Hough's stupid face made a fine pair with Daniel Secord's sharp one.

When Joseph was very close they jumped down from the palisade and planted themselves in the mud.

"Greetings, Joseph Brant," said the oldest of the Houghs.

He nodded to them.

"We heard you were back," the other man went on. "We'd almost given up hoping. They say when you were in England you met the king."

Joseph nodded.

"Goddamn, so it wasn't bullshit!" Johnny remarked.

His brother struck him with his elbow.

"Then perhaps you can satisfy my curiosity." He pushed his face forward. "Is it true that His Majesty has nine children?"

"The Queen was pregnant with the tenth."

Henry Hough nodded to himself. "A great nation, by God. Our monarch's vigor is unequaled in the world."

"The king has sent troops," said Joseph. "The counteroffensive is massive."

"He sent them to New York," Secord said with a wink. "We haven't seen hide nor hair of them here."

Joseph looked at him for a long time. Daniel still wore the Seneca amulets, but he was pale and emaciated.

"Here the war is my task," he said. "It's why I came back."

Henry Hough's neck stretched again.

"Those are the words we wanted to hear. God bless you, Joseph Brant, and bless King George as well. When do we start?"

"When we're ready."

"The list is already a long one," said Johnny. This time his brother didn't shut him up. "From Unadilla to here we've counted at least five traitor farms."

Three pairs of eyes fixed themselves on the Indian.

Joseph knew that from that moment every word he uttered would have a different weight. He was prepared; his two-month stay in New York had given him time to think and come up with a plan.

"We need gunpowder, ammunition, provisions, money." He saw them nodding. "And men willing to fight."

"We can rustle up some pretty good men," said Hough. "Committed loyalists."

"Determined people," Secord added.

"Do it. I'll go to Fort Niagara to get what we need. I'll ask for support from the Six Nations. The rendezvous is here for the start of the spring."

Henry Hough faked a coughing fit.

"Speaking with respect, Joseph Brant. There are four of us, which isn't many for the task at hand."

"We're more than enough, if we spread the news."

"What news?" asked Johnny.

Joseph looked him up and down with the scowl of an officer inspecting a subordinate.

"That Chief Joseph Brant will fight the Albany rebels in the name of the King. And that he won't stop until he has defeated them."

An avid sneer appeared on the faces of the three men.

Isaac felt himself being gripped by the collar and started wriggling like an animal on a lead. Susanna held him back. He had run out of hiding to reach the central square of the village, where all the inhabitants were assembling. Instead of hiding, he had stayed to watch them: elders wrapped in their tribal blankets, young men in worn woolen jackets and misshapen hats, Oneida children peering between the legs of the adults. Someone had thrown planks into the square, so that they could walk without sinking into the mud. His father clutched his walking stick, holding it aloft, to call for silence. Next to him, but some distance away, there were those three men. Isaac had immediately worked out what they had come to do. They had come to get his father and take him away again. So he would be left on his own with the women again. Susanna, Christina, Grandma Margaret.

His father started hoisting up the pole the flag he had brought from London. He had shown it to Isaac the night before, when Isaac had slipped outside, unable to get to sleep, drawn by the noises. He had found his father unfolding the piece of fabric with the double cross on it.

"It's the flag of the kingdom," Joseph had said. "Your cousin Peter brought it for his regiment."

It was beautiful. Isaac had thought that when it was his turn to go to war he would paint his face those colors. Red, white and blue.

The wind licked at the fabric and the flag gave a snap that rang in the air.

His father spoke clearly: "This is the flag of the English King: you all know it. From today it is also the flag of Joseph Brant Thayendanegea. I will put down any attempt to bring it low. I will place under my command anyone willing to defend it. God save King George and the Six Iroquois Nations."

He drew his knife and carved into the wooden pole the symbol of his clan.

8.

New York, 19 December 1776

Dearest Mother

I am able to write to you courtesy of Mr. Lorenz, gunsmith of Albany, who is leaving New York tomorrow to settle in Oswego, so that he need no longer sell his rifles to the enemies of the Crown.

This is the third letter that I have been able to send you. I hope you received the others, so that I can spare you the news contained therein. Upon disembarking, I discovered that Mr. Lacroix had left a short time before to go to Canajoharie. I hope that he has reached the village, and that he has described to you everything about our stay in the city of London.

For my part, I knew that Sir John had been forced to leave Johnson Hall in the hands of the Bostonians, who are now seeking Uncle Joseph and threatening to bring you to Albany so he will be forced to hand himself over. These events fill my heart with rage, and were it not for my duties as a soldier, I would do anything to be by your side and defend my brothers, our properties and my father's grave. At the moment I am not doing anything interesting or useful and I would be very happy if His Majesty's army would comply with the customs of our people, that is, fight a battle and then let the living return to their families, to hunting and trading.

When he received me, King George, said he hoped to meet me again once I had reached the rank of general, and that wish contributed greatly to my decision to enlist. If one day the Lord wished to grant me that privilege, I would certainly be the first Mohawk general to command the troops of the realm and I believe that my father would be proud of his son, he who was Irish by birth and warrior chief of the Six Nations.

When I think of that day, I imagine propagating among my subordinates some of the warrior habits of our people, meaning that it is not only the number of guns that makes the difference between two armies, but also the courage and skill of those who shoulder them.

I took part in my first battle fighting with the Indian troops, in Fort St. Johns in Canada, and then again not far from Montreal. Now I have fought two more, in the red uniform and with the flag in my hand, in New York and White Plains. All ended with our victory, but while I could recount for you the first two moment by moment and recall in every gesture the warriors' deeds, of the last I can tell you only: I held the banner high, and of my companions I know that they fired and nothing more.

At a certain point they ordered me to return to the field, and if someone hadn't told me that the enemy was in flight, I might still be wondering about the outcome of the battle.

Neither do I know what our next destination will be. They say we are about to transfer, perhaps to Philadelphia, but it certainly won't be established by a council, and none of us soldiers will be able to listen to the generals as they discuss what is to be done and take the decision. For that reason I cannot tell you where to write to me, if that is even possible, but I will try to do so as soon as possible, because I am very apprehensive and would be very happy to have your news as soon as possible.

I have no time to add anything else but

I remain always your
most affectionate son
PETER JOHNSON

P.S. Please pass on my affectionate wishes to Betsy, to all my brothers and sisters, and my greetings to my friends in Canajoharie. May Christmas bring you peace and good cheer.

9.

Soon Ohséhrhon will come, the end of the year, the start of winter. At night, the Big Dipper will be high over our heads. We will wait for the first moon, we will pass five nights of sleep and the next morning we will start the ceremonies. We will thank the spirits: the plants and the animals, the wind, the sun, and the farthest stars. We will thank God. We will burn tobacco in the fire. The Big Heads will go from house to house poking the embers and reviving the fires. We will dance, and at night we will dream hard. Upon waking we will sacrifice a white dog, to confirm our loyalty to the spirits and the Master of Life. We will invent riddles and play at sharing dreams. Night will pass like a cloud carried by the wind, and on the third day we will dance dressed in feathers. On the fourth day we will chant: the guardians of the faith will start, then the sachems, then the matrons of the clan, all the others last. After the chants, we will give names to the children. The next day will be the day of drums. On the last day we will play with peach-nut dice, divided among the clans. We will amuse the Master of Life by challenging him, joking, betting. The team that wins will lead the final dance. Again we will speak and thank the spirits, and that is how the new year will begin.

Molly knew what the new year would bring. War and hardship, loneliness. The dreams of the village went only in one direction. Apart from Ronaterihonte's. He claimed not to dream, but everyone dreams. The warrior kept the truth silent with his mouth, while saying it with his eyes: he didn't want to tell his own visions. Every day he lunched with Molly, then vanished like a shadow. Who knew where he passed his afternoons? He certainly didn't need to hide, for the Whigs never came to Canajoharie. It was Molly's pact with Herkimer: Don't challenge Sir William's ghost again. Now you sleep in his house, walk on precious carpets in boots heavy with mud. You abuse his hospitality in every way. If my husband has not asked God for permission to come down and exterminate you, to return to Paradise loaded with scalps, it is because he knows that we, his people, will pay for it. The ghosts return to the beyond, the reprisal is carried out against the living. But if you importune his wife, the mother of his children, the mother of his son who has distinguished himself in the eyes of King George, not even the Master of Life will be able to restrain him.

Molly knew it: Ronaterihonte was sleeping in Thayendanegea's empty house. Beneath that roof, it would have been impossible to sleep without dreaming.

*　　*　　*

The snow was a floor of ice, millions of scales of ice, millions of tiny reflections making up the white that assaulted the eyes.

In the vigor of winter, the *baggataway* field turned into a track for *gawasa*, "snow snake," a game common to all Indian nations to the east and north of the Great Lakes. Philip had played it as a boy, with the Caughnawagas from the mission.

On the frozen snow, players took turns throwing a straight, smoothed stick shaped like a sleigh runner. The stick plunged to the ground and slipped quickly away. The winner was the one who made it travel farthest.

He had been invited by Oronhyateka and Kanenonte, the two young warriors who had been in the Canadian expedition the previous year. They hadn't seen the Great Devil for many moons, but they had given him a rather brusque welcome. Things were getting worse by the day, they had told him. As the most vicious of the white men besieged the nation, the warriors' desire to fight was rotting on the chain, a slave to the prudence of the women and the sachems' lack of resolution. Johannes Tekarihoga spent his days befuddled with rum. Because of his lineage, he was the only one of the general store's customers exempt from the rationing.

The Mohawks of Fort Hunter, for their part, were timid and insincere, always ready to reach an agreement with the enemy. If it were up to their sachem, Little Abraham, soon there wouldn't be a nation to defend.

Philip thought that when he was a youth he would never have spoken irreverently of a sachem. He was about to say so out loud, but Kanenonte cut him short.

"We say harsh things, but it is because the young men's hearts have hardened, and their muscles are as cold as this snow."

"Our sachems are the children of days gone by," added Oronhyateka. "Their footsteps were firm and fast in Hendrick's day, but now they walk with a stick. War is for the young."

That was what Oronhyateka and Kanenonte thought, and they weren't the only ones. Suspicion and anxiety filled the souls of the warriors of Canajoharie. They all described the Oneidas as untrustworthy and distant, silent and sly. They were certainly preparing something, enchanted as they were by that reverend of theirs, Samuel Kirkland, who supported the rebel settlers. Their sachem, Shononses, was a good speaker: his speeches were swarms of fluttering butterflies with wings of a thousand colors.

"Butterflies don't defend themselves," Oronhyateka had said. "They don't fight. Bees and hornets fight, but such insects are never on the lips of Shononses."

Kanenonte looked into the distance, narrowed his eyes and thought he could see, at the end of the level ground, the *gawasa* thrown by Oronhyateka. He picked up his own between his thumb and index finger, whirled it around and threw it. The wooden snake slipped over the whiteness.

It was Oronhyateka who spoke next. "We must take up arms, Ronaterihonte. In Fort Hunter too there are healthy and brave warriors who can no longer bear sitting still. They would come with us if we set off. They would come with le Grand Diable to attack the militia and free Johnson Hall. The enemy is numerous, but we can draw them into the forest and kill them one by one."

"And afterward?" Philip interrupted. "Reinforcements would come, from Albany or who knows where. People without scruples, not like Herkimer. Vengeance would be unleashed. They have women and children as hostages. Recklessness is a grave error. We must wait for spring, brothers. Wait for the return of Thayendanegea and, above all, a new council of the Six Nations."

The two young men said nothing. From the camp there came only the sounds of the game.

Finally Kanenonte broke the silence: "Degonwadonti was wrong to warn Herkimer of the smallpox. The right thing would have been to bring the spots among the rebels, to destroy them. The white men did that, in times past. Why shouldn't we do it, too?"

Philip shivered. "Smallpox doesn't seek allies. It doesn't distinguish between its victims. If the disease had spread through the valley, it would have killed everyone, without enmity or friendship for anyone. Molly Brant stopped it. She warned the rebel commander so that she could heal our people without provoking a reaction."

They remained silent. The two young men went on throwing their sticks, until Kanenonte turned to Philip with a hiss and a half smile.

"Ronaterihonte, do you have to wait for Thayendanegea even when you're playing *gawasa*?"

Philip picked up one of the sticks from the ground. He weighed it in his hand. He studied the blanket of snow, covering grass that would soon spring up again. At last he resolved to hurl the snake.

10.

The wedge-shaped battlements that protected the southwestern side of Fort Niagara were an arrow aimed at the colony of New York and the cities on the coast. The French, not to alarm the surrounding populations, had built it to look like a huge brick general store. In fact it was a fortress, one that was hard to conquer. The battlements were tall, the casemates full of cannon.

Joseph passed by the tents and shacks that the refugees of the Mohawk Valley had built at the foot of the fortifications. Familiar faces, men and women who had set off with him the previous year to fight in Canada. Now they depended upon His Majesty's government and the benevolence of the garrison. His people had nowhere else to go.

The parade ground had become a chaotic marketplace. People of all backgrounds and religions scrambled to get hold of the last available merchandise to make it through the winter.

A wild-eyed old hunter was trying to sell furs to a group of Indians who were trying to ignore him: there was something mad about the man's manners. The white man threw to the ground the furs whose praises he was singing and began to curse. The Indians stepped back, giving him a quizzical and anxious stare.

A small group of men pushed their way through the crowd. They were Senecas, but had a young white man at their head. He bent down and picked up the fur. He examined it, handed it to one of the Indians and took some coins from his jacket pocket. "I'll give you a good price—now get lost."

The hunter walked away, muttering. The young white man turned around: it was Walter, John Butler's son.

"God strike me dead: Joseph Brant! We knew you had come back; I was just wondering when we would see you again."

He came forward, surrounded by the squad that was escorting him. Under his jacket was a wampum necklace testifying to the friendship of the Senecas. A pair of pistols hung from his belt.

"How are you?" asked Joseph.

"Well, I'd say. These are hard times, but with the help of the Senecas and the garrison we can maintain our hold in this territory."

The Senecas stared at Joseph's family without making any gestures of welcome. One of the men spoke, using the Onondaga language so that all those present could understand.

"So you are He Who Places Two Bets. What words does the Great English Father have for the Senecas?"

Joseph replied with the greatest calm.

"They are words of allegiance. Not only for the Senecas but also for the whole of the Longhouse. You will hear them at greater length at the council, in the spring."

The Seneca nodded. Walter Butler signed to the Brants to follow him.

"Come, I will take you to my father. But at dinner keep a little time for me, Joseph. I want to hear the news from the motherland."

The group passed through the crowd. Young Butler walked stiffly. Joseph felt cold, silent eyes upon him.

"My son exaggerates. We're doing a good job, but the sachems are a long way from deciding which side to take. They come here because we have provisions, rifles, blankets, and rum; they think we're at home here. They have much to gain, but they are reluctant to take the nation into war.

John Butler sat up in his chair and began striding back and forth across the room. The Spartan surroundings matched the appearance of the old Irishman, more tough and hoary than Joseph remembered.

"They may well have a point. The garrison is undermanned. News of the disembarkations in New York and Quebec comes from too far away. The Senecas and the Tuscaroras don't see the British forces deployed, they don't see what advantage there is in taking part in the conflict."

Joseph pointed to the east. "The eastern portal of the Longhouse is already under attack from the enemy. That's why I'm here. To ask you to support me and the men I'm assembling. We need gunpowder, rifles, and victuals."

"A loyalist militia? Is that what you have in mind?"

"Yes," Joseph replied.

Butler sat down again. Joseph noticed the inlaid wooden armchair, carved with scenes from the Passion of Christ.

Butler struck the gleaming arm of the chair with the palm of his hand. "A present from the Senecas. It came from a French abbey."

He seemed to meditate for a moment, and said at last, "I have a task to perform here. Its success depends on the quantity of supplies that I manage to bring in." His voice grew serious. "Winter is at the gates and I hardly have enough for my family. If I run out of goods, the Senecas will turn their backs on me, that much is certain. The only way to keep them on our side is to keep them supplied."

Joseph remained impassive.

"Are you denying me your support, Captain?"

Butler sighed. "When the time comes you will have all the support you need. But if you want my opinion, your initiative strikes me as rather hasty. We haven't received orders from high command, and the council of the Six Nations hasn't yet been called."

Joseph suppressed the impulse to raise his voice.

"In the Mohawk Valley the rebels are already doing whatever they want. Johnson Hall has been requisitioned, and Sir John's wife is in prison. It's time to defend ourselves. You say we should wait for orders, but I have the word of the king in person."

"Don't get angry, Joseph Brant," said Butler, raising his open hand. "It won't change my mind. I know what's happening at our home. My own wife and two little sons have been captured by the rebels and brought to Albany. I wasn't there to defend them, but here, doing my duty as a good loyalist."

The Indian remained silent.

Butler rose to his feet and picked up a wooden stick from the table. It was a staff of command, inlaid and painted red and black. Its grip was adorned with various scalps.

"Another gift from the Seneca sachems," said the old captain. "An admirable object, don't you think? It emanates strength and authority." He stroked one of the tufts of hair with a delicate gesture of his rough, knotty hands. "Fear."

He approached Joseph, holding the stick in plain view.

"What do you want to do?" he asked. "Sacrifice the family? Do you want to lose your dear ones, your descendants?" He looked at the Indian without expecting a reply.

Joseph saw the faces of Susanna, Isaac and Christina passing before his eyes.

"God only knows if I can wait to act," Butler went on, his voice low and grim. "But I know that when the moment comes, it will be as terrible as the wrath of Our Lord, and we must all be willing to rise to the challenge. Accept the sacrifices that God imposes upon us. Turn ourselves into a scourge." A grimace of hatred twisted his mouth. "On that day we will draw out the innards of the renegades. We will decorate the drive of Johnson Hall with their guts."

Suddenly he appeared to stir himself.

"I renew the offer I made to you in Montreal: Stay here with us. At the appropriate moment we will lead the counterattack together."

Joseph rose from his chair.

"I'm sorry, I can't wait. My decision has been taken."

Butler nodded with resignation.

"I understand. Don't leave empty-handed. We confiscated a cargo on the lake. A dozen rifles and four barrels of gunpowder. It isn't much, but. . . Take it, you'll need it."

Joseph felt his blood boiling with rage, but managed to contain himself. It was better than nothing and he was in no position to refuse. He stared at the Irishman's outstretched hand for a long time before deciding to shake it.

11.

He left Fort Niagara alone and in silence. A cascade of pins fell from the white sky, announcing frost.

Joseph looked at the long, narrow trail ahead of him. He decided it would not be a return journey so much as a pilgrimage. Winter would not stop him: he would bring the news to the Nations, the gospel according to Joseph Brant Thayendanegea. If John Butler had gunpowder and salted meat, he had a story to tell, one so fine that it would set souls alight. The story of an Indian who, like Hendrick many years before, had gone to the island of England and spoken to the Great English Father. He certainly wouldn't persuade them to fight in the snow, but the first warmth would awaken their instincts and their desire to test themselves, at least it would the younger men among them. Then something would happen—he was sure of it. Events would help him to persuade the undecided, and God would be on his side.

He reached Geneseo on Christmas Day. The curiosity of the inhabitants welcomed him like a warm embrace. His fame marched ahead of him to the Five Finger Lakes and the Mohawk Valley. It reached the Seneca villages and headed south, all the way to the slopes of the Allegheny Mountains. He told the elders about the Wise White Man who had entrusted him with the task of fighting in his name. The young men he told about the strongest army in the world. The children he told about the fireworks.

On the first day of the new year he was in Buck Tooth, then in Conewango, and then the snow stopped him and forced him to turn back.

He headed east, toward the Five Fingers, passing through villages, stopping in the houses to sit by the fire and spread the king's words. In Cayuga he developed a fever and had to stay for two weeks. Outside his dwelling a line of people waited for the story of the king and the city with its huge buildings that could hold hundreds of people. Joseph kept them all happy. He showed himself to be proud, but not vainglorious. He pretended he was in good health, suppressing his coughing fits as if choking down bitter morsels. When he had regained his strength he set off for Onondaga. Throngs of little boys and the songs of women announced his arrival. He asked the guards of the Sacred Fire of the Confederation to attend the Oswego Council in the spring. The sachems agreed, in exchange for a detailed account of his journey beyond the ocean. "Like Hendrick," the oldest of them murmured, sitting in the circle, and the name of Thayendanegea ran from one gate of the Longhouse to the other. A decrepit old chief asked him how many people lived in London. Joseph replied that their numbers were greater than the termites in a termite's nest and the sachems talked about it for a whole day, closed away in a conclave like papist bishops.

"Brothers, this rebellion is the greatest threat that the Six Nations have ever had to confront. The American Englishmen have declared their independence from England: they no longer recognize the authority of the king. This means they believe that the bar placed upon their expansion into our lands has fallen. They will spread westward like a great sea. Only by fighting can we hope to save ourselves from catastrophe. Fighting for England and fighting for ourselves."

Some of the men nodded, but most of them remained puzzled and pensive. No one followed him. Undaunted, he continued on his solitary way, leaving the villages and the winter behind him. He reached Oquaga at the end of March, pulling behind him two mules laden with whatever supplies he had managed to procure. He was alone. He was the most famous Indian in the Six Nations.

1777

12.

They left without fuss, moving toward the gilded sunset. With them they dragged two cows, the cart horse, sacks of maize. William Adlum contemplated the half-empty granary and thought of the effort it had taken him to fill it. The children peeped out from the little window of the attic, where they had taken refuge when the men had appeared in the courtyard. Their head chief had spoken kindly, asking for food and animals in the name of King George. Meanwhile, the other chiefs showed their rifles.

Two generals had blockaded the battlefront: Winter and Smallpox. Through the fog of that April morning it was clear that the first of these was now beginning to give ground, while the other was no longer attacking as virulently as before.

Now it was up to other officers to pick up the staff of command, make decisions, move on to the final confrontation.

Joseph Brant was finishing his clothing ceremony, in Oquaga's house, with slow and detailed care, aware that the time had come for its completion, as it had for the role that he had chosen for himself. Command. He didn't have a general's stripes, but that was of no importance: war appointed its greatest executors in the field. By taking the initiative at the right moment you can easily topple the most hierarchical structure. And by choosing the right time for action you can decide the outcome in many conflicts. The valor and courage of the warriors takes care of the rest. Joseph knew there were difficulties. Their equipment was sparse, only a few rifles, and they were short of gunpowder and money—all things you need to win a war. And their contingent wasn't large enough, but more men might join as more victories were won. Enthusiasm and the desire for booty would swell the ranks. If the volunteers going into battle beside Joseph Brant earned a solid reward, without costing the king's coffers a penny, within a few months they would be legion.

At last Joseph slipped on the scarlet jacket of the imperial army, solemnly and meticulously doing up each button, smoothing every crease and wrinkle, to create an authoritative and martial appearance. Now he was ready. Outside, the rays of the sun pierced the morning fog. Only at that moment did he notice that Isaac was behind him, studying him, grim and spellbound. He stared at the little boy for a few seconds, enough to make him feel worried.

"Come with your father. We have to talk to the men."

The boy jumped behind him like a dog.

*   *   *

The faces told stories. They spoke of lives spent turning clods and sowing seeds in untamed land, of wounds from claws and knives. They wore the stolid expressions of peasants and hunters. They lived deep in the interior of the colony, and Joseph knew that he could rely on their hatred of the Albany Assembly and the New York speculators.

In front of all the others, the Hough brothers and Daniel Secord were resting on long rifles. They greeted Joseph's arrival by touching the brims of their hats. Some of the others did likewise.

Joseph, with a hand on Isaac's shoulder, took up his position under the flag, as he had done the previous autumn.

"You have come of your own free will," he said in English. "I can't give you any wages, as the officers of the army do, because I have no money. I can't supply you with weapons and ammunition, or give you rations. But I can tell you that you will be obeying a single chief and no one else. And you will be able to leave whenever you wish. Only the honor of your word binds you to this company. We have only one purpose: to fight the enemies of the king. Our enemies."

"Hurrah for Brant's Volunteers!" cried Henry Hough.

"Hurrah!" repeated Johnny.

A silence followed, broken only by coughing and the spitting of tobacco.

"I shall set up our headquarters here," Joseph went on. "But in order to fight we must get hold of food and ammunition."

"We know where to go and get them, Captain Brant." It was Henry Hough's rasping voice again. "From the farms of the traitors. Those sly dogs who don't openly support the rebellion, but do so in the shadows. Spies and jinxes. We will requisition their animals and their granaries. We will take their weapons and their gunpowder."

"And what if you're wrong and they are really patriots?" objected a scrawny young man with a shock of red hair.

Henry Hough spat tobacco juice on the ground and darted him a malevolent glance.

"If they are good patriots they'll let us have it without complaining. We are defenders of the king."

A murmur of approval ran through the group.

Joseph raised a hand and silence fell.

"May God be with us."

William Adlum thanked God for being alive, along with the rest of the family. The shadow of the flag stretched across the land until it licked the farm itself. The soldiers were ghosts returning to Gehenna.

No, they were thieves and cowards.

His wife called to him from the doorway of the house. The children were crying.

William Adlum clenched his fists and turned to go back in. The world was collapsing, and all he could do was pray. The Day of Judgment was plainly near at hand.

13.

New York was all rain and grey outlines. The carriage wheels sank into the mud of Wall Street, as the horse hobbled wetly along under blows from the coachman's whip.

Guy Johnson thought of the letter that had arrived the previous day.

Since returning to America he had seen his former associates leaving one by one for the Great Unknown that began on the far shore of the Harlem River. He had been left on his own, camping out on a scrap of New World that wasn't even dry land. Now events were paying him back for his inactivity.

His joints had started creaking again: rust between his vertebrae, a sense of clumsiness and slowness, migraine headaches. It was time to move, he needed to make a jump.

General Howe, the hero of Boston, would welcome him right away. A kind of understanding had arisen between them. Now he was going to ask permission to equip a boat and set sail. Not a pin moved in New York without the general's approval. He could be compared to a dictator from ancient times, ruling the city in the only possible way, with a fist of iron and the support of the fleet commanded by his brother, the only person he really trusted.

A difficult pair, the Howes. The New Yorkers had had to learn that at their own expense. They were riotous and undisciplined people, all smugglers who would rather have gone on doing business without paying taxes to the Crown. It was no coincidence that at the outbreak of the insurrection they had melted down the statue of King George to make bullets to send to Washington.

The carriage slowed down in front of a unit of redcoat soldiers patrolling the street. The people stepped aside to let them pass, glancing at them indifferently. A little way off, two sinister-looking characters were chained to the stocks, covered with filth. One of them seemed to be staring at Guy. On the other side, a second patrol of soldiers: the same red uniforms, dark skin. Negroes trying to sign up other Negroes.

The world was changing at a great rate, Guy thought. One day you're a slave, the next you're a soldier of His Majesty.

Tall and short. He thought again of the letter he had received. Daniel Claus, writing to tell him he was back from London. A year in the antechamber had won him the command of the Indian irregulars in the imminent counteroffensive. He also wrote about Montreal, where he had met up with Sir John to recruit volunteers. They invited Guy to join them by the beginning of the summer.

Fate could be mocking: Guy had left the German at the lowest point of his fortunes, and now here he was offering the superintendent a position by his side.

Claus wrote that he would expect the regular troops to get the expedition under way. He was convinced that this time he would take a few Indians into the war. Joseph Brant would also be of the party.

Joseph. His translator, Guy thought. The Department's interpreter. Old Sir William had been very clear-sighted in choosing him as a pupil. In London that Indian had become famous and sure of his own capabilities.

If he left in a few days he would be able to do it. Joining the others and taking his share of military honor, with the kind concession of Daniel Claus and Sir John Johnson. The thought bored into his stomach.

He would be able to hug his daughters again. Claus was looking after them. Had brought them back from London to meet up with their father. He wrote that Esther was grown now, that he wouldn't recognize her.

Guy wondered if the little ones would remember his face.

Traveling across the colony was unthinkable. The rebels held the hinterland, while gangs of irregulars ran back and forth in search of booty, spies and hostages. He had to obtain permission to man a ship, travel to the Bay of St. Lawrence and Quebec. To set off upriver. A long and difficult journey.

The carriage stopped in front of the military governor's residence. Guy got out quickly and saluted the sentries, who let him pass.

"I thought the English climate was hard, before I spent a summer and a winter in New York."

General Howe was standing by the window. From that position he enjoyed the sight of an expanse of roofs, interrupted by the pennants of the ships moored by the quays. Gulls with dirty feathers sheltered from the rain beneath the eaves, watching the streets below, waiting for an unexpected morsel.

"Does the bad weather put Your Excellency in a bad mood?"

"No, sir, I'm too much i' th' sun, as the Prince of Denmark has it."

"When Your Excellency quotes Shakespeare, it's usually a bad omen."

Howe glanced fleetingly at Guy.

"They're sidelining me, Colonel Johnson. What should my mood be?"

"You're making fun of me, General. King George has no better officer than you."

Howe gave a twisted smile.

"You forget that I am also a member of Parliament. On the wrong side."

He showed Guy to a chair with a high wooden back. Guy sat down. He noticed a half-empty bottle of sherry that had been left open on the table.

The general invited him to help himself, but he refused with a bow of the head.

"Look at me, Colonel Johnson," said Howe, still staring at the city. His voice was hoarse from alcohol and thinking. "You have before you the man who saved Boston. The taking of Breed's Hill cost the blood of many good men. Twice they repelled us with long-range fire. How many officers would have ordered a third attack? One of them you have before you. We took that damned hill and then the whole accursed promontory." He tapped the windowpane with a delicate gesture that contrasted starkly with his uniform and his harsh tone. "Next came New York. A forced march in stages, to get there ahead of Washington. My men held the city when the reinforcements from England had yet to arrive. We fought here in Manhattan, in White Plains, we took the forts, routed the continentals. I sent Cornwallis after Washington, to chase him to hell, but this damned country is much bigger than hell."

He broke off and sighed.

"No one put his soul into this war more than yours truly, Colonel Johnson. Do you think I did it because I think it's a just war? It may seem strange to you, but that's not the case. I was elected as a Whig, I was opposed to the politics of our government in America. I acted for the good of England, and because I am a loyal subject of His Majesty. I have done my duty as a soldier even though I didn't agree with the cause. And what is my reward? They send Burgoyne to take command of the land offensive." He sneered bitterly. "After all I have done in the field, they still don't trust me. They are afraid I'll become too awkward, you see? So they accuse me of fence-sitting, of holding off the inland attack. Rumors are born in the House of Commons, but they can be heard quite clearly over here as well."

He turned and sat down on the overstuffed red-brocade armchair.

"Let them do it. Let them force their way inland, puffed up with all their self-importance." He looked at Guy Johnson. "I don't wish to offend you, Colonel, but the presumption of the Tories suggests the frivolity. And God knows that war is a serious business."

With a broad sweep of his hand, Guy invited him to go on. He didn't seem offended in the least. From the outset their political discussions had been based upon mutual respect. Guy had been the one who had quipped that if Samuel Johnson frequented the same London club as Edmund Burke, a less famous Johnson could boast of conversing with a Whig general.

Howe looked at the bottle of sherry without touching it, as if gauging what was to be done with it.

"Burgoyne doesn't know this country very well," he went on. "He thinks he'll come down from Canada and meet a few gangs of farmers armed with pitchforks and old muskets. I'd love to know how he thinks he's going to keep two-hundred-mile supply lines going." He shook his head. "As far as I'm concerned, I'm going to stay within reach of the coast. I tell you, in America a good backup fleet is your best insurance. We, too, will attack. But to the south, toward Philadelphia. Before the winter I will have taken that city as well." He gave a slight shrug. "As long as they let me," he added. "That way, all the ports in the North will be ours. Holding the ports means holding trade and the communication routes with Europe. What else does a naval power like England need?

Someone knocked on the door. An attendant came in with a stack of papers, which he set down for the general's attention. Howe picked up his pen and dipped it in the inkwell.

"You must forgive me, Colonel. You have certainly requested an audience for a reason, and I have bored you with my ruminations."

Guy cleared his throat, but the words didn't come out. He thought of Claus's offer and the position of second in command that would be his. He thought of the Mohawk Valley in the hands of the rebel militia, of Johnson Hall transformed into a barracks. Who knew who was sleeping in the rooms at Guy Park? Yokels and stable boys, thieves and looters. Their stench could well have contaminated the walls, never to leave. They might even have found the family treasure.

He thought of the long days at sea, the pirates attacking the boats in the name of a new and hungry nation. He thought of the mosquitoes and again of Daniel Claus, who was extending a hand to him.

He looked at the city outside the window, behind the general. A ray of sunlight had pierced the clouds and was pouring in through the window.

"I am here to pay you tribute, Excellency," he said. "and to assure myself that you are in good health. And certainly to offer you my services, in case they might be of use to you."

"I am grateful to you, sir," Howe replied distractedly, beginning to sign the papers. "I know I can count on your support. I am in excellent health, don't worry on that account—apart, that is, from my poisoned heart. But now please excuse me, I must sign today's death sentences, and it is not an activity that encourages conversation."

Guy got to his feet, bowed, and headed for the door.

"Colonel," the general called out to him.

"Excellency," said Guy, turning around.

Howe held the goose quill in midair, with ink on its tip, as black and dense as the blood it would shed.

"Come back and see me before I, too, throw myself into this great offensive." He pulled his face into a smile. "We'll drink a bottle of brandy and talk a little bit about London."

Guy nodded and passed through the door.

He had chosen. He felt lighter, not necessarily better.

14.

They had arrived one June morning, after a day of marching and a night on the riverbank. The people of Unadilla had sought refuge in the church, praying that they would go quickly. The minister had appeared in the door to welcome them into the house of the Lord. Joseph knew him: he was one of those white men who, when they hear talk of Indians, stroke their scalps and brandish the cross.

Without putting God to any trouble, the Volunteers left before evening, with a dozen cows, three pigs, and a bag each of vegetables and dried meat.

There had been no sign of the rebel militia.

A week later, many of the farms in the area had already been abandoned. The settlers escaped to Cherry Valley, to German Flatts and to Albany, to beg generals and settlers not to leave them alone to the mercy of the Indians.

Nicholas Herkimer had offered to help them. He had sent a message to Joseph to ask for a meeting, in the name of their old friendship.

A meeting in Unadilla, in the middle of the month.

Beneath a boiling sun that smelled of summer, Daniel Secord walked on clumps of earth. This field of alfalfa separated the Volunteers from the Tryon Militia. Those who had seen the rebel troop coming down along the shore of the Susquehanna spoke of at least three hundred armed men.

The general approached him on horseback, flanked by five of his troops, and stopped to wait in the grass, at the precise center of the plot. Secord smelled tobacco macerated in scotch and thought that only a madman could smoke a pipe with that sun over his head.

"Captain Brant sends his greetings and asks to know the reason for this meeting."

Herkimer took a long puff and emptied his pipe by striking it against his saddle.

"We have always been good friends," he replied. "They say he has spoken to King George and Lord Germain. I would like to know what he think about the case of the colonies."

"And what about your militiamen? Don't they want to speak to the captain as well? It will be a long discussion."

"It will be a friendly discussion," the general replied. "You have my word."

"Very well. I will come back in an hour with the answer to your questions. Is there anything else you want to ask?"

Herkimer's index finger seemed to be caught in the bowl of the pipe as he pressed fresh tobacco into it.

"You mean that Captain Brant does not intend to meet me?"

"I mean, sir, that a meeting with three hundred armed men is not called a 'friendly discussion,' it is called a battle. If that is the kind of meeting you have in mind, we will be happy to satisfy you."

This time the general appeared not to have heard. He finished filling his pipe and brought it to his mouth without lighting it.

"Inform your captain that I will have a shelter built on this precise spot. I will be here tomorrow morning, with five unarmed men. In this heat, I am sure that Captain Brant will not keep me waiting in vain."

Indian chatter, the most worthless of goods on the market. Herkimer wanted to take a hundredweight of it home with him.

"Tell me if I'm wrong," said Jonas Klug, as he whittled a branch with his knife. "We haven't come all this way to listen to a savage."

"Quite correct," replied Rynard's mouth, appearing out of the darkness. "Moreover, I know what he's going to say, I'd bet a Spanish dollar on it."

"I agree with you, gentlemen. Perhaps together we can convince the general."

"The general won't change his mind, Captain Neuman. Words drive him mad."

The German's knife abruptly cut the branch in two. Part of it fell into the fire, where the flames began consuming it.

"If you want my opinion, the only thing that matters is that we get the scalp of Joseph Brant. The rest is wasted effort."

Darkness swallowed up the faces. It seemed to do the same thing with their words.

"If they want to fight, don't let us stop them," observed Neuman.

"And what need is there for fighting? If I were part of the delegation tomorrow, I'd solve the problem once and for all."

Klug took his knife by the tip of the blade, weighed it in his hand for a moment, then threw it to the ground, where it landed between Rynard's feet.

Once again it was Neuman who spoke first.

"If you tell me that Joseph Brant is a danger that needs to be eliminated, then I'm with you. But knifing a man in the back is an act of dishonor."

"A man? A savage, I say. Think how much misery, destruction and death you would spare the American people. And even if he were a white man, what kind of patriot are you if you choose your honor over the good of the Nation?"

A fir cone dropped into the fire and sent up a flurry of sparks.

"He's right," Rynard observed. "If a great wrong brings great advantages, it's no longer a wrong."

"Herkimer and his Indian friend will speak," Klug continued, "and we'll go back to German Flatts, and one day we'll be told that Joseph Brant has flayed the people of Unadilla. That day I will come and ask you how you feel, Captain Neuman."

The man stirred the sand with the tip of his boot. He squashed a cockroach that was trying to crawl out and raised his head.

"What are your plans?"

"Get rid of the Indian, what else? I'd offer to do it myself, but my aim isn't up to it. It requires someone capable of taking long and accurate aim. When Brant shows his face, *bang*! The problem is solved once and for all."

"You risk the gallows pulling something like that. If I were you I'd be careful."

Klug looked around. "Why, are you saying there are spies here? Perhaps you should be careful yourself."

A frosty silence fell.

"Calm down, gentlemen. I've never seen anyone end up on the gallows for bumping off an Indian," Rynard finally declared, in the pause between two spits. "Some people would give you a medal for getting rid of the savage who met the king."

A hum of approval ran around the fire.

"I've heard lots of people boast of being the best huntsman in German Flatts, in the Valley, in the whole colony." Klug stood up. "Isn't there anyone willing to demonstrate it? No one's coming forward? You, Keller? Or you, Rumsfeld?"

The last man gulped, then nodded. "I'll do it."

"All right, then. Do we all agree?"

Silence settled once more. The men weighed up the words they had just heard. One by one they declared their agreement.

"Fine, gentlemen. Now let us sleep the sleep of the just."

Pain, pain in his ribs: they were kicks, Klug realized. He was being kicked awake. And it didn't take much to wake someone that way. His heart leaped into his mouth, he was about to sit up but felt the sole of a boot pressing on his chest.

His eyes focused on a bayonet and followed it up to a rifle, and a militiaman who seemed to find the whole thing incredibly funny. Klug looked around. Rumsfeld and Keller were being subjected to the same treatment, and so was Rynard.

Flanked by his guards, Herkimer stared at him. His face showed more disgust than anger.

"I should hang you for sedition, gentlemen. But I shall be satisfied with much less. You, Rumsfeld, fifteen lashes. Klug will have ten. The others will get away with nine. Then you will go back home. Do not cross my path again."

The pipe-smoke rolled thickly against the roof. The men dripped sweat and dust. General Herkimer held a Bible open on his knees and reread the same four lines. He was not distracted by impatience, or by worry about what he would say. The meeting was the final act in a ceremony: the meaning lay in the gesture, not in the words. When an American patriot could still travel a hundred miles to talk to a loyalist Indian, the time of massacres had not yet come.

A battalion of clouds was pursuing the sun when Joseph Brant came into the open, surrounded by his men. Herkimer set down the Bible, got to his feet and invited them to make themselves comfortable. Brant's entourage sat down on two benches arranged in a half-moon. Brant refused the camp chair and remained standing.

Behind him, the older of the Hough brothers smiled smugly and nudged Daniel Secord.

Joseph Brant greeted everyone and stared at Herkimer. "Your courage is admirable, sir. You are aware that I could sweep you away with a wave of my hand. My forces are greater in number than yours." He paused rhetorically to allow his words to imprint themselves clearly in the minds of those present. Then he went on. "It has not been an easy matter to restrain my warriors. I had to tell them that you, sir, are an old friend, and that among your men there are old acquaintances and schoolmates. For that reason I will settle for a dozen cattle as a peace offering, and the immediate withdrawal of your troops."

Herkimer gestured to his men to be quiet. "We are most fortunate to have friends like you, Mr. Brant. At any rate, I should like to check in person the state of the people in Unadilla."

"Out of the question, sir. Remember that we are at war, a war that we did not want. Consider yourself lucky not to have been brought to Unadilla in chains."

Herkimer nodded, without taking his eyes off the Indian's. "As you wish, Mr. Brant. But I warn you. Do not allow atrocities to be committed in this war. They will not be tolerated."

"I was about to say the same thing. The discussion is over. The next time we meet, it will not be to talk."

15.

It was good to reach Oswego from the lake, like coming from the sea. It didn't even seem like the same place, when it had appeared on the horizon.

The aquatic convoy was imposing and magnificent. A big ship, no different from those that ploughed the ocean, formed the arrowhead of a fleet of smaller vessels, all making for the council of the Six Nations.

Esther watched the vertex of that sharp geometry: pointing the way were John Johnson and Daniel Claus, standing stiffly in the prow of the *Barrymore*, bringing a cargo of men and victuals.

Sir John had organized their return from Montreal in grand style: he had reached the council with hundreds of men, a militia that he had christened Royal Green. In addition, the *Barrymore* overflowed with food, cannon, rifles, gunpowder, rum.

Esther had arrived in Canada with her uncles in early spring. She had to acknowledge that since being offered the job in the capital, Uncle Daniel seemed like another person. Even his manners had changed; they were more resolute. He now dressed in the London fashion, and even his German accent was less marked.

Everywhere there was talk of war: no one thought of anything else. Esther studied the men's faces, their determined expressions. She listened to speeches, unequivocal words. "Implacable revenge," "Break their bones," "The Johnsons will take command again," "His Majesty's army will reach us in ten days."

When the convoy had been sighted from the battlements of Oswego a jubilant crowd had assembled on the shore to wait for them, while others tried to board boats and canoes to go and welcome them and escort them to the dock. Their enthusiasm was unquenchable, and Esther had been filled with powerful emotions, and a confusion of feelings had swelled her heart. During the disembarkation and the frenzy of the unloading operations, men and women had run to lend a hand. Esther had taken advantage of the hubbub to vanish. There was something she should have done a long time ago.

The little graveyard behind the chapel was deserted. The wind carried away the sounds of the camp and the crowd of men preparing for war. The breeze slipped in and out of the standing crosses, bringing with it the smell of the lake.

A slender figure stood out among the gravestones, wildflowers held tightly in its joined hands.

Mother, I've come back.

I'm home again, mother of mine, even though home is far away. I love these trees, the water, our rivers. There are many Indians. Our Indians. There's an important council, it's going to decide the war. They say a great danger hangs over us, but I won't hide away and cry. Not anymore.

Here I am, I'm back.

I've crossed the ocean again, to be here with you.

Much time has passed, and I am different. I have grown.

In London I learned many things. I could have stayed, Aunt Nancy wouldn't have stopped me. I chose to come back.

To take my place, as you would have wanted. As Grandfather would have wanted.

Aunt Nancy and Uncle Daniel said my father would be here as well, but I haven't seen him. He won't be there. I stopped waiting for him some time ago. I have learned to live without him. Others have shouldered my pain. One of them I hope to meet here, a brave and good man.

That's one of the reasons I came back.

Mother, these fresh flowers are the love that still lives. They are a smile, a hope in times of hardship. They are the steady grip that banishes fear and pain.

My name is Esther Johnson, daughter of Mary, granddaughter of William. This is the land where I was born, these are my people.

16.

Philip thought that just two years before he had traveled from Canajoharie to Oswego, only to end up fighting in Canada. Now the war was everywhere, and yet it always set off from here, from the shores of the great lake, where the Iroquois had once again arranged to meet.

Paul Oronhyateka pointed to the smoke that rose above the treetops. They were close now.

There were barely thirty of them, the last able-bodied men left in Canajoharie, plus the old sachem Tekarihoga. It had been a silent and invisible journey, without fires or lengthy halts, in what was now hostile territory. At every stage, Philip had heard the hammering of the woodpecker. It was following them, flying overhead, darting in front of them, checking that the trails were free, beating with its beak to urge them onward, telling them to get a move on.

When the first tents appeared on the edge of the clearing, Jethro Kanenonte uttered a cry announcing their arrival. Kanatawakhon and Sakihenakenta echoed it, while Philip filled his lungs with the heat that scorched the air.

Some Highlanders drew pieces of boiled meat from a dented pot. Philip sat by the fire and thanked them. He watched the flames dancing among the embers under the vessel. He thought about what was left after combustion: a dry, dusty substance. Blackened splinters, grey ashes. Fire gives life, and yet it consumes. The wood is destroyed, it becomes a blackish skeleton, a pointless relic, mute dust.

It had been a strange summer: a series of storms that furiously followed one another, breaking the branches of the trees, changing the land into viscid mud. In the sun the skin of his face stung; in the shade his body shivered.

The tops of the pines swayed in all directions, like the heads of monks all chanting different verses.

All the songs were mournful. The meat was stringy.

From the other side of the parade ground a figure attracted his attention. A young woman was walking toward him. Philip heard an inner voice speaking her name.

Esther came forward, the only pale patch in the gray of the camp. On her face was a faint, inscrutable smile. Her wide skirt, a silky shade between pink and yellow, was licked by the mud; a bonnet rimmed with lace protected her hair. She radiated a tenacity whose potential Philip had sensed that day in London when he had taken her hand, and which now seemed fully developed. Around her wrist was the bracelet he had given her.

Philip got to his feet.

"Mr. Lacroix."

Her voice was mature now. She was a woman. He was aware of her smell.

Philip didn't know how to approach her. He said nothing.

Esther looked him up and down. "The little girl hiding in the woodshed, you remember? I'm nearly fifteen now."

"What are you doing here?" Philip managed to ask her. "There's a war on."

"My uncle, Mr. Claus, presumed that I would be able to meet my father. He was supposed to be coming here from New York. But I knew he wouldn't come."

Philip frowned.

"You knew that?"

A shadow fell across Esther's face.

"Not all men are brave." She stared Philip straight in the eyes. "There is only one man who is brave enough for all the others. And I knew I would meet him here."

Philip wondered how it was possible that this young woman was the same frightened creature that he had left in England. Barely a year had passed. Then he remembered that at that age time is counted in days, and that days like the ones they had faced make you grow up in a hurry.

"I've got to go now, Mr. Lacroix. Aunt Nancy will be looking for me."

Philip sat down beside the fire again. Before he could get his thoughts in order, someone squatted down next to him.

They hadn't seen each other for a year, but Joseph talked as if he were resuming a conversation interrupted only a moment before.

"Molly didn't want to come, then."

"She thinks she might still be useful down there."

Joseph nodded. "I thought so."

"Your message said they were all here," Philip said. "But there are no Oneida."

"Does that matter? Everyone makes his own choice," replied Joseph. "We are part of a big army. We will be home by the autumn." He picked up a piece of meat on his fork, blew on it and sank his teeth into it. After chewing it for a long time, he spat it out into the dust. "This meat tastes like wood." He got up and touched his friend's shoulder. "We leave in two days," he said. "We're going to take Fort Stanwix. The Senecas will be there as well." He was about to walk away, then stopped and bowed again.

"I'm glad you're here."

Philip watched him striding resolutely across the parade ground. He had done it. He was a chief.

17.

In the forests around Canajoharie, the blackberries and strawberries had ripened early, and the women went out at dawn to pick them cool with dew. Time stolen from more useful work, and a basket of berries for booty, just enough to sweeten the tongues of a family's hungry mouths. And yet none of them would have renounced the flavors of the forest, or a ritual that began the summer, a guarantee of order and beauty.

In the last year the valley had opened up over an abyss, had become a field of conquest for a new nation, but the little fruits were still scented, and covered the edge of the precipice. As sweet as hopes, Molly thought. As red and black as war.

Perhaps that was why the great vision of two summers before had returned, as clear as the air after the first snow. Sir William's funeral, the land too hard to be dug, the coffin gliding on the water, toward the spring.

According to the other older women, it was a prophecy of things to come. That which goes against the current is destined to return, and Chief Big Business, Warraghiyagey, would come back in the form of his descendants, and they would have to prepare to welcome him.

So Molly had decided to stay, even though Joseph had invited her to join him. So that Ann could eat blackberries, her lips circled with purple and her eyes bright with the new experience.

She pushed the two little children among shrubs and patches of sunlight. Ann and George knelt comfortably and began eating nonstop.

Molly took the opportunity to walk away, still within calling distance, to a granite rock hidden by the trees. She hoped the boy wouldn't be late. Certainly, his absence had already been noted. For some time the Whigs had been spying on her, checking her movements, and those of the people going in and out of the general store and her house. But no eyes could rifle through dreams, slip beneath every forest rock, search the store's customers one by one. The rebel spies looked without seeing, and Molly, under close surveillance, went on handling news, information, dispatches.

In his latest message, Joseph had told her about the major offensive planned by the English. The attack on the colony of New York would come from two sides, to trap the rebels in a vise. While General Burgoyne came down from Lake Champlain, Joseph would follow the troops of Colonel St. Leger, who had been besieging Fort Stanwix for two weeks. The situation was one of stalemate, but the rebels would surrender sooner or later.

What Joseph didn't know was that the news had traveled along the Mohawk River until it reached the settlers' villages. That night General Herkimer had set off with seven hundred rebel militiamen, heading for the fort to help the besieged forces.

The only alternative route for such a large contingent was the old Oneida path that ran from the village of Oriskany. The march would be very slow and a fast courier could get there at least three days before the rebels. That would give Joseph enough time to come up with a countermove.

Molly suddenly heard a rustle behind her and stopped expectantly.

The young man emerged from the forest and smiled at her.

"May God protect you, Degonwadonti."

The woman walked over and handed him the letter, a few lines scribbled down that morning, which the young man slipped under his shirt.

"You must join Thayendanegea. Run without stopping. Run until you burst, if you have to."

The image of the disfigured corpse of Samuel Waterbridge crossed her mind, but she banished it immediately and gripped the boy's arm.

"Come back safe and sound."

She watched him disappearing quickly among the trees. She hurried to fill the basket of berries and called the children to go back to the village.

As she walked along the path, she saw in her mind's eye Nicholas Herkimer in the drawing room at Johnson Hall, talking to Sir William and sipping black tea. Then she saw him as an older man, the last time he had dropped in at the store to persuade her to keep her people out of the war.

"Apparently Benjamin Franklin took the idea of a confederation from you Iroquois," the German had smiled at her.

"If Congress only wanted to steal ideas," Molly had replied, "the Mohawk battle-ax would still lie underground."

For a moment she hoped that her brother and Nicholas Herkimer could still avoid one another, but she knew it was too late. The valley could never hold both of them. Warraghiyagey's world had changed forever.

She looked at her own hands and those of her children, dyed with berry juice. She was frightened. Visions of blood reddening the river and flooding the forest came surging violently into her. She began to murmur a prayer. She prayed for Joseph. She prayed to the Master of Life to grant him victory over his enemies.

18.

When Nicholas Herkimer tried to reload his pistol he noticed that his hands were trembling. He had to lean against a tree trunk, get his breath back, cram the piston into the barrel, aim the weapon blindly past the tree and pull the trigger. The only sound that followed was that of the cock misfiring.

His wounded leg gave way, and he slipped to the ground and lay outstretched in the rain, which dripped from the branches and struck his face.

Hands gripped him and sat him up, resting his back against the bark. He saw the water coming down in streams to mix with his blood in a little puddle. He couldn't remember how many hours it had been since his knee had been injured; his leg felt like a piece of wood.

Dr. Van Hoek slipped his boot off. Herkimer tried not to think about the pain. He listened to Captain De John firing insults from the neighboring tree. His brother-in-law, a loyalist volunteer, was bombarding him with the same projectiles from a few yards further off, going back down the whole family tree, until before they had set off from Rotterdam.

Herkimer thought his brother must be on the other side as well. And Williers's cousins. And those great sons of bitches the Houghs. He knew those people; some of them had fought with him during the other war, along with Sir William Johnson. Good shots, Christ knew. He had to thank God for the storm that had granted a truce.

He looked at the bodies lying around him, some with their skulls showing, red with blood. The moans of the wounded struggled with the silence of death. One man stretched his arm to the sky, begging for help with his last remaining voice. Herkimer thought he recognized Sanders. He had been scalped, but he was still alive. He would have dealt him the coup de grace, if only the firearms had worked. Neuman's cries were heartrending. He lay a few trees away with a bullet in his guts, the blood pouring between fingers pressed to his belly. Two men were holding him tightly, but they couldn't make him stop calling out to God and his own mother.

Only a short time before, those men had been standing, alive. Time had suddenly speeded up, but the light said it was late in the day.

"Don't scatter, close ranks! Fire away!"

He had shouted the orders in Mohawk Dutch to make sure everyone understood. The militia had obeyed: they had behaved well, like soldiers, like a real army. He thought he would have to write to Schuyler and Washington.

They needed to know. They had repelled the enemy, by God. There were Indians among them too, quite a few. Forest demons, they emerged from the earth itself.

"Don't scatter, keep together!"

The attack had come from the sides of the path. An ambush. They were waiting for them, someone had warned them. The first to collapse had been Jansen, struck in the chest. In a moment the fusillade had erased the forest. Blinded by smoke, the men had huddled together in a phalanx.

"Two rows, in pairs, one fires and the other reloads!"

Alternately firing and reloading, not giving the devils time to approach, they had kept them at a distance. With the Indians there was no escape in man-to-man fighting. Herkimer knew that; he had learned it during the other war. The men struck by tomahawks lay face down.

Moving slowly, all together, like a gigantic spider, they had sought refuge in the copse. Salvation: for each man a shelter of solid wood, a position from which to return fire, a hole from which to fight like blazes.

But now Herkimer could feel his men's morale wavering, fear slipping its way among the trees, silent and lethal. Sooner or later the rain would stop and the gunpowder would dry. Could they repel a second attack? That was the question they held in, behind their shelters, accompanying it with a prayer.

He thought of Gansevoort, stuck in Fort Stanwix, a few miles further on. They were supposed to bring him aid, ease the siege. They had to resist here, behind the trees, as Gansevoort was doing behind the battlements. The Free State of New York was in danger. If they yielded, the English would flood into the Mohawk Valley, where they would be able to attack Schuyler on his left flank.

They must wait for the light to fade, let the Oneidas guide them out of the forest, and organize their defense farther downstream.

Neuman's wails struck their eardrums even harder. He tossed and kicked to stave off the death that was clawing at him. He gave off a sense of panic, while on the other side the Indians mocked him with animal cries.

"Shut him up, for God's sake!" someone yelled.

Herkimer knew he would have to resist this panic at all cost.

"Captain De Jong!"

"At your command, sir."

The lieutenant crept over to the tree, saw the blood-drenched sock and legging.

"Pass it on," Herkimer ordered, ignoring the pain. "Every man is to stay where he is. You must stay together. Anyone who makes a run for the forest is finished. If the Indians don't find him, he will die of hunger and thirst."

De Jong did as he was bid. The general's words traveled through the branches until they were lost in the depths of the undergrowth.

Dr Van Hoek shook his head.

"The wound is infected. The bullet has been in your knee for too long."

Herkimer glanced at the wound with his teeth clenched. Splinters of bone protruded from the flesh. All the pain in the world was concentrated on a single point.

"Do what you have to."

The doctor nodded.

"De Jong!" Herkimer roared.

"At your command."

"What happened to our scouts?"

"Sir, the Oneidas are down there. They say they've already fired enough. They say the agreement was for them to act as guides. They don't see any point in going on fighting."

"Tell them this," the general hissed. "If they managed to open up an escape route I'll see to it that they get two rifles each."

He glanced at the doctor, who was pouring rum on his equipment. He gripped the captain's shoulder again.

"De Jong, be sure that we have a massed defense. Either we stay together or it's over."

At that moment a voice rang out from the other side.

"Hey, Herkimer! Do you hear me? Next time I'll get you right between the eyes."

The general recognized the timbre and the accent. He coughed and took a breath. He managed to reply in a firm voice.

"Then we will go to our Maker together, Henry Hough."

Neuman's torments were echoing even more loudly than before. A merciful hand blocked his mouth, turning his wails into a muffled growl.

Herkimer thought of his men's morale. He nodded to the doctor to wait and, supporting himself on De Jong, he managed to get back on his feet. He spoke with all his breath.

"Tryon County Militia!"

A sparse chorus of voices replied from the surrounding forest. Everyone stopped to listen to him. Even the loyalists on the other side.

"You hear them? They think they're frightening us. Instead they're encouraging us. Let them come! We've repelled them once, and we'll do it again. This forest will be their grave."

"It will be yours, Herkimer!" croaked Henry Hough.

The general clung to De Jong's shoulder.

"Remember that Albany is behind us," he shouted, louder this time. "Even if we all have to die in this damned forest, one thing is certain: they shall not pass!"

A broadside of invective was fired from the rebel side.

Herkimer allowed himself to be lowered to the ground. Van Hoek showed him his saw, but the general halted him.

"Get yourself an ax, Doctor. There's no time to lose."

19.

Joseph watched a big ant walking on a branch. The insect was carrying a leaf the size of a playing card. If men were as strong as that, he thought, we could knock down the trees in front of us with our bare hands and flush out the Tryon militia in just a few minutes.

It had been a tough battle. After initial bursts of rifle fire the warriors had charged. Herkimer's men had borne the brunt of the attack in the clearing, and then they had been forced back into the undergrowth. The surge by the Indians and the Volunteers had dissipated into a thousand streams before finally petering out. The clash had turned into a vague chaos of shots fired from one tree trunk to another, from only a few feet away.

Joseph had lined up the Volunteers behind the trees, as the warriors furiously retreated.

Sir John's Royal Greens held their positions as well, but in all that confusion it had been hard to work out who was shooting at whom.

The result was that the living, the dead and the injured were now scattered across several hundred square yards of forest.

Only the storm had interrupted the fighting.

While the smell of rotten leaves and damp wood covered the odor of gunpowder, Joseph wondered how to interpret the stalemate.

That would surely be his day. As the English soldiers besieged Fort Stanwix, he and Sir John led the loyalist contingent against Herkimer's column.

The English trusted him, the Indian who had met the King.

Someone stepped through the undergrowth and distracted him from his thoughts.

Sir John and McLeod. Along with his new green uniform, the Scotsman was still wearing his soft beret.

"An ugly business," Johnson said, pale with rage. "Herkimer is a hardheaded German—I know him. We'll have to flush them out one at a time."

"We've already lost a lot of men," said Joseph.

Sir John nodded.

"So has Herkimer. And he doesn't know these places as well as we do. All he can do is skulk off in the dark. Many of his men will be lost in the forest, but others might make it."

"You'll forgive me, sir," McLeod cut in. "The same men who brought him here can get him out. The Oneida guides are his salvation."

Joseph nodded. According to the information he had collected, those Oneida scouts had been repudiated by their tribe; they were mercenaries without honor. He had to deal with them too. No one would mourn them.

Captain Butler joined him, followed by his son Walter and the chief of the Seneca warriors. Until that moment, his own Indians had been watching the clash from the edge of the scrubland.

"The Senecas are impressed," he said with a wink, speaking English. "They're saying that today Joseph Brant's men have demonstrated that they don't fear death."

Joseph nodded and replied in the same language, staring at the chief of the warrior group.

"Pass on my words to Sayengaraghta, Captain Butler. Tell him that Joseph Brant wants him and his men to stand aside like women and witness our courage. That way we won't have to share the honor of this day with anyone."

Butler's mouth twisted into a sneer. The Seneca listened to the translation and his jaw stiffened with rage. For a moment he looked as if he were about to explode, but Joseph turned his back on him.

He listened to the air. The forest was filled with a grim silence. He knew the moment had come.

He looked into the eyes of the white men, one by one.

McLeod's eyes shone with excitement.

Sir John nodded grimly without a word.

Butler looked uncertain, unsure that he had understood what the others were thinking. With eyes narrowed to slits, he studied the Indian's intentions.

"The powder isn't yet dry," he objected.

When he received no reply he realized that he had understood only too well. His son brandished his hatchet.

The old captain plonked his hat on his head.

"All right, then, damned lunatics. Let's get it over with."

Philip Lacroix hadn't painted his face, and yet he gave off an air of strength and menace. During the first attack he had prevented the young men from hurling themselves blindly against the enemy; he had restrained their impetuosity and found them good shelters from which to bombard the militia. At first the young men had champed at the bit and complained, but they had shut up after many warriors had fallen in the clearing, mowed down by bullets. Then they had started shooting from behind the trees and rocks.

Philip studied the patch of fir trees where Herkimer's Oneida scouts were entrenched.

A little while later, about twenty young Mohawks were moving silently, led by the Great Devil.

The howl cut through the moist air. Joseph raised his tomahawk and his war-cry joined that of the entire loyalist contingent. The signal ran through the forest, repeated from one tree to the next.

A second chorus rang out on the edge of the scrub. The Senecas were going into battle. Sayengaraghta shouted to Joseph Brant that he would show him that the Senecas knew how to die. Joseph felt pleased and excited. He flung himself forward among the trees, Kanatawakhon and Sakihenakenta covering the flanks. As he passed, the Volunteers leaped into the open and followed him, shouting his name.

They collided with the first row of militiamen, clutching at those who appeared in front of them, and rolled on the ground in a cascade of leaves and mud.

Philip waited until he was at the right distance, where he could count the enemy. There were about thirty of them, well armed and on guard. They were waiting to see how the battle went before deciding what to do. There were women among them, there to carry food and ammunition.

Philip could sense the other warriors' hatred of the Oneidas. He identified the biggest of them, an impressive bulk, then came out into the open on his own, armed with mace and knife. The giant saw Philip advancing and took up the challenge with broad gestures of agreement. Philip dodged his hatchet and stabbed him in the liver.

At that moment the Mohawks charged.

Royathakariyo, his eyes white and frightening in his red-painted face, was the first to land in the midst of the enemy, shattering their heads with the butt of his rifle. Nobody seemed capable of stopping him, until one of the women slipped behind him and plunged a knife into his back.

Oronhyateka, with two hands stamped on his chest like an eagle's wings, hurled himself to the ground and with two clean blows slashed the tendons in the calves of several warriors, who fell like puppets. Kanenonte reached the woman, who was still brandishing her knife, and struck her in the face with his tomahawk. Blood and teeth flew through the air.

Sir John had ordered the Royal Greens wear their uniforms inside out, making them less recognizable targets. He gave the command to attack and they erupted from their hiding places with bayonets fixed.

The Highlanders gripped their sabers. Cormac McLeod kissed the runic symbols on his hilt. The weapon had belonged to his father; the carved marks were put there before the reign of Mary Stuart, before there had been a king of England and Scotland, back when the secret of strength was passed on through magical formulas known only to a few.

He raised his sword to the sky.

"*Bualidh mi u an sa chean!*" he shouted

The Scotsmen followed him with the fire of ancient warriors.

Herkimer looked at the sky again, his soul leaping from his body, hanging there long enough to notice that the light was more intense and the clouds were thinning out, before plunging back into its cage of flesh with a jolt of blinding pain.

The six men who held him tight opened up like the petals of a flower. Van Hoek cauterized the stump with the red-hot blade.

Herkimer fainted. When he regained consciousness, he realized that he could still smell blood and smoke and hear the roar of the clash shattering the forest.

Broken branches, bodies hurled to the ground, cries, quick outlines running in all directions. The militiamen shielded the group, waving their rifles like clubs, and were immediately challenged by Henry Hough and his men.

The general felt himself being lifted and dragged away. He could still see De Jong retreating from that tangle of rabid dogs, saber in hand, shouting orders to the defenders to form an orderly row. Then his strength gave out and he let his head fall back. He saw treetops passing above him, alternating with thin strips of pale sky. They had to resist for a little longer, and the powder would dry. Sounds reached him, fainter now, drowned by a soft hum.

"General Washington," he murmured. "Today, 7 August, 1777, I, Nicholas Herkimer, general of the Militia of the County of Tryon, am writing to your Excellency, calling God as my witness." On the defense line De Jong ran an adversary through and planted a boot on his chest to free his blade. An indistinct phalanx of bodies swept away plants and earth, splintered bone and bark, spurted blood and guts.

"Excellency, today the voluntary militiamen of Tryon have resisted the ambush of a mixed contingent of loyalists and Indian warriors, equal if not greater in number."

De Jong parried a lunge from a green-jacketed soldier who had managed to cross the line, and with his sword he cleanly slashed his throat. He shouted again at the militiamen to close ranks, to not let the enemy through.

"None of them has retreated by so much as a foot. Every patriot under my command has struck back, preferring to fall in a mortal embrace with the enemy rather than yield ground."

De Jong received a blow to the head. The captain doubled over and then got back to his feet, blinded by the blood running into his eyes. He touched his forehead; the gash had cut through to the bone. He managed to pull his sword forward, then fell to his knees.

"General. Upon my word I ask you to put the militia forward for the Congressional Medal of Valor. God save America."

De Jong tried to lift his sword, but his arm fell inertly back. The lunge left him breathless. The last thing he saw was the runes carved into the metal sticking out of his side.

Oronhyateka was an arrow cleaving the forest. Philip ran parallel with him, a few yards behind. He saw him catching up with an Oneida, tripping him and making him fall. With a single movement he jumped on his back and cut off his scalp. He brandished it in the air, shouting insults at the enemy.

Four warriors walked backward, lined up to protect a limping Oneida. The one in the middle saw Philip and shouted, "You're the Great Devil, I recognized you. I challenge you. I am Honyere Tehawengarogwen. Today I have collected twelve scalps. I will kill you and everyone will know my name!"

The last syllable barely had time to leave his lips. Philip leapt forward, swinging his mace, a river stone set in a club. He brought it down and smashed the warrior's skull. The sound of bones crushed in a mortar. He was aware of a movement in front of him and suddenly bent down, and with a kick brought the second Oneida to the ground, threw himself on top of him, punched him in the throat and immediately rolled away. The third was on top of him, but a mace-blow from underneath split his face open. As Philip was getting to his feet, the fourth Oneida grazed him with his tomahawk. They hurled themselves on top of each other. Philip's knife opened up his abdomen from the groin to the stomach.

He found himself standing looking into the eyes of the last remaining enemy.

Shononses, the Oneida sachem.

The old chief was panting, His *orenda* had been lost in battle, his honor dissolved by flight.

Oronhyateka stood frozen, staring in awe at the Great Devil. The whole encounter had taken place in the space of a thought.

"Kill him!" he shouted. "Kill him, Great Devil!"

Philip looked at Shononses. The old man was struggling for breath, making gurgling noises. His broken ribs had pierced his lungs, which were now filling with blood. He tried to rise, tomahawk in hand.

Philip waited till he was standing.

He lifted the club and struck the old man with all his might.

Oronhyateka's shouts greeted the obscene crunch, the cry of a wordless animal.

Kanatawakhon stopped behind a tree, took aim and fired. Joseph instinctively quickened his pace, bent beneath the weight of Sakihenakenta. His muscles hurt and he was blinded by sweat, but he would never leave the warrior's body to the crows. Sakihenakenta had died beside him; he deserved a funeral and a proper burial. He couldn't remember the precise moment when the weapons had started firing again. He had discharged Lord Warwick's pistols against the enemy, so close that you could see the whites of their eyes. Bullets whistled between the branches, men fell. The continental militia was still resisting.

If he wanted to be a chief, he had to be wise.

If he wanted to command, he had to know how to make the right decisions.

He had howled out the clan war cry, which Kanatawakhon repeated with all his breath.

He had done it before the gestures of that bloody day lost their meaning, erased by the slaughter. Killing and dying had to retain a meaning within the context of war and the cycle of things, or else every effort would be in vain and chaos would prevail.

They reached a hump sheltered by trees and Joseph laid Sakihenakenta's body among the ferns. He turned to look at the Volunteers, still firing as they retreated. They were drunk on blood. One of them brandished a head as a trophy.

20.

Aching muscles, torn flesh, bullet holes. Coagulated blood between eyes and eyelids, ears thundering.

For the warriors the day had ended like that, with a roll call of fallen, wounded, scattered senses. Exhausted, they had collapsed a few miles from the battleground. Groans and snores rose from the makeshift beds of branches and blankets.

Philip sat down on a wet mossy tree trunk, arms folded and elbows pressed into his sides, unable to get to sleep. The night bathed his skin, the fires were mournful. Impossible to tell whether Joseph was awake.

The sentries were remote presences. On the other side of the clearing some other people were awake. Young warriors, too excited to sleep. Now and again a phrase breached the air: ". . .the Oneidas thought. . ." ". . .it's no longer time to . . ." The sounds of night, nothing more.

Someone was sitting beside him. Philip hadn't heard footsteps on the grass.

The man spoke in Mohawk, but with an accent that filled Philip with unease. His voice was hoarse, a protracted coughing fit. "It's always like this. I remember what I was like after my first battle: I could have talked about it for days. Funny: today I remember very little about that clash."

Philip didn't reply or turn to see who his waking companion was. He went on staring at his feet.

They stayed silent for several long minutes. Philip curled up and hugged himself tighter; he felt cold. On the other side of the camp, the voices had died away. The young men had found sleep.

"I must go now," said the stranger. "I wish you a good night, Great Devil."

He had spoken in Oneida.

Philip turned to look at him.

Shononses's head was split, one eye-socket empty, his face covered with blood. He got to his feet and disappeared into the night.

Philip thought: It's happened at last. I've gone mad.

He picked up a stick and went and poked the embers of the nearest fire. The flames flared up, drying the air in one last remnant of light.

In front of Philip, a little girl stretched out her hands to warm herself.

A little girl.

Philip knew her. He knew her well. Her lips trembled, her jaw held her soul in her voice, tears spilled from her eyes.

A cut ran across her throat, her clothes were heavy with blood.

Behind her a woman, in an equally bad way. With one hand she stroked the girl's head and ruffled her hair.

Philip fell to his knees, arms dangling, crying like a puppy.

The little girl smiled at him.

"It isn't possible," said Philip, pleading with his wife and daughter. "You died long ago."

The little girl walked over and held out her hands. She wanted her father to take her in his arms.

Philip wanted to do it. He wished he could. He had longed to do so for years, with all his strength. Not a night had passed when he hadn't dreamed of hugging her again. The warrior's face, ravaged with tears, mobilized itself into a smile, a desperate smile, Come, my child, come, but her mother called her back: "Let's go, darling. Let's go."

The little girl waved to her father. Philip's heart burst. Mother and daughter walked away hand in hand.

The fire went on burning.

Had it been a bad dream?

The worst of his life.

The worst of anyone's life, of all lives all together.

Philip stood up again, wiped his eyes with his sleeve. A sob shook his throat, and the night was colder than ever, even beside the fire.

A hand settled lightly on his shoulder.

Philip turned and saw Sir William.

The old man was almost transparent, incorporeal. He was smiling, paternal, sad.

With him was an austere-looking gentleman, solid, as opaque as a living being, nothing about him that suggested death.

Apart from his broken leg, still spilling blood.

He managed to say upright with a crutch.

Sir William said good-bye with a jerk of his chin. *Time to go.*

He left with the stranger. Philip gazed after them as far as the edge of the clearing.

They vanished, and did not reappear.

21.

The good of the Six Nations. Everyone wanted it. Each word was said for the good of the Six Nations. Each initiative was put forward for the good of the Six Nations.

The Six Nations had to live. To live, they had to heal the ill of betrayal. To heal, they had to purge themselves and expel the traitors, poisonous excrement that twisted the guts. The traitors were the Oneidas. A strike against the Oneidas was necessary.

That was the position of the young Mohawk warriors. Kanenonte set it out heatedly, his eyes full of tears, beating his bruised chest, among deafening cries of "Oyeh!"

Joseph listened in silence. In the past he would have translated those curses for the benefit of the whites. No longer. What was being spoken was a universal language, the language of hatred and revenge. It is spoken with the eyes, the wrinkles on the forehead, the folds around the lips, the movement of arms and legs. It was spoken with the drops of blood that spilled from freshly stitched wounds. It was spoken with fingers clenched into a fist, with gritted teeth and tears. No one would raise a hand to interrupt and say, "I didn't understand."

Joseph's head was a hive of doubts. There was a little Oneida village, no more than a hundred inhabitants, a mile away. Old people, women, children. The suggestion was that it should be sacked. For the good of the Six Nations.

Oronhyateka took the floor: the Oneidas had guided Herkimer's rebels and fought alongside them, against the warriors of the People of the Flint. They weren't just a few outcasts, as they had believed at first, but some of the most able-bodied men of that nation, and even one of their sachems. They had been stirred up by Kirkland, and had backed the thieves of Indian land, the rabble that contemptuously violated Warraghiyagey's house.

Joseph studied Sir John Johnson's expression, but the face of Sir William's heir was indecipherable. Beside him, Daniel Claus stared into the void.

Joseph tried to imagine their thoughts. In Oriskany, Indians and white volunteers had passed the test of battle and sowed terror among the enemies. They had played their part. Even Herkimer must be dead, or dying. That was good. No reinforcements for the rebels besieged at Fort Stanwix. It was time for Colonel St. Leger and His Majesty's army to finish the job and head all the way to Albany. As long as the siege didn't last too long. If they didn't take Fort Stanwix, the victory of Oriskany would prove to be pointless.

A skirmish between Indians was the least concern of Claus and Sir John. If it really couldn't be avoided, they saw it as a small price to pay, a peripheral incident. A toll to travel along that road, like the ones imposed in Europe. The treachery of the Oneidas was a sore to be cut out and cauterized as quickly as possible. Otherwise, the pus of rancor would swell it and make it rot. The infection would spread into open war, the Mohawks would waste lives and energies killing other Indians rather than fighting the Whigs. So, let them get on with it.

And Joseph? What decision would he make?

On the other side of the circle of men, John Butler stood with his arms folded, leaning against a tree. Sitting a few yards away was Walter, impatient and irritated. For the Butlers, "finishing the job" meant freeing the rest of their family, still prisoners of the Whigs. For Walter, sitting around talking about Indian honor was a waste of time, while his mother and brothers rotted in prison, victims of unnamed abuses. You could read it in his face. He pulled out blades of grass and tore them to mush. His fingertips were green.

Oronhyateka went on: the Oneidas had allied themselves with cowards who had been stealing the lands of the Mohawks for years, by means of deceit and in defiance of the law. The Oneidas would be punished. Immediately, without waiting. In the name of the Great Peace, of the honor of the Longhouse, the spirit of Sakihenakenta, Royathakariyo and the rest of the fallen.

"Oyeh! Oyeh! Oyeh!"

Someone asked the opinion of the white men present.

Cormac McLeod said it was a matter for Indians. The Highlanders wanted to be left out; they would neither support nor prevent a reprisal. As Scotsmen, they knew what a war between clans could be. Someone else would have to get it over with as they saw fit.

Henry Hough stood up and said that he and the other Volunteers would follow Joseph Brant, whatever decision was taken.

Everyone looked at Joseph, waiting for him to speak, but he didn't. With a nod he communicated detachment, waiting, listening. He looked at Butler for a moment. The man from Fort Niagara didn't return his glance.

No other white man spoke.

In the name of the Senecas, Sayengaraghta took the floor. He spoke solemnly. He said that his warriors had come to Oriskany only to see, but in the rage of battle they had had to unite with their Mohawk brothers. He said that much blood of many brave men had been spilled, that the Senecas had been impressed by the warrior honor of the Mohawks and their friends. He added that the memory of such a fine battle could not be sullied by irresolution only a day later. One of the nations in the League had behaved contemptibly. The younger brothers had raised their tomahawks and lit their powder against the elder brothers. Senecas and Mohawks were guardians of the doors of the Longhouse. Together, they would fulfill their duty and punish the traitors, unworthy to remain under that roof. The Oneida village would be razed for the good of the Six Nations.

Joseph listened, weighed things, reflected. He saw the Great Devil get to his feet, reach the front row and lay in the center of the circle the mace that had killed Shononses.

"The traitors died in the field. Revenge has already been taken."

The silence was absolute. Philip added nothing else, sat down apart from the rest and filled his pipe. Astonished questions slipped from one head to the next, with no need for answers. Oronhyateka's arms fell to his sides; in his eyes was the incredulous expression of someone who has received a stab in the back rather than an embrace. The Senecas seemed divided between repulsion and respect.

Joseph looked at his friend and thought that in his place he would have done the same thing. No Longhouse warrior had ever spilled the blood of a sachem. If there was a man who had settled his scores with the Oneida in battle, his name was Philip Lacroix.

The deciding vote in the Six Nations belonged to the chief. A question for Joseph Brant, the Indian of the Department who had ceased to be a mere interpreter. No longer was he to report, adapt, embellish the words of others. The words most keenly awaited were his own.

If he didn't support revenge, he would wound the pride of the warriors and displease the Senecas. Everything would start to collapse. He had to declare his satisfaction with their proposal.

He had to show that he was up to the task he had taken on.

He rose to his feet and picked up Philip's weapon.

22.

The first to arrive were the Royal Greens and the Canadian Indians.

From the battlements of the fort, Esther watched the green-uniformed infantrymen passing below. They must be yearning for a bed and a fire. Some of them had arms in slings or bandaged heads. Others were carried on makeshift stretchers. At their head rode Sir John, on a black Holstein. He gave the party on the battlements a fleeting glance. His face showed his exhaustion; his jacket was dusty from the long march. Uncle Daniel followed a short distance behind him, at the edge of the column; he too was on horseback. Aunt Nancy was waiting for him at the entrance to the fort; he leaned down and they exchanged a quick hug.

That night, Esther heard them deep in conversation. Uncle Daniel was talking about a furious battle, beyond Lake Oneida. Almost two hundred men on each side had been killed, and many others injured. The besieged rebels in Fort Stanwix had taken advantage of this to make a sortie against the British camp, raiding it and taking prisoners. As if that weren't enough, rumors had circulated that a second rebel contingent was coming to reinforce those besieged. These reinforcements had discouraged the Indians, who had decided to go home. St. Leger had lifted the siege to reorganize his forces.

The next afternoon the regulars arrived. An orderly scarlet rank emerged from the track along the river, and pairs of mules dragged cannon and supplies. Colonel St. Leger didn't look at any of the bystanders who had come out onto the level ground to welcome him. He made straight for the parade ground and then for the officers' quarters, followed by Captain Claus and Sir John.

Esther came down from the battlements with eyes burning from studying the horizon all day. She forgot to say her prayers and let her thoughts fly toward the hinterland, that marsh of water and forest that restored men a little at a time, never all together, rarely all together. She tried to force herself to dream, but found only brief and agitated sleep.

Joseph Brant's Volunteers arrived two days later. Their silent march crossed the rising sun. Their leader rode a gray mare. When he passed beneath her, Esther recognized him: his scarlet jacket with its captain's stripes, the flag of the realm hanging below the saddle, his bald head with its long, feathered tuft. And the features of Joseph Brant, huge and impressive, as if his face had been molded into a mask.

He was followed by John Butler, grim and ghostly. Walter wasn't there. That evening Esther would learn that Butler's son had hurled himself into an insane undertaking: going down the Mohawk River with a few other men, in search of hostages to take and exchange for his mother and brothers, still prisoners in Albany.

Many of the white Volunteers were dressed in the Indian manner, with war-paint on their faces and scalps around their belts. They smelled of wild animals and putrid meat. They were weary predators. One of them carried under his arm a bloody sack, besieged by insects. Esther didn't want to imagine what it might contain.

The fresh evening air slipped through the folds of her clothes. It was the last day of August, and soon autumn would be licking at the lake. The banks would be tinted with yellow and orange, waiting for the north wind to sweep the land and prepare it for the first snow. Again Esther thought of Uncle Daniel's words: that strategic withdrawal, as he had called it, meant that he wouldn't see his home again before next year. Aunt Nancy had asked if he would be spending the winter in Oswego.

"No," Uncle Daniel had replied. "We're going back to Montreal with Sir John and his men."

"And the Indians?"

"They're going to Fort Niagara with Butler."

The survivors of the expedition were keeping a secret. Something terrible must have happened on the Mohawk River. Something that had changed them forever, something that could also change their future.

She didn't sleep a wink that night. She felt that he was alive, and that he would come. A voice in her mind suggested that he might be dead, but she didn't believe it.

Shortly before dawn she fell into a disturbed sleep. She dreamed of the reflection of the leaves on the water, the prow of a boat cleaving the waters of the lake. She suddenly woke up and knew where to go and look.

Taking care not to be heard by Aunt Nancy or the servants, she crept out. Wrapped in her shawl, her hair tucked under her big white bonnet, she crossed the camp in the faint light that preceded dawn. She passed among the tents and shacks, animated by the day's first coughs and grumbles. Later that day, rumors of a ghost wandering among the bivouacs would run through the camp. She walked quickly and silently down to the dock. The ships were sleeping giants, their bellies lapped by the waves.

On the deck she saw two figures facing one another. They were exchanging words that couldn't reach her. When one of the two moved away, Esther hid below the wooden pillars and waited for his steps to pass over her. Peering out, she recognized Joseph Brant, wearing the same harsh expression as when he had arrived the day before.

She quickly reached the end of the jetty, where the other man was boarding a dinghy.

When Philip Lacroix became aware of her presence, he turned and looked at her grimly.

Esther glanced at Joseph Brant, who was heading back toward the fort. She looked at the boat.

"Where are you going?"

Philip removed the cover from the rolled-up sail.

"Where my people will go. To Fort Niagara."

"Take me with you," she said without hesitation.

Philip stopped inspecting the bottom of the boat in search of seepage and raised his head. He stared at her, as if to assess her determination.

"You must stay with your family."

"My mother is dead. My father is a thousand miles away. My sisters are like strangers. In London, every time I thought of coming back, it wasn't for anyone still alive. Apart from you."

Philip seemed not to want to listen to her anymore. He went back up on deck, untied the rope that moored the boat and began unrolling it.

"I beg you. They want to bring me back to Montreal," she added.

"In Canada you will be safe."

"I was safe in London, but I decided to come back."

"Perhaps you shouldn't have," said Philip. "Now go back to your family, before they get alarmed."

He jumped into the boat and pushed an oar against the jetty pillar.

Esther saw him drifting by yards toward the open water, in the calm rhythm of the low tide.

She looked down, then again at the horizon. Her eyes caught the light of the dawning day. The breeze lifted the edges of her bonnet, which couldn't contain her long blond hair. The boat slowed down.

She jumped.

A cold, mute darkness enveloped her, took her breath away, compressed her lungs, contracted her legs and arms.

Esther reemerged and tried to swim, but no one had ever taught her how. She sank again, the horizon disappeared and reappeared, she groped around, swallowed water. The weight of her clothes dragged her toward the bottom, her muscles were rigid with cold, and her cape opened up like a flower in the lake. A clothed statue, the pale figurehead of a shipwreck.

Esther.

In a crevice in her mind a woman's voice spoke her name.

Esther.

She opened her eyes and moved them upward, and began kicking her way toward the surface, fighting the invisible force that dragged her down. She emerged once more into the air, into sounds, into light, into light and a convulsion of vomiting. With a sob, she started breathing again and coughing. She grabbed the implement that had hooked her clothes, and a hand gripped her and dragged her into the boat.

She coughed again, vomited more water.

Her breathing became regular, and she looked at the man from under her wet locks. Philip's expression betrayed no emotion.

Esther watched the shore moving further away: they weren't turning back. A profound relief flooded her heart, as her teeth began loudly chattering.

He threw her a rolled-up fur.

"Take off your clothes and wrap yourself in this."

The girl hesitated, torn between modesty and the fear of pneumonia. Without saying anything more, Philip unrolled the sail and placed it between them, allowing it to swell in the breeze.

The boat began to gather speed. Esther quickly undressed and huddled in the warm fur, which came down to her feet.

She studied the surface of the lake and saw the leaves reflected in it as they had been in her dream the previous night. They sailed along the lake's southern coast, followed by the rays of the sun. Herons and grebes, patrolling the shores in search of food, raised their heads to watch them pass. Crouching in the bows, she peeped out from the dark fur while she waited for its calm warmth to fill her body and her soul. Her ears burned; her toes and fingers started moving again, one at a time.

Philip's voice broke the silence.

"You could have died."

"I knew you wouldn't allow that to happen," she replied.

"You think you know too much."

Esther shook her head.

"I'm here to find my place."

"Then you should have gone to Montreal with the Johnsons."

The girl looked into the west, beyond the prow.

"I'm Sir William's granddaughter. I'm going where he would have gone."

The following day they docked by a settlement of Cayuga fishermen. Philip exchanged a few words with them: they wanted to know about the battle of Oriskany, and about Fort Stanwix. One of them asked about the Great Devil. Philip said that as far as he knew, *le diable* had fallen in battle. The news impressed them, and made them quiet. They smoked a pipe in honor of the celebrated warrior. Philip bartered a tin of tobacco for a dress and a pair of very high-quality moccasins. He slept on the dock, leaving the boat to Esther, and next morning, when he embarked again, he found her already wearing the new clothes. She had also braided her hair and was sitting at the front of the boat, brandishing an oar.

Philip stopped to look at her, then climbed on board and took the tiller.

23.

Molly stuck a stone under the door of the general store, so that the wind wouldn't close it. Full summer, the sun had been away for only a few hours, and dawn split the night before the darkness could thicken and weigh down upon your shoulders. At six in the morning, the shining gilded disk, with its clear outlines, already hovered a couple of inches above the wind-shaken forest. It was still a pale fire; the eye could gaze upon it without pain. An hour later the light would wound the eye.

Molly raised her hands above her head and breathed. Another day was beginning in Canajoharie. During the night she had heard gunfire in the distance. Just beyond the horizon, dim lights, perhaps fires, an Oneida incursion. Revenge fed revenge, brother attacked brother, the farms were going up in flames. There was no brand for contagions like that, no inoculation that could defend body and soul. Maybe the fever had to run its full course, scorch the flesh, spark hallucinations. Afterward, there would have to be a council, to be held at the center of the Longhouse. Soon she would send a message to the sachems of the Onondaga, guardians of the sacred flame.

She was about to go back inside when she noticed a movement and turned around.

She saw them at the end of the path. Five of them, one behind the other, still a long way off. Perhaps militiamen.

For some time the Whigs hadn't set foot in the village. No one had been troubled: Herkimer had kept his promise. But Herkimer had died in the battle of Oriskany. Died without one of his legs, his blood turned to pus. God only knew where he was now. God knew if he had already met William.

They were coming for her, she was sure of it. To tell her something, or do something to her. The men were all far away; she couldn't call to them. Not with her voice.

She sighed and decided to wait in the doorway, arms folded.

As the crow flies, more than two hundred miles separated Johannes Tekarihoga from his village. After the council of Oswego, the sachem—too old to fight at Fort Stanwix, too weary from the hard journey to go straight back to Canajoharie—had stopped at Fort Niagara. A wise decision. When he got there, he had been welcomed with open arms by his dearest relation, his most indulgent friend, his most solicitous friend: rum.

In the room inside the fort, dazed and lying on a camp bed, the old Mohawk studied the dark ceiling and enjoyed the silence of early morning. Age and alcohol confined his sleep to a few uneasy hours. The summer nights were filled with talk and song, clouds of sound fluttered around the bivouacs, mixing with the smoke from the fires. Through the open windows, reverberations of words and the barking of dogs rode in on the quiet gusts of wind. Toward dawn everything grew quiet, waiting for the changing of the guard: the noises of night made way for those of day.

Toc! Toc! Toc!

Tekarihoga turned toward the window. A woodpecker, black feathers and red crest, banged its beak against a wooden post.

Toc! Toc! Toc!

He got up from the bed. The joints of his body creaked, and at the base of his spine a cluster of muscles wailed. His head was heavy, his tongue stirred in a mouth that felt as if it were stuffed with dung.

Toc! Toc! Toc!

Tekarihoga approached the bird.

"You've come for me."

The woodpecker raised its beak, turned his head this way and that, moved away from the post and fluttered its wings but didn't take flight.

"You have come for this poor old man, you knew where you would find him. You knew he had nothing to do, and would listen."

The woodpecker started hammering its beak again.

Toc! Toc! Toc!

A little group of irregulars. There was also a Delaware, wearing a strange dappled beret. Certainly not summer headgear.

The first in the line was Jonas Klug. He had been thrown out of the militia by General Herkimer himself, but he still gave himself the airs of a patriot.

When he came face to face with her, the German spoke. His voice was a saw scratching marble. "So are you satisfied now, Indian witch?"

Molly said nothing.

"We know, you red whore, that you informed that pig your brother, the one who had me attacked in my own home two years ago. Many brave patriots died in Oriskany. Pray to your savage god to keep us from killing you here like a dog, in front of your fine shop!"

"*Why don't you do it?*" asked Molly.

Klug frowned. The woman's lips hadn't moved. The voice had come from another direction. From behind. No, from *above*. The men, startled, looked around, and some of them quickly raised their rifles, ready to aim them at any new arrivals, but there was no one. The worried murmur was interrupted by Klug: "Silence!" Then he confronted the woman. "Do you think you can scare me with your tricks? I don't know how you do it, but I guarantee that. . ."

"*Go away.*"

This time there was no doubt: the voice had come from behind, and it was a man's voice. Klug had to turn around.

The drunken old chief. Tekarihoga. But hadn't he left with the others?

Legs spread, arms dangling along his sides. He looked sober.

Klug remembered him as shorter and more bent.

They aimed their rifles at him, but the old man ignored them. He stared into Klug's eyes.

The German turned to Molly Brant: "You should tell Grandfather that. . ."

The eyes of William Johnson's widow were red with rage, her lips tensed and white. She was trembling. Klug followed her eyes: the target of her hatred was the Delaware.

What the hell was happening?

The Mohawk woman looked at the hat. She looked at his hands. She looked at the tobacco pouch hanging from his belt.

The Indian felt he was being read, line by line. Like a book.

Like an intercepted letter.

The woman was inside his head. "*That hat was once a dog.*"

The Delaware opened his eyes wide, opened his mouth, staggered.

"Can someone tell me what's happening?" shrieked Klug.

"*That pouch was once a man of the People of the Flint.*"

The Delaware turned toward Nathaniel Gordon, his chief, as if asking for help.

Gordon ignored him, his eyes fixed on the leather pouch, his mind divided in two by a thread of saliva.

"*His name was Samuel Waterbridge. Your hands removed his skin, scrap by scrap.*"

Gordon cried out. It was the last thing the Delaware heard before he fainted.

The cutthroats exchanged frightened glances and began lowering their weapons.

"What are you doing? Have you lost your minds?" shouted Klug, before turning to Nathaniel Gordon and the rest of his gang. "Do we want to be stopped by an old man and a charlatan? Let your trained Indian sleep—let's go into this latrine and smash everything. Let the savages know what happens to people who spy!"

No one replied, no one moved.

Molly Brant stretched out an arm and pointed with her finger at a field, a patch of level ground on the edge of the village.

"Jonas Klug, your head will roll on that grass."

The German gulped. A big lump of spit and dust pressed against the walls of his throat.

"Go now. Don't come back to Canajoharie. As for you," and she pointed at Nathaniel Gordon, "you, too, will die. You will feel all the pain of this land. Your agony will leave no room for a single moment of dignity."

Klug took a step forward and was about to raise his fist, but someone gripped his wrist.

The old man. His grip was powerful.

"*Go away*," he repeated. His voice came from a long way off.

Klug could barely keep from throwing up.

Molly was exhausted, drained. She had never done anything like that. She slumped onto her favorite sofa.

Back at the fort, Tekarihoga slumped onto the camp bed. The woodpecker had flown away.

"Thank you, woman," he said. "May the Master of Life protect you always."

Before the smile had curved his lips, the old sachem was asleep.

Canajoharie was no longer a safe place. They would return in great numbers: the irregulars, the Oneidas, everybody, together or separately. The determination of a sachem and a witch's reputation were not defense enough. She would leave, taking with her anyone willing to follow her. Women and children. They would leave on foot, along the hidden paths of the forest, because the river was dangerous now. They had to reach Onondaga. There, Molly would speak to the sachems, she would tell them everything. She would leave the women and children in safety and go on her way.

Reach Fort Niagara. With William's help she would do it.

They waited in the store until the sun had risen, then they left. Molly and Betsy led about fifteen of the women out of the village, including Juba and two other slaves, three old men still capable of the walk, and ten children, the oldest led by the hand and the youngest carried on their backs, sleeping or awake.

Taking only the leather bottles filled with water and the bags of fruit and dried meat, they left all they owned in Canajoharie so that they could walk in the forest unencumbered, push branches aside with both arms, avoid holes, step over tree roots.

Just before they entered the wood, Betsy called to her mother. Molly turned around. They were on the hill; you could see the whole village.

"Mother. . ."

"Yes, Betsy?"

"Look. There's a light on in the store."

It was true. When they had closed the door behind them, the store had been in total darkness.

The Whigs, or their spies, had wasted no time.

24.

They marched on long paths hidden among the trees, led by the most powerful woman in the village. They trusted her: they had placed their lives in her hands. They read signs where a white man would have seen nothing, they picked the fruits of the forest, stopping when the weakest of them ran out of breath. In the clearings the heat was turning the grass yellow, but beneath the roof of branches the air was cool and the bushes soft, and all that could be seen of the sun was splashes of light, covering the earth with gold freckles. How long had they been walking?

On the evening of the third day they had met a Tuscarora hunter. He had emerged from a hole in the long grass and greeted the convoy with raised arms, his voice thick with sleep. Molly knew him; he had been to the general store several times, bartering skins for other goods.

"Don't go to Onondaga, Degonwadonti. It's a ghost town."

"What happened?"

"Smallpox passed from body to body, swift as an arrow. Streets and houses are full of corpses, covered with flies and ants. The survivors went west."

A murmur of dismay ran through the people of Canajoharie.

"What about the sacred fire?" asked Molly.

"It went out," the hunter replied. "The guardians died. Don't go to Onondaga, Molly Brant. Follow your way."

Onondaga abandoned. The sacred fire extinguished after five thousand moons. A crevasse, wide and deep, was swallowing up the history of the Six Nations.

"How do you know this? Have you been there?" someone asked.

"No, but I believe the one who told me. And you, too, will believe me. Go on walking westward, and by dawn you will smell the stench of death."

The hunter was right. When the sky between the branches grew lighter, the sweetish stink suddenly fell upon them. It was like an ambush: where the trees thinned out, a pestiferous breeze ran through the forest, bringing to their noses and mouths news of swollen bodies, exhalations, worms sucking rotten flesh. The creeping militia of Smallpox.

They didn't approach the town. Because they didn't want to sleep near the carnage, they marched until the sun was high. Sleep came down on them, but managed to take them only after many chaotic attacks.

Molly woke up. They had to march as far as Fort Niagara, with women, old people, and children, some of them very young. She asked Warraghiyagey to give her strength, and to send her a sign.

In the afternoon, on the path they had just walked down, she heard footsteps and breaking branches. She grabbed a rifle and darted to her feet.

A woman and two children emerged from the forest. They were Oneidas. They saw Molly and gave a start. The woman bent down and shielded the children with her own body.

"Don't shoot! We know you, you're Molly Brant from Canajoharie. We're going to Canadaigua, to our Seneca relations. We're afraid of the war. We have nothing against the Mohawks, you're our big sister."

Molly lowered the weapon. She had asked for a sign and perhaps she had just had it.

"We're going to Fort Niagara. You can travel with us."

The woman's name was Aleydis, her daughters were Myrtle and Marjolin.

Aleydis had learned of the end of Onondaga from a Protestant missionary, shortly after she left Canowaroghare. According to him, the sacred fire had not been extinguished because of the epidemic; the guardians had decided to snuff it out until Mohawks and Oneidas stopped killing one another. Molly had many doubts about this version of events, but took it as part of the sign sent by William: the Six Nations had to go on their way together.

They left at sunrise. Molly led the convoy toward Fort Niagara, toward Thayendanegea, leaving death behind her.

25.

Half a mile away from the fort, snakes of smoke twitched in the wind beneath a clouded sky.

The bark boats were steered to a patch of level ground and moored between mud-caked wicker stakes.

Seen from the street it looked like a Seneca village, not very different from many that Molly had passed through on the way. They would have to get near enough to make out people's features to tell what kind of place it really was. They saw weary, scratched faces, bent backs, hurried gestures, eyes opened wide to conceal exhaustion. A group of crows wandered among the fires, and dirty, frightened children pressed cobs of maize protectively to their chests. Three years before, in another land, they would have put grains in their palms and invited the birds to peck from their hands. Puppies didn't roll around with the human children, but nervously followed their pack, hoping for scraps. Spades and hoes rusted, forgotten behind the sheds. Everywhere there were bits of smashed boxes, pots scattered around the hearths, barrels, tangles of rope, rotten tree trunks, piles of wet sawdust, puddles as big as pools.

A refugee camp, where even the spirit of man became provisional.

Cries of welcome rose up from the bivouacs, sounding shrill above the barking of the dogs and the muted thunder that echoed over the lake. Tears and smiles gave her a taste of a homecoming, as if Canajoharie were being reborn, four hundred miles to the west. As if the river, the maize fields, the pines on the hills, the graves of the ancestors, were a limb that could be severed from the body of the nation without killing it.

Molly's eyes slipped from one family to the other, reconstructing their stories—struggles, births and marriages. Molly remembered them all, when they had gone and what they had left behind—apart from one well-groomed young girl who watched motionless from the door of a shack. She was white, certainly the only white in the whole camp, and her big, clear eyes had a familiar expression. On her right wrist, the girl wore a bracelet. Too far away for Molly to see the design, but she didn't need to. Her other senses told her: Philip Lacroix's adoption wampum.

Molly noticed that the voices had fallen silent. The Mohawk women's eyes were cold; they exuded menace. One of them spat on the ground.

"Degonwadonti, I see that you bring us a gift of the wives and daughters of traitors." The woman came and stood in front of the Oneidas with her legs wide. "For too long we have eaten no meat. Two young hearts will be fine."

Aleydis held her gaze, her body trembling.

Molly's laughter swept the camp like autumn wind. "I'm here now: the rations will be adequate. What Canajoharie family has no Oneida relations? For me, the Law still holds, and these are my sisters. They will share the bitter days that we endure, and when our people win, they will celebrate with us. This is what I have to say."

Molly looked around. There was a terrifying smile on her lips, and a storm in her eyes. There were murmurs of approval. The hungry woman waved her hand, turned her back and left.

The mad woman's attention turned toward a cart coming up from the lake. In the confusion of voices she made out phrases, women wishing each other a cargo of provisions and clothes, men already tasting rum in anticipation.

The cart reached the first shacks. Under the tarpaulin, everyone imagined boxes and barrels piled up willy nilly. The children hid among the legs of the adults, immediately followed by the dogs. Molly recognized John Butler sitting on the coachman's seat, though he looked much older than she remembered. Beside him was an English officer, a black three-cornered hat balanced on his head. They came forward as far as the press of bodies allowed, and then Butler pulled the reins, got to his feet and spoke in a tired voice.

"Listen. Colonel Bolton and I have come to bring greetings to Molly Brant, in the name of the Indian Department and the Fort Niagara garrison. Her arrival is a precious event for which we are all most grateful, and it is our wish that she should be duly celebrated. The Great English Father has granted you a richer cargo than usual. In it you will find sausages, smoked salmon, biscuits and rum." Butler silenced the cries of enthusiasm, cleared his throat, and continued. "News has reached me that the last cargo provoked great confusion, with shameful episodes that do you no honor. For that reason I order that only five men remain to empty the cart, and that all the others return to their own business until we have left."

With muttered protests, the people of Canajoharie left the square, while five strong young men untied the ropes of the cargo. Molly thought that she had never seen her people so enslaved to the alms of the white men.

John Butler jumped to the ground, along with the English officer.

"It's really a relief to have you here," he began. "Your people have dispersed, and order must be reinstated."

"I am glad to see you, too. Have you news of your wife and children?"

The captain shook his head.

"No, unfortunately. And there's worse. The Whigs have captured Walter, too. My whole family is in chains."

"I'm very sorry to hear that. The war takes us away from our loved ones. For two years I have not seen my son or my brother."

"Joseph is here at the fort. We have rooms and provisions for you as well."

The dark belly of the clouds hung low over the shacks, where women and children stood staring at the mountain of boxes rising up in the middle of the camp. Ann's voice cried *Mama* at the sound of a clap of thunder.

"Thank you," said Molly. "I accept your hospitality."

"You're welcome," Colonel Bolton quickly replied, then turned, saw that the men had finished their work, and waved them away.

The first drops of water wet the earth. Molly turned to look at the white girl, but the door of her shack was shut.

26.

For more than two years Joseph had been a sheet of paper, a rough scribble, a presence to be traced in dreams. Two years of voiceless words, bodiless meetings, questions still unanswered. His voice had become crisper, as if dried by drought. His face looked the same—only the hair at his temples had whitened slightly. New questions put the past in the shade.

The room was modest. A camp bed, two stools, a stout table, a narrow window. Joseph wore a woolen jacket and trousers; there was a black handkerchief round the neck of his shirt. He hugged her and then immediately asked for news from Canajoharie.

Molly sat on one of the stools and rubbed her aching legs.

"Since Herkimer died, no one has been keeping tabs on the rebels," she replied. "Staying was too dangerous."

Joseph's face darkened.

"How is the war going?" Molly asked.

"Not well. General Burgoyne was defeated in Saratoga. The Canadian offensive failed. We'll be forced to winter here, while the front moves south."

A thoughtful silence followed. The noises of the camp were far away.

Then Molly spoke again.

"The Sacred Fire went out."

Her brother checked a movement of rage.

"The Longhouse is falling to pieces," he said. "The Oneidas are with the rebels and the Tuscaroras are succumbing to the same temptation. God's curse be upon them."

"Your wife and children are Oneidas. Will you have them brought here?"

"They're already on the way."

Joseph went to the little window and looked out.

"Only fear can make the settlers retreat," he continued. "If we want to take the valley back, we will have to isolate them, leave them without food or air."

Molly sensed the urgency hovering about his words. She saw blood drench the forest. The frontier would become a battlefield. If that was what awaited them, they would have to prepare for even harder times.

"Strange signs mark our days; it isn't easy to interpret them. Why is Esther Johnson here?"

"She came with Philip," Joseph replied. "She lives hidden at the camp. She doesn't want the white men to send her to Montreal."

"And where is he?"

Joseph pointed outside. "Still in the woods, hunting. The Senecas conceded their lands as long as he led the strikes. They tell strange stories about him. They say he doesn't sleep at night and in the morning he comes back to the bivouac with huge amounts of booty." He sat down again and looked at his sister. "Something has changed in him. It happened after Oriskany, after he killed Shononses."

"I knew about that. Ronaterihonte has many ghosts walking beside him."

Joseph touched her shoulder.

"Your eyes have changed as well. There's something my sister hasn't told me."

Molly's face hardened.

"My children and I have been subjected to insults and threats."

"Who was it?"

"Jonas Klug."

Joseph's jaw tightened.

Molly closed her eyes and let hatred burst from her heart.

"I dreamed of kicking his head. I dreamed you brought it to me as a present."

She saw her brother's muscles contracting.

"The day will come."

27.

"Play for us, sir. That Irish jig, or something else, so that we can dance."

Sergeant Bunyan's face was gaunt and exhausted. His voice was slightly thick with alcohol. The old soldier could endure forced marches, inadequate food, moonshine liquor: his constitution was equal to every ordeal, as long as it wasn't deprived of music or pay.

Colonel Percey had distributed the rum. The rebels, with George Washington at their head, were retreating toward Philadelphia, with His Majesty's army in hot pursuit. The alcohol dulled pain, it blunted hunger, it spread a blanket over weary bodies, it made the men sing and dance, laugh and weep.

Peter had no wish to play. He set down his own cup, still full of yellowish liquid that contained an implicit order: Be happy.

"Go for *An Faire*, Mr. Bunyan." Peter took his first sip and went on. "Let me tell you one thing, Mr. Bunyan: if you really want to dance, you are a man of steel."

Bunyan took the standard bearer's words as a compliment. His mouth formed a girlish smile that seemed out of place on his rough face, already well on in years. After a brief hesitation, Peter opened the violin case. The violin had a good wood smell, and the hairs of the bow smelled of rosin. Everything seemed to be in order: he picked up the instrument and hefted it in his hand, as if to gauge its weight. He raised it to his shoulder, passed the bow over strings that were already worn. The instrument was out of tune. Peter couldn't summon the will to tune it.

He no longer took pleasure in his playing. The reason for this disaffection was not exhaustion, and neither was it a passing ill humor. Days before, he had caught a conversation between two guides, a Munsee and a Southern Indian. The Munsee said that the fire of the Iroquois Confederation had gone out: Oneidas, Mohawks and Senecas had spilt the blood of brothers and cousins. Peter had felt himself shiver. His thoughts had turned to his mother, to Uncle Joseph, to the days in Canajoharie, now as far away as London, as far away as China or the moon. The world he had known was dissolving before his eyes, snow in the April sun. Living men and faces had become painful memories.

Peter felt the notes vibrating. The soldiers took a few steps. He played like a machine, his fingers finding the chords mechanically. But his tempo was slow and melancholy. Impossible to dance to. After a good minute, Peter gave a start, and noticed the men's embarrassment.

"Forgive me, sir. Doesn't that seem a little slow for a jig?"

The young man nodded. "You're right, Mr. Bunyan. I don't feel very well, I've drunk too much. Please excuse me."

Peter put the violin back in its case, took his leave and disappeared into the tent, followed by a murmur of disappointment.

The light burned slowly, sending darting shadows. Lying on his camp bed, Peter stared toward a point high above his head, beyond the tarpaulin that covered his body and his worldly goods. Then he looked at the violin case. For a while, to open it had been to reveal the contents of a treasure casket, a trove of images and memories. Now he performed the gesture reluctantly. At home, a thousand miles away, perhaps only the river and the trees were still in their proper place. He felt another shiver shaking his limbs: images became ghosts, memories faded. Day after day the course of events was removing him from himself. He felt like a mushroom that had risen from the earth, foam on the stream. Uncertainty weighed down on his chest like a boulder. What fate had his people met with? Inner voices wove a tangled web of thought, but all that emerged from it was doubts, alarmed presentiments and gloomy premonitions.

It was exhaustion, he decided, that kept him from catching the meaning of his agitation. He prayed that sleep would come soon.

Two hours later he was still awake, his head filled with the same shadows that the light drew on the fabric, his legs heavy. He picked up the Bible and flicked through it distractedly. He read a passage about the birds, which need not think or toil because the Lord provides for them, and in fact they don't: they live and fly and that's it. God provides for all life—the lilies of the field, birds, men.

But men have to work and fight, while women suffer in childbirth. Lilies and birds hadn't sinned, back in the beginning.

His mother had told him that birds weren't animals like the others. They were angels that bore the spirits of men.

Peter imagined a bird unfolding its wings above him, becoming bigger and bigger. The wings covered the sun, stretched from one end of the ocean to the other. The bird was a shadow, black as night, silent and impenetrable.

28.

That night, before going to sleep, Molly prayed. She prayed to the winds to blow softly. She prayed to the sun to shine its rays on their victory. She prayed to the spirit of Hendrick to bring wisdom to her decisions. She prayed to Grandmother Moon and the Master of Life not to spill too much blood. To allow them to return home, to think of their children's future.

Molly prayed to William. To guide her eyes and senses, to control her passions, her anger, her pride.

Molly asked for help, then went to sleep.

The church is packed. Eyes and heads reach the ceiling, like sacks of maize piled up for the winter. Irish landowners, Scottish tenants, Mohawk warriors. Bears and wolves crouch on the stone floor.

Huge turtles hold up the altar on their backs.

The pastor, standing in the pulpit, leafs through the prayer book.

Peter gets to his feet. He raises the violin to his shoulder, plays: it's the old Irish march that his father had his pipers play on the bagpipes before going into battle. Two sachems in black gloves and mourning cloaks approach the coffin to lower it beneath the altar, but the hole has not yet been dug.

The congregation step forward, one at a time, to pick up a spade and try to dig. In vain. The earth is harder than iron. The handle breaks.

Joseph tries to use his tomahawk as a pick. Ronaterihonte is beside him, his face in shadow. He digs with his nails until his fingers bleed.

Beyond the wall of backs, I see the coffin, still open, but can't see a body, only a scrap of blue.

The church vanishes. In its place, a forest of autumn maples. Sitting on a rock, Sir William blesses Joseph and Philip's efforts with a smile. He has a tortoise rattle and his face is painted.

He approaches me, I sit on his knee, stroke his lips.

"Who is in the coffin, William?"

He replies, but in an unknown language. A mountain wind carries his words away. A canoe appears on the river. A girl is on board. William gets in and holds out a hand to me.

"Come with me to the Garden, my love, in the middle of the Water."

Joseph and Philip load on the coffin; the canoe goes back upstream.

I grip the girl's hand. She wears an adoption bracelet on her wrist.
Her eyes are the color of the river.
It is Esther Johnson.

29.

"War isn't really war until brother kills brother. It's a French saying, but I can't pronounce it as well as you do, Mr. Dalton. So I report it in our language, or rather in the language of the realm for which we must fight, kill and die."

Colonel Abercromby paused for effect.

"But don't we have brothers on the other side? Distant relatives, perhaps. And yet, even if we did have them, right now we would already have disowned them." He passed the spyglass to the aide-de-camp and stroked the neck of the thoroughbred on which he was mounted. "It seems that for once the Yankees intend to hold their position and resist. They are favorably situated, there is no denying it: Sullivan knows what he's up to. A decent artillery, a few French uniforms, and they've turned into an army."

"We're just out of range, sir," said the orderly. "The men have fallen in."

"Very good." Abercromby gave his mount another caress. "So all we have to do is await Howe's order."

The clouds had thickened since the morning, filled with rain, but—as if by some sinister miracle—they hadn't yet burst.

Peter had slept and eaten badly. That morning, along with the bulk of the army, he had forded the Brandywine to the north, performing a wide maneuver to circle Washington's troops and launch a flanking attack. Meanwhile the Hessian mercenary units were simulating an attack on the ford further south, to distract the rebels.

Though it had survived the long march that brought him there, his quick young body had become a weight—like the uniform, like the flagpole. His arms ached. The pole felt like lead as the wind swelled and stirred the banner of the realm, a sail exposed to the violence of the elements. He was the one who must provide a visible reference to the first light infantry contingent as they prepared to attack the hill. The flag wasn't merely a symbol; it was the needle of the compass, the vector for the army's arrangement in the field.

The colonel's garrulous voice interrupted Peter's reflections.

"Lieutenant Johnson, today is the day for you to earn your second medal. Fly the Union Jack over Birmingham City Hall and you will win it for sure."

"If God wills it, sir. I don't ask too much from good fortune."

The colonel touched his shoulder with the tip of his riding whip.

"You won the first in the forest, fighting the *petite guerre*. But today, sir, today we are fighting the real war." He chuckled nervously. "With all of its rules." He studied the sky. "And you may be sure that this will not be like White Plains. Today it won't rain."

Abercromby's loquaciousness betrayed his nerves. No one else among the marshaled ranks had any desire to speak. The tension snaked silently around.

A drum roll made the air vibrate. Repeated three times.

The order to advance. The standards of the regiment began to move.

Peter turned to look at Osborn Hill. On top of it, Generals Howe and Cornwallis aimed their spyglasses toward the hill opposite them. The cannons rang out, and the penetrating shrill of bagpipes invaded the battlefield.

Peter shivered. In the few seconds before he forced his body to move, before the horrible mechanics of war took charge of him, he saw his mother's face. She looked furious and terrifying. Warriors followed her, tall, fit, painted in bright colors, wearing the expression of men who have decided to look death in the face. His mother called to him to bring her black stallion; there was no time to talk. Peter felt his legs moving. His body seemed to be capable of marching all by itself: it had done nothing else for months. The pain in his arms was far away, in a corner of his mind, further away than his awareness of the blood beating in his ears.

Cannon fire devastated the land just in front of the first lines. He could see the sergeants closing formation, putting the infantrymen in the right place, striding along the sidelines, sabers unsheathed, faces grim. The wind carried the smell of fear.

Thunder. Explosions. Cries. "You are His Majesty's soldiers, for God's sake." "Sooner or later they will be within range."

Peter thought of the colonel's words. *War is not war until brother kills brother.* Before his eyes, men, men, and men were going to their deaths in orderly rows. They marched until the world exploded, the land was disemboweled, limbs and heads flew skyward. Death sent up the smell of blood, excrement, wet earth.

The fiery mouths of the continental forces roared again and again, opening up craters among the English forces, voids that had to be hastily filled by reinforcements from the rear. The pikemen had trouble keeping the formations in order; officers and NCOs urged and yelled encouragement, red in the face. Peter watched the scene as though in a dream, forgetting his weariness, his pain over the fate of his people, over the end of his world.

The bombs fell. Shattered bodies piled up. Twenty yards to the left, a captain with a bloodstained uniform raised his saber and harangued his men.

An explosion obliterated him. Clods of earth and scraps of body rained down all the way to where the standard bearer stood. Peter stiffened, closed his eyes. He heard the cries of the sergeants.

"Forward! For the King! Forward!"

The first rows were already under rifle fire, but their artillerymen must have brought their guns closer and adjusted their aim, because they were starting to hit the rebel defenses, granting the infantry a little cover and room to maneuver. Peter could just see the outlines of the Yankees on the line of defense. Others were firing from the windows of the village houses.

The first two lines of redcoats stopped, one standing, the other on its knees, and fired back. The third and fourth lines came forward and repeated the operation, while the others reloaded. The march continued inexorably.

"Standard-bearer Johnson!" someone shouted his name. "Standard-bearer!" The colonel loomed over him on his mount.

Peter stirred and tried to control his trembling.

"At your orders, sir."

"I want to see our flag upon that hill. Forward! Show what you're made of, by God!"

Peter pushed himself onward, as bodies fell around him. They were now out of range of the cannon, and it was the rifle fire that was bringing in the greatest blood tribute. The rebel fusillades were dense and accurate.

So this is my death, he thought.

He stepped forward again.

So this is my death.

A bullet snapped the flagpole, and the Union Jack landed on the ground. Peter felt a sense of grim liberation and slipped down after it.

So this is my death.

Someone landed on top of him.

"Get up, Johnson! Pick up the banner!"

It was Sergeant Bunyan, his faze frozen in a grimace. A bullet caught him right in the chest, and he fell. He tried to get up again, but only managed to hoist himself up on his elbows, gasping for air.

Peter drew himself up on his knees. He felt the shadow of the great wings above him.

Before the stunned eyes of the sergeant he took off his shirt and jacket. Bunyan gulped.

"What the hell are you doing?" he struggled to say. "You'll be court-martialed. . ."

Court-martialed. Peter had never heard more meaningless words. This had been the day of his meaningless death. But he had not lived his life without a meaning.

The great bird of prey dived.

Peter bent down. He picked up blood-drenched soil and with his dirty fingers drew dark red marks on his face.

Bugles sounded the bayonet charge. The ranks broke up: the charge by the English soldiers unleashed a murderous cry that seemed to shake the barricades and the clutch of houses on the hill.

Peter got to his feet, his chest bare, the flag in his fist. He pointed it in front of him like a pike. The war cry of the Wolf clan echoed in the air.

The young Mohawk warrior flung himself against the line of rebels, as fast as the thought that was running through his mind.

His soul had taken wing.

30.

The hunt had gone badly, and Philip was worried, though it was nothing new; things had been like that for days.

Hunting with the Senecas had borne no fruit: their pursuit of a big deer had gone on for hours and then, when they were sure they had surrounded it, the animal disappeared, vanished at the end of its trail into an impenetrable patch of brambles. Their uncertain eyes had met, and some of them had cursed in low voices, as was the wont of the Senecas. All together they had decided that the hunt was over.

On the way back to the fort, the man bringing up the rear of the line said that there were some dead birds along the way that no one else had noticed. Philip asked what kind of birds they were, but the hunter didn't reply. The unit marched in silence until the fort came into view,

When they reached the shacks of the refugees they met a Mohawk Valley settler and received the terrible news. The man was shaken, and he spoke to Philip deferentially, in a small voice.

Peter Johnson, the son of Sir William and Molly Brant, had died in battle.

The hunters uttered words of respect and grief, and Philip dismissed them, saying that he would be back later, and they walked away. He was left on his own, near a big maple tree, bewildered now that the darkest of his forebodings had come to pass.

Peter, the future and the hope of the nation, Peter, the violin and the sword, Peter, English studies and Mohawk hairstyle, dreams and electricity. The Valley shaped by William Johnson had died with him.

His feet led him to the fort. He thought he could hear painful thoughts filling the air until it was saturated with them.

It had come down in the evening, when torches cast sinister shadows. Philip took a deep breath of the pungent air that scraped his nostrils, and set off in no particular direction.

The figure of Joseph Brant emerged from of the shadows. The man who had appointed himself chief appeared in front of Philip, but with his eyes focused on some vague point behind him. His face was distorted by the reflections of the flames and by his suffering.

"I should never have let him go." His voice was like the screech of iron.

"He had chosen his fate and no one could have stopped him," Philip replied.

He was aware of his friend's grief like an animal nestling in his mind, ready to pounce.

"We owe it to him to take what we have done to its conclusion."

A shiver kept Philip silent. Joseph stood a like wall of sorrow and spite that absorbed the light from the torches until it darkened them. A group of ghosts danced in the darkness behind him.

"I will pursue this war to the bitter end, along with anyone willing to follow me. I will do it in the name of Peter and what he was fighting for. I will do it for all of us. We must take back what belongs to us."

"What does that mean?" asked Philip.

Joseph seemed not to have heard the question.

"I will let winter pass. I will let them feel safe."

"What does that mean, Joseph?" Philip's tone betrayed his anxiety.

"There's only one way to get our lands back," the other man replied. "Act as the French and the Hurons did during the other war."

"Attack the settlements?"

"Raid their cattle, destroy their harvests. We must strike them in their houses, drive them out one by one, if necessary. Force the settlers to leave."

"In those houses there are women and children," Philip objected. "Do you think you will be honoring Peter's memory that way? Is this your war?"

"It's what is done."

"My wife and my daughter died because of people who thought like that."

Joseph looked at him angrily.

Philip came very close, until he stared straight into Joseph's eyes.

"Yes. I know where your path ends. In a bog of blood."

"I am a chief," Joseph replied. "I have to fight for my people, I have to give them some land. If the hardness of oak is not enough, we will become rock. But we have to try, we have to make the effort. Or else there will be no dawn for the Mohawks."

Philip thought again of when they had repelled the attack of the pirates on the open sea. That day Joseph had the same look in his eyes that he now saw directed at the darkness.

He spoke as if his blood had turned to ice.

"Many years ago I inflicted on others what I myself had been subjected to."

Joseph gave a start, as if he found himself on the edge of an abyss.

Philip went on.

"When they massacred my family, my rage was blind, just as yours is today. I let myself be guided into revenge. I took an eye for an eye, without making distinctions. My tomahawk didn't stop even at the unarmed and the innocent." His voice was low and forceful, the words rolled between their feet. "What I discovered then is that there is nothing that I am not capable of. I was horrified by myself, by what men can unleash. I won't follow you, Joseph."

The other man didn't move. He had received the confession with the stoicism of a priest. His anger seemed to have cooled down. The die was cast.

"When Molly asked me to come and call you, I thought I wouldn't know what to do with you." He looked at Philip again. "I was wrong. You're the one who doesn't know what to do with yourself." His words contained desolation and bitterness. "Good luck, Ronaterihonte."

The darkness swallowed him up. His outline remained imprinted at the point where he had disappeared, hanging in the night air.

Philip would have liked to reach a destination, if only he had had one. He approached one of the bivouacs and sat down in silence, thinking that Peter was no longer in the world.

31.

I went to see her at dawn. The woman that many call a witch. The mother of Peter, my cousin, dead in battle. The woman who gave Sir William, my grandfather, eight children. She was praying, arms outstretched, palms turned upward. She was reciting phrases in her language, a mysterious music. I had to talk to her about the dream. Fear and anxiety gripped me all night. She has seemed a witch to me, too, I'm well aware of it. I remember the shyness, the anxiety.

They say that she can stop rapids, deviate rivers, reduce her enemies to ash. That she can heal the sick, encourage harvests, induce fertility. Call the dead back to life, turn herself into an animal. I didn't know how to approach her, and yet I had to. I stayed and looked at her, I watched the gestures of prayer at sunrise, until she noticed me, watching her from the other side of the window, and beckoned me in. She put water on the fire, returned my hug, listened to my words of grief.

I told her I had dreamed about Peter. She looked me in the eye and said, "Tell me."

I told her what I remembered: Peter was digging a ditch, but the earth was hard and the spade broke. Philip and Joseph Brant loaded a coffin onto a boat. Grandfather William was on the boat. He helped me in.

As I told the story, Molly's expression changed, becoming less pain-stricken.

She asked me if Grandfather had said anything. I replied that I couldn't remember.

She told me there are ways to help you remember, to make images clearer. She asked me for my bracelet, held it up with both hands to her lips, which whispered phrases. She exposed it to the smoke that rose from the brazier, and blew on it before giving it back to me.

She said the bracelet was precious, and that it was no coincidence that it had come to me. She asked me about London, about Peter, about what I had seen.

She said she was about to send her children to Montreal. Uncle Daniel will supply their needs. They will have a stone house, enough food, lessons in English and mathematics. She asked me if I wanted to leave with them. She listened to my reply: I wouldn't leave even in chains. She sighed and smiled. "You will live in my house," she said. "It isn't good for a woman my age to remain alone."

The sun wasn't yet high. The anxiety had gone.

A strange calm is walking toward me.

1778

32.

Crouching in the shadows, his bones shrinking in on themselves, no taller than a little boy before he becomes a man, digging through his hair in search of lice, coughing, spitting.

You have the decorations of a man of rank. Time has left a network of wrinkles on your face.

Johannes Tekarihoga, the last of the Tekarihogas, spiritual chiefs of the Tortoise clan since the time before the time when Woman of the Sky fell from above, the noble people who support the world on their back. If the world comes off its axis, it isn't your fault. Exile, in fact, seems to have granted you glimmers of an ancient dignity. The eldest of them say you resemble the Tekarihoga before you. How can they know? No one is older than you anymore.

Only he who is like an arrow finds his way, they say. Perhaps there may exist such a thing as an arrow that wobbles, slowly, the tip disconnected from the wood, and yet capable of passing through the air until it reaches its destination. The flank of a deer. A target fixed to the trunk of a tree. The ground, after drinking the air while its invisible wings supported you. People talk about straight arrows, not young arrows.

Mysterious things happen in the cotton-wool limbo where your best friend, the one who drinks pints and demijohns, has confined you. Things happen every day: the spirits have impalpable wings that sometimes brush past you. Your alcoholic exile is less coarse, less squalid than many people thought it would be.

So, when the going gets tough, you withdraw from the eyes of the women, you leave the field, wander in the forest shouting under your breath, cursing to yourself, or laughing and laughing, trying out dance moves, lifting your hands to the sky and giving thanks for another day of life, one more day in spite of everything, a long life to you and your best friend.

Many people still think you wise, and you are well liked. The women smile at you, the little boys greet you deferentially: you have always been generous. All gifts come from your hands; you have always kept for yourself only what you needed. If Tekarihoga were rich, now, his people would not be hungry. That's why they love you: you are the image of days gone by.

When Woman of the Earth dreamed for the first time, fertile fields were born from that proud body. A cloud from the west took different shapes to please her, until it finally became a young man. Woman of the Earth fell instantly in love and wanted to have the cloud-man inside her. Now Woman of the Earth desires only that the insects cease to swarm, to form columns, to fight. The clouds from the west have the shape of ships, of cannons, of huge funereal birds.

The world spins on its axis, and you are like all men: you follow your thoughts—if you are cheerful you laugh and laugh, and if you are sad you weep and curse your fate.

The old man was sitting on a rock. He looked at the reddish surface of the waters, where the sun seemed to be extinguishing its strength to force itself into a night of exile. His face was motionless, his eyes looked like pieces of lake sent to give light to a face tested by the seasons. Coming back from fishing, Philip had been able to study his face for more than an hour, as he rowed toward the shore. He hadn't moved an inch. Philip moored the boat and approached him, taking care to remain in view.

"How are you, old man?"

Tekarihoga turned his head and looked at him expressionlessly.

"The lake is barely rippling. It's very strange for this time of year."

Philip nodded. "The weather will change with the new moon."

Tekarihoga said nothing. Philip heard the lapping of the water on the rocks, slow and lazy. Then the old man went on. "I have never been a good fisherman, Ronaterihonte. There are few things that I know how to do, to tell the truth."

Philip was startled. Persuading Tekarihoga to utter more than a few monosyllables was extremely difficult.

"You are a good chief, even in these difficult days."

Tekarihoga raised an eyebrow. "Oh, it isn't difficult. The days are filled with signs; I am sure you have noticed. Giving good advice is easy, you just have to take yourself as an example of madness."

A night bird called shrilly. Tekarihoga stared again at the surface of the water. "You are a good warrior, Ronaterihonte. The young men are afraid of your shadow, and for that reason they don't know what to make of you. You can't be a father, or a brother: they don't understand your ways."

"I know."

Tekarihoga nodded. "Once, in Albany, I saw a Dutch butcher. He was much better and faster than our best hunter. He did nothing else all day. Skinning, cutting, boning. This is not the time of warriors, Ronaterihonte. It is no longer the time of the Mohawks."

Philip smiled. It was as if the old man's mind had touched his own. The present generation might disapprove of the choices of the Great Devil. It didn't matter: madness pervaded everything.

He said good-bye to the old man and set off toward the fort. When he turned back, the figure stood out against the dusk, motionless.

33.

Throughout the winter, wishes and prayers had kept the thirst for revenge at fever pitch. Every day the Senecas remembered the warriors who had fallen at Oriskany. The tears of the Mohawks were still hot for Peter Johnson.

As soon as the paths were free of snow, Joseph left Fort Niagara and reached Oquaga.

The king's flag still stood in the middle of the village, wet with rain and incapable of flapping. Thanks to the rum requisitioned by the Houghs, after two days of partying the number of Volunteers had already doubled.

At the end of May, two hundred of them attacked a group of farms high up the Schoharie River. Some settlers got away in time; the others were captured along with their animals. Joseph ordered that all the women and children be assembled inside a granary in Cobleskill. By the time the warriors left, not another building within a three-mile radius had escaped the flames.

On the way back, Joseph found a message fixed to a post. It was signed by Captain McKean, in the name of the inhabitants of Cherry Valley. They asked him to stop threatening them and face the militia in an even contest. If he wasn't a coward, the message read, they would happily show him how a *brant*, a wild duck, could be turned into a farmyard goose.

In Oquaga, Daniel Secord was waiting for him with three rebel spies captured in the vicinity. The first had been heading back to Fort Stanwix to inform Gansevoort that on the day of Pentecost Chief Brant had killed and skinned six men near Springfield.

The second had passed, at Pentecost, by Lake Orsego and seen with his own eyes the impaled heads of two known rebels and the symbol of Thayendanegea carved at the base of the poles, beneath a rain of still-fresh blood.

The third informer bore a letter for General Schuyler. The Schoharie Committee of Safety asked support from the army against Brant's Volunteers, who on the day of Pentecost had descended upon the village and tortured and killed men and beasts.

Happy to have received the gift of ubiquity, Joseph immediately set off again toward the west. Butler and Sayengaraghta were waiting for him in Tioga to plan a joint attack. In reality, the Senecas had chosen the theater of revenge some time before. The Wyoming Valley, a land of dreams that the settlers had taken from their fathers by means of deceit. Joseph decided not to follow them; he didn't want to be too far away from Oquaga. There were rumors that the rebels were preparing to attack the town at any moment. John Butler and his Rangers had joined their boats to the warriors' canoes. Joseph traveled up the Susquehanna on his own.

The news reached him a week later, as he led the Volunteers northward.

Fort Wyoming had fallen, along with another seven strongholds. In less than four days, fire had destroyed a thousand farms, stables and granaries. Butler's men returned to Tioga with four hundred head of cattle, two hundred and twenty-seven scalps and five prisoners. The ferocity of "Monster Brant," who was wrongly supposed to have taken part in the Wyoming Massacre, was already the subject of dispatches, curses, and newspaper articles.

On July 11, 1778, the fourth anniversary of Sir William's death, Joseph bathed in the waters of the Mohawk after three years of absence. Then he came down the valley, filled with *orenda*.

In Andrewstown he set fire to the houses without checking whether they were empty. Eight scorched scalps decorated the belts of the Volunteers and the tomahawks of the warriors. In Springfield he spared the farms of the loyalists, and the church. He had a few spies shot, loaded up what could be transported and burned the rest.

In German Flatts, the Germans managed to barricade themselves inside the fort and Joseph cursed himself for not bringing a mortar. With nothing but rifles, attacking the palisade was an impossible undertaking. Jonas Klug had to be left unharmed, his only punishment the sight of his house devoured by fire.

Meanwhile France had entered the war alongside the rebels and George Washington had put a price on Joseph's head. A hundred, two hundred, perhaps even five hundred pounds. In the new world no wealth-creating strategy was as quick and sure as killing Monster Brant.

He was the most hated Indian since the days of Pontiac.

34.

The wood to light the festivities was piled up in the field, amid the yellow grass of late summer.

Over the past year, the fallow land between Fort Niagara and the shacks of the refugees had shrunk considerably. For three winter moons it had lain under a pack of hard snow. The last white patch had melted at Pentecost, just in time for the earth below receive new evacuees. Incursions and reprisals were driving refugees out of the frontier villages.

Butler and the Senecas had just returned with a huge booty of scalps and animals. Susanna had asked for news of Joseph, so as to have one single, banal certainty. Her husband had detached himself from them and planned to go on fighting along with the Volunteers. Other than that, no reply to her question about him resembled any other. That was true of anyone's questions about Joseph Brant and his undertakings.

Susanna remembered the prisoners of Springfield, when they arrived at Easter. They said that Chief Brant had locked them in a church, and from there they had witnessed the destruction: devastated fields, cattle with their throats cut, the harvest and the farms in smoke, the fruit trees sawn off at the base. Then they had let the women and children go and taken the men away.

Three weeks later, a Dutch doctor escaping from Cobleskill had described the inferno: the valley covered with a forest of poles, with the symbol of Monster Brant carved into the base and the heads of rebels skewered on top.

Two slave families had turned up at the fort in mid-June. They said they had fled while Brant's Volunteers were attacking their master's farm. Some of them reported excitedly that the Indian had fed the old man to the pigs. Others were convinced that the master had shot himself so as not to fall into the hands of the savages, and that Joseph had entrusted his daughters to a friend who lived nearby.

After a thousand stories of that kind, Susanna had stopped wondering where the truth lay.

The hatred that springs from a lie is even heavier than that which is born of the truth, and her husband carried a burden of hate that was impossible to bear.

The sunlight still lingered over the summer day. The water of the lake became a huge sheet of copper. Meanwhile the countless stars lit up and a moment later five fires were also alight, arranged in a long line. The procession traced rings and spirals around everyone, and soon enveloped them in a single embrace. Men and women danced to the beating of drums, struck their chests, stamped the earth. Then the crowd assembled and everyone sat in a circle. Molly set a basket of tobacco in the fire and began the liturgy of the scalps.

A warrior rose up and danced, competing with the flames. The colored ribbons hanging from his arm whipped the air like a stallion's mane. He pointed a branch adorned with human hair at the sky and hundreds of throats paid tribute to him.

The man got his breath back and began declaiming the story of his trophies. Behind a row of heads, a gang of young men went on jumping and shouting in chorus. They seemed to be drunk, and when an old man turned around to tell them off they ran away laughing. As they left, Susanna recognized Isaac's outline and gate. She was tempted to follow, but remained. She couldn't go running after him, not at every opportunity, and certain gestures lose their meaning when they lose their consistency.

Once the tale was told, the warrior removed a scalp from the stick. It had belonged to a colonel, a brave man. The warrior declared that Molly Brant had appeared to him in a dream, had given him instructions about how to take him by surprise, and asked him to bring her the scalp, to avenge the death of her son Peter.

All heads turned toward her, and the water drums fell silent for the first time since the beginning of the festivities. The woman's face was a mask of rage; her eyes blazed.

"Keep your gift for the others. A thousand scalps wouldn't be enough to placate me and ten thousand wouldn't be enough to placate my son's spirit, which still wanders on the battlefield."

The other women nodded and it was the turn of the prisoners.

A fair-haired little boy was undressed and wrapped in a blue woolen cloak, as his old clothes burned in the fire. His new mother stopped crying and shouting and walked toward him, as if he were her son who had returned unexpectedly from a very long journey. She made him get up off the ground and led him to his new brothers.

The other women also asked for children and husbands. None chose to give death. Susanna thought this was a rare event, in a cruel and desperate time.

A nation of three hundred refugees couldn't afford to waste a life.

35.

In Albany prison they dined on rancid bread and warm water, a soggy soup often enriched with the flesh of worms.

If you learned to hunt, you enjoyed a more varied diet. Spiders and cockroaches, rats, earthworms. Lizards were the most coveted prey. With your eyes shut, you could convince yourself you were eating eel.

For eight months, Walter had touched no other food.

The jailers were bored to death. Among their hobbies, whipping the captives was by far the most innocuous. For eight months, Walter had undergone humiliations that his tongue refused to relate. Then he had faked an illness and managed to escape.

He gripped the reins and looked back to banish his memories.

Two hundred Rangers were marching in formation along the path. Most of the Senecas had scattered into the forests, to anticipate ambushes. Sayengaraghta, wrapped in a black cloak, brought up the rear on a thoroughbred. The animal was a present from his father to the great war chief. Unfortunately John Butler had not been able to join the new expedition because he was suffering from pneumonia, so Walter had been put in command and given the task of recruiting along the way.

He lacked his father's experience, he knew that, but winter was at the gates and there was no time to lose.

His mother and brother were still in jail, and he needed to take prisoners to get them out.

Walter was hungry for revenge and old enough to get it on his own.

Wintering in Fort Niagara had not been part of Joseph's plans. He would have preferred Oquaga, a more comfortable base, richer and less cold. But Oquaga no longer existed, and neither did Unadilla. The continentals and the militia had attacked the villages, taking advantage of his absence.

They had reduced the finest farms in the county to blackened ruins. Provisions had been burned, maize plants decapitated. The orchards were rows of stumps. The animals lay in pools of blood, their throats slashed.

The women and children had fled in advance, but now the families had dispersed, and with them the Volunteers. Joseph knew that reassembling them in the spring would not be an easy matter.

On the way west, about eighty men struggled to follow him, many with their families in tow. More mouths for the Fort Niagara refugee camp to feed.

In the early afternoon, Daniel Secord returned from reconnaissance with news: Young Butler had camped at Tioga, with a regiment of Rangers and at least three hundred Seneca warriors.

"Walter Butler? Wasn't he a prisoner in Albany?"

"Not anymore. He escaped and he's here to meet you. He says the hunting season isn't over yet."

They arrived after sunset, a twisting river of torches. The night was cold and the wind smelled of snow. Walter Butler welcomed them with great enthusiasm and a plate of beans to still their hunger.

As their mouths were being filled he made his suggestion. They would join forces for an incursion to Cherry Valley, the wealthiest settlement in the whole valley. A few months before, the rebels had built a fort there, but it was said that Colonel Alden knew more about women than he did about garrisons.

"A lot of loyalists live down there," Joseph observed. "Good people like Judge Wells. We'll have to warn them before we attack."

The other man sank his teeth into a calf's head. "Better not risk it. Kill the lot, God will know his own."

God doubtless would, thought Joseph, but the Senecas certainly wouldn't. He didn't like the boy's impudent tone, or the chosen target. Instinct suggested that he should withdraw. Reason told him that only by remaining could he avoid a massacre.

"We'll come with you," he said at last.

"Very good. Tell your men that the pay is generous. They have to sign by tonight."

Henry Hough lifted his face from his bowl. "Sign what?"

"The enlistment," the young man replied, with the insolent air of someone explaining something obvious. "John Butler's Rangers are the only formation authorized to fight in this area."

Joseph understood that the boy hadn't spoken as a simple ally. His father had an official post and received a gratuity for every new recruit. For him, Brant's Volunteers were a missed opportunity for profit.

The desire to get up and leave was increasingly difficult to control.

"Don't be an idiot, Walter. My men are volunteers, they have chosen to fight with me and they will go on doing so for as long as they want."

The young man's eyes roared but his mouth stayed shut. He threw the calf's skull into the fire and got to his feet.

"So be it," he said loudly and clearly. "But they mustn't wear any distinctive marks, not even the yellow drawstring they put in their hair. And the white men will have to avoid war paint."

A dome of silence descended on their bivouac. From the nearby fires, shouts and singing rose up.

Sayengaraghta had had to wait for the translation of the last line, but was the first to speak.

"Captain Butler is right, brother." The Seneca chief's English creaked like a dented wheel. "We have seen these white men of yours in Oriskany doing battle in paint, and I say that we will all fight harder if every man is loyal to his ancestors."

"Your grandfather did not know the rifle," Henry Hough exploded. "Mine worked his arse off all year to maintain a bloody parish priest. Sod the ancestors."

He threw his bowl in the dust, got up, brushed his trousers down and disappeared into the darkness. His brother did the same, followed by the other Volunteers sitting around the fire. Last of all went Daniel Secord: he spat a wad of tobacco into the fire and followed the group.

Joseph saw the little procession swelling as it approached the other bivouacs. He understood that in Cherry Valley he would be a captain without an army. Again he assessed what needed to be done. He decided to stay.

36.

It had snowed during the night, but by dawn the flakes were starting to melt into a soft, dense rain, like the haze that hovered over the river.

The Volunteers had set off in a crowd, heading for Fort Niagara. Only Kanatawakhon had stayed with Joseph. When they reached Butler on the ridge of the mountain, a faint ray of light lit up the valley, the skeletons of the cherry trees, the tongue of water that licked the shores. The houses looked like elements of the landscape, silent as stones.

Even on a day like that, Cherry Valley couldn't conceal its beauty.

It stopped raining and the fog climbed the hills to merge with the clouds.

The men were impatient to attack. Walter Butler held them back, wanting to be sure that the powder was dry enough.

"We have the tomahawks," said Sayengaraghta, and with a nod of agreement Butler let him go.

Joseph and Kanatawakhon joined the Senecas and followed them between the fir trees, as far as a tangle of branches and juniper, but as the band struggled to open up a passage, the two Mohawks turned back half a mile and went down in a different direction.

The dogs of Cherry Valley started barking.

Mr. Mitchell woke up when the stars were still shining outside.

He broke an egg into a cup of rum, added black coffee, butter and maple sugar. As he drank, he glanced at his wife and children, still wrapped in sleep.

Wet snow was coming down, and he had to bring in the last logs before they were wrapped in an icy cocoon.

He went outside, untied the mule's halter and went up the hill.

Leaving the forest, Joseph and Kanatawakhon saw the farms. The sounds of reawakening reached them from below. Ax-blows in a woodshed, voices, the cries of the cows ready for milking. Judge Wells's residence was very big, an estate on the other side of the village.

They started running, but the sods in the ploughed fields tripped them up. The Senecas had passed through the undergrowth and swarmed into the open like wolves. A pack of three hundred warriors.

They ran faster, fell, got up with wounded knees.

Mrs. Wells had been a guest at Johnson Hall and had given Molly a mohair scarf.

They saw the pack reaching the first farm. A group of them stopped; the others went on. Joseph pointed out the next house to his companion. Meanwhile the Rangers entered the village at the double.

Mr. Wells had bought a horse from old Butler and drunk the liquor that his wife made. The judge's safety must also have been close to Walter's heart.

Along the road there flowed a stream of animals, men and blood. The Seneca warriors scalped the fugitives from behind, still running as they did so. Bodies piled up against a horse with its legs in the air. From the river came the screams of those who had tried to escape through the river and who were now drowning in the icy water.

Judge Wells leaned against the post, on his knees, hands together beneath his mouth. In the middle of his head, the white bone of his skull poked out like a rock from a black bog. A man leapt from the first-floor window, crashed down into the farmyard and started running down the hill.

"It's Colonel Alden. Don't let him get away!"

The voice exploded from the stairs. Joseph didn't have time to turn around before two Seneca warriors came out of the house, knocking over Wells's corpse as they threw themselves forward in pursuit. Young Butler reached the door and fired a few shots, but without success. He called to the men upstairs to come down immediately and get ready for the attack on the fort. Then he noticed Joseph's expression and pointed to the judge, on his face in the dust.

"He was hiding a rebel colonel. He got what he deserved."

Joseph pushed him aside and went into the house.

In the antechamber there was the body of a young man. Two more in the kitchens. An old man and an old woman embraced beside the fire. Scalped.

Outside, the wind carried the smell of burned meat and the smoke of dozens of fires. Walter Butler was trying to organize the siege of the fort. Joseph watched the young captain waving his arms around and sweating, and he saw the complete indifference of the Senecas. The boy had thought he was using the warriors for his own revenge, and now he didn't know how to stop them.

Before midday, Mr. Mitchell turned for home. Where the trees thinned out, he noticed smoke that couldn't be coming from the hearth. He threw himself down the slope, his feet crumbling stones and roots.

The little stable was being devoured by fire. The house was in flames, but the blaze had not yet reached the supporting beams.

His wife and children were under the blankets, as they had been the last time he had looked at them. At the sight of their skulls, the impulse to vomit bent him double. Eleanor, his youngest daughter, was missing.

Mitchell ran into the farmyard, filled two buckets from the cistern and started throwing water over the flames, inside and out, inside and out, as he called to his daughter with all his remaining breath.

When the slap of the water struck the cupboard, he saw a hand emerging from the splinters and scratching the floor.

Using part of a beam as a lever, he freed the little girl from beneath the shattered piece of furniture, hugged her and led her outside to get some air into her lungs. With his fingers he washed tears and soot from her face, brushed aside locks of hair, stroked her cheek, incapable of speech.

Once again he pressed her to him, as if he had never done it before, and at that moment he spotted them, a hundred yards away, wearing the green jackets of the loyalist militia.

Mr. Mitchell thanked heaven that they weren't savages and said to himself that the best thing was to stay there, without attempting an impossible escape, to raise his hands and entrust himself to the mercy of God. He whispered to his daughter to stay calm.

Joseph looked for the house of the Mitchells, a modest family he had known years before. He peered through a window and saw a strange woman sitting on the ground, husking corn. His two children had been the same age as Christina and Isaac: she helped her mother, he poked the fire under the pot.

"What are you doing here? Why don't you escape?"

"We're on the side of the king," the woman replied calmly.

Joseph opened his eyes wide. "Not even the king could save you now."

"I heard them shouting the name of Chief Brant. If the Indians are with him, they won't harm us."

"I'm Joseph Brant, but I have no power over these men."

He moved away from the window and gazed into the valley. Flocks of crows glided over the corpses. He saw Kanatawakhon and called to him.

With a fistful of dark dust moistened with saliva, he drew on the family's cheeks two vertical marks and a diagonal line running across them. The mark of the prisoners of Thayendanegea.

"Perhaps you'll be safe like this," he said to the woman, as he entrusted her and the children to Kanatawakhon, to escort them down to the river.

He walked away and went on searching, until he recognized a shack.

The black smoke twisting above the roof told him that he was too late.

He went in. The woman looked as if she were asleep. Her two children lay there with her.

The first of the three aimed his rifle at Mr. Mitchell and told him not to move.

The second raised a hatchet and brought it down on the little girl's head. Not a cry came from her mouth.

The third said, "Answer, worm. Is it worse to live like this or to die like a dog?"

Mr. Mitchell said nothing.

The first of the three opened his throat with a hunting knife.

The Rangers entered the house, to see if the savages had left anything.

As he left the house, Joseph tripped over a statue of flesh: the corpse of a little girl, clutching the corpse of her father, a diamond in its mount.

37.

The trunk was still full, the contents in order.

Joseph lowered the lid. He thought of Peggie, his first wife, buried with her belongings in land that had ceased to belong to the Mohawks.

He thought of Peter. He wondered what he would have chosen to bury with him if his corpse had not been thrown into an unknown grave along with a thousand others.

His old violin had been left in Canajoharie. The books were at Johnson Hall, had perhaps been burnt by now. Ethan Allen's sword: he might have taken that to the grave. He wouldn't be going back to London to return it to the king.

Joseph thought of himself, of the funeral procession that his children would one day prepare for him, of what he would wish to bring.

A copy of the Gospels that he had translated. The pistols he had been given by Lord Warwick. The walking stick with the symbol of the Wolf clan.

He thought of Susanna. She had filled the trunk to move to the new house, and hadn't had time to empty it. Perhaps she had understood that she might need it for her final journey. The plague of pneumonia had struck the shack-dwellers first, the starving ones, the ones without a refuge, who in order to seek shelter from the wind slept in craters dug in the snow. Then the sickness had scaled the walls of the fort and Susanna had died of the fever three days before he came back. The attack on Cherry Valley had kept him from embracing her one last time.

He looked at the roof beams, the walls plastered with clay, the still-gleaming wooden floor.

Before the summer, Molly had persuaded Colonel Bolton to build two farmhouses. She lived in one, with Esther Johnson, the servants, and the usual army of guests and pilgrims. The other was for Susanna and the children, to protect them from the rigors of winter.

Now no one would plant fruit trees when spring arrived. No one would pick flax and prepare the land to welcome the Three Sisters.

Through the windowpanes, the water of the lake looked pale; a blanket of ice guarded its shores. Streets and paths were thin crevices in the white of the field. Another few weeks and Fort Niagara would be a motionless vessel in a sea of ice.

In the spring, the new house would be left empty,

Joseph had to go off to fight again. Isaac and Christina couldn't stay. They would go and live with Margaret, at Lake Cayuga.

When he came back, Susanna wouldn't be there to put Christina in her father's arms. Her voice wouldn't be there, to speak of Isaac's latest feats and prevent him from keeping them a secret.

Joseph got to his feet and picked up the trunk. The front door opened silently and there in the doorway stood his son, dirty and weak.

His eyes were swollen, his face and shoes covered in mud, his woolen jacket nothing but a rag. He stood motionless, one shoulder leaning against the doorpost.

Joseph walked around the table, took him by one arm and dragged him inside.

"What on earth has happened to you?"

The boy's face lit up with pride.

"I fought a Seneca, because he offended me."

"In that state, you offend yourself. What did he say to you?"

"He called me a dirty Oneida."

Joseph looked his son in the eyes, and tears appeared on his lashes. He gripped his shoulder and wanted to talk to him calmly, but the smell of alcohol aroused his anger. He let go of him and boxed him on the ear.

"You stay away from rum, do you hear me? And now go and clean yourself up, I don't want to be late."

The tears began to flow.

Joseph stood silent, motionless, as the boy sobbed. He wanted to let him pour everything out.

Isaac wiped his eyes and when he looked up again, there were no tears in them, only hatred. He bared his teeth, like a frightened animal, then summoned the courage to roar again: "Susanna died three days ago. If you didn't want to be late you should have thought of that before."

He turned and was about to go, but Joseph gripped him by one arm, hurled him to the ground and, before he could hide under the table, immobilized him with a knee on his chest and started furiously beating him.

Isaac took refuge behind a wall of legs and arms. Joseph suddenly leapt to his feet and dealt him a kick.

Someone knocked at the door and a frightened voice asked if he needed any help. Joseph picked up the trunk again and tried to think of something to say, but nothing came to mind, so he left.

Outside, a crowd of weary faces appeared: refugees waiting for their daily alms. Many of them had prepared words of condolence and recited a repertoire of despairing laments. Since the time of his return from London, Joseph had received no wages, but now he wasn't far from being one of the wealthiest men in the nation. A solid house, his daily bread, and the favor of the English.

He crossed the courtyard, repelling the assault with hasty gestures. An old man irritably reminded him that a great man gives away everything, down to the last crumb. Joseph replied that that might be why there were so few great men around these days.

He thought that he no longer cared about being a great man, a rich Indian, or an invincible warrior. All that mattered now was to make the right choice, for Isaac and for Christina. So that one day they wouldn't have to carry a trunk full of rancor to his grave.

"Once, you were a woman in the flower of youth. Now those petals are dry and their perfume blows in the wind. Now we must let you go, because we may no longer walk together on the same earth. That is why we leave your body here, so that you may walk calmly toward the Master of Life. Do not let earthly things distract you. Taking care of the family was your sacred task and you have been true to it. Parties and dances brought you pleasure, but do not let those things confuse your mind: walk straight along your path."

Tekarihoga's black cloak enveloped him like a huge seashell. The old sachem was a white and grey mollusk poking out from its open valves. Beside him was Philip, dressed in leather, with a black velvet band around his right arm. The crowd stood in a wide circle, three rows thick. The whole of Canajoharie was there: Susanna's Oneida relations, Henry Hough and many families from Oquaga, the Butlers and some Englishmen. The Negroes who had dug the hole observed the scene from a little way off. The orator resumed his speech.

"Even you, relatives and friends of this woman, can but persevere on your way. For that reason, with a string of shells we wish to clear the sky of black clouds, so that the sun may guide you still. With another string we will clean the earth, so that you may go on your way without uncertainties. With the third, we clean the heart and guts within you, lest you be distracted by grief."

Philip handed the wampum necklaces to the noblest man in the nation. Joseph understood that these were not merely formal gestures.

Although he didn't need to speak, Ronaterihonte was saying something. Grief had brought them back together.

Joseph raised his head and looked at him.

Philip, too, was wearing three necklaces. They hung on his chest just below his cross.

38

Grandpa William softly sings a song between his teeth. Sitting on his knees, Esther doesn't understand all the words. They are old words, a nursery rhyme or a magic spell.

They are outside, in the big open space in front of Johnson Hall, breathing in the peaceful air. It's a bright day, perhaps in summer. Grandpa William points to the blue sky above them.

"Sky is called *speir*," he says to the little girl.

Then he touches the arm of the chair.

"Wood is called *adhmad*."

He waits for her to repeat the words, and smiles. The little girl strokes his lips with her little fingers.

The list continues, but Esther has already returned to the present. She is fifteen, and in Molly Brant's house, where this memory has suddenly returned. Or perhaps it hasn't, perhaps by following Molly's footsteps she was able bring it to light, after it had been buried for a long time.

Molly has talked to her about the dream many times. The message from Grandpa William to the living. The phrase in the language of your land, words carried away on the wind.

Who is in the coffin?

Now the words echo clearly.

Esther runs out of the house. The camp is drenched in the light of early afternoon, it is hot, the hum of insects is lulling young and old to sleep. The women wash clothes or roast maize.

Molly is speaking with two matrons, in the middle of a group of people.

Philip set down his ax and looked at the pile of chopped wood. However much they crammed into the storehouses, he had a sense that it would never be enough. He wiped away the sweat that covered his chest and face, and only then did he notice the girl.

"I've brought you something to eat."

Esther put the bundle down on the log and opened it, revealing a few ears of corn and a sweet potato.

"Thank you."

He put on his shirt and sat down on a tree trunk to gnaw at the maize.

They enjoyed the tranquility without having to say a word. There was no haze. Below the battlements of the fort, where the Niagara threw itself into the great inland sea, the water reflected a clear sky.

"I've heard that the war won't last more than another year. Do you believe that?"

Philip shrugged.

"It doesn't make much difference to those people. They can't see beyond the winter."

Esther's eyes grew sad.

Philip looked at her. They finished eating in silence.

"What will you do afterward?" the girl asked again.

"Will there be an afterward?" said Philip, as if he expected no reply.

"Certainly. The winter will pass, spring will return. Everything begins again."

Esther rows with her eyes closed. Around her wrist she wears an adoption bracelet. The coffin is on the canoe. Together we go upstream.

The white girl points the way. Isn't that true, William? Your granddaughter came to me telling me to remember. She deciphered your words, the ones I couldn't hear.

" 'The coffin holds the sky of the Mohawk Valley and the box is made of the wood of the Longhouse.' "

So is this what awaits us?

Come and find me, William, to banish the anger and fear I have in my heart. The ordeal we must go through is still great. Smile at me in dreams, because we were happy. When we meet again we will remember everything. Our days, our breath, our embraces. Peter will be there, too. He will find a way to reach you, before I come to you.

This is the time, William. Now that our world is consumed in fire. Now that the cycle is being completed. The oak becomes ash, the ash feeds new roots.

There is one thing I still have to do. I must board the canoe, and seek the Garden.

1779

39.

Orders of **George Washington**
to General **John Sullivan**
at Head-Quarters May 31, 1779

The Expedition you are appointed to command is to be directed against the hostile tribes of the Six Nations of Indians, with their associates and adherents. The immediate objects are the total destruction and devastation of their settlements, and the capture of as many prisoners of every age and sex as possible. It will be essential to ruin their crops now in the ground and prevent their planting more.

I would recommend that some post in the center of the Indian Country should be occupied with all expedition, with a sufficient quantity of provisions whence parties should be detached to lay waste all the settlements around, with instructions to do it in the most effectual manner, that the country may not be merely overrun, but destroyed.

But you will not by any means listen to any overture of peace before the total ruinment of their settlements is effected. Our future security will be in their inability to injure us and in the terror with which the severity of the chastisement they receive will inspire them.

Birds, birds of prey. Even the Indians' features and way of carrying themselves made them look like birds, somewhere between cocks and crows, turkeys and eagles. And their way of speaking was like a gurgle, a sneeze, more incomprehensible than Spanish or even Chinese. Now their nests were burning one after the other: coming up the Susquehanna along Iroquois territory, not one hovel, they had not left a single savage stronghold standing. Goigouen, Chonodote, Kanadasega. . . what was the point in giving a name to desolation, to a ruin, to the desert? Virgin Territory, that was what they would have to call it in the future. Redeemed Territory, granted to those who would exploit it.

John Sullivan had obeyed his orders to the letter. It was a new style of warfare, dictated by contingencies, made possible by the slackening of the British grip on the colony of New York. Scorching the earth, destroying the seed of disorderly nations. The task was a decisive one, even though the power of the Iroquois was a distant memory: Mohawks, Onondagas, Cayugas and Senecas atoned with lakes of tears and rivers of blood for the shortsighted arrogance of their ringleaders.

Once upon a time, the men of letters in the coastal cities had called these savages noble primitives, and the Athenians of America. Geographical distance falsifies perspective: seen from close up, the savages were sly, dirty, untrustworthy. Ready to prostrate themselves at your feet so that houses, fields, and possessions would be spared, ready to shoot you in the back at the first opportunity. Those examples of primordial nobility were vindictive animals: better to go all the way, wipe them out once and for all, to protect the future and one's own descendants. What was happening was like the Bible stories: whole peoples swept away, generations erased from the face of the earth, cities of which not so much as a stone remained. All with the blessing of the God of Armies, protector of George Washington, Destroyer of Cities.

Sullivan looked through the spyglass at the village burning half a mile downstream and felt brushed by the terrible wing of history. Groups of infantry and convoys of artillery were climbing the slope. Drums rolled, fifes trilled. Columns of smoke rose on the horizon. The air echoed with the final shots. Distant cries. You had to be accurate; that was what worried Sullivan. The nests burned, but the savages still wanted to fight: they retreated into the forests, lived off roots and bark; gaunt, dry as skeletons, they kept the last breath that they had in their bodies to stick a knife between your ribs. Just let them get away. They wouldn't find so much as a grain of millet to calm their hunger.

Some villages were made of houses like the dwellings of civilized people; others were nothing but collections of shacks. They all had palisades around them, and some looked like real little fortresses, with Union Jacks flapping around—the last, pointless provocation. But it wasn't a matter of besieging them: you took up position, set up cannon and mortars, waited for the order, and started to rain just punishment down upon the enemy.

Artilleryman André Brillemann took a sip and passed the bottle on.

The track that ran from the village was a long line of hollow faces, drained and aching bodies. The prisoners—old men, women and children—proceeded in silence. The women covered their faces with the hems of the blankets that they wore as surcoats; their infants rode on their backs or were strapped to their chests. The old men kept their eyes on the ground, on the dust and the hardened mud.

The artilleryman hated that part of his duty. Witnessing the processions of the defeated, even of those defeated, did not thrill him. Grief is a kind of aura, a mark of evil, and staying too closely in contact with suffering makes the body's humors rot, it makes you age prematurely. The weeks of the campaign seemed like months, years. When it came to setting up a gun, calculating its elevation, loading it, and lighting the fuse, André was fine; those acts were orderly, meticulous, a kind of art. The gun crew was a well-rehearsed orchestra. It was clean work.

He thanked fate for making him an artilleryman. Raiding villages and tormenting harmless people didn't suit him. But here, he was among infantrymen. They pushed the slower walkers with their rifle butts, yelled and cursed and sniggered.

An old Indian woman tripped and fell to the ground. Without thinking, Brillemann helped her to her feet.

"Why don't you give her your jacket as well, Good Samaritan?"

The artilleryman stirred. The voice belonged to an ex–Mohawk Valley militiaman who was scouring the countryside in the wake of the rebel army, along with a gang of ugly thugs: a Delaware Indian, an ex-merchant from Albany, two fur-hunters. The man's face was mocking and hostile. His name sprang into Brillemann's mind.

"What do you mean by that, Mr. Klug?"

Behind Klug another of the thugs pushed his way through.

"I can't stand emotion being wasted on people like that," he said, indicating the line of people behind him with a quick wave of his hand. "No one can call themselves an American patriot and feel pity for those animals." The guide's face radiated hatred. Behind him was the group of irregulars, angular faces, eyes narrowed to slits.

"Leave this soldier alone."

Sergeant Harinck's low, resolute voice would have dissuaded anyone. But before he could interpose himself between Brillemann and his persecutors, Klug hurled himself at the artilleryman, who fell to the ground, on his back. Klug held him tightly, pressing his left hand against his throat, battering him with his right.

The artilleryman resisted with the strength of desperation. Their bodies started rolling in the dust, followed by cries, kicks, curses, as around them artillerymen and irregulars came to blows.

General Sullivan had been tempted to inflict exemplary punishment. But he, at least, would adhere to the code of war. The men who had passed before him had swollen faces, torn uniforms. No one would confess the cause of the brawl. The irregulars who seemed to have provoked it had disappeared. He would have to punish the victims: the code of war was clear on the matter.

Sullivan thought of the blood that would flow under the lash. Never mind, the earth was drenched with it anyway. He signed the order. The men came out of the tent, cuffs on their wrists, driven on by rifle-butts.

It was the last duty of the day. He called his batsman and told him to let no one in. He poured a glass of sherry.

In the lamplight, on the table that served as his desk, Sullivan opened the book that had gone with him through the whole of his career. *De bello gallico*. It was appropriate for the context, and rereading it had brought him moments of great enthusiasm, had made him think, had given him countless models and examples. They were approaching Fort Niagara, the Alesia of the loyalists. The glory of the world is transitory. Once the fall of the Six Nations would have been unthinkable. Now the death throes of that ancient power were interwoven with the rise of a new nation.

At the start of the war, terror had run through the coastal cities. It was believed that hordes of Indians might emerge from the forests and set everything on fire. Burgoyne, who had surrendered at Saratoga, had ridden out those fantasies and published a sonnet in which he spoke of the Indians as "ten thousand dogs of Hell," ready to avenge the honor of England. Stupid. A tyrant protected by a band of savages, that was the face he had given to his own king.

There was no room for the past in America.

40.

A beating of wings and wind in the feathers. The view precedes the descent toward the column of smoke that will soon obscure the sun. The bird flies over the blazing glade. Among the fields, skeletons emerge that once were shacks, houses, storehouses. A town.

Wing-beat. Another turn above the ruins. Corpses swollen with the heat of the fire or twisted like pieces of dry wood. On a pile of bodies, the only survivor, a dog, barks madly at the snake climbing back up the hill. The woodpecker flies in that direction to get a better view. The vast creature moves over the northwestern slope, in search of fresh prey. A poisonous centipede, its tail pointed and gleaming, its back bristling with prickles. The woodpecker makes out men, animals, wheels, metal. It settles on a branch to watch them passing below. The smell they give off is frightening, and their eyes, as numerous as the stars, still reflect the glare of the fire, are reddened by its fog. At the head there's a man on a horse as black as night. He wears a blue uniform and his name is Destruction. In his saddlebag he keeps a book. With his gaze he guards the future. At his side he carries a golden sword for the head of his enemy.

Wing-beat. The woodpecker flies away in alarm, heading west. It passes the army, flies over the forest and the hill. The air is cool and clean again. It looks down, scouring the dense growth of trees along the torrent. A rank of men is climbing the ridge, moving rapidly to reach the best position.

The woodpecker flies down. At the head of the group an Indian runs, blood-red uniform open to show the marks of war. Crossed on his chest are two big pistols, Hatred and Revenge. He is a warrior and a chief. A thousand of them follow him, a pack of wolves, fangs bared to gnash with rage in the face of destiny. They dart among the trees like arrows, they vanish and reappear, forest ghosts clutching at a glimmer of good fortune. They are Indians. They are white men. They have been fighting together for too long to tell the difference.

Another beat of the wings. The woodpecker dips to the side, performs a wide turn and comes back above them, just in time to see them arranged on the rocks, rifles aimed and hearts in their mouths, waiting for the advancing horizon.

Wing-beat. The flight gains altitude, climbs over what remains of Seneca territory. The monster tears up one piece at a time. The fire burns the foundation of the Longhouse and climbs along the walls.

The bird heads further to the northwest, very quickly, until it glimpses the shore of the great lake and the squat battlements of the fort overlooking the water. It passes over the camp of tents and shacks that clings to Fort Niagara in a desperate embrace. It sees the English sentries throwing the remains of their rations over the palisade for the crowd waiting below. Children with swollen bellies slip through the legs of the adults, hunting for the best morsels.

The bird's descent reveals a little ship that has recently docked. An effort to slow down and settle on the wall.

The woodpecker looks at the woman wrapped in a rough woolen shawl, standing firmly on the fo'c'sle. The sun lights up her resolute features. The sailors don't approach or speak to her. She turns and stretches out her hand to stroke the plumage of the creature, which takes flight again a moment later.

Molly's visions abandoned her. Again she saw the flat expanse that separated her from the time to come, and her thoughts were honed by the cold air of morning.

Come with me to the Garden, my love, in the middle of the Waters.

You are near, I feel it, on this lake that reflects our sky, the sky of the valley that we will never see again. I bring it with me, tied to the thread of hope that sustains the fate of our people. So little remains. Our life is running out, and another must begin, if that is what our Heavenly Father has in store for us.

He makes the wind blow and fill the sails. I need the speed of flight. To Montreal and Quebec. They will have to help us or receive my curse.

Peter died fighting the enemies of their king. My family left behind lands, estates, farms. My people abandoned the belly of the nation. They will have to grant us our due, or lose the last crumb of honor before the generations to come.

We are due a house, to welcome the children that still remain. We are due a land, to plant the seeds that we have saved from destruction. To make the grass grow above us, when the time comes.

We are due a new sky, free of cannon smoke, a sky we can ask for a sign of the future with the serenity of the past.

41.

They reached the fort at midday. Marching at their head was Joseph Brant, followed by a meager unit of Volunteers and Rangers. Kanatawakhon, Oronhyateka and Kanenonte brought up the rear, like dogs guarding a herd.

The Hough brothers and Daniel Secord had remained behind with the bulk of the troop, along with John Butler's Rangers. Many others had gone back to their farms and families, too weary to keep fighting. Some would turn up again in the spring, ready to start over. There were few Seneca warriors still willing to fight; most of them, exhausted, wanted to negotiate a separate peace with the rebels.

Colonel Bolton had lined up the garrison for the present arms.

As he crossed the camp and threw open the gate to the fort, Joseph saw nothing but wretchedness. Fear had abandoned these places, leaving only resignation. Refugees and prisoners mingled in the large expanse of tents and shacks, crushed by the same fate. Season after season the waves of human beings had superimposed themselves upon one another, stratified within the battlements, growths of moss on a tree trunk.

Another autumn was quickly approaching. The leaves slipped onto the lake, to form moving islands of yellow and orange. Joseph thought it might be the last one for all of them.

Bolton invited him into the officers' quarters. Joseph followed him, too tired even to reply.

"Captain Brant," Bolton began when they were sitting down. "I don't imagine you bring good news."

Joseph raised his chin to elude the sleep that had been pursuing him for days. The march on Fort Niagara had been uninterrupted. He said, "Sullivan is heading for Geneseo. In Newtown we set an ambush for him, but he smelled a rat and started firing at us with cannon. We could only look on as he destroyed the Seneca villages one after another and burned the fields. He has four thousand men with him, and heavy artillery. We are organizing the last defense. I've come to recruit all able-bodied men."

"I won't beat around the bush, Captain Brant. The situation is desperate here. Half of these people won't survive the winter. Needless to say, when the continentals arrive I will be able to evacuate only my soldiers."

"Where's my sister?"

Bolton sighed. "She has left for Canada. She wants to meet the governor. They need ships and somewhere to take your people."

Joseph thought of the mass of desperate people out there. He thought of Molly on the far side of the great lake. He thought of his son, who had sought refuge with Margaret in Cayuga. There was still something he could do.

They hung on his lips as he showed them how to take aim. The target was a log forty yards away. One at a time the boys tried to fire, and received advice from Philip.

"You must never stay where you are after firing, but always run after your prey."

One of the older boys objected that if he missed, his prey would escape and he would certainly never catch up with it.

Philip nodded. He said, "But what if it was injured? It will carry on until it runs out of strength. Then you will be there beside it, to take its life. You will thank its soul for granting you its flesh and skin. You will thank God and your strong legs." Then he noticed a silhouette at the edge of the shore and stopped speaking.

"When will you take us deer hunting?"

Philip ignored the question. A familiar figure stepped forward. Behind it he recognized Kanatawakhon, motionless as a statue, his rifle held in the hollow of his elbow. The young men watched the new arrival with big, attentive eyes.

Joseph spoke.

"You won't be hunting deer this year. A more important task awaits you." His voice was firm. "An army is threatening the fort and your families. You will have to fight for them."

Silence fell.

"Who will lead us into battle?" someone asked. Everyone turned toward Philip, waiting for an answer, but the hunter remained impassive.

"I, Joseph Brant."

The name made an impact: they knew it well. They craned their necks, murmured to one another.

"We set off tomorrow at dawn. Get hold of a rifle. But any other weapon will do." With a nod he dismissed the boys, who ran excitedly away.

Philip got up and walked to the water, letting the waves lap his moccasins. Joseph joined him. Their footprints mingled in the sand until they stood side by side, looking out at the great liquid surface.

Philip noticed that Joseph had aged. His face was lined, his body a heavy hulk.

"Have you come to recruit the little boys?"

"And the old men," Joseph replied. "We're marching against Sullivan. I came to say good-bye. We might not see each other again."

The sun was beginning to extend its trail of light across the water. Philip said to himself that in view of such peace it was strange to think that the world was coming to an end. Long blond hair flashed through his mind.

Something remote touched that final foothold in that slow wait for the end. Molly had gone beyond the stretch of water, in search of a future. There was no telling whether she would come back in time.

"You remember many years ago, when we escaped the ford in the river?" asked Joseph. "One of the two of us could have died then. And yet we were the ones, and not the more expert warriors, who killed the enemy and came out alive."

Philip watched the waves smoothing the sand and erasing their footprints.

"After all, we have been walking the same path since the start, Joseph Brant."

"There's still a way to go," added Joseph.

Philip gazed at the lake again.

42.

The unit was ready at dawn. They filled their knapsacks with provisions and ammunition. Boys with rifles longer than they were embraced their mothers. Men bent beneath the weight of time displayed old tomahawks and said good-bye to their ancient wives.

Tekarihoga witnessed the scene from a distance, murmuring a litany. Wrapped in a colored blanket and with a crest of feathers on his head, he looked like an emaciated rooster. In the Niagara winters he had lost weight and a fair number of teeth.

A young child hid beside the box he was sitting on and peered out at the preparations from behind the flaps of the blanket. The old man peered at him from the corner of his eye. He looked intense and adult. Poverty and hunger make you grow up in a hurry. War makes you decrepit.

"Don't let them see you, or they'll give you a rifle too," he said.

The child retreated nervously.

"Master of Life, listen to me," murmured Tekarihoga, as Joseph emerged powerfully from his quarters. "Guide Thayendanegea's arm and keep his heart firm always."

Joseph Brant wore a scarlet jacket over deerskin trousers. He had shaved his head, and the tuft stood out on the top of his skull.

"See that he leads these men into battle like a great chief," Tekarihoga went on. "And if his day should have come, grant him an honorable death."

Joseph reached the middle of the clearing, where Kanatawakhon was waiting to hand him his weapons. He crossed the handles of the pistols over his chest and gripped the rifle. At that moment he saw the old sachem approaching.

"Bless me, noble Tekarihoga."

The old warrior touched his forehead with his hand.

"The right way can be found within all men. May your star shine over your path." He raised his hand and kept it open. "I salute you, noble Thayendanegea."

Joseph thanked the old sachem with a nod of his head.

He turned toward the throng, toward their tired and frightened eyes.

It was not the night's dreams that had put her on the alert. She had woken before dawn, in Molly's house, and understood why, the previous evening, she had found a garland of wheat outside the door. She had been stupid. She had been as excited as a little girl. That nuptial symbol was not a gift, but a message. Joy had clouded her mind. Now all was clear, though she would have given anything to be mistaken.

She froze in the cabin doorway.

Philip was putting his bag over his shoulder. His rifle was beside him, his knives were in his belt.

Esther was seized with rage.

"Why?" she asked.

Philip came over to her and touched her hand.

"They're younger than Peter. I'm not leaving them on their own."

Esther shook her head, unable to speak, and felt the tears finding their way again, after staying buried in the depths of her soul for a long time.

He shook her hand. She hugged him, her mouth very close to his cheek.

"Take me away from this destruction."

Philip stroked her hair and her face.

"Prepare a boat. I'll be back."

Esther clung to him, breathing his breath.

"We must live, Philip. We must live for those who cannot." Her voice cracked.

He dried her tears with a caress.

Esther felt short of breath. She realized she couldn't think about the next moment, the coming hour, the next day. She was frozen on the brink of an abyss, and begged heaven that she might really fall, that they might be turned into statues, that nothing could dissolve that embrace.

Philip hugged her harder.

"I'll come and get you and we'll go away from here."

"Swear you will," she said.

"I swear it, Esther Johnson."

He pulled away from her and stroked her face once more.

"Say it again," she hissed, holding back her sobs.

"I swear it."

She felt him picking up his rifle.

She didn't look up to watch him walk away.

Tekarihoga saw him reaching the group. The young men smiled. Some raised their rifles in the air and uttered cries of enthusiasm. Joseph gave the order and they began to run.

They passed swiftly and lightly in front of the sachems.

"Look, little one," said the old man, turning to the child crouching at his feet. "Look very carefully. One day, when I am long dead, you will be able to say you saw Thayendanegea and Ronaterihonte running together."

43.

When he felt a splinter stuck under his eye, Henry Hough decided he wouldn't be caught like a rat in a trap. Time was on the enemy's side. Trusting to speed had been the only mistake in a simple plan.

Sullivan's vanguard had lost contact with most of the army. The cannon hadn't been able to cross a ford, and the soldiers had had to stop and build a bridge. Meanwhile the men ahead of them had gained at least a day's march. The idea had been to attack this advance guard on the track, take them prisoner and then rejoin the others for the great ambush. If Joseph Brant came quickly with reinforcements from Niagara, so much the better. Otherwise they would do it on their own.

John Butler had given the plan his approval. The encirclement had gone smoothly, but those twenty bastards had taken refuge in a clump of rocks, and they seemed to be the most accurate shots in the whole of America. There was no way of flushing them out, and the others might catch up to them before they used up all their ammunition. Four thousand men and a battery of cannon. Some rat in a trap.

Hough joined the Butlers, who were spying on the enemy from behind a tree.

"They can keep us here as long as they like!" he roared. "We've got to flush them out of there."

Walter Butler glared at him, as his father's jaw flexed nervously.

"To hell with us!" he shouted in Hough's face. "If they get away from us, they'll warn Sullivan and the ambush will fail."

Hough looked beyond the smoke from the guns. He could make out the red hair of one of the snipers. He assessed the distance as about seventy yards. They had to close in on them: there was no alternative. Force them to give up those damned rocks, push them even farther toward Secord's unit, like birds in a net. Their own numerical superiority was crushing, and if they stayed together they would sacrifice no more than twenty men. He hoped he wouldn't be one of that number.

As he started running, weapons in his fists, he saw that the others were quickly gaining on him. He fired straight ahead, without even aiming.

A few steps and the impact nearly threw him to the ground.

The bastards had launched themselves not back toward net, but forward, toward the beaters. Birds never did that.

He saw his brother spitting blood, impaled on a bayonet.

He unsheathed his hunting knife and flung himself onward, striking his adversary in the leg, the arm, the neck, until he slumped to the ground.

He clung to his brother, who was panting on the ground. He wrapped his arm around his shoulder to support him.

Blood stained his hands, his jacket, his face.

"Holy Christ, Johnny."

"Henry. I'm dying, Henry. . ."

"Johnny." He tried to lift his brother's head, which had fallen back. "Johnny."

His brother's body slumped lifeless in his arms.

Secord's unit was the first to return to camp. They brought battered-looking men, with ropes around their necks.

"We took these four; left eleven more lying on the ground," said Secord. "If we counted properly at the beginning, five got away."

The last words cut through the warriors like a knife. The survivors would alarm Sullivan. The ambush would fail, and the capital of the Senecas was less than ten miles away. If they couldn't count on surprise, there was no way of avoiding its destruction. The rebel army would perform its task, with the attention to detail for which it was already legendary. The western door of the Longhouse would collapse, and from that doorway Sullivan's cannon would aim at Fort Niagara.

John Butler was grimly silent. He glanced at the prisoners. He ordered the two white men to be brought to his tent and left the Oneidas to the warriors, so they could vent their rage.

Henry Hough appeared in front of him.

"Why do they get to have all the fun?"

Butler stared into his eyes and what he saw there made him shudder.

"It's what prisoners do," he said. "Indians against Indians."

Secord appeared behind his mate's back, standing near the entrance of the tent to which the rebels had been brought. Walter Butler came and stood alongside his father, ready to pounce.

"Whites against whites," said Hough.

Butler understood. He glanced around: no one was paying any attention to what was going on. The warriors danced in a circle. They had pulled out the intestines from the belly of one of the Oneidas, and were using them to tie him to the trunk of an oak tree.

Sweat poured into his eyes. Hough was drenched as well, and he lifted the brim of his hat slightly and ran a hand over his cropped hair before turning to stare at him again. Butler felt his son slumping forward, and stopped him with his hand.

"To hell with it," he hissed, before walking away, dragging Walter with him.

In the doorway they waited for their eyes to get used to the darkness. They recognized the prisoners, sitting down, hands bound behind their backs.

Secord went and stood in a corner, found the tortoise rattles and started shaking them. Hough went and sat next to the fair-haired man and looked at him for a long time.

"I'm Lieutenant Boyd, of the continental American army. I declare myself a prisoner of Captain Brant."

Hough nodded seriously.

"Lieutenant. Would you like to become captain? Or even colonel?" He took out his dagger and began to clean his nails.

The prisoner looked at him in disbelief.

"I wouldn't," said Hough. "I'm a volunteer, I have no responsibilities. I'm leaving this war when I think the time is right, and no one can tell me otherwise."

He turned to the other bound man, who eyed the blade nervously. Henry Hough leapt forward and cleanly cut through one of his nostrils.

Blood splashed on the tent wall. The cries roused no one.

Boyd shrank, his face pale and terrified.

Secord shook the rattles again, with false cheerfulness.

"I'm here for only two reasons," Hough went on. "The first was to defend my house, down in Oquaga, but one of your men burned it down."

He walked back to the lieutenant, grabbed the hair at the back of his neck and slipped a handful of earth into his mouth. Then, with his thumb, he began to press out one of his eyes, with the same mechanical determination he would have used to remove a stone from a peach.

"The second is that I've developed a liking for it," he said as his fingernail plunged into the eye-socket.

The lieutenant groaned, gulped down the earth, tried to speak, but a second clod shut him up.

The other man stirred himself. Blood ran down his neck and chest. He said they had information to barter in exchange for their lives. A punch in the mouth put him right, and the invitation to express himself openly if his split lip permitted.

"Let me have a word with Captain Brant," the lieutenant panted before the other man spoke.

Hough looked at them, and without a word he left the tent.

He came back shortly afterward. Secord had stopped shaking the rattles, the prisoners were naked, and one of them was sobbing.

The lieutenant was speaking agitatedly to the Indian who crouched before him.

"Tell Captain Brant, in exchange for his clemency we can let him know General Sullivan's plans."

"What is he saying?" asked the Seneca, addressing Secord in his own language.

"It doesn't matter. Go on."

The Indian got the embers ready. Hough took a bag of pigs' ears out of his knapsack and started chewing them along with his friend, enjoying the scene. Secord picked up the rattles and started shaking them again, to drown the screams.

At last the lieutenant raised a hand. Secord interrupted him.

Hough gulped down his mouthful, came over and listened to the prisoner's whispers.

"Good, Lieutenant Boyd, you were keen that Captain Brant should know this," he said. "I will tell him, you have my word."

"Mercy," Boyd managed to mumble.

His head slumped forward onto Hough's shoulder. The other man began stroking his golden hair, ignoring the prisoner's pleas.

"Listen. My house isn't there any more, as I've already told you, and neither is my brother. He was an idiot, but I loved him and he was all the family I had. Maybe you killed him, maybe you didn't. As chance would have it, you were the one who crossed my path today. The unfathomable will of God. For us, the war ends here. I'm taking you with me to Geneseo. I will receive your general in an appropriate fashion."

44.

They had been running for four days. They had allowed themselves just enough time to eat and rest, to gather their strength. The oldest were starting to lag behind. Philip had decided to march at the back of the column, to be sure that no one collapsed. Even the boys were tired. They had never made such an effort.

It wouldn't be long now. Geneseo was about twenty miles away. The next day they would reach Butler's camp, join up with the bulk of the contingent.

This could be their last moment of rest before the clash.

Sitting in the middle of the bivouac, Philip studied the faces one by one, as if looking at a fresco. These bodies exuded an energy that didn't smell of blood and lead. They looked like the residents of an unknown city, marching to stop a hurricane or a flood.

He looked at the little boys with their incredulous eyes, and couldn't imagine them fighting with knives. He saw them in the forest, hunting deer, or swimming in a river. He watched the elderly warriors and wondered not how many enemies they might kill but where they would take their families at the start of winter. He saw them surrounded by children and grandchildren, dying in their parents' village, not covered by dust and blood. He looked at the white volunteers who escorted Joseph, and saw merchants, farmers, blacksmiths, and carpenters.

He had new eyes. Perhaps he would see the same things on the faces of the enemy.

Sullivan's men were Germans, Dutchmen, English and Irish Whigs, Corsican exiles, Swiss mercenaries, Oneida and Tuscarora guides. Certainly, some of them were fighting for a principle, but others for money, others still out of fear or a desire for glory. Some had followed their older brothers, some had enlisted against their fathers' will. Some were driven by hatred, others by personal gain. Philip knew about the motto that Sullivan carried on his banners: "Civilization or death to all savages." His soldiers yelled it in chorus, in a toast to destruction. They yelled it at the stone houses and the cultivated fields, at the woolen clothes and the rifles. They yelled it at an alliance of peoples who had long ago adopted a law of peace. They yelled it to say that anyone not like themselves deserved extermination. And yet none of them resembled one another.

Philip looked at the plain again. After many moons he was ready to fight once more, even if he no longer had a people to defend.

We must live, Esther repeated in his mind.

Had coming events permitted, he would have gone back to try and find that new beginning she spoke of, that spring.

The sentries who signaled their arrival seemed to have picked up the mood of the camp. A feeling of demobilization.

Joseph led the column of old men and children around the fires that were still lit, so that they could rest and eat something. Philip came up beside him and touched his arm. He pointed to the war poles: under a cloud of flies, two eviscerated Oneidas. The younger men looked at them, impressed.

Joseph froze. He saw John Butler coming toward him.

"The news isn't good, Joseph Brant."

In a few phrases Butler told them about the failed attack on the enemy vanguard.

Joseph took the blow.

"Sullivan is too clever to be taken by surprise, now that he's been warned," Butler added. "We can't fight a battle in the open field. There are too many of them. Geneseo is doomed."

Joseph looked at Philip. He saw his own disappointment reflected in his friend's eyes. Running had been pointless. He gestured at the men taking down the tents.

"Where are they going?"

"Home," Butler replied, as he studied the ragtag band that had come from Niagara. "Send these boys back. Let them go home to their mothers." Then he noticed gray hair. "And their children," he added. "There's nothing more we can do. It's over, Joseph. The Senecas were fighting for Geneseo, nothing else. Now they'll come back to die of hunger and cold in Fort Niagara." He bit into a piece of tobacco. "Our men want to go home as well. Those who still have one. The others I'm taking with me to Oswego. When Sir John comes down from Montreal with reinforcements, we'll resume the war."

"Are you abandoning Fort Niagara?"

Butler sighed and came closer, as if to share a secret.

"We have extorted information from the prisoners. Niagara isn't Sullivan's objective."

Joseph said nothing, assessing this most unexpected piece of information.

"He's heading east," added the Irishman.

In the silence that followed, Joseph's thoughts traveled quickly, covering the plain as far as Five Fingers, and then still further, to the Mohawk Valley.

"He wants to destroy the other towns," said Butler. "Sweep everything away."

Joseph stared at the embers. The temptation to call it a day was strong. The weariness of the journey was about to defeat him. He had used up his strength keeping anxiety at bay.

He thought of how the Six Nations would soon be ashes. Abandoned to their fate by the allies. First Guy Johnson. Then Sir John and Daniel Claus.

Now, finally, John Butler. He had fought by Joseph's side until the last, but now, even for him, the Indians were a millstone of three thousand starving people.

His son's voice claimed Butler's attention. Walter was ready, the Rangers were arranging themselves in a column.

"Come with us," said the old Irishman.

Joseph remained motionless.

"We will wait for you in Oswego," added Butler, his face grim.

Behind him, the Rangers began marching, silent and weary. The Senecas set off in dribs and drabs, little groups of warriors disappearing along the path. Joseph checked the provisions and the water in the canteen.

"Sullivan's heading east," he said, turning to Philip. "The first town along the way is Cayuga. My children are down there. My mother."

"It's nearly ninety miles away."

"Bring the old people and the children back to Niagara," Joseph ordered him.

"They've come as far as this. They'll find their way back," replied his friend, slinging his rifle over his shoulder. "In Cayuga there are old people and children. We must get them all out."

"Just us two?"

Philip pointed behind him.

"Apparently not."

Joseph turned and saw Kanatawakhon standing a few feet away, leaning on the barrel of his rifle, ready to leave. Without another word, the three men headed toward the edge of the camp, but the figures of two warriors appeared on the path in front of them.

"Do you want to face Sullivan on your own?" asked Oronhyateka.

"We are going to save my children," Joseph replied.

"A memorable venture?" asked Kanenonte.

"One worthy of a son of the Wolf clan."

Kanenonte smiled, and Oronhyateka launched into the ululation of war.

They walked across the plain and into the depths of the trees, urged on by the twilight and by fate, an army of five men and many ghosts.

They ran to save a clutch of souls from the Apocalypse. They ran, because it was written thus. Time was ending, and everything was reaching its conclusion.

45.

Left-Hand Twin is ice. He is the lord of winter, cold, slippery, sharp as rock crystal. He is a storm from the northeast, a chill that slips between the chinks of the shacks. Man of Ice, Cold Cold Heart, Mirror of Stone: some say that his true nature is the Whirlwind.

Right-Hand Twin is fire. He is the lord of summer, hot, damp, soft ground. He is a warm breeze from the southeast, he is a flame that boils water and cooks food. Master of Life, Support of the Sky, God the Father: some say that his nature is the Sun's Ray.

Destruction, too, comes from the southeast, but it is a cloud full of hailstones that gathers, filling the sky. Lightning rains down from its belly; its messengers devastate the earth. In the cloud there is fire, but it does not belong to Right-Hand Twin. The whites have usurped its direction— since they crossed the ocean everything has been confused, and mourning often comes from the east. Rum smallpox on a skeletal horse, and now this: columns of rifles, bayonets, and cannon. Fire drives the white man's heart. Incessant, frantic blood feeds endless expanses of men, more than one could possibly imagine, more than the greatest flock of migrating birds. They wait for Destruction to spill out like locusts and put an end to our days.

At the dimming of a short, cold day, General Sullivan made the decision. A pale rain fell on the canvas of the tents and on his tricorn; the horses' nostrils gave off puffs of steam. The men walked with their heads lowered. No drums, no fifes, flags drenched with water. Weariness. Once past Geneseo, the next stage could only be Niagara. An English garrison, refugees, many warriors. They would certainly have received provisions and ammunition from Canada. Winter threatened to be long and cold. It would be a terrible siege, not only for those inside.

Sullivan had thought for months and months about the wedge-shaped fortifications. The walls were solid. There, even the Tories had cannons. Sullivan thought again of recent events. War between different peoples, without laws, is inevitably cruel; there are no pauses for pity, and the beast reveals itself in its most repugnant forms. In his mind Sullivan saw Lieutenant Boyd tied to a tree on the path to Geneseo. Decapitated, eviscerated—his own innards the cords that bound him, like a grotesque ornament, a hideous offering to the demons of the savages. He felt in the depths of his soul that his mission must be pursued to its conclusion, coldly and intelligently, to free the future nation from such scandalous and immoral neighbors.

Sullivan had made his mind up. He would turn back, he would not contravene Washington's orders: to lay waste the territory of the Six Nations, and sow their fields with salt. *Delenda est Carthago.* Every house had to be destroyed, all farmland ruined, all traces of the presence of the Indians erased.

The right thing to do. Veer eastward, toward Cayuga and the Mohawk Valley.

There are times when wisdom is folly, recklessness the only wisdom. The death of a man gives life to worms and larvae. Then they, too, die, and from the loam arise the village fires. Children nurse, and young men paint their faces, preparing to deal out more death.

Sky Woman asked the Twins: "Do you know where you came from? And do you know where you will go when your journey on this earth is over?"

Right-Hand Twin replied: "I know: we descended from the sky, from the world above the clouds. I will not forget it. When the time is right, I will return to the place I came from."

Sky Woman rejoiced. "I will call you He Who Supports the Sky."

Then she turned to the other one. Left-Hand Twin said: "What need have I to know where I come from and where I will go when I leave the earth? Don't give me a headache by talking about another world, because now I am in this one. I am young, I am strong, and there is plenty of amusement here."

They were always like that. Following the army, finishing its work. Sullivan concerned himself with laying waste, destroying, uprooting: the plundering wasn't too accurate. After the last rearguard action came the turn of the irregulars.

When the soldiers had passed the horizon, or lost themselves in the dense belly of the forest, the women who had managed to flee returned, the bravest first of all. They came back in dribs and drabs: if you concentrated on the first group, you had all the time in the world to do what you needed to do. You had to stay in hiding, spy on their movements, see where the savages had hidden the most precious things. Usually they buried them. Then Nathaniel Gordon and his men came out of hiding and began the dance. There is no war without plunder, no plunder without rape, and a good rape is crowned with a killing.

Klug counted the gold coins drawn from a coffer of wood and leather. There was a lot of money in there. He told himself again and again that his choice had been right: after being thrown out of the militia, he had thought he would need a bit more war and a few more scalps before returning to German Flatts as a patriot.

He glanced inside. Nathaniel Gordon was giving orders to the others; the Delaware guide was laughing and running after a dog. His hat with the ears fell and rolled in the dust.

At some point the dog stopped, turned around, legs straight, and started barking and baring its teeth. The Delaware crushed its head with his tomahawk.

Christ, what was the savage doing? He had taken out his knife and opened up its belly, started skinning it, exposing the muscles and thin layer of fat to the cold. The others had lit a fire.

"Do you want some, too, Klug?"

"Christ, no! I don't eat the food of savages, for God's sake."

Nathaniel Gordon sniggered. "You really are a peasant, Klug. And I thought these weeks would have weaned you." His cold eyes stared into the German's. "As far as I'm concerned, this meat is excellent." He bared his yellow teeth and bit into a haunch of the dog. He chewed complacently. "After waging war, I get incredibly hungry. I'd even roast the savages' kids, if I could find any."

The company burst out laughing. The Delaware cleaned his teeth with the tip of his knife. Nathaniel Gordon went on: "Come on, Klug, you don't know what you're missing. I don't want you to offend your primitive friend."

Klug noisily exhaled. His companions were scary. All too easy to displease these people. And yet he hadn't pulled out, not even of the most repugnant ventures.

The crows described broad circles above the smoke of the ruins. A cloud of steam formed in front of mouths and noses, before quickly vanishing. Klug gulped and accepted a piece of meat. He brought it to his mouth and began to chew.

46.

Another month, then the frost, the snow, lethargy. Big prey was rare in the cold season, and the forests around Lake Cayuga were no exception. That month would let everyone know whether Isaac Brant was a good hunter. Whether he could kill his first deer at the age of twelve, like the best warriors of the nation.

As he cleaned his rifle he studied the day ahead. Veils of mist passed over the village. The big houses of squared-off tree trunks came into view, and beyond the palisade the crests of beech trees broke through the gray.

When he emerged, the sun was behind the mountains and the toads were out enjoying the damp air. He took a little flask from his pocket and poured into his throat rum that tasted of molasses and tobacco. He checked his gunpowder, cartridges and knife one last time, then had another swig. He could take it easy: no one was waiting for him apart from the deer he had dreamed of. For months he had gone hunting on his own. There wasn't much choice of company in Cayuga: little children, women, old men with poor eyesight who didn't want to make fools of themselves in front of a boy. Other young men hunted in groups, but they made so much noise that they never caught anything.

Grandma Margaret's voice struck him in the back of the neck. Isaac saw her and stayed at a distance: the old woman's stench turned his stomach. She was always wrapped up in that blanket, sitting in her armchair, all day and at night as well.

"There's a dark patch on the sun and the wind smells of fire and carrion."

Isaac walked away, cursing. The sun hadn't yet appeared and the wind hadn't breathed for days.

In the road, a little boy waved to him over his mother's shoulder. Isaac quickened his pace: a real hunter has eyes only for his prey. Women and kids are pointless distractions.

He took a path into the forest that crossed a deer track, five miles uphill. He hadn't walked two hundred yards when a sound made him freeze. Feet running, branches breaking. A hubbub that no hunter would make, not even when following a fawn at breakneck speed.

Isaac hid behind a tree trunk, his mind in torment. His right half hoped they were strangers, his left that they were enemies.

He raised the barrel of his rifle and at that precise moment the sound stopped. Silence, except for the distant wailing of doves. Then a rustling sound that started at a point high up the hill, multiplied, and ran in several directions.

They were surrounding him. He instinctively ran down the hill. One of his pursuers yelled, and Isaac recognized the war cry of the Wolf clan, slowed down for a moment and turned back. Out of the corner of his eye he spotted a shadow coming toward him, but didn't have time to move. He found himself on the ground.

"Isaac? Stop, it's Isaac."

It was the voice of Jacob Kanatawakhon, who was already getting to his feet and holding out his hand.

Immediately after him came Isaac's father. "Where are Christina and Margaret?"

Other men from Canajoharie appeared. Philip Lacroix, Jethro Kanenonte, Paul Oronhyateka.

"Get up, we have to warn everyone. Sullivan's army is a few miles from here."

Isaac ignored the hand and got to his feet by himself.

He opened his eyes wide. He was surrounded by the bravest warriors of the clan, and felt that this day would stay in his memory more than any great hunt.

He beckoned them to follow, and set off headlong for Cayuga.

The nights were cold and tense, a dark abyss. Beneath the weight of the blankets, Klug lay cramped like a sick animal, his back and legs shivering. After drowsing for a long time, he fell asleep just before dawn, only to be immediately woken by a kick in the ribs, a furious cry. The life of a raider was hard. And then there was that business about the dog meat. He didn't know why, but he had a sense that after that episode something had changed.

Now they were on reconnaissance. They couldn't light fires to cook, so for days they had lived on dried meat, and Klug had a knot where his guts should have been. He never dreamed. For a few minutes he went into a funnel of darkness, when the thoughts running through his head left him free. For days, that was the only sleep he had had.

A damp sensation on his forehead and his cheeks. He opened his eyes and looked up. The face struggled to take shape, emerging out of a vague blur: Nathaniel Gordon, tall as a giant, was pulling on his breeches. Klug suddenly sat up. The band exploded into grotesque laughter. The Delaware's body shook, his eyes streamed, his mouth laughed and laughed, coarsely, shrilly. A wail came from his throat, like a skinned pig or an Indian squaw when you opened her legs.

Nathaniel Gordon suddenly changed expression. Everyone fell silent.

"Move yourself, Klug. You're always the last, you're a millstone. I don't know if I can be bothered to take you with us."

He turned to the rest of his mates. "Come on, the village is waiting for us."

One of the raiders broke in. "That's right, Nat. The village *is* waiting for us. Perhaps it'll be like it was in Secondaga, an old man jumping out of nowhere and shooting at us. Wouldn't it be better to wait for Klug as well? There could be some surprises, so the more of us the better."

Nathaniel Gordon shook his head. "By the time we get to the village, Klug will have joined us. Even if he stays behind, it'll be no great loss."

The gang walked along the path that went down toward Cayuga. Klug moved as quickly as he could. His bones ached, but he hated being left behind, on his own, in the middle of the forest. He looked anxiously around, pricked up his ears, as his companions' backs disappeared toward the valley. He quickly gathered his things together, hoisted his rucksack onto his back, then stopped for a moment. He set down the rucksack and quickly loaded his rifle. The first cartridge fell, spilling its contents on the damp ground. He cursed and finished the operation—cartridge wad, stuff it right down to the end of the barrel—and slung the rifle over his shoulder, looked at the path and set off.

His companions had disappeared into the half-light of dawn, behind the last bend.

Philip walked slowly. He reviewed the column of refugees. Everything was ready for their departure.

About fifty people, perhaps sixty. Women, children. Old men whose arms couldn't have supported the weight of a tomahawk. Children clutching sticks, knives, even, some of them, rusty rifles left over from the last war. At best they could have been used as cudgels. Oronhyateka and Kanenonte were joking, weighing those wretched weapons in their hands, prompting admiration by relating their feats of war.

Kanenonte struck his chest with a fist, then pointed at Philip. "You see? We're fighting alongside Joseph Brant and the Great Devil. They trust us."

Philip walked on. Kanatawakhon stared at the trees around them, and the bushes, and the rocks in the path, as if waiting to see enemies emerging in the shape of lizards.

Isaac was at the head, first in line, armed, frowning, proud. He looked straight ahead and took a deep breath, swelling his chest. He was shivering and trying not to let it show. *He looks like Joseph when he was a boy*, Philip thought.

Joseph was at the rear, busy persuading his mother.

"I told you, Margaret. We have to leave right away, we can't wait as much as the flutter of a wing."

The old woman, wrapped up in her musty blanket, pressed Christina to her and looked at the trees, like Kanatawakhon.

"I tell you that the wind smelled of carrion. Of fire and carrion. We can't leave now, we'll end up in the stench and the flames."

"There isn't so much as a breeze, mother. The fire will break out here, if we don't leave quickly."

"I don't recognize you any more, Joseph, you seem like a white person! Can't you smell the stink? The carrion is further down the path!"

Philip felt the hairs on his arms standing up. He walked over to Kanatawakhon. "What's worrying you, brother?"

"Noises, Great Devil. They are faint, but I had them in my ears, I'm sure of it."

"With all this shouting, your hearing might have deceived you."

"No, Great Devil. I have trained my ears not to make fun of me. I heard something *beneath* the voices."

"Sullivan?" asked Philip.

"No. Those would be big noises, heavy as bears. These are insects."

They walked over to the mother and son, who were still squabbling. Philip put a hand on Joseph's shoulder. "Maybe your mother is right," he said. "Strange movements around here. Better go and see."

Joseph frowned.

"Listen to your friend, Joseph," said the old woman. "He's a good Mohawk, even though he's French."

They called Oronhyateka and Kanenonte. After a swift confabulation, it was decided that the column would leave, but cautiously and in silence. The five warriors would walk half a mile ahead, along the sides of the path, moving swiftly from one tree to the next. If they intercepted the enemy, they would try to surprise and eliminate him, as the column proceeded along the path. Then they would rejoin the column, to escort it upon its long journey.

Joseph called Isaac over. "You're a man now. We must check that the escape route is not dangerous. Until we come back, I entrust to you the protection of Margaret and Christina."

Isaac froze as if standing to attention, lifted his chin and said between gritted teeth, "I will defend them."

Joseph heard a hiss. He turned around and saw Philip crouching behind a tree, sniffing the air that came down from the hills.

A click of the tongue from one warrior to the next brought the group together. They started to climb the ridge, then Philip gestured to them to spread out. Oronhyateka and Kanatawakhon squatted down in the shelter of a big pine tree. Philip, Joseph and Kanenonte hid in the tall grass. Philip hunkered down, supporting himself with his rifle. He looked at the ground, breathing slowly.

Klug walked quickly. He realized that he could put a foot in a trap. The path was steep and uneven, and his back was burdened with the weight of the sack and the rifle. He was utterly exhausted, in pieces, wrecked, and with each step he swore he would go home to German Flatts and immerse himself in politics, now that he'd been in the war and everyone knew it.

Where were the others? Klug looked for the rest of the unit, then saw them eighty, ninety yards ahead. He gazed after them as he quickened his pace.

There was a shot, a cloud of smoke. One of his companions fell. The others picked up their rifles. A crisp, shouted order. Nat's men threw down their arms. Indians emerged on either side of the path.

A cold shudder ran through Klug. He felt his guts twisting. He squatted down behind a rock.

Joseph studied Nathaniel Gordon. "Your face is familiar."

The man spat contemptuously on the ground. "I've never seen you before. I don't know who you are."

Joseph's face was ice. "Soon you won't want to defy me any longer."

Oronhyateka lifted the fur hat off the Delaware's head and turned it around in his hands. Kanenonte pointed his finger at the tobacco pouch that the Delaware wore on his belt. A sudden awareness spread through the minds of the Mohawks. The Delaware shivered. Kanenonte emitted a high-pitched, terrible cry.

Christ, it looked as if they hadn't noticed him. The path sloped downward, and it wasn't yet broad daylight. Klug felt an impulse to turn around, to flee as quickly as he could. But there was a figure, there at the end, that he couldn't take his eyes away from.

He gave a start. Holy Christ, it was Joseph Brant. Lobster-colored jacket and war paint. His way of moving was unmistakable. Careful as a cat, Klug took out his spyglass. Nat Gordon's face was livid. The Delaware was a wall of stone. And the chief of the savages really was Joseph Brant.

His heart beat like crazy. Klug felt the cold determination of hatred stirring his limbs. Before wondering if he was capable of carrying out his task, he had raised his Kentucky carbine. He pulled the trigger.

Just a faint metallic click and the spark of the flint. He thought he'd loaded the rifle, but the barrel was empty.

He cursed between his teeth, prayed that he would be granted enough time. He reloaded carefully, heard cries, looked down the hill. The situation was coming to a head.

He shouldered, aimed. The hero who would wipe out Monster Brant was there, behind the rock, and his name was Klug. He pulled the trigger. A cloud of smoke hid the scene. Klug tilted his head to one side to check the effect of the shot. There was a man on the ground, the Delaware was fighting with another savage, and perhaps his companions would prevail, but Klug's legs decided to flee.

Run, one step after the other. He, Jonas Klug, the man who had wiped out Joseph Brant.

47.

Philip saw Molly, in pale blue, and took a step forward to climb the hill. He breathed in air and light, the world was calm, the corn was ripe and meditative, the wounds of the world were cool dew. Molly was far away, up at the top, but he knew he would reach her. After so long his feet moved lightly, and the grass responded to their touch, bent and allowed him to pass. The universe listened curiously. The war was over and there was sun everywhere.

Molly waved and smiled. Come, from here you can see everything, fields and lakes, mountains and oceans, cycles reaching completion.

Philip was close to her, looking straight ahead. The world no longer had a horizon, it stretched as far as the eye could see, and went on, increasingly narrow and dense, vague and drenched with air, without ever disappearing.

Peoples and colors, lives and destinies, all alive in that thin strip.

There at the end, we are seen from behind, thought Philip Lacroix Ronaterihonte. If the arrow of my eye reached so far, it could stick into the back of my neck.

Molly Brant Degonwadonti took him by the hand.

The air formed hesitant little whirls.

Philip spoke.

It's time for me to know why you chose me.

Cast your eye to the end, drummer boy. And behind us, and all around. We are at the peak of time, where the reply precedes the question, the effect precedes the cause, death precedes birth.

You had to climb that hill to understand your journey.

Without your mother and father, you died as a Frenchman to be born as a Mohawk, the day Hendrick fell in battle.

That day Sir William's world put down roots.

You had to die to avenge Hendrick. But you escaped, and a new cycle opened up.

The nation gave you a father and a mother. You have been a great warrior. You have endured ordeals. You walked with the Mohawks.

Then the nation lost you, and you lost the nation. The incompleteness of your cycle unbalanced the world, and the Master of Life knew it.

You had to come back to the world, Ronaterihonte, to be able to die, to illuminate the fate of the Longhouse.

Philip spoke.

I, without a mother, no longer know how many times I was born.

You are the first midwife and the last. You turned me into a Mohawk and
you have called me back for the first time.

Now you are death.

Molly spoke.

One circle is closing, another is opening.

Molly spoke.

The Six Nations will live.

Philip sighed, his eyes filled with tears.

The lead had torn the flesh to pieces, severed a vein, freed the blood.

Someone called a name: "Ronaterihonte!"

Someone intoned a question.

Someone grunted a reply.

The last human figures crowded into the corners, increasingly veiled.

Teeth would be ground, fists clenched.

Weeping, and singing, and farewells.

Philip was ready.

I'm returning to the world's womb, mother, my origin, my nation.

In the warm, welcoming darkness of the earth.

48.

Joseph remembered the first time he had seen Philip. A frightened boy, in uniform, maybe white or maybe Indian.

Joseph, too, had been a boy, too young to fight. Molly had brought him with her to Lake George. He had to help the women treat the injured: run to fetch water to wash the wounds or rum to anesthetize those with bullets stuck in their flesh. Help support the ones who could barely walk.

That day she had seen Sir William coming back from the camp on a stretcher. The men escorting him had told her: Hendrick was dead.

Shortly afterward, standing next to Molly, he had witnessed the arrival of the convoy of prisoners, among the shouts of rage and pain of the warriors and the groans of people being dragged along and kicked.

The little boy was exhausted. Joseph was sure that his blood would soak the grass. Instead, his sister had darted forward, proud and furious. She had defied the warriors, had shamed them, made them feel stupid and irrelevant to the history of the Six Nations. At one point Joseph had seen himself being pointed at, for Molly had used him as an argument: *that boy is the same age as my brother.*

That day the nation adopted the future Grand Diable. And Joseph's life changed forever.

Now the world had opened up its mouth full of ulcers and rotten teeth and swallowed Philip up.

Joseph could feel it: the bullet been meant for him.

A note of pain rang out among gums, temples and eyeballs. Overlapping orders roared in his ears, mumbled and lost in echo, increasingly meaningless.

Around the dying, everything was quickly changing.

Joseph would see. He would have time. He would speak to the ghosts. Time to think, remember, blame himself, exculpate himself. And live in the place of the dead, *live*, because that's how it is, you live or you die. And the living take care of the living, of those left behind.

Sullivan was a threat hanging over them. They had to assemble a stretcher for Philip's body and reach the column of survivors. Christina, Isaac, Margaret. Save them all, leave this crazy world.

"We're staying here, Thayendanegea," said Oronhyateka, pointing to the prisoners. "There's something to be done, at long last, you know."

"Since this story began," added Kanenonte.

"Sullivan's on his way," replied Joseph. "There's no time. . ."

"You and Kanatawakhon can escort the refugees without our help," said Oronhyateka.

Kanenonte smiled. "We'll see each other where the Great Devil waits for us, one day."

Joseph narrowed his eyes, sucked air through his nostrils, hunched his shoulders as if he were cold. He opened his eyes again and said, "So be it."

The man who had introduced himself as Nathaniel Gordon, sitting on the ground with his wrists tied behind his back, looked at Joseph with pleading eyes.

"I can tell you the name of the one who fired at your friend, Joseph Brant! He's a fellow villager of yours! Klug! Damn the day that German joined us!"

The warriors gave a start, glances flew from one face to the other. Joseph clenched his fists on air, until he felt pain in his wrists.

"Everything finds its place, Thayendanegea," said Oronhyateka, then turned toward Gordon: "Nothing you tell us will save your life. You and your friends must pay much more than this."

Gordon uttered a wail and deflated like a pierced water-bottle, drained of all energy. "Please, Joseph Brant."

Joseph stared at him contemptuously. "You have done nothing for yourselves. How could I do anything for you?"

Kanenonte and Oronhyateka wept and laughed, covered their faces with their hands, slapped each other on the back. They looked as if they had lost their senses, yet they were getting drunk methodically, they were skillfully reviving the flames, and however much rum they drank, they always came back to torture the prisoner tied upside down by the fire. Each scrap of flesh cut away bore a name: "This is for Samuel Waterbridge. This is for Royathakariyo. This is for Sakihenakenta. This is for Ronaterihonte."

The Delaware didn't cry out, not so much as a grunt. Scalped, skinned, arms burned and hot ash on the exposed flesh.

The others had to watch, kicks and slaps if they closed their eyes. They prayed like children. Each of them had vomited and pissed and shat himself. Gordon had no more tears to weep.

"Did you hear that lovely phrase of Thayendanegea's?" said Kanenonte, laughing and showing his teeth. "I wish I'd said it! 'You have done nothing for yourselves. How could I do anything for you?' "

"Thayendanegea is a great warrior," observed Oronhyateka.

"And what about us? Are we great warriors?" Kanenonte asked.

Oronhyateka didn't reply. For the umpteenth time he walked over the prisoner.

He raised the knife, carved out and removed a scrap of skin.

"This is for Oronhyateka."

He immediately cut away another.

"This is for Kanenonte."

Laughter, sobs and prayers. Crackling flames.

49.

The earth was damp and soft; the digging spades encountered no obstacles. Joseph and Kanatawakhon worked quickly. Isaac wrapped an arm around Christina's shoulders. Margaret hovered around the two warriors and looked at them as if making sure the work was going well. The rest of the column was bivouacked a short distance away, but only the Brant family witnessed the burial of the Great Devil. A burial without rites, neither Christian nor pagan, before resuming the journey. Fort Niagara was a long way away.

Philip's body was wrapped in Margaret's blanket. The old woman had seen him dead, lying on the stretcher of branches and vines. Murmuring something, she had taken off the big dusty rag and stepped forward.

"Are you sure, Grandma?" Isaac had asked. "The air is cold."

"No matter. I have not many moons remaining. Soon I will put it back on."

Joseph had given his mother his own woolen jacket. The old woman wore it sleeveless, as if it were a shawl.

In a few minutes, Joseph and Kanatawakhon had dug a ditch five feet deep.

Now it was time to lower the body. Joseph felt duty and effort constricting his throat, like two hands attempting to strangle him. He felt himself tottering on the edge of the hole. Kanatawakhon gripped him by an arm.

"This grave claims me too," Joseph said, "but the time has not yet come."

"Sit down, Thayendanegea, you're tired," said his companion.

"How long is it since we last slept, Kanatawakhon?"

"I've lost count of the days, brother."

"So have I." Joseph walked a few feet away and called his son: "Isaac, give me a hand. Learn to bury the dead."

Isaac broke away from his sister, and Joseph took his place. The little girl gripped her father's leg.

Kanatawakhon and Isaac lifted the body by the shoulders and the feet, carried it over with abrupt solemnity and dropped it into the ditch.

Ronaterihonte's final journey was a quick flight, and his landing made no sound. The soft earth received the body and seemed to shape itself around it. The warrior and the boy gripped their spades. Joseph stopped them.

He turned to his mother: "Margaret, you are the oldest. You represent the clan, the nation. Say a word for this warrior."

Everyone fell silent. The old woman moved, bent and tottering. She stopped a foot away from the edge.

"My dear ones loved you well, Philip *Lacrosse*. My daughter gave you life. Part of my son dies with you."

Joseph felt the vise tightening around his throat, squeezing his head, forcing it to throw out tears. His eyes welled up.

"My grandson buries you. I shall be the last to salute you. We will all pray for you."

Having said these words, she walked away. She passed by Joseph and Christina and walked one step at a time toward the refugee bivouac.

Joseph gave the signal. The spades lifted piles of earth.

50.

"Master of Life, you have been joined by a great warrior, who knew the People of the Flint in their adverse times and wove his destiny with theirs, like the wampum I clutch in my hands. His name is Ronaterihonte. The rivers and valleys have known his fame and his courage. He has defended the nation in danger, has lived with us through times of famine and wretchedness. He has taught us that when the shadow falls upon the earth it is not honor that counts, but the safety of those under threat. Our brother Ronaterihonte obscured his light to pass through the darkness along with his people. Master of Light, welcome him as you would welcome the noblest of men. Amen."

Johannes Tekarihoga lowered the arms that he had stretched toward the sky, lit by the sun. By the rock where he liked to go and contemplate it, the lake glittered golden.

When he heard the beating of wings, he smiled. He turned his head and saw the woodpecker flying along beside him.

"You have come back, my friend."

He was aware of the warmth of midday, although the bite of November was already there. He took a deep breath and felt a sense of ancient vigor, of renewed energy passing through his limbs. He savored the wind that slipped among the willows. He felt the water around him flowing in his veins, as he seemed to hear the announcement of a propitious event. The surface of the lake was populated by spirits: birds, warriors, sachems and matrons of the land, aware of the fate of their own descendants.

The woodpecker alighted on his shoulder. The old Mohawk's face relaxed.

"There. Our fathers await me." The chief of the Tortoise clan breathed in deeply through his nostrils and looked at the woodpecker again. "My heart will be with you, in the Garden in the middle of the Water," he whispered quietly between his lips. He half-closed his eyes and seemed to be sleeping. The woodpecker flew away, toward the lake, where dark outlines of ships appeared on the horizon.

A salvo of cannon-fire and the cries of the lookouts rang out from the towers of the fort, while the body of the old sachem slipped into the water.

Guy Johnson was striding back and forth on deck, slowed down by the mass of wretched figures boarding the ship, with clutches of children, household goods and scrawny animals. As soon as he stepped on dry land he was struck by their silence, as if everyone had decided not to be heard, fearful that the road to safety might close as it had opened.

He understood that he had arrived just in time. The journey had lasted more than a year. Soon after he sailed from New York, at the beginning of autumn in 1778, a terrible freeze had left him stuck in Halifax until the spring, when he had continued on to Montreal. Then down along the St. Lawrence to the lake, and now Niagara.

The tales of poverty and hardship had not prepared him for the impact with the reality. A proud, tenacious people had known defeat and abandonment, famine and death. Little scraps of other peoples had also coagulated in that corner of the world. They followed the fate of the Iroquois, and now all were mixed together in a great mass of flesh. Still loyal, whether from convenience or conviction, to the king in London.

He managed to make his way through the crowd and reach the slope leading to the fort and the refugee camp. He stopped to get his breath and studied the spectacle of all that activity under a bright sky that turned the walls white. Aching bodies, consumed with hunger, dragged their feet along the shore. The few soldiers of the garrison regulated the flow without much effort.

A lugubrious procession, it was all that remained of the Six Nations.

Little more than five years had passed since William Johnson's funeral, but they had been worth a century, and upon a dream that had once looked like solid rock was heaped a pile of misery and death. He thought of how much he had struggled and risked to obtain the post of superintendent of the Indian Department, and how little that meant now.

He studied the crowd once more. In each of the faces, whether familiar or unknown, he traced the common feature of the material they were shaped from. Dark soil from the night of time, the faces of the old people. Red soil of striated rock, the faces of the last warriors. White marble dust, the faces of the young women.

One of them came over. Guy was struck by her grief-stricken expression.

"Father," she said.

He looked at her in astonishment, unable to recognize his daughter in that woman. She wore her hair in the Indian style.

"Esther. Good God, Esther." He wanted to hug her but didn't know how: a whole ocean had interposed itself between them, and then a continent. They were strangers, but Guy hoped he could still offer her an ally and a new life. He had crossed America for this.

"What are you doing here?"

Guy read grief in his daughter's eyes, but also the innate strength that had disconcerted him since she was a little girl. Now he recognized it: it was the look of William Johnson.

"I'm bringing you back to New York. We will leave this place."

"It's too late," said Esther.

She let her father take her hand between his.

"That's not so," Guy insisted. "We can go back to London, far from the war."

"You know I won't come."

"I'm your father, I'm not leaving without you."

The woman did something unexpected. She smiled at him.

"The future is not behind us, but in front of us," she said. "Beyond this lake. The Thousand Islands. That's where we're going."

"I must forbid you."

"But you won't." She came over to him and stroked his cheek with her hand. "Take care of yourself and my sisters." She pulled away from him and immediately checked herself. "Please, have no regrets. It's how it had to be."

She went down toward the deck, where Molly Brant stood waiting for her, wrapped in a white cloak.

Guy wanted to restrain her, but could neither speak nor move. Arms dangling at his sides, mouth tightly closed.

Joseph recognized the solitary figure at the top of the hill. Of all the white men he expected to see, Guy Johnson was really the last. He felt a twinge of compassion, as if aware of the effort that it had taken him to get there.

"Joseph," said Guy, stunned. "I've lost everything, even my daughter."

"She has found her place," said the Indian, watching the woman walk away. "Can we say the same thing about ourselves?"

Guy looked resigned.

"What will you do now?" he asked.

Joseph answered without thinking.

"I will use the time I still have left to fight. I will die with honor."

The Irishman straightened his back, regained control of himself. "I wish you good luck."

The Indian took the outstretched hand. Under his tricorn hat, Guy Johnson's bitter expression disappeared. Joseph watched him walk off toward the dock and pass through the crowd gathered around the boats. For a moment his hat reemerged from the sea of heads, and then it disappeared completely.

Joseph nodded to Kanatawakhon and went down to the lake.

Molly supervised the boarding, watching the slow exodus that was about to begin. The final act of a journey that had begun four years before.

"You have come to tell me you aren't coming with us."

"We still have scores to settle." She hugged him. "Protect my children and our mother."

Isaac, Christina and Margaret were already on one of the boats, watching him uncertainly. He himself had ensured that they were among the first to board. Isaac turned to look in the other direction.

"We will wait for you," said Molly.

Joseph picked up his knapsack and slung it over his shoulder. He walked slowly behind Kanatawakhon, against the current of human beings pouring toward the shore.

Esther watched the land drifting away one last time. She touched the wampum that she wore around her wrist.

Soon she would see Philip again. She knew the road, she had traveled it before.

There is no grieving for those capable of dreams.

You said you would keep a boat ready for me, my darling. Here it is.

Philip would climb on board. Together they would cross the lake, so big you couldn't see where it ended.

Esther looked at Molly, standing on the fo'c'sle. The sight of the woman gave her courage.

There is no destruction for those who understand the law of time.

She thought of what she had seen in her sixteen years and the world that had collapsed around her.

She thought of the life that awaited her and the new world they would build, in the Garden in the middle of the Water.

The Thousand Islands.

Manituana.

Epilogue

Valley of the Mohawk River, 1783

The man slipped in the mud and got back to his feet. He trudged across the plain toward the forest, his hand pressing against his injured hip.

The rain had transformed the field into a bog, and his feet sank into it.

One knee gave, and the man found himself on the ground once more. He pulled himself up, and went on walking bent forward, his lungs filled with fear and the sharp smell carried on the wind. Houses were burning less than a mile away. He uttered a strangled cry, a sob of terror as he rolled in the mud. He managed to sit up and slip the pistol from his belt. The gun misfired. He threw it at his pursuers with the yelp of a hunted animal.

They caught up with him easily and stopped to look at him. The man was panting with terror, his eyes filled with tears.

The two Indians nodded to one another. One of the two raised his saber. The man screamed.

His head rolled away.

The rain was falling thickly, in little drops, enveloping everything in gloomy peace. Kanatawakhon pointed the blade downward, letting the blood soak the earth. He murmured words in the language of his forefathers.

Joseph picked up the severed head. He took a fistful of mud and stuffed it into the open mouth.

"You wanted my land, Jonas Klug. Here it is. It's yours now."

He put the trophy in a sack and threw it over his shoulder. The weariness of the long years of war made the burden even heavier.

Revenge. His gift to Molly. He had put the valley to the sword and flames, once, twice, but Klug had always managed to escape. He had flushed him out only now that the war was ending.

The air carried the sound of distant gunfire, signals of assembly. The Volunteers' work was over. From the Schoharie to German Flatts, the houses of the settlers were in ashes. Sir William's dream had vanished forever; no one else would take it on.

The two Indians walked slowly to the top of a ridge. They stopped to look at the devastation that surrounded them. Smoke rose from the four points of the compass, the fields were burnt or ruined, cattle that had escaped the raid wandered aimlessly.

Kanatawakhon spoke a few words.

"Yes." Joseph nodded. "We won't be coming back."

The war had been lost. The latest news was that in Paris the white men were talking of peace. The English were negotiating surrender, but no Indian sat with them. Joseph Brant was an inconvenient ally now. The survivors of the Six Nations lived on a handful of islands at the mouth of the St. Lawrence.

Joseph's mind rose above the rubble of Iroquireland, traveled back up the river, flew across the lakes. The vision of Christina playing in the sun lightened his heart. Isaac swam to the shore and splashed his sister with cold water, making her laugh, then followed her inside the log cabin Molly had had built for them. There were others, blazing fires, vegetable gardens, boats coming and going. And there was she, Degonwadonti, the living image of Sky Woman, telling the littlest ones the legend of the Garden of God and the thousand fragments that escaped destruction. A thousand drops of Paradise where hope could be reared. In the yard, a young woman with fair hair chose the seeds that would germinate in the spring. The descendants of Corn, Bean and Squash.

Joseph knew: he would not see that harvest. Not after the end of a war that had cost him everything and expected to dismiss him without noise or compensation. He would hold the white men to their promises, with his last remaining breath. He would go back to London, if necessary, to ask the king in person. There was still a long journey to travel. He gripped the edge of the bag.

"We will have to get marching again."

The two Indians went down toward the river. Their outlines blurred until they vanished beyond the curtain of rain.